Praise for

Dubravka Ugresic

"An astonishingly perceptive, elegantly witty, utterly original exploration of the age-old question 'How Do Stories Come About.'"—Alberto Manguel

"It is a book of ideas, of losses, of love and sorrow, of wars and migration: it is a book, in other words, perfect for our 21st century."—Micheline Marcom

"Ugresic is also affecting and eloquent, in part because within her quirky, aggressively sweet plot she achieves moments of profundity and evokes the stoicism innate in such moments."—Mary Gaitskill

"Like Nabokov, Ugresic affirms our ability to remember as a source for saving our moral and compassionate identity."—*Washington Post*

"As long as some, like Ugresic, who can write well, do, there will be hope for the future."—*New Criterion*

"Ugresic's wit is bound by no preconceived purposes, and once the story takes off, a wild freedom of association and adventurous discernment is set in motion. . . . Ugresic dissects the social world."—*World Literature Today*

"Ugresi⌐ the
dreame:

"Dubrav ......pher of evil and exile, and the storyteller of many shattered lives."—Charles Simic

"A unique tone of voice, a madcap wit and a lively sense of the absurd. Ingenious."—Marina Warner

Also by
Dubravka Ugresic

FOX

Dubravka Ugresic

Translated from the Croatian by
Ellen Elias-Bursać and David Williams

OPEN LETTER
LITERARY TRANSLATIONS FROM THE UNIVERSITY OF ROCHESTER

"Part One" translated by David Williams
"Part Two" through "Part Six" translated by Ellen Elias-Bursać

Copyright © 2017 by Dubravka Ugresic
Translation copyright © 2018 by Ellen Elias-Bursać & David Williams

First edition, 2018
All rights reserved

Library of Congress Cataloging-in-Publication Data: Available.
ISBN-13: 978-1-940953-76-2 / ISBN-10: 1-940953-76-6

This project is supported in part by an award from the National Endowment for the Arts and the New York State Council on the Arts with the support of Governor Andrew M. Cuomo and the New York State Legislature.

Printed on acid-free paper in the United States of America.

Text set in Caslon, a family of serif typefaces based on the designs of William Caslon (1692–1766).

Design by N. J. Furl

Open Letter is the University of Rochester's nonprofit, literary translation press: Dewey Hall 1-219, Box 278968, Rochester, NY 14627

www.openletterbooks.org

Contents

PART ONE

A Story about How
Stories Come to Be Written

The real literary fun begins the moment a story slips an author's control, when it starts behaving like a rotating lawn sprinkler, firing off every which way; when grass begins to sprout not because of any moisture, but out of thirst for a near source of moisture.

—I. *Ferris,* The Magnificent Art of Translating Life into a Story and Vice Versa

1.

How do stories come to be written? I'm sure many writers ask themselves the question, though most avoid an answer. Why? Maybe it's because they don't know what they'd say. Or maybe it's because they're afraid they'll end up sounding like the doctor who only uses Latin terms with his patients (the ranks of whom are, admittedly, ever thinner!), wanting to parade his superiority (when was *that* ever in doubt?) and keep them in an inferior position (one they can't escape even if they wanted to). Maybe this explains why writers prefer to shrug their shoulders, leaving readers with the belief that stories grow like weeds. And perhaps that's for the better. Because if you collected the many thoughts writers have ventured on how stories come to be written, you'd end up with an anthology of inanities. And the more obvious the inanity, the more acolytes the writer wins. Take the global literary star who babbles on about how his moment of creative epiphany arrived during a baseball game. As the ball flew through the air, at that very moment, he realized he was to write a novel. So when he got home, he sat down at his desk, took pen in hand, and he's never looked back.

The Russian writer Boris Pilnyak begins his "A Story about How Stories Come to Be Written" (which stretches to all of a dozen pages) with a short line about how in Tokyo he "quite by chance" met the writer Tagaki.* As relayed to Pilnyak by a third party, Tagaki had won fame on the back of a novel in which he describes a "European woman," a Russian. Had Pilnyak not come across the repatriation request of Sophia Vasilyevna Gnedikh-Tagaki in the archive of the Soviet consulate in the Japanese city of K., Tagaki would have slipped his memory forever.**

Pilnyak's host, Comrade Dzhurba, a secretary at the consulate, takes Pilnyak into the mountains above the city to show him a temple to the fox. "The fox is the totem of cunning and betrayal; if the spirit of the fox enters a person, then that person's tribe is accursed," writes Pilnyak. The temple is located in a grove of cedars, on a stone cliff that falls to the sea, and houses an altar on which foxes take their rest. From there, in the eerie quiet, a view of the mountain range and ocean unfolds. In this sacred place, Pilnyak poses the question of how stories come to be written.

The temple of the fox and the autobiography of Sophia Vasilyevna Gnedikh-Tagaki (which Comrade Dzhurba makes available to the writer) inspire Pilnyak to commit pen to paper. It is thus we learn that Sophia finished her schooling in Vladivostok in order that she might become a teacher "until she could find a suitor" (Pilnyak's aside); that she was "exactly like thousands of other girls in old Russia" (Pilnyak's aside); that she was "as silly as poetry can be silly, and it is right for an

---

* All cited passages are from Beatrice Scott's translation of the story in Pilnyak's *The Tale of the Unextinguished Moon* (New York: Washington Square Press, 1967). In one or two instances, the translation has been slightly adapted.

** As Pilnyak reveals in *The Roots of the Japanese Sun*, the city in question is Kobe.

eighteen-year-old to be silly" (again, Pilnyak's aside). Her biography piques Pilnyak's interest from "the moment when the boat docked at Port Tsuruga. It is a short and unusual biography, distinguishing her from thousands of provincial Russian women." These women's biographies were "as identical as two peas: first love, injured innocence, happiness, a husband, a child for posterity, and very little else."

How on earth did this young woman from Vladivostok find herself on a boat sailing for Tsuruga? Using fragments of Sophia's autobiography, Pilnyak *fills in* details of her life in Vladivostok in the twenties of the previous century. Sophia rents a room in a house where the Japanese officer Tagaki also has lodgings. According to Sophia's autobiography, Tagaki "took two baths a day, wore silk underwear and pajamas at night." Tagaki speaks Russian, but his *l* comes out as an *r*, which sounds rather strange, particularly when he reads Russian poetry aloud. Something akin to *the night smerred sweetry . . .*

Although Japanese Army regulations forbid officers from marrying foreigners, Tagaki proposes to Sophia "in the style of Turgenev."*

Before his departure for Japan—the Russians are about to sweep into Vladivostok—Tagaki leaves Sophia a list of instructions and money for her to follow him.**

---

* This is but one of Pilnyak's many allusions to the emptiness, vapidity, and false sentimentality of provincial Russian women.

** Although he twice underscores that "it is not for me to judge other people," Pilynak wonders to himself how "the woman should have managed to miss the experiences we had known during those years. As everyone knows, the Imperial Japanese Army was in the Russian Far East in 1920 in order to occupy this region and was driven out by the partisans; there is not a word about this in the biography." Here Pilnyak's "I" quickly becomes a terse, declarative "we," as if the threatening shadow of a "Comrade Dzhurba" were hovering over him, and as a consequence, he must reproach Sophia her political indifference. In another section Pilynak again reacts like a Party comisssar, remarking: "The Japanese were

Sophia makes the voyage from Vladivostok to Tsuruga, where she
is detained by the Japanese border police and questioned about her
relationship with Tagaki. She confesses their engagement, and the
police eventually question Tagaki himself, suggesting that he call off
the engagement and return Sophia to Vladivostok, which he refuses.
Instead, he puts Sophia on a train for Osaka, where his brother is to
collect her and take her to his village, to his familial home. Having
put himself at the disposal of the military police, Tagaki's case is soon
favorably resolved: he will be discharged from the army and sentenced
to two years banishment, which he is to serve in his village, in his
father's house, "concealed by flowers and greenery."

The newlyweds spend their time in sweet seclusion, their nights filled
with tumultuous physical passion, their days in peaceful and unhin-
dered routine. Tagaki is pleasant, yet reticent, and prefers to spend his
days sequestered in his study.

"She loved, respected, and feared her husband: she respected him
because he was omnipotent, courteous, taciturn and knew everything,
loved and feared him for his passion, which burned her out, subdued
her utterly, left her powerless, but not him," writes Pilnyak. Although
she knows little about her husband, marital life agrees with Sophia.
When Tagaki's banishment officially ends, the young couple remains
in the village. And then suddenly, journalists, photographers, and the
like spoil their seclusion . . . And it is thus that Sophia discovers the
secret of her husband's daily withdrawal into his study: in those two
or three years, Tagaki had written a novel.

---

hated along the whole far eastern Russian coast. The Japanese caught Bolsheviks
and killed them. They burned some in the boilers of battle cruisers, others they
shot to death and burned in the morgue, situated on one of the hilltops. The
partisans used all their guile to annihilate the Japanese: Kolchak and Somenov
died, the Reds from Moscow poured down like mighty lava. Sophia Vasilyevna
did not mention a word of all this."

She isn't able to read Tagaki's novel. She requests he tell her something of it, yet he remains evasive. With the novel's success, their life changes; they have servants to prepare their rice, a private chauffeur drives Sophia to a nearby town to go shopping. Tagaki's father "bowed to his son's wife with even greater respect than she offered him," and Sophia begins to enjoy the fame of her husband's unread novel.

She learns of the novel's content when they are visited by "the correspondent of a city newspaper" who speaks Russian. Tagaki has devoted the entire novel to her, describing their every moment together. The journalist serves to bring her in front of a mirror, where she "saw herself coming to life on paper. It was not important that the novel described in clinical detail how she shuddered in passion and how there was a turmoil in her belly. The frightening part—the part that frightened her—began after this. She came to realize that her whole life and every single detail in it was material for observation and that her husband was spying on her at every moment of her life; this is the point at which her fear began and became the cruel accompaniment of everything she did and experienced."

Pilnyak asserts, and it is up to us whether we believe him, that the sections of this "rather silly" woman's autobiography devoted to her childhood and schooling in Vladivostok are a complete bore, while those in which she describes life with her husband contain "authentic words of simplicity and clarity." Whether or not this is indeed the case, Sophia gives up "the rank of a famous writer's wife, love, and the touching jasper days," and requests return to her homeland, to Vladivostok.

"And that is all.

    "She . . . lived out her autobiography and I wrote her biography. He . . . wrote a splendid novel.

"It is not for me to judge other people, but to reflect about everything and, among other things, about how stories come to be written.

"The fox is the totem of cunning and treachery. If the spirit of the fox enters a person, then that person's tribe is accursed. The fox is the writer's totem."

Whether Tagaki or Sophia ever existed is hard for us to know. Whatever the case, not for a second does it occur to the reader that the Russian consulate in the city of K., the story of Sophia, her request for repatriation, and the writer Tagaki are, in fact, invented. The reader remains struck by the story's cruel veracity, by the power of a short biography made up of two betrayals: the first committed by the writer Tagaki; the second, propelled by the same creative impulse, by the writer Pilnyak.

2.

In mythology and folklore the fox's symbolic semantic field presupposes cunning, betrayal, wile, sycophancy, deceit, mendacity, hypocrisy, duplicity, selfishness, sneakiness, arrogance, avarice, corruption, carnality, vindictiveness, and reclusiveness. In myth and folktale the fox is most often associated with a "lowdown" enterprise. The fox meets frequently with affliction, and is thus consigned to loserdom, its personal attributes preventing contiguity with higher mythological beings. In any symbolic reading, the fox is situated among the lowly mythological kin. In Japanese mythology, the fox is the messenger of *Inari Ōkami*, the Japanese totem of fertility and rice; as a messenger the fox is located in human orbit, in the earthly sphere, while "higher" realms, the divine or the spiritual, remain out of reach.

Among Native Americans, the first nation peoples of Canada, and Siberian and other Eskimos, the legend is widespread of the indigent whom a fox visits every morning, shedding its pelt and becoming a woman. On discovering the secret, the indigent hides the pelt, and the woman becomes his wife. When the woman eventually finds the pelt, she again takes the form of a fox and leaves him forever.

In both western and eastern imaginations the fox is invariably a trickster, a shyster, yet also appears as a demon, a witch, an "evil bride" or—as in Chinese mythology—the animal form of a deceased human soul. In western folklore, the fox is invariably gendered male (Reineke, Reynard, Renart, Reinaert), and in eastern, female. In Chinese (*huli jing*), Japanese (*kitsune*), and Korean (*kumiho*) mythology, the fox is a master of transformation and the art of illusion, a symbol of the death-dealing female Eros, a female demon. In Japanese mythology, *kitsune* have different statuses: the fox can be a commonplace wild fox (*nogitsune*) or become a *myobu*, a divine fox, for which it must wait a thousand years. The tail announces a fox's status within the hierarchy: the most powerful have nine.

All told, it seems that Pilnyak was right; there is much that qualifies the fox as totem of the traitorous literary guild.

3.

Who is Boris Pilnyak?

The photographs of a handsome man with thin, round glasses on his nose, dressed in a fine suit to which a butterfly broach is pinned, dandy through and through, in no way conform to the "western" image of a Russian revolutionary writer. Yet Pilnyak was such: a Russian revolutionary writer.

His real surname is Vogau (Pilnyak a pseudonym), the son of Volga Germans, his childhood and early youth spent in the Russian provinces.

One of the most prolific writers of his time, his opus is broad in genre and style. His creative diapason ranges from traditional and documentary prose (with discernible traces of both naturalism and "primitivism"), to reportage, travelogue, the "written-to-order" socialist realist novel, and modernist "ornamental prose," the best example of which is his masterpiece, *The Naked Year.*

Pilnyak was loved and hated, famous and influential, his literary style imitated by many. He was widely translated into foreign languages, and free to travel to places of which others could only dream, including Germany, England, China, Japan, the United States, Greece, Turkey, Palestine, and Mongolia . . . His "Japanese cycle" includes the travelogues *The Roots of the Japanese Sun, Rocks and Roots,* and "A Story about How Stories Come to Be Written."* To America he devoted the book *Okay! An American Novel.*** Pilnyak also devoted a

---

* As a beneficiary of the tangled relationship between the two countries, not to mention a benevolent cultural and political moment in history, Boris Pilnyak visited Japan on two occasions, in the spring of both 1926 and 1932. Indeed, the history of cultural relations between Russia and Japan is curiously absorbing, in that Japan has traditionally shown strong interest in Russian culture, from the realist period and first translations of Tolstoy into Japanese, through to the well-established Slavic tradition at Japanese universities, to interest in Pilnyak himself, whose works such as *The Naked Year* were known to Japanese readers in advance of his visit to the country. The new Japanese translation of *The Brothers Karamazov* sold in the millions, something, I sense, that wouldn't even happen in Russia today. Yet the relationship between the two countries is not based on reciprocity: the Japanese have always shown far greater cultural interest in Russia than Russia has ever shown in Japan. In this respect, the writer Tagaki, who speaks Russian and recites Russian verse by heart is an entirely believable character.

** At the invitation of MGM, Pilnyak traveled to American in 1931 to assist with a film about an American engineer working on an enormous construction site in Soviet Russia (Pilnyak's novel *The Volga Falls to the Caspian Sea* centers on the construction of the Dnieper Hydroelectric Station). Pilnyak tore up his contract shortly after arrival and bought a second hand Ford, traveling coast to coast across America. On his travels he met fellow writers such as Theodore Dreiser,

book to England, the collection of short stories *English Tales*, and a work to China entitled *Chinese Diary*.

Perhaps because many women have a weakness for writers, women loved Pilnyak, Russian women in particular, it seems. He married three times. With his first wife, Maria Sokolova, a doctor at Kolomna Hospital, he had two children. His second wife was an actress at the Maly Theater in Moscow, the beauty Olga Scherbinovskaia; and his third, the actress and film director, Kira Andronikashvili. With her he had a son, Boris. He owned an almost unbelievable *two* cars (he brought an American Ford back to the Soviet Union!), and enjoyed the use of a spacious dacha at Peredelkino, the famous writers' colony near Moscow.

Pilnyak's bibliography is substantial. Apart from the classic *The Naked Year*, his other significant works include *Machines and Wolves* and *The Volga Falls to the Caspian Sea*. His story "The Tale of the Unextinguished Moon," about the murder of communist leader Mikhail Frunze, provoked a scandal. It was alleged that doctors acting on Stalin's orders had poisoned Frunze with an overdose of chloroform.

Pilnyak was a close friend of Yevgeny Zamyatin. Zamyatin, an engineer in the Russian Imperial Navy who wrote in his spare time, is the author of the most powerful words a writer has ever dispatched to his executioner. In a letter to Stalin seeking permission to leave the Soviet Union (permission that Stalin, persuaded by Maxim Gorky, granted), Zamyatin wrote: "True literature can only exist when it is created, not by diligent and reliable officials, but by madmen, hermits, heretics, dreamers, rebels, and skeptics."

Sinclair Lewis, Floyd Dell, Regina Anderson, Wald Frank, Mike Gold, Max Eastman, W.E. Woodward, and Upton Sinclair.

Zamyatin's novel *We* (published in English in 1924) has been pla-
giarized by many writers, George Orwell (*1984*) and Aldous Huxley
(*Brave New World*) among them. Only Kurt Vonnegut publicly admit-
ted his debt, others preferring to engage in finger pointing (Orwell
at Huxley, for example). Happiness in emigration proved elusive to
Zamyatin: he spent a miserable six years in Paris, dying of a heart
attack in 1937, the same year Boris Pilnyak was arrested. It seems
that Stalin's bullet, which mowed down so many Russian writers of
the era, refused to bypass Zamyatin's heart, even though Zamyatin
had taken shelter well out of range. This, however, is not a story about
Zamyatin, but one about how stories come to be written.

4.

"A Story about How Stories Come to Be Written" was composed in
1926. My mother was born the same year. That year, many things
took place that one could link with my mother's biography. I, however, prefer to imagine the existence of a poetic connection between
Pilnyak's story and my mother's.

"He settled her in a train, told her that his brother would meet her at
Osaka and that he himself was 'a little busy' just now. He was hidden
by the dusk, and the train left for the dark hills; she was abandoned in
the cruelest solitude, which emphasized all the more that he, Tagaki,
was the only one in the whole world, well-loved, loyal, to whom she
was beholden for everything, without understanding anything. It was
brightly lighted in the carriage, but everything outside was swallowed
in gloom. Everything surrounding her was frightening and incom-
prehensible, as when the Japanese traveling with her, both the men
and the women, began to get undressed before going to sleep, quite
unashamed to go naked, or when they started selling hot tea in little

bottles and supper in pinewood boxes, with rice, fish, radish, with a paper serviette, a toothpick, and two chopsticks. Then the light in the carriage went out and the people fell asleep. She did not sleep all night, feeling lonely, bewildered, and scared. She could not understand anything."

Twenty years after Pilnyak's story came to be written, my twenty-year-old mother set off on the journey of her lifetime, quite literally. Her train ticket gave entry to the unknown. Choosing this journey, and not some other, the skein of her fate began to unwind, which, it seems, together with the travel signs and railway stations, could already be traced in the lines on her palm. In Varna, on the Black Sea, where she lived, attended high school, and adored films and books, she met a sailor near the end of the war, a Croat, with whom she fell in love and became engaged. At war's end, she set off for Yugoslavia, to her now fiancé. Her parents settled her on the train, placed her gently in her compartment, as if in a dinghy that would carry their child to safe harbor. They knew something of such journeys: my mother's father, my grandfather, was a railway man. My mother traveled from Varna to Sofia, from Sofia to Belgrade, and from Belgrade to Zagreb. The train made its way through a ruinscape, and it is this journey, through swathes of scorched earth, that would irretrievably scar her. Following the sailor's instructions, she would get off some fifty miles before Zagreb, and find herself in the darkness of an empty and abandoned provincial railway station. There was no one waiting for her. This black and desolate railway station burned itself into my mother's heart like a branding iron, the first overwhelming and aching betrayal.

"A Story about How Stories Come to Be Written" adheres to the form of fairytale; the one about a mysterious creature from another world, an "unknown force" (the Beast, Raven Son of Raven, the Dragon, the Sunman, the Moonman, Koschei the Immortal, Bluebeard, etc.) that carries the princess away over seven mountains and seven seas to a distant kingdom (alternately known as the "bronze," "silver," "gold," or "honey" kingdom). Jasper is Pilnyak's synonym for Japan and for Sophia's days of happiness ("her days resembled a rosary made of jasper beads"). The secretive Tagaki takes his Russian bride to his "jasper" kingdom. Tagaki has little in common with the ensign Ivantsov, who Sophia ceased greeting because he had "gossiped about their rendezvous." The mysterious Tagaki, as opposed to the ruffian Ivantsov, kisses women's hands and offers gifts of *chocorate*. At first, this "racially strange Japanese man" holds no appeal, is in fact "physically terrifying" to her, but—as if in a fairy tale in which the "beast" morphs into seductive lover—he promptly vanquishes her soul.

And herein lies the paradox: if Pilnyak's story didn't bear the *blueprint* of a fairy tale, there is little doubt that it would be so believable. The moment she consents to chase after the golden skein of her *womanly* fate, Sophia, who in no way differs from thousands of others, becomes a convincing heroine. But what is meant by *womanly* fate? The history of world literature offers a strong hint. The classics (both the minority written by women and the majority written by men) pass an almost inviolable template (a kind of memory card) down from generation to generation like a hereditary illness. The heroine must act in accordance with this template in order that we recognize her as such. In effect, she must endure a trial of some humiliation or another in order that she might win the right to eternal life. In Pilnyak's story, the heroine is doubly betrayed, laid bare, and "robbed": the first time by Tagaki, the second by Pilnyak. Pilnyak calls this "a journey through death" (!). In this way, Sophia, the young heroine of the story, joins the thousands of other literary heroines who bear this imprint to this very day, not least in novels that sell in the millions, wherein She shudders, entralled by the mysterious Him. He will put a spell on her, subjugate her, humiliate her, and betray her, and in the end She will arise as a heroine worthy of respect and self-respect.

Going back to my mother, her young and buoyant heart will quickly heal. As luck would have it, Fate, that clumsiest of writers, forgot that my mother was supposed to be met by her sailor. Sailors don't wait for their sweethearts on railway platforms, their place is in the harbor, and perhaps that's why Fate forgot about the sailor. And then, like a belated happy end, in the light at the end of a metaphorical tunnel, He appeared, the real hero of my mother's story, my future father. This, however, is not a story about my mother and father, but a story that wishes to say something about how stories come to be written.

5.

I visited Moscow for the first time in 1975. I traveled from (today non-existent) Yugoslavia to the (today non-existent) Soviet Union to take up a two-semester scholarship. A particular incident marks the memory of my first trip to the center of Moscow. I needed a restroom, yet it wasn't easy to get into a restaurant or café because of the queues that stretched out front; public restrooms were almost non-existent. Yet by some miracle I ended up finding one. Upon exiting the cubicle, I was surrounded by a group of Gypsies, five or six of them. I hadn't a clue what they wanted from me. With little gobs of spit shining from every reflective surface, they gently patted me down, taking my hands and opening my palms, mumbling this or that, all at the same time. And then they withdrew as quickly as they had appeared. Dazed, I walked out into the street and noticed that I was clenching a ball of paper. I opened my palm. A bunch of tattered lottery tickets fell out. I checked my handbag. About two hundred rubles had disappeared, which at the time was around two average Soviet monthly salaries. The loss of the money didn't bother me in the least; to the contrary, it seemed that on landing in Moscow, I'd flown into the everyday of Bulgakov's *The Master and Margarita*. Just as Pilnyak's heroine Sophia saw the world through a romantic, Turgenevian prism, I (at least at the time) saw it through a Bulgakovian one.

I was placed in the student dormitory of Moscow State University. I lived in room 513, in Zone B, sharing a bathroom and vestibule with a countrywoman, a student of mathematics. It took me forever to work out the building's entrances and exits, how to locate anything in the colossal labyrinth that was divided into zones. On my floor, in zone B, there were Yugoslavs, Finns, and Arabs. The latter's presence was made known by the warm scent of unfamiliar spices wafting from the communal kitchen on our floor. One of the three Finns had won a scholarship to do doctoral research on Mikhail Sholokhov, who at the time was still alive. All three Finns, two guys and a girl, soon forgot why they'd come. Behind the closed doors of their rooms, they drank themselves to unconsciousness, unrelenting until it was time to return to their homeland. Various restrictions meant that for locals, vodka was hard to come by. Aided by their passports and hard currency, foreigners bought vodka in exclusive stores to which only they had access. The chain was called Beryozka. And vodka at Beryozka was a lot cheaper than in Finland.

In contrast to the Finns, I had come with the intention of collecting material for my master's thesis on Boris Pilnyak. Of the nine-month academic year, I spent the first two or three in the Leninka, the Lenin Library (today the Russian State Library). Just getting into the library was tortuous: first, you had to wait in an interminable line for the cloakroom; then in an interminable line to pass through a security checkpoint manned by the library police (I remember the daily emptying of my handbag) before entering the library itself; and then you waited for a book delivery mechanism that resembled a model train and railway (I hope I didn't dream this up, that it really existed!). Maybe this explains why so many slept at the library, quiet snoring an ineluctable part of the general ambience. Given you were only allowed to copy twenty pages a day, the two or three photocopiers always had long queues. Copies were printed on coarse, cardboard-like paper. Anyone who could finance it could hire a "surrogate" to wait in line and do his photocopying for him. Yet the smoking area in the library attic was most repulsive of all—a small, poorly ventilated room with a few chairs and a table, dishes overflowing with butts and ash. At the foot of this butt mountain sat the martyrs, the smokers. Even the cafeteria didn't offer the expected modicum of humanity and warmth, because there too one had to wait in a long line just to get in the door, yet the wait wasn't worth the effort: crap coffee, good tea, and, it goes without saying, the miserable hotdogs that jumped out at you from everywhere, staples of student cafeterias, street vendors' pots, and cheap Moscow lunchbars.

Work in the library was painstaking and required patience, and I, evidently, didn't have the charismatic qualities it demanded. Incomparably more interesting was Moscow's parallel literary life. In this parallel life, people hustled their way through with the help of friends and connections: a friend of mine who worked at the library would photograph the books I needed. Afterwards we'd develop the films and arrange the photos like pages. I had several boxes of such books, all on photographic paper. This parallel life was inhabited by witnesses to the previous epoch, and meeting them was infinitely more powerful than studying in the library. As if in a kind of Hades, it was here that one could meet senescent representatives of the Russian avant-garde, those who had the blind luck to survive; it was here that books were secretly copied and distributed, foreigners, like me, frequently rendering assistance. We could buy rare Russian editions in Beryozka, smuggle works of Russian *tamizdat* into the country, and, like postmen, smuggle manuscripts out of it.

6.

In this Moscow—where philologists, both local and foreign, hunted witnesses to the previous epoch; where famous writers' widows were worshipped (Nadezhda Mandelstam, for example); where anyone who had survived, outlived others, and was in any state to testify about it, was worshipped; where the world burst with memoirs, mementos, and diaries, with collectors and archivists, with artists real and phony, with those who had "sat" (*"sidet"*), i.e. been in a camp, and those ashamed that they hadn't—I met Pilnyak's son, Boris. I never thought of myself as a "hunter"; the pervasive zeal for biographism held no appeal, though I understood where it came from. In this milieu, the battle won by the Russian Formalists—the great battle for the text of a work of art—proved futile. Innumerable authors saw their texts vanish beneath a stampede of biographical details.

Boris Andronikashvili was Pilnyak's son from the writer's third marriage to famed Georgian screen actress and director, Kira Androni-kashvili. Boris was tall, strong, and handsome, also a trained as a screen actor. He felt himself Georgian, was proud of his aristocratic surname, spoke Russian with a heavy Georgian accent (as all Georgians do), and in his house they drank *chacha* and ate *khachapuri*: his true home was not cold and scentless Moscow, but "the city of roses and mutton tallow," as Isaac Babel wrote of Tbilisi. By the time we met he had abandoned film and now occupied himself with the administration of his father's estate. With no experience in such matters, he did so in an amateur fashion. He himself had written several works of prose. He was in his second marriage, from which he had two children, five-year-old Kira, and two-year-old Sandro.

I never wrote my master's thesis on Boris Pilnyak; I gave up halfway. Later, I translated *The Naked Year,* "Snowstorm," and "A Story about How Stories Come to Be Written," into Croatian, and I did write a master's thesis, but on something entirely different. I saw Boris twice more, the last time on September 6, 1989, during a short stay in Moscow, when he gifted me his father's volume, printed the same year, the foreword to which he had written himself. Were it not for his dated dedication in the inside cover, I wouldn't remember the details. I almost didn't recognize him, his expression one of indeterminate internal capitulation. We exchanged several letters, and then lost all contact. The Soviet Union fell apart, then Yugoslavia fell apart, and I left the country. I have closed many files, among them, the year in Moscow when I was supposed to delve deep into the work of Boris Pilnyak, but instead, in place of literature, I delved into life, even though at the time, the two appeared difficult to separate.

Boris Andronikashvili died in 1996, in his sixty-second year of life. I found that out on the internet. His collected works were published in 2007, in two volumes. His daughter Kira did her master's and published a book on her grandfather, also editing two impressive volumes of Pilnyak's letters. I'm not sure I'll read those books. I travel a lot, crisscross borders, and try to carry as little luggage with me as possible. I've closed many files. And once closed, files gradually become unreadable.

7.

The biography of Sophia Vasilyevna Gnedikh-Tagaki attracted Boris Pilnyak like a magnet. Pilnyak stole Sophia's soul (the fox as a mediator between two worlds, the world of the living and the world of the dead), yet in doing so, also erected a literary monument to her. In a given moment and constellation, her biography was significant to him; had it hooked him in another, the encounter with her story perhaps wouldn't have given birth to a new story. Many stories in the life of a writer end as *lithopedions*, as calcified embryos.

In those years, Moscow was a city of philologists, both expert and autodidact, those who had taken on saving forgotten manuscripts and resurrecting neglected authors as their sacred mission. The gaping hole in which millions of human fates disappeared gave rise to a fever-ish hunger for restoration, which to us, "foreigners," seemed akin to a real illness, albeit one with its own allure, like passage to the other side of the mirror. Many self-declared literary archivists truly burned for their voluntary rescue mission, saving books from oblivion. The "forest people" of Bradbury's novel (and Truffaut's film), *Fahrenheit 451*, came to mind. It was as if everyone knew a book by heart. Many dreamed of manuscripts lost to flame (manuscripts burn after all!), and the time for such dreaming was in abundance. People neither expected nor hoped for anything. In this frozen time one was left alone to his or her fever.

Writing this story, I opened a thin, yellowed folder at random to see whether its opening might light a spark . . . Inside were two notebooks, slender, with soft, light green spines, stamped with the word *Tetrad*. (Many years later I stumbled upon this kind of notebook again, in Berlin, I think, in a chic boutique selling nostalgia for the bygone era of communist design.) In scribbles in my own hand, a bibliography of articles on Pilnyak snaked along the checkered paper. Presumably, I had read or intended to read them in the library. It was the scent, a musky and unmistakable scent, not the content, of which there was little, that imbued the folder with meaning. Two xanthous pages of folded A4 paper slipped out, both bearing lists of words, one word under the other:

Album, games: cards, chess, spinning top, sherbet (Günter Grass); lethal objects: spike, revolver, pitch-fork; socks, ribbon, hairband, hair-piece, walking stick, fireplace; silk, cinnamon, pepper; tunic (Joseph and His Brothers); candles, matches, goblins, powder box, wig; shears, Krleža; Zola, nail ("Nana"); Hamsun, pencils, Pan; paddle, Dreiser; bed pan, skullcap, shirt, pipe, candied fruits; objects that migrate, Francis Ponge, Bachelard, Rilke; dagger, underwear, sheets, family photographs; Desdemona, handkerchief; key, barrel rum, mirror, medallions; Kafka, odradek, "The Cares of a Family Man"; music box, coffer, piano, window, tortoise-shell comb, amber; 12 chairs, The Glass Bead Game; sun umbrella, poison ring, signet-ring, garter, corset, curtain, prayer-book, flintlock, watch, monocle, lorgnon; Gogol, cake; Cortázar, sweets; cigarette-case, pawnshop.

The fragment seems incomphrehensible—a gulf of almost forty years lies between my former and present self. The words are definitely written in my hand, in ugly, gray, and cold Moscow, where, seized by the atmosphere of *underground* life and a world view rent from Bulgakov, I spent an academic year. I'm only guessing now, but the things or objects on this haphazardly compiled list were supposed to be "triggers," the kind that propel a story, play a crucial role in a fable, or otherwise function as a central compositional element in a story. Objects with magical properties play a crucial role not only in fairy tales, but often too in what we call *belles lettres*. I'm guessing that a literary exemplar lurks somewhere behind each entry, or at least a vague idea of such. But if this were the case, how did I overlook so many obvious triggers? I mean, what happened to Gogol and his overcoat? How is it that of all the possibilities, it was these very things, and not others, that raced around my young and bursting head? As it turns out, in my biography Moscow is a story barely begun, a *lithopedion*, a calcified embryo. It remains there, static, I forget its presence, if coexistence of this kind can at all be called presence.

8.

I met him in the bar of Moscow's Hotel Belgrade, a well-known meeting place for the city's Yugoslav population, students, embassy workers, representatives of Yugoslav firms, not to mention the Yugoslav tourists who, for this reason or that, stopped by in search of their countrymen. He was exceptionally good-looking, and with his vulpine, copper red hair and trimmed beard, light-green eyes and chiseled frame, it was hard not to notice him. He was my countryman and he was a liar, the kind who lies even when he doesn't have to. A man strolling about in a red English sweater, a light blue shirt with fine white pinstripes, a cashmere coat, white cashmere scarf around his neck, claiming he's studying painting in Moscow couldn't be anything else. He was, however, a tight-lipped liar, which righted the picture to some extent. He put a spell on me; against Moscow's gray and depressing backdrop, green-eyed and fair, he looked like something from another world. He had a carpenter's hands, the biggest, broadest, warmest hands I had ever touched. He made love with conviction, one moment hot, the next cold, as if melting ice cubes in a well-heated pot. We were wild together and I fell in love with him, a love with the scent of a promise, a lovesickness that overcame me and made me ready to die for him. When he left, I cleansed Moscow's Sheremetyevo Airport with my tears. Evidently unused to overtly emotional scenes, the airport police asked me for ID, asked me why I was crying, and I couldn't answer, because I was dying: my copper-haired lover was swimming away in a sea of my tears and, reaching the shores of passport control, forever disappeared from my horizon. In my hand I crumpled imaginary winnings, worthless lottery tickets, ripped in two. My heart slipped from my chest and vanished . . . He didn't leave me his address, and as I pressed mine upon him he told me that letters were silly, and that he was sure we'd meet again someday. And here's the thing that I've never been able to explain: although prepared to venture to the end of the earth with him, I never forgot anyone in my life with greater ease or speed!

He knocked on my door a year or so later, by which time I was already back home. The meeting left me stunningly indifferent, and moreover, his surprise, unannounced appearance irked me somewhat. He seemed to avoid my gaze, yet my gaze was not focused on anything in particular. I got out of him everything that needed be known: that he was married, that he had a son, and that he was in Zagreb not to see me, but to see one of my countrywomen, who (oops!), was the mother of his unwanted child. Although a story excruciatingly banal, a moth of compassion escaped my unventilated heart.

He appeared one final time a few years later, again unannounced, but this time a new, powerful, and unanticipated spark was lit, and we eloped to the Adriatic coast for a brief and torrid affair. Again he didn't say much about himself (oh, the sly fox!), but with an almost inappropriate tenderness recalled our distant trip to Leningrad.

"But we never went to Leningrad together!" I replied in shock.

He tried to convince me we had, and offered details, the name of the hotel, the number of the hotel room, happenings from a visit to the Tsar's Village, the names of restaurants where we had dined, the ballets we'd seen, scenes from our lovemaking, remembrances of our return on the night train to Moscow, of people we'd met along the way . . .

"I was crazy about you, girl . . . I'd never been like that with anyone . . ."

"Why are you mocking me?"

He was lying, of course, but his little "Leningrad fabrication" worried me. The lie had no function, nor had he a motive of any kind. We started to fight, packed up our things, and returned to Zagreb. I cowered in silence the whole way home, dying of fear as he drove like a man possessed. He let me out in front of my building, we never said goodbye. In the darkness, shadowed by sandy eyelashes, his green eyes flashed with a coldness I'd never known.

A month or two after his departure a book slipped from one of my library shelves and from the book a bundle of papers I'd absentmindedly saved. Among the papers were theater tickets for a ballet in Leningrad, reservations for a hotel in Leningrad, my name and his and the date of our stay all there, even tickets proving a visit to the Tsar's Village. For whatever reason, this little "ikebana" also contained a pressed and dried four-leaf clover . . .

This, however, is not a story about me and my time in Moscow, but a story that is trying to tell a story, and that story is trying to tell a story about how stories come to be written.

9.

So really, how do stories come to be written? Pilnyak lived in a time when the literary word was powerful and central, the cinematic image exciting and young. I live in a time when words have been shunted into a corner. How can one expect users of new technologies, those who have undergone physical and mental metamorphosis, whose language consists of pictures and symbols, to be willing and able to read something that until recently was called a *literary text*, and today appears under the widely adopted term *book*?

I am haunted by the feeling that I live in a time in which enchantment has been forever banished, although I can't explain what that magic is, nor the purpose it serves, nor why the past was better than the present. Anyone daring to compare different time periods is not only afforded the possibility of being wrong, but more often than not, is wrong. Many moments in the past seem magical to us, simply because we were not direct witnesses to them, or if we were, those moments are now irrevocably gone.

Why does Pilnyak's heroine Sophia remain as alluring as she ever was, irrespective of Pilnyak's attempts to strip her bare, and why do I return to Pilnyak's story again and again, equally enchanted by his talent in its telling? It is entirely possible that *magic* is a poorly chosen word.

What, for example, are we to do with the central symbol of Pilnyak's story, with the fox? Judging by the innumerable amateur video-postcards to be found online, the Fushimi Inari shrines are a kind of Japanese Disneyland. In today's social codes, Pilnyak's fairy tale about the ethics of the writerly trade, about the fox as totem of treachery, would be read in reverse. The motto of the present would go something like: the fox is the totem of cunning and treachery: if the spirit of the fox enters a person, then that person's tribe is blessed! The fox is everyone's totem, there are no privileged few!

Today, Sophia would be scurrying to write her account of her erotic life with Tagaki, her novel lavishly buffeted by promotional video material. Putting one's life and the lives of others on display is, at this moment, no longer a question of ethics and choice, but one of automatism: everyone does it, and everyone expects it of everyone else. Could Pilnyak have imagined, for example, that his granddaughter would leave her innocent fingerprint on a random website, explaining that she loves Turgenev's prose and Bunin; that she likes running; that she doesn't believe in political parties; that she's convinced things would be better if everyone loved their work and performed it honestly; that she is temperamental and easily offended; that she doesn't wish anyone harm. What separates the short biography of Pilnyak's granddaughter from the thousands like it?

"In the hills above Kobe . . . there is a temple, dedicated to the totem of the fox. On cliffs that fall to the sea, high above the ocean, nestled in ancient pines, an entire city has been raised. In the silence sounds a Buddhist bell. The deeper one enters the mountain, the more deserted and quiet it becomes. There stand small altars, on them industrially produced porcelain foxes, their quality worse than the puppet fox-heads sold for small change at fairgrounds. One evening in Kobe, I bought ten such foxes at the market for a single Japanese yen," Pilnyak writes in his book *The Roots of the Japanese Sun*.

What would Pilnyak say were he able to cast an eye over the billion-dollar Japanese manga and anime industries? I cast such an eye, and learned that foxes (little blue foxes, in an anime film!), eyes enormous and round like billiard balls, are popular in Japanese comics and films; that these foxes are *morphs* (just like in the old Japanese legends), able to leap freely from a fox's body into a teenager's, the teenage body not in the least uncomfortable with the addition of vulpine ears and tail. When if Pilnyak today visited Japan and saw young people girded with artificial tails, which, operated by remote control, signal their owner's emotional state to those around them (lowered tail–raised tail–wagging tail); what would Pilnyak have made of all of this? The journey from the silence and mystery of a temple on whose altar foxes lie in repose to vulpine *cosplay* and fake tails took barely a century.*

---

* But perhaps we should be going back a few centuries, to the painting "The Beggars" by Peter Bruegel the Elder. The garments worn by the crippled figures

A volcanic dust of oblivion constantly falls upon us, slowly burying us, like insoluble snow. We are all footnotes, many of us will never have the chance to be read, all of us in an unrelenting and desperate struggle for our lives, for the life of a footnote, to remain on the surface before, in spite of our efforts, we are submerged. Everywhere we leave constant traces of our existence, of our struggle against vacuity. And the greater the vacuity, the more violent our struggle—*mein kampf, min kamp, mia lotta, muj boj, mijn strijd, minun taistelu, mi lucha, my struggle, moja borba* . . . Behind us we leave thousands of photographs and video recordings that we never find time to look at or watch; if, but a few years later, we chance upon a clip, we no longer even know where it was filmed, nor when, nor who the people are around us; we're not even sure that's us in the clip or not. Behind us we leave volcanic dust, new layers covering the old. With their little blue tails, eyes as round as billiard balls, little blue foxes from Japanese anime films cleanse, sweep away, and erase Pilnyak's story, their own mythological history too, and in the end, put us to sleep with a blue smile of oblivion.

This, however, is not a story about the past and the present, but a story about a story that tells of how stories come to be written.

10.

Boris Pilnyak was arrested on suspicion of being a Japanese spy at the very hour his son Boris was celebrating his third birthday. He was arrested at his dacha in Peredelkino, on October 28, 1937, and shot several months later, on April 21, 1938; a bullet to the nape of

---

of beggars in Bruegel's painting are festooned with fox tails. Bruegel's colleagues Bosch and Dürer portray a fool who carries a fox tail strung from his belt. Perhaps the fox tail was used to mark social outcasts: vagrants, beggars, cripples, fools, and madmen.

the neck, the customary way. He was forty-three years old. Some two thousand Soviet writers were arrested in the same period, an estimated fifteen hundred of whom lost their lives. In a purge unprecedented, both people and their manuscripts disappeared.

The circumstances of Boris Pilnyak's arrest are detailed in his son Boris Andronikashvili's piece "About My Father," the account based on the testimony of his mother, Kira Andronikashvili.

"At ten o'clock in the evening a new guest appeared. He was dressed head to toe in white, although it was fall, and the hour late. Boris Andreyevich had met him in Japan, where 'the man in white' was an employee at the Soviet consulate. He was painfully courteous. 'Nikolai Ivanovich requests that you come urgently. He needs to ask you something. You'll be back within the hour,' he said. Noticing the doubt and fear on the face of Kira Georgiyevna at the mention of Yezhov's name, he added: 'Take your car so you can drive yourself home.'* Then he repeated: 'Nikolai Ivanovich just wants to verify something.' Boris Andreyevich nodded: 'Let's go.' Holding back tears, Kira Georgiyevna brought out a little package. 'What for?!' Boris Andreyevich refused. 'Kira Georgiyevna, Boris Andreyevich will be back in an hour,' said the man in white, scornfully now. Mother kept offering the package, souring the game the nice man had imposed, but Boris Andreyevich didn't take it. 'He wanted to leave the house as a free man, not a man under arrest,' said mother."

---

* Nikolai Yezhov was head of the NKVD (the People's Commissariat of Internal Affairs) between 1936 and 1938. In Russian, the time of his purges is known as "Yezhovschina." Although Stalin's right-hand man, Yezhov was also to be accused of "anti-Soviet activities," and arrested and executed in 1940, just three years after having ordered the arrest of Boris Pilnyak. He became known as "the Vanishing Commissar": following his death his likeness vanished from sight, particularly from photos in which he had appeared with Stalin.

Brutal fate assigned Boris Pilnyak an end akin to a fable: the fox came for the writer's head in order to place it at the feet of Hedgehog the Terrible.*

Could this be put a little better?

Brutal fate assigned Boris Pilnyak an end akin to that of an unknown work from his unfinished opus. His angel of death differed from popular conceptions of the angel who brings news of the end. Pilnyak's angel of death:

a) Was painfully courteous

b) Was dressed in white

c) And was an employee of the Soviet consulate in Japan.

11.

At a certain point in his narrative, Pilnyak observes that "this is how one could end the story of how stories come to be written," yet continues apace.

---

* Translator's note: in Slavic languages, the word *jež, ёж, еж, ježek, ježko, їжак,* means hedgehog, which explains how the terrifying "Yezhov" here becomes Hedgehog the Terrible.

"The fox knows many things and the hedgehog but one," is the Greek aphorism Isaiah Berlin used as a motto for his noteworthy 1953 essay, "The Hedgehog and the Fox," in which he establishes the dichotomy between monistic and pluralistic moral values. Put baldly, authoritarian and totalitarian ideas are grounded in monism, and tolerance and liberalism in pluralism. In accordance with these categories, Berlin divided eminent writers into hedgehogs and foxes; into those who write, engage, and think with recourse to a single idea (hedgehogs), and those who merge manifold heterogeneous experiences and ideas (foxes). Dante, Plato, Pascal, Dostoevsky, Nietzsche and Proust are hedgehogs, and Montaigne, Erasmus, Molière, Goethe, Pushkin, and Joyce foxes. One could draw a connection between Berlin's essay and Pilnyak's "A Story about How Stories Come to Be Written," yet it would be somewhat forced. In any case, in Berlin's typology Pilnyak would be rather among the foxes than the hedgehogs.

Pilnyak's "A Story about How Stories Come to Be Written" is organized on the principle of juxtaposition and the relationship between three incomplete stories narrated in fragments: the **first** story is attempted by Sophia Gnedikh-Tagaki in her short biographical notes, whose narration Pilnyak usurps; the **second** is that contained in Tagaki's novel, of which we know only indirectly (via the short dispatch of an anonymous journalist), Pilnyak's own admission that his friend Takahasi relayed the contents of Tagaki's novel to him, and Pilnyak's claim that Tagaki had written "a splendid novel"; the **third** that in which Boris Pilnyak writes of Sophia and Tagaki and of his own visit to Japan. Having focused primarily on the story's obvious complexity and virtuosity, few literary scholars have taken an interest in that which interests the majority of readers: are the writer Tagaki and Sophia Gnedikh real people?

In her article "Pilnyak and Japan," the Japanese Russianist Kyoko Numano maintains that Pilnyak used celebrated Japanese writer Jun'ichirō Tanizaki as a living prototype for the character of Tagaki (Tagaki-Takahasi-Tanizaki!), and more explicitly, Tanizaki's novel *Chijin no Ai*, which translates as "A Fool's Love" and was published in English as *Naomi*. Tanizaki's novel was serialized in the Osaka newspaper *Asahi* in 1924, and appeared in a single edition the following year. Pilnyak set off for Japan in the spring of 1926. On a visit to Tokyo, a Japanese Russianist by the name of Semu Naboru brought Tanizaki to Pilnyak's attention, describing it as the literary sensation of the day.

The hero of Tanizaki's novel, Jōji Kawai, is obsessed with fifteen-year-old waitress Naomi. Jōji is enamored with western culture, and Naomi, who reminds him of Mary Pickford, becomes the incarnation of his cultural and erotic aspirations. In this respect, Jōji is a kind of

Japanese Pygmalion: he pays for Naomi's putative "Western" education (piano lessons, singing lessons, ballroom dancing lessons, English lessons), and having quickly acknowledged his erotic obsession with the girl, he marries her, only to end up the girl's slave. In Tanizaki's novel Naomi is characterized as a beautiful yet cunning, vulgar, lazy, and manipulative *modan gāru*, or "modern girl." She is, not incidentally, a representative of the new class that emerged with the Japanese industrial revolution, where the role of women radically changed.

Tanizaki sets out his novel as *shi-shosetsu*, an "I-Novel," or "novel of the self." At the time, literary naturalism, which centered on the details of a narrator's personal life (particularly those of a sexual nature) had developed into a literary school or movement. The first such work in Japanese literature is Katai Tayama's *The Quilt* (1907). Like Tanizaki's novel, it caused a scandal on publication. Together with Roman Kim, a Russian expert in Japanese literature, Pilnyak published an article in 1928 on the affair in the Russian literary periodical *Press and Revolution*, their claim being that contemporary Japanese literature had given birth to a specific form of literary creation, which they referred to as "autobiographical belles lettres." According to Pilnyak and Kim, this form of literary testimony was authentically Japanese, and a form of which "European literature has almost no sense," and that "autobiographical belles lettres" were, at that very moment, dominating Japanese literature.

It's hard to say whether Pilnyak's "A Story . . ." was inspired by Russian formalism (Boris Eikhenbaum's *How Gogol's* Overcoat *Was Made*) or intended as a kind of moral polemic with Japanese authorial confessionalism, or whether his intentions were otherwise. Whatever the case, the fascination with Japan—both that of Pilnyak and of his heroine Sophia—ends in a sense of defeat. Sophia leaves Japan having suffered the devastating betrayal of everything she held dear,* while Pilnyak's Japanese cycle appears to evidence that the Russian writer tried "with all his heart to fathom the soul of Japan." Yet as in the case of his heroine Sophia Gnedikh-Tagaki, it appears that Pilnyak's "Japanese affair" left a bitter taste—quite aside from the fact that some years later it would cost him his head. Perhaps it really was, as Pilnyak suggested, that the East expels the westerner like the cap from a bottle of kvass.

Pilnyak fails to solve the puzzle of Japan, and instead becomes a small fragment of its whole. First clue down: Russian avant-garde writer who wrote about Japan, surname beginning with the letter "P." Perhaps Pilnyak wasn't really interested in Japan. Perhaps his feeling of defeat is rooted in something else, perhaps, for example, the realization that even after the books he had written, the countries he had traveled, the literary fame he had won, and the inescapable bullet that awaited him in mid-life, he, Boris Pilnyak, Ivan the Fool, was still standing at the very beginning, obsessed by the question of how, exactly, do stories come to be written?

12.

I read Jun'ichirō Tanizaki's *Naomi* in an English translation,** certain

---

* In his text on the image of the Japanese in Russian literature, G. Chkhartishvili writes that Sophia Gnedikh-Tagaki finds herself not only in a foreign, "but in an *inhuman* foreign world" (Chkhartishvili's italics). For Chkhartishvili it is the corporeal freedom enjoyed by the Japanese, which also shocks Sophia, that is "inhuman," yet this suggestion of alterity likewise brings to mind the connection between Pilnyak's heroine and the template of the fairytale. In the code of the fairytale, Tagaki, "the alien," becomes the Beast, Bluebeard (the *inhuman*), and in such a reading Sophia fails to withstand the test of the genre, which explains the sense of defeat and lack of any happy ending.

** Jun'ichirō Tanizaki, *Naomi*, translated by Anthony H. Chambers (New York: Vintage, 2001), p. 237.

that the story I am obviously still writing was, well, finished. Given its theme, an older man's obsession with a manipulative fifteen-year-old, Tanizaki's novel better compares with Nabokov's *Lolita* than Pilnyak's "A Story about How Stories Come to Be Written." I have no doubt that somewhere a studious Nabokovophile has already investigated any similarities between *Naomi* and *Lolita*. As for Tagaki and Tanizaki, the latter of whom Pilnyak is thought to have employed as a prototype, there is almost certainly a link. If nothing else, having read Tanizaki's novel it must have been easier for Pilnyak to imagine the way in which the fictional writer Tagaki might describe his Russian wife, Sophia.

Only superficially are Sophia and Naomi alike. Both are "foreigners," Sophia Russian, Naomi Japanese—the latter's pale "Western" skin and western visage making visible her difference. Both are characterized (the former by Pilnyak, the latter by Jōji, the narrator of Tanizaki's novel) as ill-educated and somewhat vacuous. While Sophia evolves from a "stupid girl" to a mature woman who endures the betrayal she suffers with unexpected strength, Naomi goes from being a problematic teen to a capricious, promiscuous, and selfish young woman, an adept dominatrix, who, revealing an infallible instinct, turns Jōji into a willing victim, her slave.

"It seems that once a person has a terrifying experience, the experience becomes an obsession that never goes away. I'm still unable to forget the time Naomi left me. Her words echo in my ears: 'Now do you see how frightening I can be.' I've known all along that she's fickle and selfish. If those faults were removed, she would lose her value. The more I think of her as fickle and selfish, the more adorable she becomes, and the more deeply I am ensnared by her."*

---

* *Ibid.*, p. 237.

Among the novel's expatiated themes are Jōji's obsession with Naomi,
the arc of Jōji's descent into total submission, and ultimately, the
female body and corporeality. Tanizaki is a master of the lens. In his
narration, Jōji takes up the camera, photographing Naomi in various
poses and attire. Tanizaki captures perfectly the relationship between
light and shadow, a hunter of details, always just small details, never
the whole, creating an atmosphere of enigma and understatement.
Jōji is infatuated with the whiteness of Naomi's skin (an infatuation
usually understood as an obsession with a superior "westernness"),
with her toes, her nails, her clothing and its fabric, her hair, her darting glances, the various parts of her body and its scents. Although
the fifteen-year-old Naomi allows Jōji to bathe her, which he enjoys,
she nonetheless forbids him all bodily contact. Near the end she even
allows him to shave her, but only on the condition that he not touch
her skin, which affords him a masochistic pleasure. In the novel's
closing pages, it seems that Naomi herself has become obsessed with
the whiteness of her skin, and before going out in the evenings she
"applies white makeup to her entire body."*

Jōji often thinks of Naomi as a creature, not human. More than once
he describes her using the adjective "animal" (calling her, for example,
"a wild animal"), and if the English translation is reliable, the colloca-
tion, "animal electricity" (the latter appearing several times).

"If there's such thing as animal electricity, Naomi's eyes had it in
abundance. It seemed beyond belief that they were a woman's eyes.
Glittering, sharp, and frightful, they brimmed with a certain mysterious allure. And sometimes when she shot her angry glance at me, I
felt a shudder pass through my body."**

---

* *Ibid.*, p. 236.
** *Ibid.*, p. 47.

Whether perchance or perforce, there is a connection between Pilnyak's story and Tanizaki's novel. Just as Sophia experiences many
things as foreign, and just as she is amused by Tagaki's Russian accent,
Tanizaki, through his hero Jōji, makes merry at the expense of west-
ernized Japanese women, in particular, a certain Miss Sugizaki, who
mangles her English pronunciation to such an extent that "more"
becomes *moa moa*, "gentleman" *genl'man*, and "little" comes out as *li'l*.

There is, however, another person in Tanizaki's novel in whose
"accented English *three* became *tree*."* That person is Madame Alexandra Shlemskaya, a Russian countess who fled to Japan in the wake
of the revolution, and now supports herself and her two children by
giving dancing lessons. Jōji and Naomi enroll in a ballroom class, yet
unfortunately Shlemskaya makes but a brief appearance in the novel.

"I've already reported that Naomi stood about an inch shorter than I.
Though the countess appeared to be on the small side for a westerner,
she was still taller than I am. It may have been because she wore
high-heeled shoes, but when we danced together, my head came right
up to her prominent chest. The first time she said, 'Walk with me,'
placed her arm around my back, and showed me the one-step, how
desperately I tried to keep my dark face from grazing her skin!."**

Tanizaki intends the countess to serve as the embodiment of an alluring, superior, and untold West. Infused with an inferiority complex,
Naomi is but a stunted Japanese substitute, all that Tanizaki's narrator
Jōji can afford. Yet this East-West relationship comes across as somewhat forced and unconvincing; Jōji's obsessive and limited gaze only
registers physical details, skin color in particular, but very little else.

---

* *Ibid.*, p. 61.
** *Ibid.*, p. 69.

"What set her apart from Naomi most of all was the extraordinary whiteness of her skin. Her pale lavender veins, faintly visible beneath the white surface like speckles on marble, were weirdly beautiful. (. . .) Naomi's hands weren't a vivid white—indeed, seen after the countess's hand, her skin looked murky."*

Anthony H. Chambers, Tanizaki's translator and author of the foreword to the novel's American edition, offers an interesting tidbit: Tanizaki apparently loved "Western" dancing and dance halls, so much so that he once registered for a dance competition in Yokohama, which at the time was run by a Russian named Vasily Krupin. In this respect, in the novel Vasily Krupin becomes the Russian countess Alexandra Shlemskaya.

In his story, Pilnyak deploys the powerful symbol of the fox, the mythological embodiment of treachery, cunning, and betrayal—and, as Pilnyak would have it, the most likely candidate for worship as totem of the literary guild. The fox in Tanizaki's novel gets only a passing mention in an intimation that Naomi herself might be a fox, an incalculable and seductive female demon.

"Taking care not to awaken her, I sat by her pillow, held my breath, and stealthily gazed at her sleeping form. In the old days, a fox might decieve a young man by taking the form of a princess, only to reveal its true form when it slept and gave itself away. I recalled hearing such stories in my childhood. Rough sleeper that she was, Naomi had shed her coverlet and was gripping it between her thighs. One elbow was raised, and the hand rested like a bent twig on her exposed breast. My eyes moved back and forth between the pure white Western paper in the book and the whiteness of her breast. Naomi's skin looked yellow

---

* *Ibid.*, p. 68.

one day and white another; but it was extraordinarily limpid when she was asleep, or just awakened, as though all the fat in her body had melted away."*

13.

So really, how do stories come to be written? Perhaps Pilnyak subconsciously fumbled his way to an answer in using the verb *sozdat'* instead of the verb *sdelat'*. It's all in the nuance: *sdelat'* infers to make, to produce, to render (in the sense of Boris Eikhenbaum's *How Gogol's Overcoat Was Made—Kak sdelana Šinel' Gogolja*). *Sozdat'* infers to create, shape, mold, form, develop . . . Furthermore, Pilnyak uses the imperfective verb in the present; this, thus, is not a story about how a story came to be, but a story about how stories come into being. The imperfective verbal aspect suggests that stories are never finished, that the process of their formation remains ongoing. Perhaps this explains the title's absence of a creator, the story's author, he who conditions its continuation.

In his "essay on aesthetics," *In Praise of Shadows*, Jun'ichirō Tanizaki eulogizes the aesthetics of Japanese everyday life: wooden handicrafts, candles, lamps, and rice paper lanterns, lacquered wooden dishes, soft lighting, all of which engender opacity, placidity, and discretion, a penumbral quality and pliancy, a tranquility and mysticism. Tanizaki contrasts this world of shadow, the world of traditional Japanese life, with the modern world and its opposing aesthetic values, those of glare, squall, vulgarity, and clamor.

"I would call back at least for literature this world of shadow we are losing. In the mansion called literature I would have the eaves deep

---

* *Ibid.*, p. 120-21.

and the walls dark, I would push back into the shadows the things that come forward too clearly, I would strip away useless decoration."*

Isn't the purport of the excerpt above entirely contradictory to the principles of *shi-shosetsu*, the "I-novel," under which *Naomi* is shelved? Because nowhere in the novel does Tanizaki strip himself bare, but does, rather, the opposite: having laid him bare, he pushes his narrator Jōji farther into the shadows. All told, where lies the secret of a well-told story? In the interplay of light and shadow, the hidden and the revealed, the declared and the suppressed? Or, to use the formalist lexicon, in the organization of the material? And moreover: did I choose Pilnyak's story or did Pilnyak's story choose me? Am I telling a story about Pilnyak's story or a story about myself? And in any endgame, isn't Pilnyak's story also telling me?! Do the revelations connected to Pilnyak's story alter its meaning or does it remain as it always was? What role do reader and literary interpreter play in a story's becoming? Am I destroying Pilnyak's story or am I its co-creator? Is Pilnyak's story material of the same value to me as Sophia's short biography and Tagaki's novel were for Pilnyak, or moreover, material worth the same as Sophia was for Tagaki?

14.

Here is where the story could end—a story about how stories come to be written, notes Pilnyak at a certain point before, naturally, continuing his narration. Perhaps here, amid the unanswered questions that mingle spritely beneath my fingers, could my story about how stories come to be written come to an end?

---

* Jun'ichirō Tanizaki, *In Praise of Shadows*, translated by Thomas J. Harper and Edward G. Seidensticker (Leete's Island Books, 1977), p. 42.

In the early years of our puberty (years that today appear almost painfully innocent), my friends and I would engage in a kind of fortune-telling during our childish horseplay. Seeing a loose thread on a friend's clothing, we'd gather it in our fingertips, and as if with a broom of sorts we'd sweep the spot where we'd seen the thread with our palm and intone: *Someone fair is thinking of you* (if the thread was white) or *Someone dark is thinking of you* (if the thread was black). Of course, by this we meant either a blond or dark-headed boy. We'd say it even when there was no thread, just pretending we'd found one. Recalling this innocent horseplay, I wondered how it was that later I never met anyone, anyone at all, on whose clothing I spotted any kind of thread. Where did all the black and white threads on our clothing come from? It was as if we were all daughters of the plump neighborhood seamstress, her clothing always laced with a smattering of multicolored threads. As young girls, this harmless superstition involving cotton thread had a magical allure, perhaps because of its murky undercurrent of sexuality. I wonder where the enchanting magic of black and white threads was lost. Where did it disappear? Where are those vanished threads? I think they still exist, but are now invisible. Who knows, perhaps walking the world, we exchange threads; in passing we brush against an unknown body, we slip by or collide, graze one and other . . . and thus the threads travel, from shoulder to shoulder, sleeve to sleeve. Threads are breath and body, the means by which the souls of the living and the dead travel, lodge themselves under our nails, and it is in this way that we, unknown to us, are all connected.

It was at the "wishing tree" that I remembered my childhood superstition. I tied a strip of paper, my wish inscribed. A hot gust of wind occasionally nudged the tree, from which *omikuji* dangled, strips of paper tied by thread to small branches. The August night in Kyoto was warm and wet, and the asphalt glistened with a cheap glow. The night absorbed background noise like a dry blotter, and the little tree appeared like a ghostly apparition. The pieces of paper jostled with every stirring of the breeze, producing a dry, rustling sound; some threads caught and became entangled, and some will remain so, and when a stronger wind blows and the rain falls, the letters will run on the paper and the wishes slide down like tears. Perhaps here, in this place (in early August, the time of *Tanabata*) a story about how stories come to be written might end? I went to Kyoto, and I drank their sake, and if you don't believe me, check, my tongue is still moist, even now.

I never actually visited the Suwayama Inari temple in Kobe, which Pilnyak describes in his story. In its place I visited the Fushimi Inari temple in Kyoto. There I bought a cheap fox's mask made of papier-mâché, the kind Pilnyak mentions in his Japanese travelogue. In one of the many souvenir shops, which stood honeycombed next to each other, I bought an amulet, a miniature fox made of pelt. I avoided the Japanese cookies filled with *azuki*, a sweet green bean paste, the outline of a fox stamped onto their surface. In neighboring Kobe I visited the house where Jun'ichirō Tanizaki had lived. The house stands in Uozaki Street and is only open to visitors on Saturdays and Sundays. It was Monday, which I had completely overlooked. Perhaps a story about how stories come to be written might end with a photograph of Tanizaki's wooden house and abundant garden, of which on tippy-toes I managed to sneak a shot above a high wooden fence.

Perhaps a story about how stories come to be written might end in my conversations with K., who generously offered to be my guide to Kyoto and Kobe. K. had traveled endlessly through Asia, North Africa, and Europe, and read Vietnamese writers with the same interest he did Austrian or North African. He wore brightly-colored, rubber-soled *tabi* boots, and in a kind of modernized Japanese *hakama*, a bag from Laos slung over his shoulder, his Moroccan *gandora* and flat cap on, his attire signaled that cosmopolitanism and global culture were a fusion of both his intellectual positioning and way of being in the world. While living in Vienna, K. managed to visit wartime Croatia, participate in demonstrations against Milošević in Belgrade, and learn Polish and several words in almost every Slavic language. He had traveled to Portbou, where, kneeling at the grave of Walter Benjamin and thinking of the *Arcades Project*, he tried in contemplation to revive the tragic end to Benjamin's life. Of "world literature" Benjamin had this to say:

"World literature is like a whale around which suckerfish gather like practiced pirates. They attach themselves to the whale's body and vacuum the parasites from its skin. The whale is a source of food, protection, and means of transport. Without the suckerfish, parasites would settle on the whale's body and the body fall apart . . . I have no illusions about my own literary talent. I am a literary suckerfish. My mission is to attend to the whale's health."

While K.'s English was probably decent, his accent made it almost impossible to understand. All the same, having come from opposite ends of the earth, K. and I didn't get "lost in translation," in fact, perhaps *thanks* to mistranslation, we found each other.

Perhaps my story about how stories come to be written could end with a detail from the novel *Dōhyō* (*Mileposts*) by the Japanese writer, feminist, and communist, Yuriko Miyamoto. In 1927, Miyamoto traveled with a friend, Yuasa Yoshiko, to Moscow, where the two women studied Russian language and literature and befriended Sergei Eisenstein. Three years later the two friends returned to Japan, where Miyamoto became the editor of a women's Marxist literary magazine, and Yuasa a respected translator of Russian literature. Yuriko Miyamoto lobbied for proletarian literature, joined the Japanese communist party, and married its general secretary, the literary critic Kenji Miyamoto. Her communist engagement made her a target for Japanese police and she spent more than two years in jail.

Yuriko Miyamato wrote of all of this, and much more besides, in *Mileposts*, which is a kind of fictionalized autobiography. Written in the third person, the novel takes as its heroine the writer Nobuko Sasa, who travels with a friend from Japan to Moscow. Nobuko is invited to a gathering at the house of a Russian writer named Polnyak. The gathering becomes a drunken affair, yet Nobuko refuses alcohol (*I can't!*—*Ya ne mogu!* she repeats in Russian). Polnyak's wife is there and to Nobuku resembles a kind of doll. At some point Polnyak and Nobuko meet by chance in the hallway and he pushes her into a room where he tries to rape her, but is disturbed by other guests.

During their time in Moscow, Yuriko Miyamoto and Yuasa Yoshiko really were invited to a farewell dinner, organized by Japanese professor Masao Yonekawa at the home of Boris Pilnyak. It is thought that there were twelve people present at the gathering, including Pilnyak's wife. The episode from Miyamoto's novel was kindly narrated to me by A. O., a Japanese scholar of Slavic literature. In his memoirs, Masao Yonekawa, a respected translator of Russian literature, writes of Miyamoto's account to him of Pilnyak's attempted rape. Perhaps Yuriko Miyamoto decided to take revenge on Boris Pilnyak: in her novel he is reduced to an ugly incident. Or perhaps there is an internal polemic at work, the irreconcilability of the two types of writer sketched by Isaiah Berlin in his essay "The Hedgehog and the Fox." Apart from being a woman, Miyamoto was obviously also a hedgehog.

Perhaps I should end a story about how stories come to be written with my return from Kyoto to Tokyo, at the very moment the spectacular *shinkasen* approached Tokyo's main railway station, an architectural colossus and magnificent replica of Amsterdam's Central Station. The train bolted through a line of skyscrapers that stood like trees, rays of sun cutting through a melodramatic sky filled with darkened clouds. The glass expanse of the skyscrapers reflected both the hurtling *shinkasen* and the skyscrapers on the opposite side, transforming the real landscape into the surreal, at once intricate, fragmented and dislocated. It was a moment of visual delirium, more perfect and true than anything reflected by reality. I raced through a multiplied world. In the train sat men-boys in business suits, haircuts like anime heroes, and women-girls whose fingers as thin as chopsticks silently tapped the screens of their digital toys. Others, both men and women, simply slept, gently nibbling the air with their beguiling heads. The multiplied reflections in the skyscraper glass were suddenly joined by vulpine shadows, chasing each other, playing tag, trying to outrun the train. On the tips of their tails these vulpine shadows spun balls, skillful jugglers, tricksters, shape-shifters, masters of the shell-game con, illusionists, foxes with one, with three, with five tails . . . Vulpine shadows floated across the sky like illuminated globes, producing a bluish scintilla and exploding like firecrackers. *Kitsune.* This was their illusionistic orgy. It was somewhere here that I sensed my story about how stories come to be written had come full circle and returned to its beginning, like a fox tired of playing that lies down to rest, and blinking lazily descends into sleep. In a dream she sucks the tip of her tail like a baby its thumb.

PART TWO

A Balancing Art

It was late afternoon, and she sat, smoking, in the corner, in the deep shadow cast by the tall cupboard onto the wall. The shadow was so deep that the only things one could make out were the faint flicker of her cigarette and the two piercing eyes. The rest—her smallish shrunken body under the shawl, her hands, the oval of her ashen face, her gray, ashlike hair—all were consumed by the dark. She looked like a remnant of a huge fire, like a small ember that burns if you touch it.

—Joseph Brodsky, "Nadezhda Mandelstam
(1899–1980): An Obituary"

1.

Literature and Geography

I was once traveling by train from Antwerp to Amsterdam; across from me sat a young man, engrossed in his book. The book title was stamped on the cover in raised, gold letters. The young man was a manual laborer whose muscles were his bread and butter. "I have a library of five hundred books," he bragged. He read only thrillers, the plots of which were situated in scintillating, geographically exotic locales: Hong Kong, Bangkok, Singapore, Tokyo . . . "And everything about the place has to be exactly right, like in a travel guide," added the young man. "Why?" I asked. "Because I enjoy traveling to the city where the story takes place and visiting all the sites described in the book!"

The young man ran his finger over the raised gold letters of the title, *Murder at Kuala Lumpur Motel*. "I have not yet come across a thriller that takes place in nature. Nature is no good for thrillers," he added with the cadence of a seasoned reader, and I envied momentarily all those writers who situate their exciting stories in exciting cities, without skimping on topographic detail.

But I was skeptical as to how meaningful topography (and geography) could be for a plot as it unfolds; how essential is it to the story? How much do the two elements—plot and topography—work in tandem and how much are they at odds? Will any link between them occur to the readers only later, in their interpretation? I wondered then what role chance plays in all this, and whether an "urban scenography" helps the story or hurts it. Because if the plot locality is a "strong place" (one that is, at the same time, a *cultural text*) while the event is "weak," our entire literary effort could end up as some sort of fictionalized travel guide. If, on the other hand, the event is "strong" and the place "weak," the reader might rightfully wonder what point there was to insisting on the topography.

I hadn't given this much thought before. Now, when these two things, the event and the place where the event occurs, are bouncing and colliding in front of my nose like balls in the hands of a slipshod juggler, I am thinking about it. I feel sure they are essentially irreconcilable, that between them—between *my* place and *my* events—there rules a thematic and stylistic incompatibility. Linking a fictional literary text and its geography is most often "artistically" risky. One is tempted to do so by the hope—supported by nothing—that these "partners" will conform to one another and join in a harmonious marriage, like orange juice and the ice cube.

I was invited for three days to Naples as part of a meeting on European migrations. The meeting was an international academic conference, attended mostly by historians, sociologists, and political scientists. We, a few of my colleagues and I, belonged to the category of "entertainers." We were the mavens of migration, the acrobats of exile, the people of rubber, the tightrope walkers (who knew how to stretch a wire and, ambulating along it, inch our way to Europe from Africa), writers who were thought to have something first-hand to say about émigré life. I agreed to go, not because of the draw of the subject matter (this was a topic I had long since plumbed), but because I'd never been to Naples.

2.

The Hotel

I arrived at Grand Hotel Santa Lucia on Via Partenope around noon. At the reception desk they asked me to wait for at least an hour as my room wasn't yet ready. I strolled along Via Partenope by the sea and then came back and explored the little streets right behind the hotel. It was a Sunday, but this part of the city seemed somewhat forsaken and deserted. In a small restaurant I ate a sad little pizza and then went back to the hotel. At the front desk I picked up a brochure for guided tours, went up to my room, and drew the curtains across the breathtaking view of the sea and Castel dell'Ovo. I turned on the light and looked for the schedule the organizers had sent out at the last moment (Ah, those slapdash Italians!). A second perusal of the schedule made things no clearer, but I did understand what mattered most: the meeting with the organizers would be held only in the evening of the next day. Before I slid between the impeccably clean, cool sheets (Ah, bless those Italian women!), I called down to the front desk and asked to join the full-day tour: "Pompeii & the Amalfi Coast."

I slept—stirring now and then—until morning, exactly as if I'd landed on the moon instead of Naples. Like cotton candy I chewed my dreams. At one moment I gurgled, started awake, cleared my throat from the gunk of sleep, and with deep breaths continued greedily sipping sleep like oxygen.

In the morning I lingered for a time in the shower, then dressed and went down to breakfast. Along the way I surveyed the hotel guests, guessing which ones might be my "colleagues." The best known among us, I'd heard, would be the widow of a famous writer. Her husband had been an émigré and had died long ago; only recently had people begun thinking of him as a great writer. In the front hall, however, there was not a single woman who looked the way I imagined the widow of a great writer might look. The minibus soon arrived and enthusiastically I joined the smallish knot of tourists.

3.

Pompeii & the Amalfi Coast

The minibus delivered us to Pompeii and left us there to wait. There were dozens and dozens of people milling around as they waited patiently for their guides. Around us were a few cafés, vendors hawking plastic bottles of water, hats, and caps (for protection from the sun), and stands, tents, and booths with souvenirs. Costumed figures dressed as Roman soldiers mingled with the crowd so tourists could pose with them for a photograph. In time the crowd dispersed, groups formed, each was assigned its guide. The guides made sure they were visible by holding up umbrellas or flags. For my "umbrella" I chose a couple, tourists from my own group, a young Estonian woman and her husband, for she—dressed in loud green pants, green T-shirt, green jacket, her hair black as a crow's feathers, with a perturbed, dark look in her eye as if copied from the face of a tragic silent-movie actress, her full lips done in loud red lipstick—was simply impossible to miss.

Our guide, too, was a striking young woman with an impressive mastery of the genre of eco-catastrophe. "Pompeii was laid out like New York City," she said, sketching a map of Manhattan in the air with her red, buffed fingernails, gesturing to the Pompeii streets that lay there before us. When she said the word *up* she pronounced it with a broad "a" and drawn-out "p" (aah-puh) while pursing her lips, which her lipstick made look three times their natural size. Telling us about the vanished life of everyday Pompeii as if it were her very own intimate past, our guide completely entranced us. And when she drew our attention to a penis engraved on a paving stone—meant to point eager sailors to Pompeii's red-light district—the men from our group snorted with childish glee. They smirked softly, in hoarse, geezerly tones, with the stolid wordless backing of their wives who moved, sentry-like, to their men, tucking an arm silently under theirs or leaning just slightly into them. The collective male delight, bubbling over at the sight of that twenty-century-old symbol of manhood, was comical, especially coming as it did from mainly older men. The collective female reshuffle after seeing the penis carved in the street was nearly unanimous. When I remarked in passing to the Estonian woman something about how it's only the unreliable things—the things women cannot seriously depend on—that require monuments carved in stone, she breezed right by my sentiment and reached, instinctively, for her husband's arm

With dramatic language, the Neapolitan woman painted for us the catastrophe of two thousand years ago, comparing Vesuvius to a pressure cooker, pronouncing the word "eruption" (erruppshoooon), rolling her eyes framed with their thick, brush-like lashes, so the men—their foreheads scorching in the hot afternoon sun—now also smirked at the word "eruption." The young woman buoyed our flagging attention by frequent use of the phrase "Now, surely you can imagine . . ." and repeating that the people of Pompeii were buried under twenty tons of volcanic ash. I don't know where she pulled the fact from, but she trotted it out at least five times.

Our guide also relied heavily on a book, *Pompeii Reconstructed*, which she flipped open to show us how certain places had once looked centuries before and how they looked now. We all hastened to inquire, of course, where we might buy it. The book, if our group's reaction was any indication, pressed our mental *before-after* button. It was a *total-makeover* toy and crystalized for us what life had been like in Pompeii before the "erruppshooon." The book's photographs of a Pompeii staged free of tourists, and even the town itself today thronged by hundreds of tourists, us included, looked far better than the reconstruction sketched in the style of a classic, high-detail comic strip. The drawings gobbled up the imagination with the speed of a termite, leaving absolutely nothing behind.

I think the unconscious appeal of Pompeii for tourists lies in vague memories of a childhood game that we called "statues," or something like that. The person who is "it" tags the players and then they have to "freeze" like statues and stay where they were when they were tagged. Whoever moved was out. The carbonization of daily life, frozen at the instant of the eruption, evoked a similar childish thrill. Pompeii was like a sweet dream of our own funeral that we dreamed with ease, knowing we weren't dead.

As I observed the people who trudged obediently along behind their guides, their bottles of water in hand, their canes, hats, and sunglasses at the ready, as I recalled the collective male smirk at the sight of the penis in the shape of an asymmetrical clover carved into the paving stone, I was overcome by a sudden attack of misanthropy. In another fifteen minutes they would be ushering us into the vast hall of what used to be a workers' cafeteria, a "restaurant" in name only. Spry waiters there would shovel into us lousy spaghetti, rotting lettuce, and vinegar-sour wine; an aging singer with guitar in hand would gallop through several *canzone Napoletana* because outside was another tourist group waiting impatiently. As I watched the human circus, the frenzied waiters reeling from the tempo, the countless plates sailing above our heads, the voluntary humiliation to which we acquiesced as if we had paid for the right to be humiliated; as I watched our stampede emptying the lunch room so the next group could stampede in, I suddenly longed for Great Vesuvius to do its damnedest, spew its lava over all of us, carbonize us, and blanket us with twenty tons of volcanic ash . . .

Life is so short, says Ingrid Bergman when she visits Pompeii in the movie *Viaggio in Italia.* Guided tours are organized precisely as if designed for attacks of misanthropy. They seem to exist mainly to run adults ragged as if they were children, have them scarf down every food served up to them so that they drop off to sleep, dead tired. My spell of misanthropy would soon be assuaged by the beauty we'd already seen, the beauty of Pompeii, and the beauty washing over us through the windows of the bus on the road to Amalfi. The sea shimmered below us; in the distance we'd see the eternally "pregnant" island of Capri, charming Praiano, Positano, Galli, Isola di Nureyev, magical Amalfi . . . From time to time we'd step down out of the bus and inhale the air, aromatic with oranges, lemons, and salt, while the shimmering blue of the sea and sky caressed us like silk . . .

At the "restaurant," as cavernous as a basketball court, we perched on long wooden benches. Across from me sat the Estonian couple. The Estonian woman was earnestly assisting the waiters to hand out the plates with spaghetti, passing them on to others. She was adept, exactly as if she had spent her entire life vacationing in girl-scout camps. She and her husband would be continuing on to Vesuvius while I went on to Amalfi. She was the proprietor of a fashion boutique in Tallinn. I handed her a brochure with a guided tour of outlets where one could purchase clothing by famous Italian designers at deeply discounted prices.

"Not interested," said the Estonian woman, sucking up the spaghetti with youthful vigor. "I want to laze around, savor fine wine,

and roam," she said, and her husband nodded his shaved head. "Emma
Bovary, somewhere in the first chapter of the novel, says that for one's
honeymoon one should travel to countries with sonorous names. The
country she has in mind is clearly Italy because right after that Emma
mentions the sea shores and the scent of the lemon trees. And then
she adds that in some places happiness flourishes like a plant peculiar
to that place, which cannot thrive anywhere else. I'm certain Flaubert
was thinking of Naples. Happiness blossoms in Naples like those red
Neapolitan bougainvilleas. Nowhere but in Naples have I seen such
a color . . . Jesus! As if it grows straight out of a blood vein instead of
the ground!"

I was astonished. I hadn't told the Estonian woman what I did for a
living. The unexpected literary reference rang in the air like the ping
of a crystal goblet. I looked at the slender, green-clothed creature
with her big eyes shaded by the dark bags under them, like the ones
actresses have in silent films, her lips the hue of Neapolitan bougain-
villea, and I thought I had never seen anyone like her. Just then the
bus driver appeared, going from table to table and shouting, "Amalfi,
Amalfi coast, Amalfi . . . !" I rose, reached over to shake the hand of
the husband with the shaved head and then hers.

"Ciao, bella," I said foolishly because I didn't know what else to
say, and off I hurried to my bus.

4.

Hakuna Matata

The Italian academic institutions had their reasons for organizing
a meeting on migration in Naples, of all places. The statisticians
had been claiming that the number of refugees in Italy was within
the "permissible" seven-percent range, but in southern Italy this had
reached an "alarming" twelve percent. Italy and Greece are the "gateway

to Europe." Using any means available, people had been flocking to this gateway from Tunisia, Morocco, Somalia, Ethiopia, Nigeria, Rwanda, Burundi, Burkina Faso, from the former Yugoslavia, Albania, Ukraine, Poland, Romania, Bangladesh, Pakistan, China . . .

Almost every day, there was news reported in papers, on television, and online regarding "incidents": scores of refugees suffocating below the decks of old fishing boats before they reached their destination; boats sinking, overloaded with refugees; refugees trampled by the unbridled behavior of the anguished human herd as it disembarked; cruel traffickers making their riches off the suffering of others; families selling everything they owned to pay the way for their sons and daughters to the promised lands; African gangs who, knowing the routes, kidnapped refugees and demanded ransom from their families, holding the young female refugees in sexual slavery; the small percentage of lucky ones who made it alive to the Italian shores; the despair they faced as they disembarked . . . Stories poured in daily from the news outlets about the shabby treatment refugees had received in Lampedusa and other Italian cities; they claimed they felt as if they were in an "open prison" in Italy, which was no lie because they could venture no farther. Other European countries were refusing to accept them, politicians were toying with the unfortunate people, nobody knew what to do with them. In Italian refugee ghettoes, people were identified by number, not name; this was, among other things, the dismal practice at the refugee centers. The mayor of Lampedusa allowed refugees to be accommodated in the city museum, thereby infuriating the local population. Documentary film scenes— of "anti-drug patrols" cruising on nocturnal forays through the small towns of southern Italy supposedly to help the police in their battle against criminals—were reminiscent of the not-so-distant fascist past and were stirring anxiety and dread at the prospect of its possible resurgence. On the other hand, in front of television cameras, Italians had been clamoring their agitation, their concern for their daughters, they called the migrants of color "ugly snouts," speaking of them with scorn (*What they really want is a BMW or a Mercedes!*), and there had been calls for forming new units of the National Guard. The furious people of Lampedusa (where a large number of refugees fled after the "African Spring") spoke of the "invasion" of migrants and demanded that they be stopped at all costs (*Execute the invaders, every last one of them*); the onslaught was interfering with tourism—their livelihood. And indeed, many tourists had canceled their plans to vacation in Lampedusa. The people who fled their homes found themselves in a "European hell"; nobody offered them an acceptable solution, or compassion, or a job, or anything. They'd embarked on a "journey of epic proportions" (in the words of poetically inclined journalists) and were met by what they had left behind at home: poverty, powerlessness, jail.

Language was the perfect gauge for the attitudes toward the refugees. The more delicate the wording, the worse the attitudes about the "newcomers." The European bureaucracy wrestled with its terms—migrants, emigrants, immigrants, asylum seekers, exiles—until they finally settled on "migrant," suggesting by doing so that this is a mobile work force, choosing of its own volition which destinations suits them best in terms of geography, culture, climate, and finance for temporary work in this globalized world, at their own risk, of course. The language of journalism could be viciously cynical (*dehydrated migrants!*), even as it claimed the opposite. Equally confusing was the language of the pundits (sociologists, historians, political scientists). That language had tagged me, as well, with categories such as *hyphenated identities, hybrid selves,* and so forth. The language that followed the strictures of supposed political correctness and courtesy, language that took a stand, at least declaratively, in opposition to the language of outright fascism, had only, in fact, broadened the linguistic repertoire of discrimination.

The conference panels were being held in several venues both in the center and on the outskirts of town, so participating required physical effort and the organizers were not inclined to trouble with the handful of us "colleagues," to transport us from various discussions in one venue to those in another where our participation was not planned anyway. I was surprised when I saw in the program that I would be appearing in a discussion with the widow of the famous literary exile. Several colleagues were speaking before our turn came, and, full of good will and solidarity, I sat in the devastatingly empty hall at the exquisite complex of the IBC, the *Instituto Benedetto Croce*.

In *Paradise: Love*, a film by Ulrich Seidl, there's a scene that takes place in the half-empty restaurant of a hotel at a vacation spot somewhere in Kenya. There are two or three middle-aged German women sitting at the tables with a man who is dozing, and they are being entertained by a listless musical group dressed in what was supposedly local attire: long robes and caps sewn of cloth with a black-and-white zebra design. The "Zebras" give a lackluster performance of the song "Hakuna Matata" from *The Lion King*. In the film, the local Kenyans use this phrase with aggressive frequency.

Many tourists, when they went home after vacationing in the former Yugoslavia, brought with them the phrase *nema problema*—no problem. I heard it countless times from Germans, English, Italians. Apparently *nema problema* was the only thing foreigners took away with them from Yugoslavia and about Yugoslavia. After hearing *hakuna matata* it occurred to me that kindred countries produce kindred phrases with which to gratify tourists, offering them services along the way that symbolize "the real thing" as opposed to the unreal thing, which is, of course, the life lived by those unimaginative foreigners.

Onto the stage stepped a young Chinese man; he had made his way to Italy and there published two collections of poems. Now he was serving as an example of the successful integration of Chinese emigrants into Italian society. An Albanian woman had been scheduled to appear, but she had recently received a major Italian literary award so she had, I assume, outgrown participation in such events. A pretty writer wearing a turban who looked as if she had tumbled out of an old-fashioned colonial advertisement for bananas was also here. She had flown to Naples from New York. There was also a Berlin Turk, an Amsterdam Iranian resembling an aging Omar Sharif, and a gray-haired African. The African was showered with the most attention by the organizers simply because he symbolized the most pressing problem: the African refugees in Italy and Italians' attitudes about them.

I chatted over breakfast with the African man, who came across as the most genial in our group. In the twenty years he had spent in western Europe, he had succeeded in schooling his four children; now they were employed and scattered around various European cities and he had returned to his country to wage local political battles. He had his moves down pat: all he had to do was put on his "robe," don the little cap, and he immediately looked the part. In our lively conversation over breakfast he did not hide what I could have guessed: the older man had married a young woman when he moved home and with her had two very small children; the western European routes of exile were finished, the generosity of donors, no matter who they had been, had dried up, and all he could rely on any more was a pittance from domestic sources. True, the return was eased by the fact that his importance at home had skyrocketed. He had not received a Nobel prize, but his countrymen had begun, for some reason, to show him respect. While he had been merely one of thousands of people in exile "abroad," here he was potentially the father of the African *non-fiction narrative*, or something like that. He was rattling his ethnic and racial *rakatak*, but I had to know that in his country many of the people were illiterate, so literature functioned in an altogether different way. And while we were on the subject, the rattle of the "ethnic and racial *rakatak*," believe it or not, was the only sound everybody heard and understood, both those at home and the hosts here in Europe who'd invited him.

"The time of internationalism and cosmopolitanism is over and done with. Period," declared the wry old man, and then, as if he were suddenly afraid of what he'd said, he went on with a mantra about the goodness of the European countries: "The Netherlands are good and France is good, England is good and Italy is good, Sweden is good, and Finland is good . . ."

All of us were like the characters in the Ulrich Seidl movie; we'd donned our robes, some brightly visible, others invisible, sporting what were supposedly ethnic and racial designs, and we were all offering a lackluster performance of the only routine we knew: *Hakuna matata, Nema problema*. It was too late for condolences. Human hearts had in the meanwhile turned to flab. Our boats had capsized, we were swimming as best we knew how, some with life jackets, others without, that being the only difference. This was our modernity—the age of survival. Life had become a luxury, literature all the more so, except that nobody had informed the conference participants accordingly. They were convinced that the empty hall was the exception, not the rule. They assumed there must be a major soccer match on. That is exactly what the organizers said, by way of apology.

5.

The Widow

So this was why the hall was now standing-room-only! The Widow and I first met on stage at the conference table where she warmly offered me her hand. The moderator introduced us and then gave us the floor.

The Widow breathed a genteel charm, as if she had just stepped out of a BBC adaptation of some great English classic, a more sensual version of Maggie Smith. She had thick, gray hair plaited in a short braid that she wore down her back like a bashful high-school girl. Curls poked out in all the right places around her ears, softening her face and making the wrinkles less pronounced. Yes, she had wrinkles, after all she was over eighty; her teeth were just slightly crooked, but they were still hers and they were all there. Her face was well put-together, the only trace of makeup the discreet strokes of eye shadow on her eyelids. Her hands were angular, wrinkled, scattered with liver spots, and tanned, as if she gardened. Her posture was elegant, her back was, age-wise, surprisingly straight. Her nose was slightly hooked, her eyes, the color of honey, were a little slanted. She was wearing a black linen dress and black espadrilles. Around her neck she wore a necklace of string and a pendant of black veneered wood, its symbol reminiscent of African amulets. She had a warm smile and she was generous with it.

She spoke first, in a pleasant voice, modestly, about quite ordinary things; how she and Levin had lived in Paris in the 1960s. The Widow was candid, at least she gave that impression. She did not treat her role in Levin's life as significant, she said they'd lived together for only three years and had married, for practical reasons, not long before he died. She said she couldn't speak about Levin's earlier life because he had not been able to tell her much about whatever he hadn't "processed through literature," meaning that the so-called autobiographical fragments could be, and most often were, in terms of factuality, quite unreliable. Levin did not feel he deserved any particular credit for the fact that his life, unlike most, had cast him up on so many shores, though he saw his "geographic and cultural good fortune" as his lottery jackpot. He did, however, feel he deserved more acknowledgment for his writing than he'd been accorded. The Widow spoke about details from their shared life; the poverty, how she'd found two crates of canned food in the basement of the house where they were renting an apartment. The package was from Norway, who knows how it had ended up in the Paris basement, condensed milk and—reindeer meat! A genuine treasure trove, a windfall. Never before or since had she eaten reindeer meat. "I remember the years I spent with Levin as years of hunger," she said. Levin himself had been too ill to go anywhere and she no longer had anywhere to go back to. She'd lost her parents in quick succession. Levin, whether he wanted to or not, had become her new "home." Each exile longs for some form of home. Levin was at the core of her symbolic domicile, a home which, after his death, she built herself, said The Widow modestly.

When my turn came, I "expounded" on exile, which turned out to be embarrassingly stupid. I would have earned far more sympathy with a witty anecdote about passport-control officials than with my flimsy disquisition on the subject of the literary dynamic; the inclusivity and exclusivity of cultural environments (only great cultures are inclusive, which is what makes them great; only small cultures are exclusive, which is what keeps them small). Everything I said left the audience cold.

Never in my life have I felt more invisible than I did during my appearance with The Widow. After the panel, journalists and several television cameras thronged around The Widow: nobody bought a copy of my book, which had just come out in Italian, but they did buy Levin's; nobody felt the need to come over and say a kind word, they were all waiting in line to speak with The Widow. My presence turned out to be superfluous.

The moderator and I went out into the garden of the IBC and waited for The Widow to finish talking with the journalists and members of the audience.

"Did I handle everything to your satisfaction?" asked the moderator, as if apologizing for my more than obvious defeat.

"Yes, you were top-notch," I said.

"I'm a historian, you know, I study European migrations in the Middle Ages. I'm not big on literature . . ."

"Were there any then? Migrations, I mean?"

"There have always been," said the historian. "The Neapolitans moved everywhere and people moved to Naples from everywhere else . . . the Romans, Goths, Lombards, Byzantines, the Normans, Saracens, Spanish, French, Austrians, Germans . . . This region was settled by Jews from the very earliest days, who were first brought as slaves. There are remnants of a synagogue in the catacombs of Naples. There were some cities, like Capua, that were 'Jewish' . . . The richer families later moved to the north of Italy . . . In the seventeenth century tens of thousands of slaves were shipped in from Africa. And there are Chinese communities today in the poorer neighborhoods of Naples," she explained in a way as if she, herself, couldn't quite believe what she'd just said.

The Widow stepped into the garden, bidding farewell to the charmed throngs who'd attended the event, and came over to us.

"Let's go for a drink," she said brightly.

The historian begged off, she was due at another panel, but, honored by the invitation, I agreed immediately.

6.
Gran Caffè Gambrinus

The Widow and I strolled from the Instituta Benedeto Croce to Piazza del Gesu Nuovo.

"We'll catch a cab here . . ." she said. "Do you remember the old De Sica movie *Marriage Italian Style*, with Sophia Loren and Marcello Mastroianni? About Filumena and Dumbi?"

"Why do you ask?"

"Because Filumena and Dumbi are married at last in this church, Gesu Nuovo, and the final scene is at their house, with its windows facing the church. There, and in front of the house today there is a cab stand . . ."

The Widow spoke in a confident tone, like a native. At her side I felt like a lazy tourist. The cab soon dropped us in front of the famous Gran Caffè Grambrinus, a haunt for Guy de Maupassant, Oscar Wilde, and many others, which meant that the coffee cost twice as much as it did anywhere else. I learned only later about the famous history of Caffè Gambrinus when I studied the fancy travel guide I bought only after coming home from Naples.

"How did you and Levin meet?" I asked, startled by my own audacity. Even as I asked I wasn't so sure I was interested in the answer.

She brightened. Her vigor did not, I assume, spring from having the opportunity to tell for the thousandth time how she and Levin had met; who knows where it came from. Whatever the case, in no way did she indicate that the question irked her.

"To tell you the truth, I've almost forgotten everything. I have only the vaguest memory of details. From today's perspective those seem to be precisely the details I resolved to remember at the time, and now, many years later, when I 'reach' for recollections, I'm appalled that they are all I can bring up, nothing else. The things one fixes in one's memory later act like a police cordon, a human wall. Memory has, of course, a strong, built-in, conciliatory mechanism encouraging our secret impulse to forge myths about ourselves and others, and

once a myth is launched seldom does anything come along to compel
its revision. Levin had that impulse. A little episode with Nabokov
illustrates this best. Whatever the case, I chose Levin, and I have a
crystal clear memory of when . . ."

Somebody had picked her up and brought her to Levin's apartment,
to a party reeking of tobacco smoke and cheap wine. She had heard
of him but hadn't read a single line of his writing. She was put off by
his arrogance, pomposity, and scorn. He sat on the spacious bed as
if it were a throne. He behaved like a lord, and treated those present
as his subjects.

"He was court jester and lord all in one. On the bed he looked like
the crazy captain of a sunken ship."

With gestures he commanded attention and "awarded" his subjects.
He would gesture to somebody to pass him their cigarette; he'd take
a puff or two and back he'd send it; from another he'd sip from their
glass and give it back. It was as if he loved commanding everyone to
serve him but the things he required were so paltry that turning him
down would have seemed silly. Some sat next to him on the bed. She
remembered an episode with a friend of Levin's. Because of her smile,
which seemed frozen to her face, the woman had resembled a toy
doll. Levin loved to "terrorize" his friends with gifts, something The
Widow only later figured out. He gave the woman something warm
and woolen—between a kerchief and a shawl. His "show" in doing so
drew the attention of everybody at the party: first he insisted on having the woman unwrap the gift but she did so too slowly for his taste.
Levin nervously grabbed the present from her hands, impatiently
ripped off the paper, and draped the shawl over her head, which was
obviously uncomfortable for the woman, she felt in all of it an act of
violence, not goodwill, and she was right. Levin arranged the kerchief
on her head, adjusted it as if he were a photographer preparing his

subject for a photograph, and then, having had enough, he yanked the kerchief off and announced loudly, "Ah, Masha, you'll never be Ingrid Bergman!"

The Widow had been slightly sickened by the scene and asked where the bathroom was. Out of curiosity she opened the medicine cabinet, where she was greeted by vials of medicine lined up on the shelf like little soldiers. And here, one thing completely unrelated to the other, in the indifferent space of somebody else's lavatory, as she read the labels on the little bottles, she burst into tears, precisely as if the milligrams, medical terms, and instructions on the containers (3x1, 1x1) were ciphers encoding her destiny going forward. She was swept by a dull inertia, although the feeling also electrified her. Perhaps this was how people contemplating suicide felt . . .

"We never know what attitudes or situations contain the potential to enthrall us. There are moments in which we can slip and careen off in some different direction than we'd meant to go. Such situations or attitudes might, for instance, be decisive for me but not for you. Levin had perfect intuition, perhaps only misanthropes have such intuition. I think he sensed that a change of some sort happened during my brief absence, because when he caught sight of me he slapped the bed with an imperious whack and commanded me, with a gesture, to sit next to him."

She sat down so compliantly that she surprised herself. He ordered her, again by gesture, to put her feet up on the bed, and she, by gesture, responded that she probably first ought to take off her shoes, and he abruptly, and almost roughly, pulled her legs, still shod, onto the bed, and then, arms crossed over chests, they sat next to one another without a word.

Levin seldom looked people in the eye. Instead he'd tuck his head into his shoulders and sniff the air around him. That's how it was then, he watched her out of the corner of his eye, obviously pleased with the outcome of the situation. He stretched out on the bed with the same ease that other people walk or sit. She felt a peculiar lassitude, whether pleasant or unpleasant she couldn't say, course through her veins like a drug. She had the feeling that on the bed, on that anchored craft, she'd be afloat for a long time to come . . .

The Widow grinned . . .

"Who knows what was buzzing around in my crazy young head at the time! I loved reading. Love of letters and a fascination with a living writer are not so very original at that age, are they? Literature has kept itself afloat on that, on the enchantment women feel for books and writers. Into the foundation of every male national literature (there are only male national literatures) are built the time, energy, and the imagination of nameless female readers. But you know that full well yourself, *lelkecském* . . ."

The Widow's pleasure at alluding to her age, more by tone than words, and in addressing people younger than herself with *lelkem* or *lelkecském* (Hungarian words she had kept in her vocabulary, meaning *darling* or *my dear*), and her unassuming theatricality—all this belonged to the stylistic repertoire of now-vanishing East-European intellectual mannerisms, which The Widow herself had identified, with Levin, as his "pomposity" . . .

"And then again," she went on, "we are all vampires and feed on the blood of others. In this free-for-all of 'promiscuity' there are people who do not depend on others, and this makes them unusually attractive, but also despised. Levin was one such person. Literature was his only abiding fascination, perhaps because everything else could be taken from him. Literature nobody could take from him. Does that kind of allure make writers great? This I can't say. Levin was obsessed with literature his whole life, literature was his only passion . . ."

"You mentioned an episode with Nabokov?" I asked cautiously.

"Ah, this was an innocent detail, yet so embarrassing . . . At one time Levin wrote to Nabokov, asking if they could meet. Nabokov never replied. Once, however, Levin blurted to a journalist that he'd exchanged a letter or two with Nabokov and Nabokov had written a few lines praising Levin's literary talent with words so laudatory that Levin couldn't actually bear to repeat them. Nabokov never openly exposed Levin, if he even knew of the little fabrication. And besides, Levin died first; Nabokov outlived him by ten years, so any such dis-avowal would be interpreted as churlishness on Nabokov's part and malevolence rather than the truth. And so, *lelkem*, began the legend of how Levin was Nabokov's sole equal as a literary rival, and that for years he'd languished in Nabokov's shadow, mainly because of 'damned geography,' which only seems foolish at first glance. How-ever, if you think a bit more about it, 'damned geography' really does determine literary destinies, as do gender, class, social status, good luck—the sort gamblers rely on . . ."

Levin, a Russian Jew, had had a complex biography, or more precisely a bio geography. After the revolution, instead of heading West as did most Russians, more by chance than deliberate decision he went in the opposite direction, eastward to China and then Japan, and from there to Hong Kong, whence, in 1954—thanks to a gesture of the Dutch government's with a commitment to accept four hundred Rus-sian refugees from the Hong Kong refugee camp—he arrived in the Netherlands in 1955. Upon his arrival, he settled at Lange Voorhout 78 in The Hague, at *Het Russenhuisje*, the Little Russian House, in the former offices of Queen Wilhelmina, who had donated the royal

property to an ecumenical foundation that turned it into a haven
for elderly Russian refugees. Six years later, Levin moved from The
Hague to Paris. There was a curious twist between The Widow's and
Levin's biography. After the Hungarian revolution of 1956, she and
her parents found themselves among two hundred thousand Hungarian refugees in the Netherlands, whence, after her parents died, she
moved to Paris, where she and Levin met. Although the Dutch were
kind and generous hosts, The Widow remembered the Netherlands
as a mind-numbing limbo, like the half-life of Sleeping Beauty's glass
casket. Levin described the same process of mind-numbing when
he sojourned in Hong Kong, in the refugee hotel he wrote about
in his novel *The Peninsula Hotel*, and waited for destiny to catapult
him to the other side of the world. Like Levin, she and many other
émigrés developed a certain sensitivity to spaces, cities, landscapes,
street names, hotels, places, as if the environment in which we find
ourselves is nothing more than the symbolic staging for the higher
powers that determine our lives. "Take Switzerland, for example . . ."
sighed The Widow with a touch of drama. "It's the most dangerous
country in the world! The Swiss make the finest watches, but when
you're there you can never tell the time; the minute and hour hands
melt away as soon as you cross the Swiss border, the watch on your
wrist goes haywire. In that little country, it's as if you might drown
in a glass of water, lose your way so completely that no one will ever
find you again . . ."

I knew that the story of the Far-East routes of Russian emigration
had not been given even a tenth of the attention dedicated to the
Russian diaspora in western Europe and America, perhaps because
they were both more modest and more complex and (to Europeans
and Americans) more challenging to understand. All in all, the émigré stories about Russians in Iran, Indonesia, China, in Harbin and
Shanghai, Japan, in Australia remained incomplete, untold, or simply

out of focus. Levin himself was a cynic who expressed no sympathies for the Whites or the Reds. Sometimes he would merely defend his geo-biography, which was understandable. He had spent too much energy on continually conquering, adopting, and abandoning places to allow himself the luxury of indifference.

"Triviality is the salt of everything, triviality is the wind that moves the whole mechanism, *lelkem*," continued The Widow. "The great names of art survive thanks to the trivial; the artwork by itself is clearly not enough. Indeed, why are we so sure that Van Gogh is still relevant thanks to his genius, while underestimating the detail of the severed ear? What do you remember living modern artists by? Is there a single one of them, man or woman, who has done nothing to scandalize the public? Where is a selfless, modest artist, show me! All artists are myth-makers. Some succeed in becoming famous while others do not. I am certain that Nabokov belongs to the myth-makers, that he was consciously or unconsciously raising himself a monument . . ." said The Widow brightly.

"Are you sure?"

"Well, if you think about it, what all of us experience as 'artwork' is always related in some way to the circus, the art of the country fair, the oldest art in the world."

"An example would make it easier for me to follow what you're saying . . ." I said.

"Clear examples are more readily found in the modern visual arts, in theater, performance art, than in literature. Still, here is a fresh one: of late, the literary marketplace has developed a penchant for long novels and many writers seem to be competing for who can write the longest-winded work. Everybody is suddenly awed by page count and they automatically declare these novels remarkable . . ."

"Well, many of them are, indeed, good."

"Perhaps. But that initial awe at the number of pages has become, too readily, an aesthetic category. Is a novel of over a thousand pages the only 'true novel'? This includes awe at hyper-productive authors; then the cruel declaration of the demise of authors who have not succeeded in coming out with a new book every year or two. What about the bookies who place bets on literary awards! All this is closer to categories of tenacity, brawn, and circus strongmen than it is to traditional aesthetic categories. Or take, for instance, what we call experimental literature. Experimental literature, today, implies themes of the bizarre, the weird, a literary manuscript that is more invalid-like than it is a work of literary skill, concept, and knowledge. The Modernist concept of experimental literature is quite different from today's. The freak-show equivalent to today's experimental literature would be 'little people,' 'bearded ladies,' 'men of rubber,' and so forth. The circus act is the oldest 'artistic' formula in the world, which many of us still carry in our cultural memory. As academic aesthetic arbitration is disappearing, and as the significant theories of art are all dead today, the only compass available for determining the difference between artistic and non-artistic work remains what is closest to the proto-idea of art, meaning the circus act," concluded The Widow.

"We are on our way back, metaphorically speaking, to the art of the country fair?" I asked.

"So it would seem. What about the literary festivals that have recently become the most popular form of literary entertainment? In each European country you have a dozen international literary festivals every year. This money could be spent in more useful ways, everybody knows that, but it bothers no one. Today literary festivals are not so different from medieval country fairs, where the fair-goers stroll from tent to tent, from fire-eaters to jugglers. Writers today no longer burden their audience with a reading, they 'perform.' The audience, whose standards for reception have been honed by television and the internet, are more and more ignorant about literature, what they want is fast, unambiguous entertainment . . ."

Everything The Widow said sounded convincing. We had coffee and the famous Neapolitan *sfogliatella*, a little pastry with ricotta and thin layers of pastry shaped like a seashell, and then we went back to the hotel. I was planning to leave early the next morning, but The Widow warmly proposed . . .

"Why not ask the organizers to change your flight? Stay another day or two, *lelkecském*. I have nothing scheduled. We'll explore the city together. Have you been to Naples before?"

She was right. Here I was in Naples for the first time in my life and I was in no rush. I kept having the feeling there was something else The Widow meant to impart.

7.

Museo Capodimonte

The kind organizers not only changed my flight, but they moved me from the expensive hotel, for which they had been paying, to an inexpensive bed & breakfast for which I would pay. The B&B was on Piazza Bellini. I was in the very heart of Naples, in the *Centro Storico*, and I had another whole day and a half free.

The next morning, after breakfast, I bid goodbye to the organizers and conference-goers and arranged to meet The Widow at Piazza Municipio. Three tourist buses were leaving from there to tour Naples: the red one, Route A, Luoghi dell'Arte; the purple one, Route B, Veduta del Golfo; and the green one, Route C, San Martino. We chose the Luoghi dell'Arte tour with the option of hopping afterwards onto a bus that was going in the opposite direction, along the Bay of Naples through Chiaia.

We took our seats on the open roof. The day was dazzling, the sky blue, and Naples spread out before us like an accordion. *Pitura pompei-ana* streamed down the façades, washed out and worn in some places, crackled in others, and yet in others, glistening and fresh . . .

We got off the bus at the Museo di Capodimonte. The museum was housed in a grandiose, pleasantly cool palace. We strolled through, examining at a leisurely pace several of the museum's treasures by Titian, Caravaggio, Breughel, stopping before Parmigianino's breath-taking *Antea*, and then lingering before what must have been the most hideous exhibit in the entire museum: the canvases of Joachim Beuckelaer, a Flemmish sixteenth-century master who instructed the Italians, particularly Vincenzo Campi, on the depiction of food. We were enthralled for a time by these grotesquely sumptuous composi-tions of people and food, the contrasts between the silk sheen on the women's finery and the slabs of lard-streaked pork flesh on their laps; between their mother-of-pearl complexions and the kitchen knives as long as swords in the women's white hands. Parmigianini's was a grotesque gigantism of abundance: chickens, hens, turkeys, partridge and quail, game, and sides of pork, beef, and lamb, an array of fish and shellfish, fruits and vegetables . . . People with detached, solemn expressions sank into the food they were displaying to the eyes and brush of the painter, and blended with it.

At the museum café we bought bottles of juice and went out to the park. The air was fragrant and sweet. I'd almost forgotten the mean-ing of the phrase "heady air." The air truly was heady. The Widow and I sipped our juice and listened to the chirping of birds. Then The Widow looked over at me with her frank gaze . . .

"I owe you an apology for our performance together on the panel, *lelkecském*. The people yesterday came to see me, not you. I'm so sorry about that. Especially because defeat could be read on your face. Your chin quivered, you were on the verge of tears. I'm sorry, but somehow I'm guessing this is not the first time this has happened to you. Literary life is exciting only when you're at your desk between four walls. All else evokes a feeling of defeat, both human and professional, if serious writing can even be deemed a profession. I was the 'little Buddha' yesterday, people came to bow down to me. Not to me personally, who knows to whom or to what, really. And literature lovers do adore their celebrities. Compared to you, I'm a literary celebrity. Don't frown, you, yourself, know this to be so, the less genuine the grounds there are for fame, the more a person qualifies for the celebrity orbit. For it's the members of the audience who set the bar, not us. And once the public reaches a critical mass, they disapprove of standards they would not themselves be able to meet or at least grasp. For the people who sat in the hall yesterday, I was a walking spool onto which they could wind their fantasies and their never-articulated beliefs. Am I a creative person? No, I am not. I have spent years working on Levin's books, publishing new editions, signing contracts for the translations, managing and maintaining his archive. From time to time I'd find a misplaced poem, story, or a page from his diary . . . He was a master at misplacing his things, have I not already told you this, *lelkem*? Did I say anything worthwhile yesterday? No, I did not. And if you were to take all those people who attended our panel yesterday and lay them on a psychotherapist's couch, not a one would be able to admit to several glaringly obvious things . . ."

"Such as?" I said, taking a breath.

"Men value me. Why? Because I know 'my place.' Obediently I served and facilitated the literary talent of a man, I served the mind of a man, I am, therefore, a dream-woman for many men, I am also their dream-widow. I was Levin's secretary and archivist, his spouse, editor, agent . . . I have not re married, I have served him long since his death and I will serve him until I die. He left me, after all, with his symbolic capital, which I built on with careful stewardship. Anyone who has had anything to do with Levin knows we were husband and wife for barely three years; that we married when he was already seriously ill, at a time when that marriage was not, nor could it be, consummated, nor was it ever likely to be. Levin never kept any of that from me . . ."

I was at a loss for words. The Widow's monologue, with her hushed and slightly monotonous intonation (that is how the English language spoken by a Hungarian sounds to my ear) in that setting of the beautiful park, the dazzling day, the blue sky, and the heady air, came across as surreal. Her words were heavy and filling, and exerted a hypnotic effect, much as Beuckelaer's canvases had done moments before.

"Having said that, I should say that this story is hardly unique to us," continued The Widow, "I assure you, if you were to poke around in the biographies of artists you would find many similar stories. All of Levin's fans keep failing to note the key details and would rather believe in an image that has nothing to do with the facts. For them I am a marvel of a woman, I have sacrificed myself for literature, because of literature I live permanently in widow's weeds. And they are pleased when they see my age, because they insist on forgetting the fact that when I was getting to know Levin I was nearly forty years younger than he. The older I get, therefore, the more 'suitable' I become for the image of me they cherish. If they were to accept the factual state, they might be led to conclude that Levin was an aging pervert who turned a young émigré woman into his nurse and typist . . .

"Women value me for the same reason. The thing is, you see, I know 'my place.' Others find me easy to identify with. They can't do the same with you, you don't know 'your place,' you dare speak in your own voice, as good a reason as any for them to despise or resent you. I know you disagree with me, what I say is not exactly how things now stand, you're thinking, perhaps they stood that way in the old days but today they most definitely do not. That's why you brushed off your defeat of the other day and shooed away your momentary humiliation as if it were a buzzing fly, and turned to the new day, ready to wage your battles. The first and most important was your battle against mediocrity. Yet the very vocation you so fervently pursue thrives on mediocrity. Mediocrity is the underlying principle of every artistic venture. There is no industry that can thrive only on first-rate quality and still enjoy success. Yet here you are, a diligent toiler in the vast creative industry and you stubbornly believe you will turn the situation to your advantage. Where's your early warning system for defeat?"

It seemed to me we two had both lost our sixth sense for defeat, I, who listened breathlessly to a person I hardly knew, and she, who said so much to somebody she knew not at all. For just a moment I flattered myself. Perhaps she had read one of my books, I wondered, then dismissed the thought. All this had merely been an interlude, a rare gift that comes with fraternizing at literary gatherings, time to relax. So why was I all ears, icy with fear and disquiet? Fear of what? Of whom? Of a lonely old woman who was a bit too chatty, though everything she was saying felt so apt? There is definitely something wrong with me, with my ability to listen. It was I, not she, who'd lost my early warning system . . .

"I became acquainted with a writer whom I saw again after many years. He'd been anxious his whole life about how to insure his own survival, because, by taking care of himself he was taking care of his books, the ones already written and the ones he'd yet to write. I heard he'd married for a third time to a much younger woman. His wife, however, 'betrayed' him by dying suddenly. His face twisted into an ugly grimace right there in front of me. He looked as if he'd burst into tears and kept saying, 'This is not what we agreed, not what we said . . .' Of the whole performance the only sincere part was his horror at the possibility that after his death his work would end up in the wrong hands, or in the trash, essentially the same thing. No need to add that the unfortunate woman had been a literary historian . . ." said The Widow.

"Writers are a little like motorcycle enthusiasts . . ."

"How!?"

"Haven't you noticed how motorcyclists always choose compatible life partners, feather-weight, petite little women who fit snugly on the back seat . . ." I said.

The Widow was amused.

"Women are no different, *lelkem,* once they muster the courage. And Alma Mahler, by the way, is the queen of all widows. Thomas Mann dubbed her '*la Grande Veuve.*' To her celebrated shish kabob of marriages to Mahler, Gropius, Werfel, one can add her lovers, such as Gustav Klimt and Alexander van Zemlinsky, whom she called her 'ugly little dwarf.' She railed the most personally against Franz Werfel, whom she was married to the longest and who left her a financially comfortable old age. Known for her anti-Semitic outbursts, Alma called Werfel an 'ugly, fat, little Jew.' Twice-over a widow, she buried Mahler and Werfel while Gropius outlived her by a few years. Her children—a daughter Maria with Mahler, eighteen-year-old Manon with Gropius, and a ten-month-old son whose father was Franz Werfel—all predeceased her. She had admirers, including composer Franz Schreker and biologist Paul Kammerer—who threatened to kill himself on Mahler's grave out of unrequited love . . ."

"And Kokoschka . . ."

•

"Oskar Kokoschka, indeed . . . All in all she left behind a heap of broken hearts, the insults she lambasted men with, and yet everyone adored her, she outlived many of them, she was a mega-parasite, many fed her, dedicated their works to her. Her life today is performed as theater with the title *Alma* and travels around like a biography circus. We have to admit: 'Who, today, has heard of Werfel?' Many, however, know of Alma Mahler. And she left us with only seventeen poems . . ."

"Did she have promise as a composer?"

"I couldn't say. Her main talent was a deep and abiding knowledge of the economy of love. She was fully versed in how the shares rose and fell on the love market. Alma's biologist, Kammerer, threatening suicide on Mahler's grave, defined the essence of that economy."

"And that was?"

"That through women, men find their way to other men. It is, perhaps, in poor taste for an older woman to speak of such things, but I know a little something about this from my own life. I've had lovers, suitors, friends thanks to the fact that I am Levin's widow, though I could have sworn it would be the other way around. A young woman married to a fast-fading older man is hardly the most attractive sight in the world. Yet after his death, many rushed to make my acquaintance, though it was Levin they were interested in. This did not diminish the sincerity, passion, solemnity, or comedy of my relations with men. The fact is, however, that Levin's shadow was carousing right there along with us, just as we, I assume, were carousing with his ghost."

At this point The Widow fell briefly still. She closed her eyes and seemed to be listening to sounds. I didn't know how to respond to all she'd said, or whether I should respond at all. Fortunately I didn't say anything, because The Widow, leaning back on the bench, had dozed off. Above her wrinkled lips, barely visible droplets of sweat glistened exactly like droplets on a spider's web. She slept sitting almost fully upright, with her head tipped just a little to the side like a bird's. She snored softly. I felt a glow of satisfaction spread through me, the pride of a guard dog. It was a comical yet touching feeling. I enjoyed listening to the birds and sniffing the sweet air around me.

Her nap didn't last long; evidently it was part of her daily routine. She apologized, she was embarrassed. And for a moment she wasn't sure where she was.

"What did you dream?" I asked.

"Ah, *lelkem* . . . I have no idea," she said.

A famous Croatian woman poet—in her youth a beauty with flashing black eyes, a broad face with pronounced Slavic cheekbones, long, curly dark locks—grew ugly, unfortunately, as she aged. She developed logorrhea and people began avoiding her, though I assume they might have avoided her no matter what. Her lovers had long since jilted her, life was gradually pushing her away, and then quite literally: from a large apartment she was pushed into a smaller one, then into a smaller one yet, then out into the street . . . A goiter swelled on her neck, which in time became so large that it engulfed her face and throat. The famous Croatian poet looked like a wig-wearing Humpty Dumpty. She was stubborn: just as she'd refused to cut her hair she would not allow them to operate, although in her case the operation, or at least so they said, would have been routine. She strutted around with the goiter like a crazed turkey, claiming that inside it, right there in that unsightly swelling, dwelt her creative powers. In time she learned how to swathe it with fetching shawls, but the ragtag wrappings, under which the big, bulging mass could still be seen, only made matters worse. As her shares on the literary and social scene fell with age and unsightliness—men are forgiven such things, but women never!—her shares rose in her other, parallel, world. In the morning on a certain day each week, those who revered her magical powers, all of them neighborhood men—the butcher, cobbler, postman, tailor, and barber—would knock at her door. She, the great priestess, defiant, her hair flowing loose, messily dyed dark with a good inch of gray roots showing, still in her nightgown, would open the door, and they, on tiptoe, would slip quietly into the apartment and take seats around her little kitchen table. In the solemn silence she'd make coffee, serve it to everybody in demitasse cups, and then she, too, would sit, shut her eyes, and turn the huge goiter, smooth and shiny like a soothsayer's crystal ball, toward her visitors. (The postman even said that in the mornings the goiter of the great poetess shone with a bluish light.) And then, ruminating numbers through the goiter as if spinning a lottery drum, she'd speak in combinations. The men, who already had slips of paper and pencils poised, would jot down the numbers, then race off to the nearest kiosk and buy lottery tickets. Legend had it that one of the number combinations always won a sizeable sum. The men divvied the take in equal parts and gave the poetess her share.

The Widow brightened.

"That sounds just like a fairy tale! Did you know her?" she asked.

"Barely."

"Interesting that you thought of that story on this very spot . . ."

"Why?"

"The book called *La smorfia* is the bible for all those who play the lottery. It was first published in the late eighteenth century and has been in print ever since. *La smorfia* is a book for interpreting dreams. With its help the dreamer translates dreams into numbers and uses the numbers obtained to fill out the lotto card. We should go to 17 Via del Grande Archivio . . ."

"Why?"

"Because every Saturday they announce the results there," she said.

"But shouldn't we buy lotto tickets first?"

"First you need to dream something."

"But what if there's no number for what I dream?"

"*La smorfia* has sixty thousand entries. I doubt your dreams are so original that a number can't be found!"

"You don't know me. As far as dreams are concerned, I'm like one of those snow-making machines," I said, wondering where I'd dug up the snow-making-machine.

We began walking slowly toward the bus stop where the red hop-on, hop-off bus was waiting. I don't know why, but again the feeling wormed its way into me that there was something else The Widow meant to tell me.

8.

Museo Archeologico

As we rode on the bus toward the Museo Archeologico museum where we planned to get off, I thought about how city-goers are so eager to confirm stereotypes about their cities, as if the stereotypes are themselves the city's very foundation, and as if, without them, cities would crumble. I remembered the driver of the bus that took us from Pompeii to Amalfi. After speaking to us in the Neapolitan language, he juggled with Spanish and English, and, while barreling along a dangerous road, he sustained a constant stream of chatter. With dramatic intonation he described for us the beautiful scenery that was rolling by us, and listed the names of famous Neapolitans: Enrico Caruso, Sophia Loren, Toto—meanwhile aping the Neapolitan stereotype given to us by Italian cinema. His was a collage assembled from many, from Marcello Mastroianni, Giancarlo Giannini, and right up to the American, Jack Lemmon who, in the movie *Macaroni*, plays the "American," thunderstruck by the beauty of the Neapolitan surroundings . . . The driver's favorite words were "confusion" and "chaos." Confusion and chaos, according to the bus driver, ran in the veins of Naples. But every catcall I felt rising inside me at his shabby performance, my every urge to resist stereotypes, was handily quelled by Beauty. Beauty silenced my internal protests, laid a finger across my lips. Shshshshshs, thaaaat's better, good girl . . .

The Widow, seated next to me, was caught in the same trap and was compelled to resort to her own stereotype; if she were to relinquish it she'd be disqualifying herself. "The writer's widow" was hers, another was the "professor's wife"—produced by the reality of life on American university campuses, while the "Neapolitan gigolo" was yet another. The gigolo erodes his own sex appeal with his stream of chatter, but, if he shuts up, he undermines the stereotype, and, hence, his appeal.

Beauty. This was unequivocal beauty, beauty with no need to justify itself, beauty that humbles and leaves one breathless. "Beauty is truth, truth beauty—that is all ye know on earth, and all ye need to know," whispered The Widow. The verse may be a platitude, but it had a poignant ring to it, and nothing felt more apt just then. The Widow and I hovered with melting gazes over the Pompeii frescoes, over comely faces, Paquius Proculus and his wife, the fetching expression of a young woman who for two thousand years had been resting a stylus on her lower lip, over the flora and fauna, the gods and mortals, the mythic scenes and exquisite landscapes . . .

We peeked as well into *Il Gabinetto Segreto*, the Secret Museum, where we found ourselves surrounded by placentarii, bronze figurines with long penises. There were big penises, circumcised penises, lazy penises, pudgy penises, flying penises, heavy penis-oil lamps, figurines of men, penises bared, juggling trays and dishes, statuettes of satyrs, frescoes of impressive Priapus . . .

"In the context of Pompeii, these penises are comic relief . . ." I
whispered.

"Ah, and when have you, in your lifetime, encountered a trage-
dian?" asked The Widow, choking back laughter.

Although our conversation might easily have slid that moment in a
joking-vulgar direction, my response, wisely, was silence. The rooms
of the secret cabinet were overcrowded, crammed with visitors, and
this meant we had to view the exhibits quickly and leave as soon as
possible.

"Bellezza . . ." she said. "You are still young, *lelkem*, you have not
yet arrived at this sensation . . . Some older people become suddenly
hyper-sensitized to beauty. This is the best and worst thing that can
happen to you in old age. On the one hand you can see clearly what
you let slip in life, while, on the other, you realize you no longer
have the time to make up for what you've missed. It's as if your focus
sharpens while your vision weakens, but it sharpens only for beauty,
the beauty of nature, the heavens, faces, bodies, art, music . . . This is
Gustav von Aschenbach syndrome. Levin had it, too. Homosexuality
has nothing to do with it, at least I never read *Death in Venice* that
way . . . Authentic beauty for women and men of my age may usurp
us like a real earthquake."

The Widow seemed shaken. When I rubbed her shoulders in a gesture of comfort, I felt her shiver a little under my hands.

"I feel like Ingrid Bergman in the movie *Journey to Italy* . . . At every
tourist sight in Naples, including this very museum, Ingrid Bergman
weeps. True, her hyper-sensitivity comes from the fear that she has
lost her husband's love, while mine may well spring from senility," she
added and chuckled.

She had style. Although I hadn't said so to her, I was pleased that before the trip to Naples each of us had watched *Journey to Italy* by Roberto Rossellini.

We went off to find the Herculaneum papyri. I think this was more as a nod to the prophetic power of Bulgakov's famous phrase, "manuscripts don't burn," than to a wish to examine the actual carbonized scrolls of paper. The story about these papyri—touchingly intriguing and open-ended—stirred the imagination, especially because hundreds of people had toiled for almost two decades on their reconstruction. Some two thousand carbonized scrolls were found in the mid-eighteenth century when the villa of a rich family in Herculaneum was excavated. It took one hundred fifty years, hundreds of enthusiasts and experts, the advent of computers, technological advances, digitalization, and micro-computer tomography, to make legible the valuable original works by Greek philosophers.

"It transpires that, as fragile and sensitive as paper may be, it is, in fact, indestructible. Imagine, these carbonized scrolls lay under tons of volcanic ash for a full seventeen centuries, and today on a screen we can read all the letters that were penned on them in ink! How exhilarating! We will disappear, but paper will outlive us . . ." she said

9.

In the Museum Arcades

Before leaving the museum we sat down on a stone bench in the arcades to rest. Our gaze swam around the lovely atrium before us and the walls of the arcade secured a refreshing coolness . . .

"Elderly people often cajole those around them. Hence their smiles and simpers that seem awkward, especially in older women. Their simpers are apologies, as if the smile is meant to mask their knowledge of their own lack of physical appeal. When we are young, none of us bothers with such things. And then we start taking care, at some point, not to 'offend.' Why? Because we depend on others to move through life. We only realize this when it's too late to fight back. If people around us gradually begin pulling away, this means they've assigned us a one-way ticket in their thoughts, they've written us off. The reasons for this may be banal and most often are: they haven't time for us, we're taking up too much space, we're ugly, we're old, we're useless, we're tiresome, we're weeds . . . So we step out of the way, we retreat, we have even learned to roll our shadow up behind us, we grow quieter, hush our breathing . . ."

"What are you saying! You yourself saw how many people came yesterday, and they all came to hear you."

"The bitterness aired by elderly people used to surprise me but now I understand it. There is a point when you find you've stepped through the looking glass and what you're hearing everywhere is *jabberwocky*, you can't grasp the language, you no longer understand others and they don't understand you. You pick up mimicry, similar to the way older people who are reluctant to admit they're losing their hearing go on pretending to hear in hopes of holding on to their place a little longer in the world of 'normal' people. This is the moment when loneliness begins to settle within us . . . But that is not your story, you aren't old enough yet, and besides, loneliness has already settled in with you, has it not?"

"Think so?"

"I recognize the scent of loneliness. It has soaked your hair, your pores, your clothing, it trails behind you. Now, don't you worry, very few people can pick up the scent. I can. I have spent my entire life alone, I know all there is to know about it."

"I believe you exaggerate . . ." I said calmly, though I didn't like her shift to such personal territory when I hadn't allowed it.

"Work a little harder, why don't you, to avoid set phrases when you talk. You are a writer, after all . . ." said The Widow with an edge of mild irritation in her voice.

"I'll do my best . . ."

"Women long to converse," she said. "This is a hunger we've felt for centuries. Not so with men. They're forever in conversation. With other men, of course."

"What are you trying to say, exactly?" I asked calmly.

"This . . . A man besotted with his own voice is on his way home from fishing, carrying the fish he caught in a bag on his back and singing with gusto. By the road he spots a dead fox, scoops it up, and drops it into the bag. The fox, which was only playing dead, eats the fish along the way, then wriggles free of the bag and goes bounding off. The man, besotted with his voice, continues along his way with no fish and no fox pelt. You're besotted with your own voice and you neglect to keep an eye on the things around you. You think the beauty of your voice suffices, everybody will hear it, and it's your job to sing. Yet you, yourself, know things don't work that way. And meanwhile, you're no fox, the fox is most definitely not your totem."

"What does that mean, being a fox?"

"Celebration of betrayal."

"How can I be something I'm not?"

"You sound as if you're in a state of constant internal mutiny. On your face I can see you are forever bumping into things; you can't walk by things without them brushing against you. You're always in friction with your surroundings. Always championing justice. Yet there is no justice, as, I presume, you've realized by now. You feel it was not worth the effort, you sink in quicksand, time has crushed you, you're on the outside looking in, and everything seems beyond your control. You are obsessed by a sense that no matter what you do, you're no longer visible, nobody hears you, you don't exist . . ."

"No, really!"

"Irony is hardly your strong point at this particular moment. I've spent my whole life among *your* kind, I am a diagnostician. I've perfected this. Just as a blind person heightens their sense of hearing, I have heightened my sensitivity to your type. You're not artful, you're only occasionally cynical. The world doesn't change, it is constantly crumbling and generally it will tend toward greater stupidity than it should . . . And by the way, at airports you can hear, for free, God's commandment: 'Mind Your Step!'"

"Can we talk about something else . . . ?"

"Sorry . . . It's just that I have the feeling nobody has ever spoken to you of such obvious things. Because in principle people do not take care of other people. It is only those who hate us who take care of us. And you're still in somebody's sights. You're visible still, yet you go about with no protection. A perfect target. Never has it occurred to you that there are people poised with erasers to erase you, people prepared to stab your flesh with their knives, people ready to trample you . . . Why? For the simple reason that you are a little more visible than they, taller by a centimeter. Most people cannot bear that. You have no children, you're not an invalid, you aren't sufficiently ugly, you aren't married, you're a woman, you've ventured out into the world, you 'sing,' you're accountable to no one—all this is an excess of freedom, something that is not so easily forgiven. Those you left behind do not forgive you, nor do those whose community you joined. That's why you have had to adopt little self-defense tricks. The way you bow your head, the way you avert your eyes, the way you hunker down and wait for a threat to pass . . ."

"What are you even talking about?"

"I see by your wince that you're tired. Your spirit is sluggish and drained. And no longer can you expect the little vials in somebody

else's medicine cabinet to glisten at you with the brilliance of diamonds . . ."

The Widow touched my cheek. She did this with her thumb, describing a line from the corner of my mouth to my chin as if brushing away
a trace of spittle, a lipstick smudge, a crumb of food. Hers was the
lightest of touches, something almost like a blessing.

"How old you are, yet you haven't yet come clean with yourself
about a few of the basics. Would you, for instance, rather dream about
a work of art than create it? Do you imagine yourself taking part in
literature as a footnote that can easily be dropped, or as an indispens-
able work of art?"

"I cannot believe . . ."

"What?"

"That I'm sitting here calmly swallowing all these banalities . . ."
I said.

"Sincerity always sounds hackneyed . . ."

"And palm-readers are sincere! And manipulative! Like you!" I
said, though I'd meant to say something else. But the words, nevertheless, hit home. The Widow, a master of conversation, knew that
the words one says never matter as much as the tone. And with my
tone I had brusquely shoved her to the side of the road.

She got up, swaying slightly as if she might fall. A deep wrinkle slith-
ered downward, lizard-like, from the corner of her mouth. I wondered
where my sudden outburst of intolerance had sprung from. Perhaps I
couldn't forgive her the fact that she, and not I, had stolen the show
during our panel; that her story, not mine, had piqued their interest.
Had I been hurt by what she said, but couldn't admit it? Because
everything she'd said was true but her words would have been just
as true if she'd said the opposite. In this type of communication,
translation is key. And we steer every reading of palms—whether it

be a conversation with a palm-reader or a psychotherapist—to our advantage. I will have a chance to apologize, there's still time for apologies, I thought, and then sat there as if glued to my seat.

The Widow flashed me a cool look in which there was still a shred of warmth, and then she stood up and slowly made her way off. The rays of sunlight streaked her hair and blazed it orange. Her slow advance under the arcades of the Archeological Museum was splendid and achingly photogenic.

Just then I suddenly remembered another, much younger woman. As if the deep wrinkle on The Widow's face had served as a magnet and drawn to me the other, who came into sharp focus . . .

10.

Marlene

Marlene was Polish (in age she could have been my daughter) and she occasionally cleaned my apartment for ten euros an hour. Who knows how she'd found her way to Amsterdam and from where, but in the flood of words she showered on me in her poor, strongly Polish-accented English, I remembered mention of a collective somewhere in Belgium with its leader whom she referred to, reverently, as "Baba." She still went there from time to time to lend a hand in the garden or the kitchen. My guess was that this was some sort of new-age commune for the treatment of drug addiction or something like that, where she met a fellow from Negotin . . .

". . . where she met a fellow from Negotin. The boy had two brothers who were living in Amsterdam. Hardworking, capable fellows, they got here before the Poles, who are also hardworking, capable fellows. Marlene got to know all three brothers. She also knew their mother, who would visit her sons from time to time and stay for a month. The sons were good boys. Before going to sleep they'd read a page from the Bible, which their mother appreciated. One of the boys from Negotin spent all day painting apartments, and on Saturday and Sunday he'd dance the salsa. He even took a salsa class. He enrolled in a school for shiatsu massage. Marlene's Negotin boyfriend repaired bicycles. The third brother, who did nothing but smoke hashish all day long, had recently returned to his mother's in Negotin. So Marlene learned Serbian instead of Dutch. Though I never met the young man, I have to say he couldn't be worth even as much as her little finger. Because Marlene is tall and slender as a birch tree, with a transparent, milk-white complexion and light blue eyes, a true northern beauty. Only her hands are large, red, and chapped, as if somebody had attached them to Marlene's fragile arms by some terrible mistake. Marlene works as a maid in a cheap Amsterdam hotel on the sly. Working as a maid in a cheap hotel means spending half the day with your nose buried in people's shit. And the boss is a nasty woman, to all of them—to Marlene, a Bulgarian woman, a Croatian woman, and a Serbian woman—she treats them all like slaves. Sometimes Marlene cleans houses as well, and in her spare time she makes cute little bags that can be worn around the neck. Marlene looks after her family, her grandfather (she has a special fondness for her grandfather), and for her newfound family. She identifies with the stories about Negotin though she has never been there. When one of the brothers gets sick, she cooks healing chicken soup for them. Marlene also looks after her own little 'Dutch' family: a turtle, a rabbit, and a cat who live with her in her miniature Amsterdam apartment. The rabbit and cat can hardly wait for her to come home, and they are happiest when she lets them sleep with her.

"But Marlene is not entirely without dreams of her own. You can see by the gleam in her eyes that she is no ordinary young woman.

Something is cooking in Marlene, though for now she has no idea where to take herself, to the left or the right . . .

One day Marlene told me . . . 'I've decided to move up . . .'

'Up? What do you mean, move up, Marlene?'

"She had met some people by chance who ran a puppet street-theater, and the actors needed somebody to stand on stilts, and Marlene, thinking of her grandfather—who had delighted her by walking around on stilts—said, 'I will!' And what do you know, she stood on stilts. At first she wobbled dangerously, of course, but now she struts around with the ease of a fish in water. Marlene wears a giraffe costume. Her head is in the clouds and somewhere way down below are the nasty hotel manager jostling with her friends from Negotin; her rabbit, cat, and turtle; her family in Poland; her mother; her grandfather . . . She uses the money she makes on the stilts to buy everybody a little something: a terrarium for the turtle, a carrot for the rabbit, a ball for the cat, a scarf for her boyfriend from Negotin, a little basket woven of matchsticks for me . . . It isn't the money that matters, it is how Marlene feels. Up there, her head in the clouds, her eyes two and a half meters or more above ground, Marlene feels like somebody who has finally reached the height she deserves. Some Dutch people feel that Marlene's integration into Dutch society has been a success. The only thing they hold against her as a giraffe is that she hasn't yet learned to speak Dutch."

I wrote that fragment about Marlene and worked it into an essay about recent European migrations. I'd published the piece some time ago and forgotten about it, and Marlene lost touch with me. I don't believe she'd ever come across the passage I wrote about her, because I don't remember her ever expressing an interest in any sort of writing. I ran into her boyfriend from Negotin after Marlene had gone from my life. I happened to wander into a shop with used bicycles:

the Negotin fellow had short legs, he slurred his words, and avoided eye contact, a cagey guy, all in all. I was right: he wasn't worth even Marlene's little finger.

After an exploratory phone call, Marlene showed up some seven or eight years later at my apartment, pale, her disheveled hair sweetly tamed with children's barrettes, still slender as a birch, with thin-framed glasses perched on her nose that only served to accentuate her air of fragility. Her English seemed even more speedy and garbled and her Polish accent even stronger. Oh, yes, she'd broken things off with the Negotin fellow ages back, she had a new boyfriend now, a Pole, she was no longer cleaning houses, nor did she work in the horrible hotel, her hands showed it, the red chafing was gone, she was busy with, ha-ha, "creative work." Ever since she'd left the Negotin fellow she had been sharing an apartment with a friend, her friend had a child, a seven-year-old girl, and a former husband who stopped by now and then, the ex-husband was a shaman, yes, why was I surprised, no, he wasn't from Negotin but he was from *that part* of the world, clearly she was destined to be around people from *there*, whether they were bicycle repairmen, or shamans, or their wives . . . And I could see the picture of her new boyfriend on her smart phone, a nice, sharp picture, and this is her grandfather, over ninety and still sprightly, and these are pictures of the little rice-paper shades she made, and colorful bedspreads . . . No, she hadn't made the bedspreads herself, they were the work of her new boyfriend's mother in Poland, maybe her future mother-in-law, a hundred euros a piece, if I liked she could get me one, or two, or how ever many I wanted, and these are pictures of clown shoes, she made a pair, and a little trunk, she made them all for the theater . . . Yes, she was still working with the giraffes, she traveled with them, though she'd been thinking she might split off and form her own street theater, for the moment she was holding workshops, teaching others how to walk on stilts, there were people interested, especially in Poland, because there were no jobs there and young people were casting about for ways to survive . . . True, she'd held only two workshops so far, she told the students it isn't so much a balancing act as it's about the movements, you have to have a knack for stilts, people often think it's enough to take those first steps, but what matters is *full-body expression*, that's what she called it, *full-body expression*, that was the catch, to know how to *act with your body*, because your face is hidden, after all, by a mask . . . She had, meanwhile, made her peace with the idea that she'd remain a giraffe as long as she was working at the theater, because nobody would allow her to be anything else, oh, yes, she could have been a zebra had she wanted to, but what difference would that make, which is why she decided she'd break away as soon as possible and open her own school in Poland, no, she wouldn't do it here, her boyfriend was giving English lessons, that was how he supported himself, the people who were tutored by him cared nothing about his qualifications, true, they were older people, lonely souls, anxious about signing up for proper language classes, but they were glad to learn a little English . . . the times are new, the internet age is here, an interested party can be found for every service offered, and, by the way, I, too, might give it a try, age plays no role at all . . .

I don't know why—perhaps because of the smoke screens Marlene needed to obscure her genuine state of affairs—rage, instead of pity, stirred in me. Rage is another form of sympathy. Perhaps it was her school for walking on stilts that sent my blood pressure skyrocketing, maybe it was because of her repeated use of the word "career," though she had barely completed elementary school, and maybe it was because of her advice that, *by the way, I, too, might give it a try* (that an interested party can be found for every service offered), *age plays no role at all* . . . All in all, I said something, lashed out with harsh words at Marlene's invisible stilts, I don't even remember what, the tone mattered more than the words, a tone Marlene understood, my tone sent her swaying like a crystal goblet, she looked as if she might shatter, but she didn't make a sound or cry, instead she spat out something like *I do what I know the best I can*, and then she got up and left. We promised each other, of course, that we'd be sure to see each other more often now, but I knew she wouldn't come by any more and she wouldn't call, she'd never forgive me for lashing, out of the blue, at the image she'd so carefully fashioned for herself.

After Marlene left, I sat down in front of my computer and searched on the internet for her street theater with its permanent address in Amsterdam, and on their site I finally watched a video clip with the giraffes. There were a lot of them, a whole family, big ones, little ones . . . A herd of giraffes ambled through an Amsterdam park, and to them flocked the delighted audience. The people stroked the giraffes on the muzzles as if the puppets were real animals, as if the public didn't know or successfully pretended not to know, that these were only big puppets being maneuvered by stilt walkers. Here, too, Marlene was right, with her stammering effort to articulate *full-body expression*, indeed, what mattered was not authenticity, but the art of illusion. The giraffes bent their necks gracefully and, stretching out their sweet muzzles, big eyes, and long lashes, they did some sort of not very nimble dance but the clumsiness was endearing, they rubbed their necks together, the little giraffes nudged their way under the legs of the big ones . . . Among them was Marlene, but I couldn't tell in which giraffe beat her heart.

Marlene had asked nothing of me, I could so easily have said a few words about how marvelous it was that she was doing this, how she'd given it a shot when so many others were floundering, how resourceful she was in these times of hardship when many people were finding it so difficult to get a job, and how she'd chosen an admirable, old-time skill . . . I said none of these things; only somebody who is better, or at least feels themselves to be superior to the person they're talking with, can say such generous things, and I was blindsided by the realization that I, myself, am a "stilt walker," but less skilled and far older than Marlene, and hey, I, too, *do what I know the best I can.* Of course, under the cheap truth peeked an even cheaper one: Marlene had showed up at my door not because she was particularly keen to see me, but to check on whether I needed somebody to clean my apartment as she had done before so she could she pick up a little extra cash, just as my sudden outburst of anger at Marlene was provoked by the fact that I did, indeed, need somebody to clean my apartment, but I no longer had the wherewithal to pay for it.

11.

Piazza Bellini

The next the morning I sat in a cab and had the driver take me to Santa Lucia. I thought I'd find The Widow at breakfast so I could apologize.

"The lady left this morning," said the man at the front desk.

"When this morning? It's only 8:30!"

"She had a very early flight," he said.

"Did she leave any sort of message?"

He handed me a hotel envelope. "Yes, this is for you," he said.

The whole secret is in good posture! This is the sum of what I've learned in life. So straighten up! And don't forget—mind your step!

I held The Widow's note as if it were a lottery ticket. Like all great quotes, this was a clichéd *fortune-cookie* message. The Widow's courteous gesture, which I had in no way deserved, touched me. I was most moved, in fact, by her shrewd insight (How had she known I'd come looking for her that morning at the hotel?!), and also by a certain childish tone to the note. And I, what about me? Did I not come running less to apologize than to hear yet another word or two about myself, and then about the secret of success of the magical package people call a "work of art"? Is there anything more childish than these expectations, which The Widow, to be fair, never betrayed? Could the whole trick really be in good posture?

I went out into the street. I thrust my shoulders back, feeling a mild twinge at the stretching of my shoulder blades. The sea and Castel dell'Ovo were glistening there in front of me. I took a cab over to the other side, to the hilltop, to Castel Sant'Elmo, from where there swept a magnificent view of Naples. The city shimmered in a sunny haze in front of me like a big Neapolitan treat, a *baba* soaked in rum, a tasty symbol of the vitality of a human race that survives, and the beauty that reconciles it all: the poor and the rich, the handsome and the ugly, the old and the young, the new arrivals and the local denizens . . .

Down the hill I went into the *Centro Istorico* and roamed its narrow streets. I bought a few *portafortuna* charms, key chains with a *corno*, a Toto, a Pulcinella . . . I let somebody talk me into purchasing a little pot with a robust local basil plant, which was silly since I was sure the customs officials wouldn't allow me through with it, and I'd have a terrible time juggling the pot at the airport. I sat in a little café at Piazza Bellini, passing the time until I went to retrieve the suitcase I'd left at the B&B and wait out in front for the cab promised by the conference organizers. In front of me gaped a large archeological excavation, the main attraction of Piazza Bellini. The site had uncovered remains of Greek walls, the oldest of the many historical layers of Naples.

If somebody were to compel me to send a message to the past ages and generations through this impressive pit yawning there before me, what would I say first? *Hakuna matata*? What can we do with the fact that right before our very noses—while we sip a cappuccino and wait for a cab—there yawns a pit and in the pit, as in a pot with hot water ready for pasta, simmers time? Around the pit is the peaceful present, sunlit, and overarched by the dome of blue sky. A few steps farther on, at Piazza del Gesù Nuovo, workers who've been laid off are protesting. A few miles farther on, the Lampedusa coastline is being overrun by hundreds of immigrants from Africa, many of whom are arriving as corpses, having suffocated below the decks of the ships transporting them to a better life . . .

If I attune my ear more finely, I'll hear the din of rage, of people scuttling, rodent-like, in search of food. And it's merely a question of days before they start, rodent-like, gnawing at one another. Things are more fragile than they seem, the Neapolitans know this better than anybody, they have learned to live with it, with their "volcano neurosis," their "chaos," for it is true that at any moment somebody might stomp on Virgil's Egg and there you have it, tragedy; angry Vesuvius spews lava tomorrow on the city and there you have it, tragedy; a capricious *jettatore* grazes us with the evil eye, and tragedy.

If I slightly sharpen my focus, the Neapolitan images begin swarming around me like giant hornets: images of refugees from North Africa kicking around in front of their refugee camps with no idea of what to do or where they might go; images snapped through the bus window of dark figures looming by the roadside like phantoms; images of immigrants rising above the idyllic landscape like desert meerkats; images of immigrants sprouting from a trash heap, from dilapidated apartments, their balconies overflowing with flowers, images from all sorts of pits where the many centuries of layers verify the history of the town; images of people taking root like graveyard crosses, blocking the view of Vesuvius; an image of a girl, her elbows planted on the windowsill, gazing at the army of dusty miniature cacti set out on the sill; an image of a market stall with piles of fruit which, lit by the bright rays of the sun, glow like paper lanterns; an image of a little girl who with her delicate fingers adroitly unwraps a *sfogliatella* like a skein of wool . . . Naples flips about before me like the splashing fish held in the wide, flat, round, display dishes used by the street vendors on Via dei Tribunali. The orgy of images, fragrances (the smells of decay, street food, trees, melons, the sea, sweet, pungent, intoxicating scents) and sounds—steals my breath, dizzies me, and prevents me from anchoring in the safe harbor of my own perspective. It, my perspective, keeps shifting, crystal clear at one moment, blurred the next, double the next, flipping between comic relief and tragedy, and it's as if nothing gets by without its double: there is no creature alive that's not lugging its own dead body on its back; there's no good luck without bad luck; there's no love without hatred toted along in its backpack.

The only thing unambiguous and constant is loss. Every person, one way or another, is always losing; we all slide downhill, what matters is only our skill at slowing things down, a skill demonstrated by the orange tree that grows out of the sidewalk on nearby Van San Sebastiano and pelts car roofs and noisy motorcyclists with its fruit.

The movie *Seven Beauties* by Lina Wertmüller, a Chaplinesque story about a small-time Neapolitan hero, ends with Pasqualino's return to Naples from a German concentration camp. *Pasqua, you're alive!* says his mother in a tone suggesting the belief that survival is the only choice we have. Her tone is, at the same time, apologetic because she and her many daughters survived thanks to prostitution, despite Pasqualino spending half of his life defending the honor of his mother and his winsome sisters. *Yes, I'm alive,* answers Pasqualino darkly, having prostituted himself, as well, to survive. For Pasqualino—as he strips off his camp tatters, sings the Neapolitan canzone "Maria, Mari" and then stands on a round rug with a swastika design in the center in the office of the kapo. The kapo is a woman whom he struggles to please sexually while she brutally humiliates him, offering him, who is starving, food as if he were a dog (*Mangia, Napoli*)—so he, too, has used survival as an alibi and an apology.

A city is a text. Every text survives by repeating stereotypes and undoing them, through trivialities and the dodging of trivialities. By penning a brief footnote to this city, I am merely going down the well-trodden path of words that have been uttered so many times before. It is not me, of course, that matters, it's the footnote. The footnote is a form of survival.

I faded from Naples like color—blending through the airplane window with the blue of the Bay of Naples *(Nel blu dipinto di blu . . .)*—and with scent. The customs officials, wonder of wonders, did let me pass, after all, with my pot of basil that lay in my lap throughout the flight. At every jostle, even the slightest, the basil, berserk, exuded its heady scent.

EPILOGUE

First Epilogue

The final frames of Pasolini's film *The Decameron*—which takes place largely in Naples with non-professional actors speaking in the local dialect—show Giotto (or a pupil of Giotto's) finishing a fresco in the Chiesa di Santa Chiara in Naples. The fresco depicts the Madonna holding Jesus in her arms. Everybody is pleased with it, the church bells are rung in celebration, the workers cheer the successful completion, but Giotto (or Giotto's pupil), played by Pasolini himself, says: *Perché realizzare un'opera quando è così bello sognarla soltanto?* Why create art when dreaming about it is so much sweeter? Is dreaming about the artwork and the author's (Giotto's or his pupil's?) lack of pretension regarding dreams closer to a woman's feel for creativity or a man's?

Second Epilogue

In his text "The Art of the Circus," Viktor Shklovsky says:

"Every art has its structure—that which transforms its material into something artistically experienced.

"This structure finds its expression in various compositional devices: in rhythm, phonetics, syntax, and plot. A device is something that transforms non-aesthetic material, imbuing it with form, into a work of art.

"As far as the circus is concerned, things are going rather strangely. [. . .]

"Neither the snake man nor the strong man lifting heavy objects nor the bicyclist looping the loop, nor the animal trainer putting his well-pomaded head into the lion's jaws, nor the trainer's smile nor the lion's physiognomy—none of this is art and yet we perceive the circus as art, as no different from heroic theater. [. . .]

"Without difficulty there is no circus; therefore, in the circus the artistic work of the acrobats under a dome is more artistic than the work of those acrobats in the parterre, though their movements were both in the first and in the second instances absolutely identical [. . . .]

"Making it difficult—that is the circus device. Therefore, if in the theater artificial things—cardboard chains and swords—were routine, the spectator at the circus would be justifiably indignant if it turned out that the weights being lifted by the strong man weighed less than what was written on the poster. Theater has other devices at its disposal than simple difficulty; therefore it can get along without it.

"The circus is all about difficulty.

"Circus difficulty is related to the general laws of breaking in composition.

"Most of all, the circus device is about 'difficulty' and 'strangeness.' One of the types of difficulty connected in literature with plot-breaking occurs when the hero, for example, gets himself into difficult situations through the struggle between the feeling of love and duty. An acrobat overcomes space with a leap, the animal trainer overcomes a wild beast with a glance, the weightlifter overcomes weight with strength, just as Orestes overcomes love for his mother in the name of rage for his father. And in this lies the kinship between heroic theater and the circus."

Third Epilogue

A year after our sojourn in Naples, I came across an article in the press reporting that The Widow had died, felled by a heart attack. Several black-and-white photographs from her younger years circulated on the internet, always by Levin's side. Levin was phantom-like in the pictures, while The Widow, with her remarkable beauty, was the focus of all the attention. In one, The Widow was wearing a white sleeveless dress with a deep-cut neckline displaying to advantage her shapely collar bone and broad shoulders, a silken polka-dotted shawl draped around her head, and big dark glasses. In all the pictures it was The Widow's arresting face, nuanced by intelligence, mystery, and a raw sensuality, that most stood out. I leafed through several newspapers, and, wouldn't you know it, the place of her death given in each was different! The Paris papers wrote that she died in Paris, the *New York Times* claimed she died at the St. Regis Hotel during a brief stay in New York, while the *Corriere della Sera* reported that she passed away at Grand Hotel Vesuvio in Naples. Was this a simple error, too minor to merit a correction or even attention, or was this something else? I had no way of knowing, of course. The newspapers quoted several lines of an ambiguous verse by Levin, which could be interpreted as romantic and might possibly have referred to The Widow, though there was no explicit indication that it did. Her obituary was eclipsed by an interview with a major New York publisher announcing publication of Levin's previously unpublished diary. The diary would carry the title *The Other Shore*, said the publisher, and he announced translations into several languages.

What a fox, I thought, even in death she's covered her tracks. I thought about how literary history can sometimes veer off in unexpected directions, and if that were to happen, The Widow—the beautiful, silent assistant who stands, reclining against the target at which the grand circus master takes aim with his unerring knives—might, in the future, be rewarded for her patient, quiet heroism. History, especially literary history, is engaged in the manufacture of illusions, as is literature, so there was, in this, a modicum of justice as well. The Widow had created Levin, not he her; he served, at first, as her modest start-up capital, which, through astute investment, she had aggrandized over the years. She was the broker for Levin's literary legacy, a canny and savvy business woman, like all those who succeed in turning a small profit—real, or symbolic, or both—from art.

I, of course, immediately bought in to the Neapolitan version (*See Naples and Die*). I was sure she'd died at Hotel Vesuvio, a haunt for famous celebrities with a view of the sea and Castelo dell'Ovo. She had a knack for the management of symbols. Furthermore, it was easier, as in tarot, to divine the reasons behind choice. She had assigned herself the role of the siren, Parthenope, a bird with a woman's head, a woman with a bird's body, a second-tier mythical celebrity who killed herself, plunging into the sea, when her divine song failed to entice Odysseus. The waves cast her body ashore where Naples stands today. Naples rose up on Parthenope's bones. Parthenope is the patron saint of Naples; the Neapolitans sometimes refer to themselves as Parthenopeans. Oh, and, by the way, according to one version, Parthenope's mother was Melpomene, the muse of tragedy.

There is another legend, the poor man's version, more accessible to the tourist's imagination, about a centaur named Vesuvius who fell in love with Parthenope. This so enraged Zeus that he turned Vesuvius the centaur into a volcano and condemned him to yearn, eternally, for

Parthenope. And Zeus turned Parthenope, meanwhile, into a city, a gem, Naples.

There is a third legend, this one Christian. During the age of witch hunts when women were put to death on a grand scale in Europe, Christian propaganda produced (for the sake of balance!) a corresponding popular genre through which certain women of myth underwent Christian beatification or "madonnization," in other words they were given a Christian *makeover*. This Christian standardization for female heroines was abetted by the strategy of introducing a double, used to expunge the power of the original. Historical appropriation began in the age of the Renaissance, and then women celebrities *suitable* to the church were produced massively during the baroque. So there was talk in the fourteenth century that Parthenope was the daughter of a Sicilian king who had sworn an oath to God. But it would seem that after centuries of vying for the role of Madonna—at least as far as the city of Naples was concerned—it was St. Patricia who won. Having resolved never to marry and to devote her life to God, she fled her native Constantinople, received the veil from the then Pope, and lived under the aegis of Catholic Rome. After her father's death she donated her worldly possessions to the poor and set out by ship for Jerusalem. The ship was wrecked mid-journey and the waves bore her body to the shores of the Bay of Naples, to the little island of Megarides, today's Castel dell'Ovo. In the seventeenth century, at a time when Naples was going through a massive Catholic and baroque transformation, St. Patricia became Naples's protectress, and, to make matters even more brutal, her relics were reinterred on the spot where Parthenope is thought to have been buried, at a monastery on Caponapoli hill. And so, as an interloper in Parthenope's temple, Patricia was declared the saint of Naples. The two women—both virgins, both foreigners, both migrants from the "East," both cast up on the shores of the Bay of Naples—were left to compete for prestige.

Yet the rivalry between Parthenope and Patricia (and who, according
to some researchers, is also St. Lucia) is not symmetrical. St. Patricia
is the product of the powerful Catholic industry, a modern figure, a
figure of our times, a typical female Catholic shyster, an "entertainer."
She's linked to legends about her healing powers; a legend about how,
for instance, a pilgrim broke a tooth off her skull to add to his reli-
quarium, and the tooth suddenly bled. The blood, collected in two
glass vials, dried over time, but it reverts to liquid every August 25th.
The miracle of the liquifying of St. Patricia's blood every year bolsters
her status as a saint, as demure Parthenope slips into oblivion. And
while Patricia is a symbol of (cheap) artistic success, behind which
stands the powerful, far-reaching industry of Catholicism, Parthenope
is victim of a historical deception, a loser-woman. Parthenope did not
succeed in enticing Odysseus with her divine song simply because
Odysseus had his ears stopped with wax. Naive Parthenope, who
knew nothing of Odysseus's ploy with the wax, experienced his stoic
indifference as a devastating blow to her artistic self-confidence and
preferred a plunge into the sea to continuing a song that no longer
enchanted anyone. Parthenope is a symbol of the struggle for artistic
excellence, for high artistic standards, a battle before the fact against
the horrors of modern artistic cacophony, but also a symbol of stunning naiveté: most people are born, apparently, with wax in their ears!

Mediocrity and loserdom in the realm of art dog Parthenope (as they
do after every gifted woman who has rebuffed their Christian ritual
transformation into "saints") like an ugly rumor. According to one
such rumor, the sirens, and among them Parthenope, challenged the
muses to a musical contest and lost. For their punishment the muses
plucked their feathers, making it impossible for them to fly. Using the
feathers of the poor sirens, the muses wove themselves victory wreaths
while the sirens tumbled into the sea. This rumor supports, at least

as far as the history of female creativity is concerned, ideas about the eternal female rivalry with, at its root, biological, procreative energy.

All in all, The Widow chose Parthenope as her symbolic double. In her early youth The Widow had committed symbolic suicide, exactly as if she knew that her song would not enchant Levin (he, too, apparently knew the trick with the wax), so she reined in her voice and fell silent. It was at the expense of her rash desire to be a nobody (her self-pruning of self-confidence) that she immortalized Levin's mortal coil. She raised a monument to him into which she inserted herself, just as famous builders have built their own silent shadow into their buildings.

In my mind's ear, provoked by nothing at all, words of The Widow's suddenly chimed like a jangling, nervous bell: *From time to time I would find a misplaced poem, story, or a page from his diary . . . He was a master at misplacing his things, have I already told you that,* lelkem? . . . Tears trickled down my cheeks. I studied the pictures of her on the computer screen. Her eyes, slightly slanted, the color of honey, watched me with taut attention, precisely as if I were her potential prey. And then, perhaps because of my tears, her eyes seemed to slant even more, as if she were choking back laughter. Or a sob. And I switched off the computer.

PART THREE

The Devil's Garden

"Hey, where do you think you're going?"
"I'm going home!"

— *Joel Schumacher,* Falling Down *(film)*

1.

The *muskrat, Ondatra zibethicus* is a variety of wetlands rat. Smaller than a beaver yet bigger than the common rat: it may, with its tail, reach to thirty inches in length and weigh as much as five pounds. It is named for the musk it uses to mark its territory. It breeds unusually rapidly; the female bears as many as four litters a year with six to eight young in each. Native Americans revere the muskrat: in their creation myths, the muskrat dredged up the primordial muck from the ocean floor. From this muck came Earth.

The muskrat was introduced in Europe in the early part of the last century when they were first raised on Czech farms. Muskrat-fur coats were all the craze in the 1920s. The rats, however, eluded control and scampered off to freedom, and from there they colonized Europe, particularly wherever there was a lot of water. Because of its lowlands, the Netherlands was their most natural habitat. For the Dutch, the *muskusrat* is a constant threat; it chose for its habitat the polders and by doing so has compromised the elaborate Dutch system of flood protection. Rat exterminators are prized and richly compensated in Holland. The Belgians have come up with a tasty dish made of muskrat meat served in restaurants (though, true, not many): after a salt-rub and an onion marinade, the muskrat is stewed in beer. In New Zealand, the muskrat has been strictly banned as a species, but, in Canada, hats sewn from its fur grace the winter uniform of the Canadian Royal Mounted Police.

These details about the muskrat are a rambling prelude to a brief incident described to me by a Dutch friend, a writer. While working on her novel she found she needed to know the muskrat inside and out. She acquired a freshly butchered one, skinned it, and, recalling dissection class in high-school biology, she cut it open. Then she pored over its innards, roasted it in the oven, and dined on it. She set aside the muskrat's larger and smaller bones, laid them out in a tin box, and buried the box in her garden.

My friend is a calm and sober fifty-year-old woman, pleased with her life. Each time we meet for coffee I remember her story and feel a rush of respect for her. Before me sits somebody who has faced *her* muskrat, dissected her problem, dined on it, digested it, and buried the inedible remains. And each time I ask myself: when will I face mine?

The reason for my reluctance lies not so much in my cowardice as in my sense of futility, and then in the feeling of "illegality" of the literary voice and literary form. A woman's voice is not, of course, illegal, but women, it seems, have still not embraced or conquered every form of literary expression. The specific "dyslexia" that readers—men and women alike—show when reading literary texts, each for his or her own reasons, has made this conquest impossible. In short, most "girls" still write romance novels, while *notes from underground* are reserved for "boys"; the rebellious confession is a male literary narrative because the rebel is invariably a man, he is our tragic hero. The story of a tragic heroine is read—with the "dyslexia" I mentioned—as the tale of a "madwoman." We come across such "madwomen" on the street, women who seem to be muttering with an invisible collocutor. An encounter with them is more likely to arouse disquiet than compassion, and passersby usually move away and avert their eyes though the "madwoman" never looks at anyone. Such women have, apparently, learned they cannot rely on anybody. They wage their battles alone.

2.

Things must have been simmering for a time so I can't say exactly when a thought first wriggled through my mind, or how much time it took for the impulse, half-hearted at first, to gel into resolve. Perhaps my intently forward looking focus, wherever my *forward* might be, had worn me down, and with only lukewarm resistance I was slipping backward, plain and simple, without the stamina to jump to my feet and begin again. Perhaps the cities I'd been traversing for years—instead of jump-starting my progress as they used to—were now slowing me down and stirring a vague anxiety that I could justify with nothing. Perhaps the "reflective" character of city spaces was knocking the wind out of me: I saw myself reflected in cities as in a mirror. Using the cityscape—as if it were a gas meter—I gauged my condition. I held my inner map up to the city map. Taking the city's pulse I took my own. The maps of the subways and undergrounds I compared to my own circulatory system. Others had psychoanalysts, I had cities.

Could my backslide be traced, perhaps, to my sojourn in Kolkata a few months before? The sight of miles of concrete pillars with jutting iron rebar—through the sun-drenched early morning mist on the road from the airport to the hotel—gripped me with a sinking sense of apocalyptic angst. It was not clear whether this was a construction job that had been begun and then abandoned, or a project that never would be finished because it wasn't meant to be, or a modern ruin of a structure that had stood there until only recently; just as I couldn't tell whether this city was a relic of the past, or of the present, or of the future in store for all of us. Kolkata had the feel of well-lived chaos, though this chaos could have been a synonym for frenetic organization. The inhabitants were slug-like parasites latching onto the city; they were devouring it like ants, trundling it off like an emptied animal hide, filling it with their saliva, feces, sweat, tearing down, drilling and rebuilding, molding it to themselves. The urban homeless behaved like tropical slugs, they conquered the city, took it to pieces but also fortified it; they created dark, smoky corridors along the sidewalks from which steamed the scents of food; their home was assembled and dismantled on the street like a cardboard box; and indeed home was, most often, a cardboard box, a sheet of discarded plastic, an old tarp, the hole in the wall of an abandoned house, a shelter below a bridge, by a railway line or standing façade. Decay as a higher principle was everywhere: in the thick dust that blanketed the city, the trees, the shrubs, the grass, from which the greenery acquired not only a clay-like hue but a clayish texture; in the mildew stains on the freshly painted walls of my hotel bathroom; in the pervasive odor of sulfur. On the street, people rolled out their rags, their sheets, their coverlets and draped them over the fences that ran along the road; the people seemed to do little else than air their mouse holes, wash, trim hair, shave, copulate, give birth, die, pray to their gods, defecate, prepare food, raise children, feed their livestock . . . and all this on the street. In the painfully open process of life there were some places that were under control, "pure places," like the golf course by my hotel where long since decolonized Indians imitated their former colonizers, strolling about with golf clubs amid the divine serenity of the greens. I experienced the view of the trim lawns and the figures moving around on them as soundless, in slow-motion, probably because only a few steps away, beyond the fence, beyond the uniformed guards and the entrance ramps, began the boundless clamor of human chaos.

Here, in Kolkata, assaulted by the swarming sounds, images, smells, and colors, I burst, with no warning, into tears. These were wrenching sobs that seemed to have been gathering steam inside me for years, and now, having found a fissure, came gushing out. Back I went to the hotel. For the first time in my life I felt a plain hotel room was *home*. There was also stowed away inside me a vague twinge of defeat.

Was, perhaps, an earlier episode in London a warning signal? I'd come to London for a business meeting, for a lunch during which we'd discuss work, or a work discussion we'd have while lunching; I was there to show the person I was meeting that a trip from Amsterdam to London was a breeze for me. And so it went until the moment when I found myself at the cheap hotel I'd reserved online and of which there are so many around Paddington station. Tourists milled around the reception area, most of them large Italian and Spanish families (do Italians and Spaniards ever travel alone?). My room was the size of a generous coffin, the bathroom miniature, a shower under which one could barely stoop; a child-sized bed and a mirror set so low that the priority guests at this hotel must have been below the age of twelve; around the mirror there was an array of items including a hair dryer, an electric burner, and two or three packets of tea and instant coffee in a small dish. And it was in such a hotel that after the meeting, instead of hurrying off to the museums and galleries or calling my London friends, I holed up until the next morning, riveted by fantasies that room No. 455 no longer existed, that—as soon as I'd walked in and shut the door behind me—the wall had closed off. In the morning I forced myself to get up; the floor covered in wall-to-wall carpeting, on which thousands and thousands of bare feet had trod before mine, creaked so painfully that it sounded about to buckle. Out I

ventured, first letting the stampede of Italian and Spanish families
rumble through the door, but after only a few steps I took a seat in
a café to sip my morning coffee and spent over an hour observing a
group of construction workers, Romanian men, who'd stopped in for
breakfast; the waitress, a Russian woman who served me my coffee
with milk; a young woman with a little girl whose face was slightly
disfigured (they, too, were Russian); and two women who walked into
the café, their breasts thrust out, marching in parade step. And they,
too, were Russian . . . In my thoughts I worked the puzzle, musing
whether the waitress was related to the Russian women who ran the
café, and what the emigrant bond was among them all. Upon leaving,
I turned left toward the underground station and then had a change
of heart and went back to the hotel, where I spent the rest of the day
and night until it was time to leave for the airport.

All the way back to Amsterdam from London, I was pressing an
imaginary remote control, yearning to turn down the volume. Several rows in front of me, young men were laughing, turkey-like, with
loud, throaty guffaws. From their laughter sprayed male hormones
and, through the haze produced by the sun, shining on the travelers
through the little airplane windows, these men resembled a TV ad
aimed at beer drinkers. I didn't know how to help myself, the throaty
turkey guffaws jangled my high-strung ears. A woman was sitting
next to me in a T-shirt and her bare arm was practically rubbing
mine. On her arm she had a tattoo, a caricature, the face of a bald
man with a bulging bluish nose and lips that slid glumly downward.
The woman's arm was meaty, larded with fat. The color of her skin
hinted that she spent a lot of time in tanning salons. I was awash with
panic. I felt I might choke. Droplets of sweat beaded the skin of my
face. The man's face on her arm with his glumly drooping lips fixed
its beady gaze on me, two black dots. It is time for me to go *home*, I
whimpered to myself. Where could I go *home* to?! Where was *home*? I

asked myself. *I don't know*, I answered thoughtfully, anywhere, just so it's *home* . . . Later, when I'd revived, I remembered an episode about *home* that happened some twenty years before that, in another city, in New York . . .

3.

I found myself in a situation at one moment when air raid sirens (whose message I did not, at first, comprehend), radio and television broadcasts, and my closest neighbors were all imploring me in a panic to hurry down to the cellar and by all means bring along a *bag with the bare essentials*. I did not realize that this phrase, part of the vocabulary of war, was signaling a radical watershed in my life. First I dutifully puzzled over what *bare essentials* ought to go into such a *bag*, only to catch on quickly to the fact that this raised a real quandary: my Yugoslav passport was no good because the new Croatian government was about to replace it; my money was no good because the banks were on the verge of shutting down and then the currency would be changed; my home was no good because at any minute it could be reduced to rubble, just as I, at any minute, could be obliterated. If I survived, then the first assumption was that I'd spend the rest of my life compensating for these losses. And something else: war is a time when the worst of humankind floats to the surface. Whoever survives must face the consequences. I know that now. Then, when it was happening, I knew nothing about any of this.

Long did that phrase—*a bag with the bare essentials*—ring in my ears after I first heard it in 1991. I often packed and repacked the imagined contents (yes, this was a form of backsliding), just as in my early childhood I agonized over which one of the three wishes I'd make if I were to stumble upon a good fairy and she'd allow me to choose what I want to be: wealthy, happy, or wise. Who knows where I got the idea that I had to choose only one and that getting one would preclude the others. Because in the world of fairy tales, Ivan the Fool, the stupidest character of all, gets all three of his wishes—wealth, happiness, and wisdom. I remember feeling sheepish about the way I puzzled over this, just as my little niece did—whether out of embarrassment or the belief that wishes don't come true if other people know of them—when she hid her Christmas wish list under her pillow. I read it while she was out of her room. Her wishes gave me an almost physical pang, maybe because they reminded me of my never-to-be encounter with the good fairy. Although I was younger then than she is now, her wish list seemed even more earnest and heartfelt than mine had been. *Wealth* was hidden in her first-place wish: *I wish for a job for my daddy.* The sentence—*I wish to be allowed to wear high-heels*—meant happiness, I suppose, and *I wish for good grades in school* could be translated, in the language of fairy tales, as wisdom. The only thing I couldn't for the life of me explain was why my precious little niece added to her Christmas list *I wish for clean teeth.* She brushed her teeth regularly, went to the dentist's for check-ups, and had the sweetest smile in the world. Maybe high-heeled shoes and clean teeth in her world were the only valid ticket to a *happy, wealthy, wise* life.

Our deepest desires pounce on us from unexpected places, ambush us, snatch us by the throat, and steal our breath. I was in New York one July after spending two semesters in a small American college town, on my way to Europe, but not going home, because I no longer had a home. I was staying at the apartment of New York friends who were out of town. This was their generous gift to me. Savoring long ambles through the scorching-hot city, I stopped to look at a store in Soho and stepped into the chilled, snow-white space: the wooden floorboards had been painted white, the shelves were white, everything was white. The store offered an upscale array of luxury household items: towels, curtains, bedding, tablecloths, napkins . . .

Silk, lace, linen. And while still standing there in the doorway, I burst into tears. The salespeople stopped and watched me with interest. I went back out into the street. The heat beating from the air, the pavement, and the concrete quickly dried my tears. And now I understood that the promise I'd made to myself after the experience with the *bag with the bare essentials*—to never, never wish for a home—was simply impossible. The urge for home is powerful, it has the force of primal instinct; the mind-set of the short-term—nourished and entrenched over time into a pigheaded moral principle—was more dangerous than I'd thought; it could turn against me if I didn't toss it a morsel and staunch its hunger, if, in other words, I didn't make a home from which, one day, if I so desired, I could catapult out again. Everything moves in circles, the greatest feat of every emigrant seems to be making a new home; emigrants, many risking their lives in the process, come pouring out of their countries only because they want, sooner or later, to purchase a home and hang out the flag of the state where they live; moreover many spent their entire lives in two homes, the one in the country they left, the other in the country where they ended up, just in case they're hit by the traumatic loss of one, or both.

When I came back to Amsterdam I decided that instead of renting an apartment again, short-term, as I had before, it was time to provide myself with more stability—and I resolved to do this almost subversively, as if stealing my own wallet, with a feeling of both victory and defeat. There may have been a cautious voice in my mind calculating that I'd been wandering from place to place for too long now, high time I settled down. Had the sheer whiteness of the New York store and that sudden attack of sobs tugged a thread inside me? I don't know. All I know is that I brought the pure white of my new home to a searing white psychotic heat. White curtains of hand-tatted lace, white towels, white linen bedding, white walls, white floor- and wall-tiles in the kitchen and bathroom, white shelves . . . Everything was white, basic white, like oblivion. It was only later that the stains appeared.

4.

I read the great works of world literature in high school—Jane Austen, Dickens, Balzac, Stendhal, Zola, Dostoyevsky, Flaubert—and found that all of them were actually about money, just as the relations among the characters were governed only by money, though our literature teachers told us otherwise. Writers like Dickens may owe their great popularity during their lifetime precisely to the way money motivates everything in their novels, something the vast majority of readers can grasp. With modernism, money slipped out the backdoor of literature. True, Virginia Woolf in her oft-quoted essay *A Room of One's Own* does say a woman cannot be a writer if she has no *room* of her own and a minimal income of 500 pounds a year. This assertion has been a magnet for the attention of the literary public for nearly a century. Indeed, ever since the essay was first published, somebody, every so often, comes up with the idea of converting the sum of five hundred pounds to today's standard of living.

So I had the *room*, but not the yearly 500 pounds. And then, in addition to my one *room*, I found myself in possession of another, thanks to the caprice of a gentleman, an admirer of my writings, who left me some property in his will. This made me uneasy; I couldn't remember when anybody had given me anything more valuable than a book and a bouquet of flowers, and now out of the blue—a house with a garden in a village I'd never heard of. I'm not one who often hears of villages anyway, the thought of life in the countryside had never attracted me. The only village I was familiar with was the English variety, the kind I watched on BBC shows in the PBTP (Property-Buying Television Programs) category. The programs had charming titles (*Escape to the*

Country, To Buy or Not to Buy, Safe as Houses, and so forth) and the narrative structure was much like that of a porn film: a good-looking young agent takes a middle-aged, retired couple around to see two or three properties in the English countryside. The middle-aged couple and the young agent tour the houses and in the end there's a final "mystery" house. My *mystery house* was in a Croatian village, not in England. Life may also write novels, but it varies the geographic setting and cultural surroundings that anchor the story, and these fundamentally set each novel apart from all the rest.

My first thought was to decline the gift left to me by this man I hardly knew, but the tax I was to pay if I were to take ownership was negligible and the lawyer persuaded me that to refuse such a thing was simply foolish. So there it was, I acquiesced, signed the papers, and set the whole story aside for a time. At the moment of his death, the old gentleman had, apparently, had no next of kin. His Zagreb apartment was left to a caregiver who'd been looking after him for years. He'd read my books with interest, or so he claimed in the handful of letters he sent me. This was something I did not find flattering; first one must get to know one's reader and his literary tastes before knowing whether to take his praise to heart.

And that was that. Even my lawyer couldn't tell me anything more about the old gentleman. Some people are so self contained that they take even their own shadow with them to the grave, while others make a museum of their life, in which even the needle they used to sew on buttons is prominently displayed.

5.

Even now, more than forty years after his death, I can summon to my memory the dark-purple stain that was an object of fascination for me when I was small. I don't know how things imprint themselves on our memory, whether we choose what we remember or it chooses us. Father refused to speak of the war, the Second World War. He spoke, in fact, very little. He never mentioned his parents. *They died in the war*, was all he'd say, slapping with his tone a non-negotiable kibosh on the subject. My interest in my grandparents was buried with that sentence. He joined the Partisans when he was barely seventeen. He didn't relish talk of that, either. He came out of the war with German shrapnel lodged in his leg, with a wound that never healed and a stain the hue of rotten flesh. He refused to have the shrapnel removed and insisted it didn't bother him. I had no idea what shrapnel was, and that's probably why the story so shook my childish imagination. The blemish aroused no disgust in me or fear for my father. I studied it with curiosity, as if studying a map. The stain was big simply because I was small. Father died before the age of forty-nine. And so he was buried with German shrapnel in his leg and a Partisan star engraved on his gravestone. The shrapnel in his body was a metaphor, but I understood that only many, many years later.

Mother outlived him by thirty years. Over all those years she managed to expunge him almost completely from my memory, though I doubt she meant to. Mother came by her victory honestly: she lived much longer than Father had and, unlike him, she told stories. I knew all her stories about close family, distant family and the very distant cousins, her acquaintances, family friends, neighbors from the building where she lived. Those people, thanks to her stories, became a part of my extended family, at least for a time. Only in the last years of her life did she begin to concoct little make-believe tales, erasing people from her mental circle, although many of them were dead anyway, many she hadn't seen for years; with time she saw fewer and fewer people. Women were gradually given the advantage on her list, particularly those who were no longer alive. Men, unlike women, faded, dropped off the list, or the ink of her suspicious nature blotted them. *He was not a good man*, she'd say for some poor fellow who was long since gone and buried, exactly as if she were chairing a celestial committee. She was not religious, indeed she despised the church. I think she was simply beginning slowly to pack and select in her mind's eye whom she would be "taking with her," and whom she wouldn't.

And yet, though he was a *very, very good man*, I am not sure Father would have been included in her mental circle. Perhaps she erased him at the last moment before death erased her; perhaps she was punishing him for abandoning her to live alone for thirty years. Because we, her children, were only a comfort to her when we were able to be at her side.

6.

Whenever I came to Zagreb I stayed at Mother's. After her death, the apartment was gradually emptied of furniture. Friends, neighbors, neighbors' friends took things, whatever each of them needed. When the big wardrobe was pulled away from the wall, ugly, old, ragged wallpaper was exposed that had been hidden behind it for years. This wallpaper flapped—like a white flag signalizing surrender—a long time in the half-emptied apartment until, during one of my Zagreb stays, it dared me to begin. I replaced the windows, because pigeons had nested in the outdoor housing for the Venetian blinds and nothing could drive them out. The new windows helped, but the pigeons kept flying into the wall above, seeking a way back to the space they'd conquered and that had been their home for so long. I glued rows of plastic spikes to the sill and this stopped the pigeons, but only for a time. I had new kitchen cabinets installed, renovated the bathroom, painted the walls and woodwork white, had the parquet floors sanded. The absence of character, the ascetic feel, the lack of furniture all soothed me. Except for Mother's books, nothing in the apartment was hers any more, nor was it mine. The whole space had an anesthetizing effect.

Only sometimes, at dusk, from the corner of the dining room, by the window, where before there was a broad sill on which Mother had kept pots of flowers, I'd have the impression I could hear rustling. The sound came from an invisible cage around which an invisible canary fidgeted nervously. Its beady black eye seared into me like a white-hot needle, penetrating straight to the malleable core of never-healing shame. At one moment (when she was the same age I am now) I had given Mother a canary. At first she was bemused, she'd never kept pets, she felt they were unhygienic, but then she understood. I'd brought her the canary to keep her company, a canary is just the pet for a woman her age, I thought (did I?). They give senile women rubber baby dolls at old peoples' homes and the residents rock them for hours, anesthetizing themselves with the rhythm. Why are doctors and therapists so certain that a doll is the woman's one and only toy? Why was I so sure the canary was the best choice?

I was writing her off. Humiliating her. I remember her surprised, slightly slanted gaze and the color of her eyes: light brown flecked with amber. It was the look of a little girl who's been dropped from a game, a moment of youthful protest flashed in her eyes that was soon stilled . . . She swallowed the insult with grace, accepted the canary dutifully as a blow she didn't know how to parry, and then with time she grew used to it and even loved the presence of the bird. Whenever I called her from abroad, I would always ask after the canary, it was silly but, surprisingly, it helped: we were winding the wool of our conversations around something living, painless and light, around a surrogate that eased the ache.

7.

The village was known as Kuruzovac. It was some thirty miles south-east of Zagreb. I borrowed a car from an old friend . . .

"Are you sure you don't need it?"

"Yes, I am. What would I do with it, anyway. It's silly to sell it for a song but right now I don't even have the money for gas . . ."

"Should I pay you something for the loan?"

"No need. When you bring it back, fill up the tank, that's all. And we'll be happy as the day is long," she said.

The phrase—*happy as the day is long*—sounded oddly out of place, although there was nothing wrong with it. Maybe it's that I hadn't heard it said in a while so it sounded odd, maybe there was something off with me. Too often, the words and sentences said by people I was talking to and strangers on the street or on a tram sounded weird. They came popping out from everywhere like broken springs. I hadn't spent time in Zagreb in years, I reasoned to console myself, although this wasn't, in fact, exactly true: I came two or three times a year and each time I'd stay for at least a month. The language, as ordinary people spoke it, had been infiltrated by something unnatural, out of kilter, insecure. It was perhaps the occasional word, phrase, or use of dialect, such as Kajkavian, for instance, where it didn't quite sit, or a twinge of inner insecurity that drove the speaker to pause for just a second before they said what they were about to say, and this mental hiccup reflected in an ugly way on what they said. The intonation had changed, young people had their own cadence now, the pace of speaking had changed, too. The Croatian dubbing of children's cartoons and animated features, American teen TV series, the gallop of ads and radio, all this had sped up the Croatian language over the last twenty years. The inflection and pace sounded to my ear like ungainly novelty.

My questions began the moment I landed in Zagreb with the intention of finally having a look at the house. Didn't I catapult myself abroad twenty-two years ago without a thought, even once, for what would become of me, where I'd go, how I'd fare moving forward?

Didn't I leave then, forsaking my home and crumbling domicile because the air was so thick with hatred that it couldn't be breathed?
And now, look, lured with a nubbin of cheese I was crawling steadily
toward the same old mousetrap. What was I thinking! Home? What
home! Why, I have a home in Amsterdam, don't I? Friends? What
friends? Didn't my friends write me off, watching silently—as the
powers-that-be batted me about: they the cat, I the mouse—showing
an indifference that iced the blood in my veins? Did they ever wonder
where I was going, would I be back, did I need any help? Look, after
all the years we'd spent as friends they weren't interested in these
trifles. So what about later? Did they ever seek me out? Isn't twenty
years long enough to think, at least once, of one's lost friends? And
what about those who declared open season on me, what about the
hunters who harvested a trophy pelt from my hide, weren't they still at
the very same posts they'd occupied in the newspapers, at the university, on TV, in the publishing companies, yes, my colleagues? Didn't
the booksellers refuse to display my books for years on their shelves?
Didn't the journalists follow my every—barely published—book with
a tomblike silence or fling their inflated, ignorant bile at it? Had any
of them ever apologized for the long years of loathing? And what
about the innocent in this whole story, the young people who hadn't
yet had time to be infected by the hatred. Would they ever invite
me to join them and set things straight somehow? Wasn't it they,
obediently upholding the rules they'd inherited in the vicious social
games, who erased me from university curricula, secondary-school
reading lists, anthologies, textbooks, publishers' catalogues? What
about my colleagues, editors, publishers? What about the publisher of
mine who, during the rapid-fire changes in government, leapfrogged
from publisher to chief of the Croatian police force and pounded, one
night, drunk, at my front door, demanding that I open up? The rush
of power had gone to his head as it did for so many and he sought the
cure for his sense of intellectual, professional, or sexual inadequacy in

a substitute, a revolver. What about my colleague who—smack dab in the middle of a crowded tram car—accused me of betraying my homeland, milking the other travelers as his eager audience? What about my female colleagues, did they show solidarity? Didn't they hasten to publish barbed texts in which there were no statements grounded in reality but only naked envy wrapped up in quasi-argument? They, too—"the girls"—stabbed their penknives into the bloodied flesh. They relished the smell of blood every bit as much as "the boys" did, and, following the boys, they flung feathers in collective retribution at the tar smeared all over me. Didn't all that, and so much more, happen then and was happening still today after a full twenty years, with the same doltish obduracy? If so, what was I thinking, plunging back in? Had I come back for a new slap in the face, fresh spittle that would slather my cheeks like pigeon shit, a new blow to knock me breathless when my righteous "volunteer," my illiterate executioner, no longer even knew why he was doing it? He stares at me with his dull gaze, his mouth slack, saliva dribbling out the corners, he musters the spittle, works it around with his tongue as if it were a piece of hard candy, and then—splat!—gloms it onto my cheek like a llama. And I wondered. Was I addicted to the humiliation? Was what I needed an even bigger dose, perhaps? And if not, then why the hell didn't I break this habit once and for all?

I am overstating my case and my importance; they'd never even noticed I was gone because they hadn't known I'd been here in the first place, and besides, hadn't I moved from address to address enough times by now? Why, then, was I tugging at their sleeve, and what, exactly, did I have in mind? Hadn't I been doing just fine where I'd settled, and wasn't it a little peculiar that I kept coming back so persistently? Each time has its music, and time had passed me by, twenty years was a whole age ago, everything that was making me itch had happened in the last century, and back then, for God's sake, people were dying. I

should have been glad nothing so awful happened to me, look, war is
war, the war is over and done with, people have put it behind them
now, they've stepped into the new century, the new millennium, there
are other, young faces on the media screens, new entertainers, new
TV anchors . . . And, of course, new writers. So why, then, would I
matter? Had I ever had anything nice to say about them in my writing? Hadn't I refused to be a Croatian woman? Hadn't I refused to be
a Serbian woman? So what was I after? It wasn't their fault I hadn't
taken sides at a moment that required only that, the taking of sides.
And didn't I declare, if you please, several times in public that I was
a *nobody*? So what did I expect? Be my guest, ma'am, be a *nobody*, heh
heh, don't let us stop you from being a *nobody*, heh heh, go live with
your *nobodies*, write your *nobody* books, find your *nobody* readers, but
us—git-git, shoo shoo!—give us a break!

It was a sunny day in late April when I went off to scout out the house
I'd inherited. I brought with me a flashlight, a sleeping bag, a blanket,
bedding—just in case I decided to spend the night—and a few other
practical necessities. I drove along back roads and this had its up side:
the sky arched above me, bright blue, and a slide-show flashed by
my window: green, dandelion-sprinkled fields, flowering fruit trees,
villages with hopelessly ugly houses. My gut resistance melted as I
caught sight of purple lilacs cascading in clusters over the fences in
the rural yards, and I capitulated when to the surface of my memory
floated the image of the thumb on a child's hand, working back and
forth to make a crease in the skin. Into the crease was poked a lilac
floret and the crease, by squeezing together the folds, held the little
blossom upright. That was how, when we were little girls, we carried
flowers around in the thumb crease, holding our hands out before
us like tiny trays bearing crystal goblets—the lilac florets. We were
junior acrobats plying our trade with rapt attention: the floret must
not tip over. That sudden image left me breathless when it surfaced

from the depths of my recollection to gulp in air, to remind me that in childhood, everything was a close-up and in high resolution—every blade of grass, ant, and leaf, every detail—I drank it all in thirstily, with attention and delight. It was a time of lilacs, a time of little wonders.

8.

The house looked far better than I'd expected. It stood at the end of a row of houses and was set back a little from the road that wound through the village. A short, unpaved turn-off led up a gentle rise to the house. It was all of wood, the sort of rustic log cabin one seldom finds intact any more. It had a capacious porch and I already could imagine myself sitting out there, staring at the blue (sky) and green (field) ribbons on the horizon. As I turned the key in the door, a powerful thrill coursed through me. The view of the interior, which I could see from the threshold, however, made it obvious that somebody was living there. I put down my silly "girl-scout" bundle and went into the kitchen to open the refrigerator. There was food on the shelves, milk, butter, eggs . . . In the living room, which opened onto the kitchen, there were a small table with a television set, an old sofa, and an armchair. I picked up the remote and clicked on the TV. It worked. There was a desk and shelf in the living room with a small, but unexpectedly good selection of books, and, what's more, I noticed a few of the most recent Croatian translations. On a side table by the sofa I noticed an older edition of Krleža's novel *On the Edge of Reason*, the same edition I had. On the ground floor was a bedroom and a bathroom with a toilet. The bed was unmade. I went on up to the attic where, clearly, nobody was staying. Up there were built-in closets, a big mattress, and a half-bath. The toiletries in the downstairs bathroom suggested that the intruder was a man.

Out I went into the yard. Alongside the low stoop there were early spring flowers, forget-me-nots, pansies, and white-button daisies. On each side of the house grew a large purple lilac bush. This almost childish symmetry touched me deeply for some reason. Behind the house stretched a spacious garden and orchard with a dozen fruit trees. It all seemed well-tended, somebody was regularly mowing the grass. Lettuce was just coming up in the garden and there were a few tufts of scallions. A portion of the garden was planted with flowers, I recognized two bushes of peonies that hadn't yet flowered and beds of ox-eye daisies. There were no houses nearby: the woods began right behind the orchard.

I called the lawyer. I told him there was, apparently, an "intruder."

"Hold your horses, no cause for panic, the intruder may turn up, in any case I'm sure there's nothing criminal involved."

I sat on a bench on the porch and watched the sun set. The fields in the distance sank into a pinkish haze. It was warm and still. The wooden wall of the house warmed my back as I leaned against it. I shut my eyes. I'd nearly dozed off. And then I heard the sputter of a car. A man got out, roughly my age, and with light step came up onto the porch.

"Hello," he said warmly. "Welcome to Kuruzovac."

"And you are?"

"Your intruder, Bojan," he said, offering me his hand.

"Who told you it's not me who's the intruder?"

"Your lawyer."

This surprised me.

"What should we do now?" I asked.

"Nothing. I'll take some of my things now and come for the rest tomorrow. Would that be OK?"

"Of course . . . I'm sorry . . ."

The man packed several items of clothing into a bag and collected his toiletries from the bathroom.

"Listen, my cat may turn up. She's out and about all day long but in the evening she comes back to the house, so please let her in," he said.

"Out of the question! I can't stand cats!"

"How do you feel about dormice?"

"Who?"

"It's a kind of rodent. Between a mouse and a squirrel. The attic was crawling with them when I arrived. Since the cat has been here, no dormice."

I stared at him in surprise. None of it made sense. This was an entire new genre I'd stumbled onto, village sci fi.

"OK, I'll feed her. I saw milk in the fridge . . ."

"Good night," he said.

It occurred to me I hadn't asked him where he'd sleep, but then I had to wonder if I was losing my mind. Was I actually worrying about where a man I knew nothing about and who'd broken into my house would sleep? But then again, didn't he say he was in touch with my lawyer? And didn't that mean that the lawyer knew about him but hadn't said a word to me? Meanwhile I caught myself noticing the lightning speed with which my ownership instinct (*my* house, *broke in*, *intruder*) had asserted itself.

If the cat showed up that evening, I never knew because I soon fell fast asleep and slept straight through until morning, when the cat's meowing woke me. She'd come for her saucer of milk.

9.

The next morning I drove to the nearest place with stores, a crossroads I'd passed through on my way the day before, to see what my

neighborhood had to offer. It was some five-six miles from Kuruzovac
and didn't look like much, a stain on the map that was best referred
to as a *place* because it couldn't be said to be a city or a town or even
a village or hamlet. There were provincial non-places much like this
all through the interior of Croatia, and they all looked the same. I
was born in one just like this, grew up and lived there till I went
to university, and along the way I developed a permanent allergy to
the provinces and provincial rituals. True, there were several stately
old Austro-Hungarian houses here gracing a park, but their façades
had been painfully strafed with shrapnel. I spotted a grocery store,
a pharmacy, a shop selling household linens and fabric, a store with
handy merchandise for village households, and a bakery. The municipal building had been renovated and a Croatian flag hung out in front.
Sullen bushes grew in the park, water sprayed in the modest fountain
in unpredictable spurts, and frozen there was a new statue, raised
to the defenders who lost their lives fighting in the Croatian homeland war, 1991–1995. I figured the new statue probably stood on the
pedestal of the earlier one glorifying the victims of fascism who died
during the War for National Liberation, 1941–1945. The situation
with monuments was identical everywhere: "Partisan" statues were
torn down and in their place were raised new "homeland" sculptures,
or sometimes the old "Partisan" ones were just slightly adapted. All
they had to do, after all, was chisel the number 4 into a number 9, and
replace the words "National Liberation" with "Homeland."

At the grocery store I purchased a few basic foodstuffs and then took
a seat at the café and ordered a cappuccino. Local kids were loitering
at the café, the boys always too loud, the girls, silent, wearing too
much makeup.

   "So what's up, Auntie? You lost?" asked one of them jauntily, while
the others smirked at his audacity.

   The children were clearly translating the word "Mamma" from

American urban street slang into "Auntie" in Croatian and that was, likely enough, how they addressed all women who didn't fit the category of "Grandma."

I averted my eyes—a defensive gesture reserved for encounters with those who are "stronger"—downed my cappuccino, stood up, and left.

"Auntie, hey, you're not scared, are you?" Jaunty hooted after me, and the rest snickered and sneered.

I wondered what kids use as their retort these days. In my time it would have been, "Change the record!" or "Switch the channel!" What would the analog be now?

"Reboot"? Whatever, the kids must be dying of boredom if they had nothing better to do than taunt a middle-aged lady. The name of the café was "Zdravko."

Back at the house I began an inspection of the kitchen cabinets. The kitchen was modest, but adequately furnished, there was almost nothing missing. I found cleaning supplies and a vacuum cleaner in a closet. The house had nearly everything I'd need. I checked the garden woodshed and there I found an orderly array of tools, hoes, shovels, a sickle for mowing grass, rubber hoses for watering the garden, and a few things for who knows what . . . The inspection was exhilarating, and the word *mine* (*my* house, *my* garden, *my* tree) clung to my vocabulary like a burr.

First I took out the vacuum and vacuumed up the dust on the first floor, then I mopped the wood floor with a wet rag. In the bedroom I changed the sheets and dumped the dirty sheets into a plastic bag. I'd fallen asleep the night before on the sofa in the living room, covering myself with my sleeping bag because I didn't have the energy or will to make the bed up with fresh linens. Then I mopped the attic floor with a wet rag and swept the cobwebs from the rafters. I discovered linens stored in a cupboard, several clean towels, and some men's clothing. All of these, I assumed, belonged to the *intruder*.

Down I went to the garden and picked some as yet unripe lettuce and onions. Along the way I cut some of the ox-bow daisies to put in a vase inside. While I was snipping the daisies the grass around me swayed; something slunk by me and scampered off into the woods. The intruder's cat? I went back into the house; the living room was now beginning to look almost presentable. The little curtains on the windows were ghastly. I took them down and tossed them out. Then I washed the windows. With a new surge of energy I went on to the bathroom, wondering as I scrubbed where this almost physical glee was coming from. Cleaning was usually more of a chore for me than a pleasure. As if all those images from long ago had poured into me—mainly from the movies—of pioneers venturing westward in America to seek a better life (although, truth be told, I was not able to dredge up a single film title), and in which the hard-working, resilient heroines salvaged abandoned log cabins. These were scenes of solace, a matronly ethics, the aesthetic of poverty, the symbolism of scrubbing. Cleaning always signals a transition to a new, better life. And when my gaze fell on the vase with the daisies on the table, which I had set there just a moment before, I realized I was performing a well-practiced genre I'd internalized years ago. This discovery, by the way, did nothing to diminish my glee at "bringing order to the chaos."

I had just showered when I heard a knock at the door. It was Bojan.

"Come in, come in, have a seat," I said.

He looked a little surprised at my words, my tone, but down he sat politely. And I bit my tongue: the man had, for God's sake, been living here until the day before, and now here I was with my voice of the newly minted housewife (where did that come from?) inviting him in to have a seat.

"May I wash my hands?"

"Yes, of course . . ."

I asked him to join me for dinner. He acquiesced. I made spaghetti with tomatoes and cheese and a salad with the spring lettuce from the garden.

"Are there any animals here? Aside from the dormice, that are now gone, and your cat?" I asked.

"Why do you ask?"

"Because while I was in the garden, picking the lettuce and scallions, something slunk by me and scampered off into the woods . . ."

"A fox . . ."

"A fox?"

"A kit I've been trying to tame. I've been bribing it with food . . ."

"What have you been feeding it?"

"Chicken. I buy it from the local farmers."

"The fox from *The Little Prince*," I said, with irony.

"Ah, yes, the fox from *The Little Prince*," he said, ignoring my irony.

"What century was *that* in! The feeling, I mean . . ." I said, instead of an apology.

"That was when we were starting our studies at the university. Cheap 'spiritualism' was the height of fashion: make love not war, Herman Hesse, Japanese Zen and the bicycle, exotic peyote and local hash, *The Little Prince* . . ."

We ate our modest repast, which he politely praised, then we moved out onto the porch. I uncorked a bottle of wine and poured us glasses.

"It has barely been twenty-four hours since you moved in and already you're completely at home," he said amicably and raised his glass to me.

I didn't answer. I didn't know what to say.

There was an internet connection, he'd had it installed because without the internet he was lost and he assumed this would mean a lot to me as well. If I had a laptop, iPhone, or iPad with me we could test it.

There was no landline set up though there was a phone jack. He used only his cell . . . He didn't have a lot to tell me, in fact. The washing machine wasn't working, he could find somebody to tinker with it but I'd be better off buying a new one, this one was ancient. He didn't know much about the village, there were a few houses, some older people who lived off the land and a little livestock, mostly pig and poultry farming. As far as he knew there were no other weekenders about, this was the only summer cottage he knew of here, but there were several scattered around neighboring villages. I'd seen the town center and it was convenient, what with the grocery store, the doctor who showed up twice a week, and the little pharmacy. There was a school some fifteen miles away. The countryside was lovely, there were a few pretty spots, a pond in the woods, for instance. He'd take me there if I liked. The woods were full of mushrooms, porcini and chanterelles, one could live off the mushrooms alone—fresh while they were in season and otherwise dried. There were blueberries and wild strawberries.

"And the orchard?"

"Come, I'll show you . . ."

The orchard seemed large to me, but he said that an orchard this size was just enough for one household. Two apricot trees, he made jam from them, I'd find a couple of jars in the kitchen cupboards left over from last year. These were apple trees, only two varieties, the Yellow Transparent, an early apple, while the other, a Reinette, ripened in the fall. There were more cherries on the two cherry trees than he could pick, a pear tree, a Petrovka, and another with smaller fruit the locals called squash pears. Over there were two plum trees, a white plum and an Empress, and every year a neighbor picked them to distill the plums for brandy. Here we had vineyard peaches, a rarity today and by far the tastiest variety. And this here? A gooseberry bush. People here weren't familiar with it, he'd planted one so he could try his hand at making gooseberry preserves, all because of Russian literature. He'd remembered the mention of gooseberry preserves. Was it Chekhov? Did I know? True, the orchard wasn't purely *eco* and *bio*, it was a challenge to keep an orchard viable with no "chemicals."

"This really is your house, Bojan," I interrupted him, chagrined.

"Now it's yours," he said. "I moved in when there was no owner around. True, I've kept the house and garden in good shape, without me this would all be overgrown. There's a lot to do around a house, I don't know how handy you are with that sort of thing."

The cat appeared in the garden and twined around Bojan's ankles.

"There you are, you little tramp," he said, scratching it on the head, and turned to go back to the house to feed it. I followed him.

"Bojan, what are you doing out here in this village?"

He stopped for a moment, and then answered with an tinge of reluctance.

"I'm a de-miner."

"A what?"

"I clear minefields . . ."

"What minefields?" I asked stupidly.

"I'm not here alone, there's a whole team of us . . . Quite a few landmines were abandoned after the war. The war was awful around here. You saw the damage to the houses at the crossroads . . . They look like Swiss cheese."

"It's all so mindless!"

"Right you are, mindless . . ."

"So where's this team of yours?"

"Not far, I can show you our work area, if you like, our MSA . . ."

"MSA?"

"Mine suspicious area . . ."

"Do you mean to say there are land mines nearby?"

"Well, that wouldn't be far from the truth."

"And then what do you do?"

"We search the area we've designated as an MSA and when we find the landmines, we de-mine them."

"How many mines are there?"

"Official Croatian sources give the number as 60,000, with three times as many in Bosnia. But unofficial tally has the numbers much higher."

"So sixty thousand potential Croatian corpses, but only according to official sources? Unofficially, every Croat might be a victim?"

"You think like a fundraiser. Luckily, only a third of the people who step on mines are killed."

"And the others?"

"They're likely to lose an arm or a leg."

"Conversation with you really does lift the spirits," I said and poured more wine.

I fell silent. The sun was going down and a chill crept in. I rose to get a sweater and came back to the porch.

"After what I told you, you have the feeling that there are mines lurking at every step, don't you," he said.

"Exactly. Does that mean I'm a coward?"

"No, it means you're normal."

"But there are none in the garden?"

He laughed.

"Or the orchard?"

"No."

"What about the woods?"

"No, these woods are not categorized as an MSA."

"Still, one never knows . . ."

"True, one never knows. But if you follow the well-trodden paths I doubt anything will happen to you. The local farmers all know that."

"Still, people are sometimes killed?"

"It does happen."

"So mindless . . ." I repeated the phrase like an ugly tic.

"War is mindless. It's over now but the landmines are still with us. And the whole problem has sunk into illegality . . ." he said.

"Illegality?"

"The war no longer interests anybody except those who think there's still profit to be made. Our heroes have been acquitted of guilt for war crimes on all sides. Most of them will never do time. The few who have gone to prison are welcomed back as heroes. New statues have been raised, veteran pensions granted, the refugees are not coming back because they have nowhere to come back to. The landmines are all that's left to remind us of what happened here . . ."

"What you're telling me sounds like the opening for a novel."

He chuckled.

"The most interesting paradox is that the de-miners are doing the job to eke out a living."

"Excuse me?"

"At first it promised to be well-paid. The European Community, but also the Croatian government, set aside considerable sums of money to clear Croatia of landmines. Private de-mining firms began cropping up, some forty of them in Croatia alone."

"But wouldn't that be a good thing?"

"It would have been good had they all been honest."

"They weren't?"

"The people working in the field are decent folk. There are even women among them. There's one woman, for example, everyone knows her, from Bosnia, Davorka from Livno, a single mother supporting six children. She is a de-mining star. But . . ."

"What?"

"The boys don't like it when there are women in the work area . . ."

"Why?"

"Women bring bad luck. De-miners are like sailors, sailors don't like women on board ships either."

Bojan stood up.

"It's late, time for me be off," he said.

"And where will you sleep?"

"Don't worry about that. I'll be back tomorrow for my things, tomorrow is the weekend. Would late morning be OK?"

"Why don't you sleep here," I said, cautiously.

He didn't miss the note of caution in my voice. He hesitated but then agreed. The bed in the attic he made up himself.

We went back out onto the porch and sat a while longer. Outside it was dark now and the sky was studded with stars, the houses were obscured, a velvety silence ruled.

"I don't remember when I last saw stars," I said.

"The stars are all we have here," he laughed.

"Stars and landmines," I added.

There I was, apparently, in the very same mousetrap I'd escaped twenty years before. From the mousetrap the moon in the sky always looks like an unattainable wheel of cheese. It now looked like an unassuming little landmine, the kind called a *pašteta* for its resemblance to a can of meat paste.

10.

I was woken in the morning by puttering in the kitchen.

"Good morning!" he said as I entered the living room.

I couldn't remember when somebody had last greeted me with "Good morning." He had an easy, deep voice, he measured his words slowly . . .

"Sorry? Come again?"

"I didn't say anything."

"I could've sworn I heard an internal comment."

"So?"

"But the day has only just begun."

"It hasn't . . . begun," I grumbled, out of sorts.

"Have a seat," he said calmly.

Black coffee steamed on the table, and there were bunches of fresh-picked radishes and scallions laid out on a dish, toast in a basket, and onto my plate slid two soft, fried sunny-side-up eggs, perfectly round.

"Fresh local eggs. The hen laid them this morning. Just for you. The hen's name is Biserka. She's become a friend of mine."

"I may start to cry," I said.

"Why?"

"Because in one of my favorite films this American literature professor, a Bertolt Brecht expert, cries every time his girlfriend, a Polish woman, fries up eggs for his breakfast . . ."

"Why?"

"I don't know. Maybe the literature professor sees this as the ultimate gesture of tenderness."

"I agree. Though I'd choose eggs Benedict as my ultimate gesture. You get them tomorrow morning," he said, joking.

"While we're on the subject . . ."

"Not yet, tomorrow," he continued, grinning.

"But what I mean is . . ."

And then with no lead-in, question, or invitation, a muddled mish-mosh of words tumbled out of me before this man I hardly knew, who had only just woken up and kindly fixed me breakfast, what I was saying was a porridge with no taste or sense, a jumbled summary of my nocturnal meditations. I said I had no idea what I'd do with the house; I hadn't come here to stay but to check and see how things stood; I hadn't known the owner; I'd no idea why the man left me the place; the house was so much nicer than I could've dreamed, in fact it felt like a "deep metaphor for home" (these were my exact words, though I had no clue what I meant by them); I found this all baffling, perhaps precisely for that reason; I traveled a lot; I didn't live in Croatia; sure, I visited from time to time; I wasn't certain whether I was ready to move back; for now I was at a loss; I was unsure about everything; I had no plans; so it was best that we didn't change anything; we'd both leave things as they were; I'd go back to Zagreb tomorrow or the day after; and I'd like to ask him to stay on as he had until then, especially as he'd become one with the house—more than I'd ever be able to . . .

I took a breath.

"Look at the miracle worked by two sunny-side-up eggs," he said easily.

We both fell silent. The morning sun shone in through the window. I got up and opened the door to the porch. In the distance, pools of water were gleaming, looking, from afar, like mirrors that somebody was playing with, ready to blind whoever looked at them.

"What's that in the distance? Water?"

"Bogs left after last winter, wetlands."

The view of the sheen in the distance, Bojan, the house, all of it together—stirred a vague disquiet. Together, wrapped up in this package, it touched on something I'd locked away a long time before and suddenly I found myself in a state of high alert, exactly as if my security system were under attack.

I didn't know where it all began. Perhaps people really did change every cell in their body every seven years, I wasn't so sure about that, but what I did know was that each big change left fissures behind. A first crack, a second, a third, and at some point the teacup fragmented into little pieces all by itself. Will you look at that, it just broke apart, we'd say. I'd seen that, that effect, on people I knew. It was easy to keep things together while the natural glues, hormones, health still worked, while the skin was smooth and radiant, while the muscles were taut, while we were at our best, while we were loved, while there was a purpose, while we loved others . . . But what happened when all that was gone?

11.

It was Sunday and Bojan offered to guide me through his work area. He was right, it wasn't far at all from the house, barely eight miles. We drove along a dirt road through the woods.

"To the left is an MSA, and to the right, it's not . . ."

"How do you know the area to the right is not?"

"We have information. There are conventions between armies. Accurate maps of where the landmines are buried are a precious commodity . . ."

"Sorry?"

"That's information worth haggling over with the enemy, it can be used to trade for the lives of prisoners, and so forth . . ."

"Can it be trusted?"

"Certain conventions must be respected."

"So the left side of the woods is dangerous, and the right is not?"

"Exactly."

We stopped and got out of the car. I can't remember when I last smelled the intense fragrance of the woods. The forest was glowing with light as if posing for *National Geographic*. The sun broke through the dense canopy in bundles of golden arrows and lit the rich undergrowth of ferns as if from within like Chinese lanterns. Everywhere there were red ribbons, markers reaching deep into the woods. The woods were like a pagan shrine. Lit by the sun, the red ribbons resembled the veins of some mystical organism pulsing among the forest ferns. Two little machines like children's toy robots stood by the side of the road. Minesweeping robots . . .

"You're right . . . The woods are like a shrine. I don't know if you noticed that the machines have fitting names, *Zeus, Titan* . . . And the landmines are, like all weapons, a designer metaphor for male sexual fantasies. Most of them are shaped like penises, when you line them up they look like sex toys at a porno shop. The hand grenades resemble testicles. Indian traditional culture reveres the lingam and they're scattered all over the place in an array of sizes. These western versions are more restrained, camouflaged, but essentially the same. Men prattle to their member and give it nicknames. You probably know that. They have the same attitude toward weapons."

"Why?"

"It probably helps them rein in their fear . . ."

"What are some of the nicknames for the landmines?"

"Meat Paste, See-saw, Corn Cob, Bell, Whitey, Sardine . . ."

And the most dangerous?"

"The Prom, an anti-personnel bounding spray mine. Deadly. Last year a crew member of ours was killed by one."

"And other kinds?"

"Sometimes we come across landmines left over from the Second World War. When our crew was clearing the area around Lastovo they stumbled, literally, on a British landmine. It killed one of our de-miners after it had lain there for sixty years, dormant."

For some reason everything felt strangely quiet, as if we were wrapped in cotton batting.

"I, too, have that feeling. Are we unwittingly bracing for a blast? You know what the Egyptians call a mine field?" said Bojan.

"What?"

"The devil's garden."

"Why are you whispering?"

"Because de-miners, like sailors, dislike noise. It's forbidden to whistle while on board a ship, did you know that?"

"And why's that?"

"Whistling attracts a storm."

Just then we heard whistling.

"The Valloner."

"Who is the Valloner?"

"A what, not a who. A metal detector. Vallon manufactures them."

We listened to the trill of the mournful "Valloner."

"Can you see him? The man in the flak jacket with the metal detector? There, to the left, just beyond the bushes."

Not far from us I saw a man in a light-green flak jacket, sweeping the forest floor.

"Has he found a mine?"

"The detector finds metal, it could be anything," said Bojan.

"Come to Daddy-o, my sweet little girlie-o, my little minie-mine, little girlie girl, come to me, baby minelet, driving me round the bend-o, mean old thing-o, I know you're in there, come out, come out, little miss Tinker Bell, let daddy have a look-see . . ." purred the man.

"That's Terminator. He's always chatting with the mines."

"Why's he working today? Isn't it Sunday?"

"He's never quite been the same since a mine blew off his right hand. He's retired but he still comes to work. We can't get rid of him. He is always on the job. He's obsessed with landmines, treats them as if they're alive. People, he says, are worse than mines, mines take your leg or arm, people take your soul . . ."

The man caught sight of us and waved.

"Hey, Judge, what's up?" he called.

"I stopped by to see what you're up to!"

The man waved again and then back to work he went . . .

"See that, Tinker Bell, girlie-o? They're seeing what we're up to, as if the two of us aren't fine and dandy all on our lonesome, we two are so much happier when we're by ourselves, aren't we, mine-o, girlie-o . . ."

12.

"So why did the Terminator man call you Judge?" I asked as we drove back to the house.

"That's my nickname. We all have them. Like the mines."

"But why 'Judge'?"

"Because I was one."

"What do you mean by that?"

"Well, for a time I was a judge."

"But not anymore?"

"It wasn't a good fit."

"Why?"

In '91, as a judge sitting on the Zagreb municipal civil court, he'd watched as the new authorities fired his colleagues, Serbs, only because their documents stated somewhere that they were Serbs or Yugoslavs. Sure, there was a war on. War is war, such things are to be expected. He, however, at that awkward moment found himself ashamed of both Croats and Serbs. He was a blockhead, he chose the stupidest form of protest. It couldn't be called the least efficient, because every protest was equally lame: once war shifts into high gear it's hard to stop. He was waiting in line at the Zagreb police station on Petrinjska Street for a new ID card, and when the woman at the counter asked him what his ethnicity was, he declared loud and clear that he was a Serb.

"But your documents state you're a Croat!" said the lady clerk.

"Wrong! I'm a Serb."

"Instead of being ashamed, I see you're actually boasting about it," said the lady clerk.

"Serb, write Serb!" he dug in his heels.

"Chetnik!" snarled the clerk, but she didn't enter that into the computer.

At a moment when all "normal" people were trying to bury any ties they might have to Serbs, when they were clamming up about any Serbian relatives, divorcing, changing their names—his protest, no matter how paltry, reverberated across the overflowing waiting room and reached the ears of his supervisors.

"You were brave."

"No, I was a jackass," he said hollowly.

From his seat on the bench he slid downward, though, true, to a soft perch, and joined a private law firm as an attorney. They were all "his boys," mostly Serbs, they'd ended up out on the street as had he, but unlike him they'd hopped to it and opened private law offices. One of them, a friend, asked him to join them, and it went well at first, but then, suddenly, the friend became a dynamo. The legal profession was suddenly the most prestigious Croatian occupation. The international criminal court in The Hague, the ICTY, had begun its work and trials of war-crimes and war-criminals were starting up, while at home, at the local level, the full depth and breadth of Croatian corruption was suddenly surfacing. His buddies threw themselves into defending the worst of the lot and showed themselves to be highly adept. At first they made excuses, the law is the law, a crime is a crime, a doctor is there to save lives, not to treat only the patients he likes, blah, blah, blah . . . And everything went along as smooth as silk, the boys got rich, and the local "godfathers" and "commandos" were received like national heroes when they were released. Something wasn't quite right. His boys became hotshots, no different than ordinary swindlers, their pictures showed up in newspapers with them in their Hugo Boss suits, looking like shysters, raking in colossal compensation for their brief spate of humiliation in '91. Now they were swamped with work and, look, riffraff, as a result, was going free. Nobody was proffering a helping hand to the innocent. After all, innocent people had no way to pay the lawyers. His boys, all Serbs, had become more avid Croats than the Croats themselves, and meanwhile, what do you know, he, Bojan, was labeled forever—a Chetnik! This is where he snapped . . .

"Anybody normal would have snapped," I said.

"It's not that simple. My snapping didn't make me a hero, nor did I snap because I'm heroic."

"What do you mean?"

The sun beat down on the car windows. Bojan's profile was limned in sharp relief. He worked his mouth, trying to nip at a flap of dry skin on his lips. Individuals were not at fault, at fault was a situation that drew out the hidden potential in most people, and he stressed *potential* with irony. From that, from that feeling of intoxication, many had gone off the rails . . . The war destroyed plenty of human lives, one way or another. All that should be forgotten. Normal people do what they can to forget.

"Are you one of them?"

"Yes, ma'am," he laughed.

"Yet you work in de-mining?"

"And why is that such a contradiction?"

13.

My little niece came home from school all in tears because she didn't know the answer to the question of why the Battle of *Gory* was waged.

"How do I know why they fought that stupid Gory Battle?" wailed the little girl.

"You mean the Battle of Gorjani? 1537? It was over real estate," I explained.

"What's real estate?"

"You know, like summer cottages, apartments."

"Auntie!" she huffed with exasperation so I'd know she knew I was only being silly.

Every war is fought over real estate. This last war, too, was waged—or so it seemed when all was said and done—for real estate. Somebody lost property, somebody else procured it, some moved in, others moved out, some smashed others' statues, some torched others' homes, some, uprooting others, grabbed control of factories, banks, media, political positions, mines, shipyards, ambassadorial posts, railway lines, highways . . . Blood was shed for real estate. The warmongers used the word "homeland" for real estate so people would have fewer misgivings. Why say *he fell for real estate* when it sounds so much more convincing to say *he fell for the homeland*? For buying and selling real estate one gets a percentage, for defending the homeland—medals. Cunning participants in the last war got the percentage and the medals and more: the real estate as well.

I visited V. in Zagreb before I came to Kuruzovac. He'd known my father, though they were never close. They were from the same village and both had run off into the partisans as boys, before they were seventeen. A few months ago V. wrote me the only letter he'd ever sent me. He expressed his fear, in the letter, that he wasn't long for this world and would like to see me. A sense of obligation and curiosity persuaded me to call him and set a date for a visit.

The old man received me, obviously overjoyed. His son, a few years younger than I, was also there. The absence of a woman's touch was glaringly evident: the old man's wife, crippled by Alzheimer's, was spending her last days at an elder-care facility. The son set the table; I declared my satisfaction with the nibbles they'd offered, which pleased the old man no end. V. was obviously eager to talk; his son, however, inadvertently filled the pauses with chatter in an effort to relieve the pressure on his father, who had slowed with age. V. groped for words too often and after several vain stabs at joining the conversation, gave up. At one moment, he did snare my attention with gestures and pulled me off to his room. He had an old elementary-school desk and on it an old-fashioned typewriter. The desk was too small and too uncomfortable for the old man. He showed me a shelf with books where I spotted two of my own. The real reason he'd wanted to see me, however, lay on a shelf: a heap of his manuscripts, neatly typed on the typewriter and bound in light-blue, cloth covers. I saw right away what I was supposed to do: I picked a volume and promised to read and return it. The old man's face shone with real joy.

And then, while he poked around the room, probably looking for something else to show me, V. quite unexpectedly toppled over. He fell the way old people and little children fall who have just learned to walk: my mother knew how to fall in the years right before she died and each time, to my great surprise, she'd get up unscathed. I froze with fear and pity. The old man's son jumped in and with a practiced grip hoisted his father up off the floor. We went on talking as if nothing had happened, but the mood had darkened. I felt an invisible alarm go off somewhere above my head, telling me it was time to leave. We said our goodbyes, the old man and his son saw me to the door, and as I was about to step into the elevator, the old man said something.

"What did you say?" I asked, stepping back out.

"My apologies for collapsing!" he repeated.

I smiled. He responded with a frail smile. I was startled by his choice of verb, it would have been more normal to say *fall*. He chose *collapse.* And the way he slurred the "s" at the end indicated there was something wrong with his dentures.

The disintegration of Yugoslavia and the new war had pushed V. back in time. The old man, like so many people in what had been Yugoslavia, slid fifty years back into the past; the society's iconography was backsliding, too, into the epicenter of Second-World-War trauma, wounds people had thought to be forever healed. V. opens his memoir with memories of his first childhood nightmare and ends it with a rhetoric of humiliation and self-denigration (he refers to himself as *one unworthy of mention*). This made me uneasy, perhaps because such things are not typical of the genre; people do not, as a rule, write autobiographies to abase themselves but, instead, to erect themselves a monument. V.'s autobiography was but a modest monument to the voluntary capitulation of the average Yugoslav citizen. His story did not stir compassion, perhaps because he wasn't seeking it. From the text emanated unpleasant stains of a shame that was never plumbed. The accusation one might have expected, an invective against the injustice of the times, slid dolefully into a wail of remorse. *My apologies for collapsing . . .*

I could see myself able to make sense of V.'s unhappiness and others like it with my mind, but only partway with my heart. Where had this hardness come from? I wondered. And didn't my lack of a spontaneous rush of compassion spring from the fact that we were beaten—on all the warring sides—not by Serbs or Croats, but by riffraff, rogues, murderers, pickpockets, swindlers, psychopaths, shysters, cowards, roughnecks, thieves, robbers, nobodies? We were undone by our lack of will to stand up to them. His awareness of the true face of the enemy was what fueled his dogged denial, followed by the wave of self-pity that many of the victims of this shakedown secrete like a sticky saliva. And on the list of things that touch our hearts, self-pity does not occupy an exalted place.

I berated myself for my lack of empathy. The average person's blood vessels are said to be about 60,000 miles in length, meaning that the veins, arteries, and capillaries of a human being—if they were tied end to end in a single long thread, and if we imagine our planet as a spool—could be wrapped roughly two and a half times around the earth. That, at least, is what my little niece's textbook claims. The very niece who not so long ago had come home from school awash in tears because she didn't know why the Battle of *Gory* was waged. And, will you look at that, her tears, like hot wax, penetrated straight to the core of my hardened heart; I understood her child's protest: she was being made to study the world using parameters that were not her own.

Perhaps my father was right when he slapped that non-negotiable kibosh on his past. He died of cancer in 1973, still so young, and slipped away soundlessly like a shadow, taking with him to his grave his real and metaphorical shrapnel. Who knows, maybe he chose to kibosh his past once and for all when he realized how entranced his little daughter was by the story of the shrapnel he carried around inside him. Is it not perverse to drop explosive family-legacy souvenirs into the backpacks of one's own children as they skip along on their way to their own *shining future*? For when facing such truths one arrives at nothing but the knowledge of banality, the banality of evil: there are no discoveries that change our lives, no justice, no remorse, no shame, no consolation, no desired catharsis, no nothing . . .

In 1971, in what was then Yugoslavia, a prequel played out in Croatia of what was to come twenty years hence. Yugoslav political censors abruptly jettisoned the Croatian prequel and processed its authors in the courts. A number of people went to prison, and, they say, the prequel rocked Yugoslavia as a country to its core. Many Croats refer to this brief period as the "Croatian Spring."

That same year, 1971 (by then my father was already seriously ill), Mother surreptitiously slipped me a list of people; on it was my father's name. I didn't understand what it said, it was some sort of semi-official document; perhaps it was even a brochure designed with the intent to rabble-rouse. It was a "hit list" circulated to a select number of addressees, and had (by chance or intent) found its way into my parents' hands; it listed the people (in the small town where we lived) who were to be kept under "close surveillance" should those who were behind the "Croatian Spring" actually realize politically what they'd set out to accomplish. The people on the list were to be "scrutinized," "sidelined," "kept under control," "liquidated," though not in so many words. On the other hand, the more vague the instructions, the more focused and effective the implementation—for the instructions sent out twenty years later to libraries by the Croatian Ministry of Culture requesting the cleansing of "non-Croatian" books from the Croatian libraries were every bit as vague. And although there was no mention of the words *burn* or *trash*, books were, indeed, burned and others ended up in the trash. There was not, apparently, a list of authors and books explicitly slated for destruction, but the literary tastes of the zealous Croatian librarians concurred: it was mainly books by Serbian authors that were jettisoned: books printed in Cyrillic—even ones by Croatian authors; books by "Yugoslav" authors; books by "left-leaning" authors; books by communists and anti-nationalists.

Meanwhile, at that same time, in 1991, apparently with no instructions from "above," Croatian "death squads" cleansed Croatia of ethnically "unsuitable" people. If these squads truly did this at their own initiative, how could it be today, twenty years after the crimes were committed, that so few of the perpetrators have gone to prison?

My father *dedicated* his life (yes, that's the word) *to building a new society* in which the crimes of the Second World War would be forgiven and forgotten, a society that would insure for everybody, without discrimination, a *better tomorrow*, a society in which *knowledge* would be *power*, a society in which *brotherhood and unity would be cherished like the apple of one's eye*, a society in which *workers, farmers, and honest intellectuals* would build equitable relations, a society whose future was *shining*, plain and simple. I have often thought since then that having seen the list and his name on the list, my father died of shame. A few months later he did die and took to his grave his shrapnel, both the shard in his leg and the countless metaphorical shards.

In 1971, Mother promptly destroyed the sheet of paper with the list of names. Twenty years later she threw away what was left of father's papers, including the letters he'd written to her during his stay at a tuberculosis sanatorium while she was pregnant, expecting a child, me, and on his way back from the sanatorium. She saved a pile of the death notices that were usually posted on neighborhood buildings, a pointless number of some thirty copies or more, and an equally pointless pile of condolence telegrams. I tossed them all out when I cleaned and remodeled her apartment. Mother had left only proof of Father's death through her muddled censorial efforts, while destroying all evidence of his life. Except for a few photographs and medals (given to him for his *self-sacrifice* in realizing the ideals of socialism), there is nothing left.

My quick glance at the "hit list" was something I'd buried deep in oblivion. The list, like mildew stains on a white wall, blossomed, only briefly, on the surface. The very next instant I'd washed it away, scrubbed it, whitewashed the mildew as if it had never been there at all. There is nothing more vital, humane, and natural than the urge to

forget a fall, and, especially, humiliation. We don't trouble ourselves
with such things, they are not the purview of the heart. Our self-
defense system sees to that, the rubbery eraser of oblivion.

14.

We got back to the house, and while we were unlocking the door
it suddenly felt as if I'd lost my sense of time. As if we'd already
unlocked the door together once, indeed more than once, many times.
The feeling was both precious and cheap, as in a sci fi movie with
humanoids who cheerfully recall things that never happened to them.

I made dinner while he showered, then I showered while he set the
table. And at dinner again I couldn't suppress my curiosity . . .

"But I just can't get it through my thick skull how you could have
gone from judge to de-miner."

"While I, for one, can't understand the position you're judging
from!"

"Why?"

"Because you know full well that our lives were upended! Wasn't
yours?"

"True, it was, I could never have imagined . . ."

"Nor I!" he interrupted, his voice slightly raised. "Nor many others! Nobody could've imagined! Why, then, should my case be any
more bizarre than the case of the Croatian truck driver who became a
Swiss millionaire overnight? I backslid, while he, don't you know, shot
upward! Does that mean I'm stupid and he's a genius? Could a poor
kid from backwoods Pakoštane dream he'd become a national Croatian icon? a hero children read about in school? the proprietor of a villa
and an industrial fish farm, all of which were given to him as a gift for
expelling some two hundred thousand Serbian civilians from Croatia?
and all because instead of going to school he fled over the border and

learned how to pull the trigger of a gun! Could a solemn little country boy from the tiny village of Repušnica have ever dreamed that he'd one day destroy an entire Croatian factory and then buy himself a villa in London and send his children to school at Oxford? And yet in this whole ludicrous affair—this *wheel of forutune*, this *round-and-round-it-goes-where-it-stops-nobody-knows*—you ask how I went from judge to de-miner? And yet I notice you're not asking how Croatian judges could become criminals! It wasn't Albert Einstein who came into power in this country, but riffraff!"

"Well?"

"You aren't giving up yet?"

"No."

"Use your imagination," he said tartly.

"I have none," I dug in my heels.

"I was out of work. I saw an ad, paid the tuition, attended the course for de-miners. At first they promised us a good salary."

"So you went into de-mining for the salary?

"Whatever I say, you won't believe me. If I say I took the job for the money, you won't believe me. You'll say I was all wrong; there are less risky ways of earning a living. If I tell you I did it for reasons of ethics, because, in the end, somebody must clean up the debris left by the war, again you won't believe me. You'll say I am flattering myself, right?"

"Well you couldn't possibly say you like doing it."

"You won't believe me, but I do."

"You're such an odd one!"

"And what is wrong with that?" he said brightly.

And then he rose slowly from the table and wished me a good night, but instead of going up to the bed in the attic, to *his room*, he turned toward the first-floor bedroom, *my room*. It was habit, he did it reflexively, it had been *his* room, after all, until now. I followed him; I couldn't say why (could I be safeguarding *my* territory?). We paused at the door, I stepped in, he, startled, stepped back, we turned to one another, there were only a few inches between us. He rested his hand on my face. The gesture confused me. And then—as if mastering, for the first time, native rituals I'd been studying—I rested my hand on his. As if we were reading each other like Braille, under our fingertips tips streamed the history of the other's body; one body paid its respects to the other, like elderly tango dancers or over-the-hill heavy-weight wrestlers. There was also something deeply ritualistic about it. The frozen instant lasted merely a second, two, maybe more, and then without a word we undressed, lay down, and made love. We made love with a tender restraint, no hurry, we made love the way, I guess, people of our age do, recovering from a long and painful lonesomeness. I fell asleep with his breath on the nape of my neck. Before I sank into sleep, I thought: *home*.

I was woken in the morning by the birds. I crawled out of bed leaving Bojan to sleep and went out onto the porch. Through the air straggled sleepy wisps of fog. The air was redolent of lilacs. Down the steps I went and picked a lilac cluster. Back on the porch, I sat on the bench, broke off a tiny goblet-like floret, and poked it into the crease alongside my thumb. I sat there, thumb out before me, elbow propped on knee, taking care that the floret didn't tip over—and breathed in the new morning. I cannot remember a morning that seemed newer.

15.

After Bojan went to work, my first impulse was to get in the car and leave for Zagreb, and then grab the first available seat on a flight to Amsterdam. The impulse was overwhelming, as if I were fighting for my last ounce of oxygen. I sat in the car, but instead of driving to Zagreb I cruised around on local back roads, dispeling my inner disquiet. Before he left for work that morning we exchanged a few words. I adeptly sidestepped any linguistic situations where I'd have to choose between a more formal and a more intimate tone. This was a kind of awkwardness I knew well, the hesitation at calling a partner by his name, the stupid, but inevitable "diplomatic" vigilance that more exposes than conceals us.

On my drive I came across a neglected, tumble-down house. I stopped, atrracted by the beauty of a huge walnut tree growing in the yard. A gaunt man was sitting out in front on a bench, smoking. Next to him was a boy doggedly bashing a soccer ball against the wall of the house. I got out of the car. A woman in Turkish trousers peered out of the house and withdrew.

"Hello," I said.

Absently, the man muttered something unintelligible.

"I seem to be lost. Could you tell me the road I should take to Kuruzovac?"

The man ignored my question. The boy kept bashing the ball, ignoring everyone. The woman in the Turkish trousers came out of the house.

"We don't know," she said.

"Aren't you from around here?" I asked, though obviously they weren't.

"From Bosnia," she said.

"He's your son?"

"Grandson. Mirsad."

"How old?"

"Twelve."

"Does he go to school?"

"There are no schools nearby."

"Shouldn't he be in school?"

"Yes, but who can take him? It's an hour's walk to the bus stop and then another half-hour ride to the school."

"Are you employed?"

"See for yourself."

"So how do you manage?"

"We eat air," she said, and her face twisted into a grimace that mocked a smile. They didn't live on air alone. Their son, Mirsad's father, had died several years ago and their daughter-in-law, Mirsad's mother, was working in Italy. She cared for an elderly woman there and cleaned houses. What else could she do? She sent them a little money, if she didn't they'd die of hunger. But for now she still couldn't afford to bring Mirsad to live with her.

From a poster plastered to the walnut tree grinned the putty face of an old acquaintance of mine who had, in the meantime, become a Croatian politician. The puffiness came from pockets of air that had worked their way under the poster and were slowly billowing it out and dropping it. I pointed at the poster and looked at the woman, my eyebrows raised in query.

"Oh, she was here, that lady, she put the poster up and promised transport for Mirsad . . . for school . . ."

"And?"

"And nothing. They pass through, they even come to this hole-in-the-wall, it's not that they never come through, but they never come back. Everyone has forgotten us: God, the Devil . . ."

I thought about how these people, the boy included, had been erased. The woman was persevering, imitating her former life, doing the cooking, cleaning, washing, but despite her diligence the family was growing more and more invisible; soon they'd vanish, leaving no trace. Together with the tumbledown house they'd slowly be overrun with ferns, vines, grass, and then they'd be completely squeezed out by the roots of the walnut tree, it would envelop the house, octopus-like with its limbs, like the exhibit I'd seen before coming here at the Amsterdam Museum of Funeral History in which a root had sucked up a human skull.

People are erased in any number of ways. Sometimes one group erases another, brutally, en masse, the way Serbs did twenty years ago in Srebrenica, murdering over eight thousand men and boys, Muslims, labeling them "packages" before putting them to death, all without batting an eyelash. Or one group kills another, either on purpose or inadvertantly, and the numbers swell to the tens of thousands of civilians who perished in Bosnia. Or people receive death threats and move away of their own volition, either individually or as a group. Or they're dismissed from work, or all their sources of oxygen are cut off, or their home is torched so they have nowhere to return to, or they are moved out and others moved in, just as the Croats around here expelled the local Serbs, and into the houses vacated by Serbs they moved Bosnians whom other Serbs had expelled from homes in Bosnia. And, look, the war isn't over yet despite the twenty years that are behind us, because many have an interest in prolonging the war, there are still "packages" on the move, seeking an address, there are human bones jutting everywhere from the ground. Both God and the Devil have forgotten these two, old before their time, and so many more. So many were moved, and not by choice, to a parallel existence, and from there, from behind a glass wall, they send us signals, open their mouths like fish, release silent bubbles, gesture a sad pantomime, point to their heart to show they're still alive. And here we are, behind us barely a quarter century since the Wall came down, and the dam burst and water swamped millions of people like ants. They didn't *hit the ground running*, well whose fault is that! They didn't know how to swim. Well whose fault is that! The numskulls swam against the current! They didn't know how to navigate the eddies! Why didn't they hold to the shore? Grab a branch? Some *hit the ground running*, others didn't—this divide, as non-negotiable as a death sentence, is the excuse for the withholding of compassion. What can they do, where can they go, this man and woman in their fifties, old before their time? The best they can hope for is that their own grandson—once he builds up more muscle mass or his mind addles or he goes off the deep end—smothers them with a pillow and puts them out of their misery.

On my return, I passed through my "neighborhood" and shopped for supplies. At the fabric shop I found reasonably good quality cotton bedding and white linen fabric by the yard for the curtains. I bought sewing supplies and scissors because I wasn't sure I'd seen any at the house. I spotted a smile on the face of the cashier and realized I'd been grinning the whole time, completely unawares. On the way to my car I passed by the Zdravko café. The same kids were sitting there, exactly as before, as if they hadn't budged since I saw them last time.

"Hey, Auntie, moving in?" jibed Jaunty.

"Do you mind?" I asked, halting for a moment.

"Not me. But everyone else's clearing out . . ."

"So?"

"Nobody normal moves here."

"So?"

"You look normal!" said Jaunty, and the boys around him met his quip with hoots of support.

"So why don't you leave?"

"Because I'm not normal. And I don't have the cash for a bus ticket!"

The boys giggled, and several approved his comment with "high-five" gestures.

I turned to go to the car.

"So, buy me a ticket, Auntie!" warbled Jaunty, laughing, behind me.

"A ticket, a ticket!" chanted the other boys in unison.

"A ticket to America . . ." someone sang out solo.

In this amateur-production provincial tragedy, I thought, these kids are like a chorus that has no clue it's the chorus, or what the function of a chorus is.

Yet that lone voice, singing out among the others with a line from a golden oldie Yugo tune from thirty years ago (. . . *buy me a pretty dress, silver jewelry, red raspberries, and a ticket to America*) touched me. Just the giftie for *Auntie*, I thought.

16.

Who knows, so maybe all the way to the house I dragged the silly metaphor of the amateur theater group along like a mental burr, because after dinner when Bojan and I were out on the porch, I didn't feel as if I were "sitting in life" ("I sit here in life as if I'm sitting in a movie theater," said a friend of mine once) but on a stage, before an empty auditorium, and somebody had switched off the sound and lights and every way of communicating with the world.

"I believe I have a problem," I said.

"What sort?"

"With communicating."

"Go on . . ."

"My little niece never answers my emails with the answer I expect."

"No?"

"Instead she covers the screen with smiley faces and pulsing hearts. It's no better when we talk on the phone. She never, for example, answers the usual questions of 'how are you?' and 'what are you up to?' Instead she breathes sounds into the phone like, chchchchchch, zhzhzhzhzh, or shshshshsh. Or she puffs air, pooooh, pooooh, she laughs, she whistles . . ."

"The child isn't used to conventional language."

"True. Now she's in the phase of juggling emoticons. When she has no computer handy, she draws them freehand. She draws little grumpy faces when she's angry, or silly-looking blobs gushing tears when she's sad. She feels that conventional language is not hers, and never will be. That is the language of schoolbooks, the language of the Battle of *Gory*, poetic odes to kin and nation, the language with which grown-up men send their messages. She's already sensing the male violence in this language and her exclusion from it."

Bojan got up and went into the living room. He came back a minute later with a book and a flashlight. He switched on the flashlight and read . . .

"*The poet is a cloud that slays with thunder, pelts with hail, soaks the furrows, and swells the rivers with its blessed deluge or merely flashes on the solemn skyline, vanishing after the blazing sun or the stars, chill and drowsy, like a sigh. The Croatian pasturelands would perforce have seared bone-dry with nary a cloud* . . . What makes you think that I've suffered any less from the male language of violence, this canonized literary pornography? Just because I'm a man?"

"Whose lines are those?" I asked. I was embarrassed to admit I didn't recognize the poet.

"That you ought to know. A Croatian classic."

"*Rings, rattles, chimes, sounds, throbs, thunders, booms, resounds* . . . *This is the language of my breed* . . . That one?"

"Ha! No, but no matter . . . What I meant to say is that I, too, am a victim, just like your niece. The study of law was harsh training for adapting to a language that is every bit as much a departure from ordinary speech as was this 'poetic baroque' of a moment ago. I earned my degree in 'bureaucratic baroque.' We are all victims of somebody's hot air . . . In that sense literature shares ground with politics."

He was right, but I didn't respond. The sky was studded, again tonight, with stars. When I gazed up at them my head spun with a mild giddiness.

"This morning I sat in my car, fully intending to flee to Zagreb," I said.

"Why?"

"I don't know."

"Scared?"

"I have no reason to be. You're a good man."

"Is that a question or an assertion?"

"A question."

"I'm not a good man. I have no stamina. But being bad requires stamina. And I'm tired."

"Of what?"

"Of us, us men, who are forever stamping our feet in our Croatian or Serbian haka, like the Maoris of New Zealand. They shout, wag tongues, flex muscles, glower, roll eyes, roar, howl, terrify the enemy. This has been going on and on and shows no sign of stopping."

"And what else?"

"Of my environs, of the unrelenting crass, witless behavior. Vulgarity and idiocy—a deadly cocktail. Our people are not kind, they'd rather die than say a kind word. We're a peasant culture, people here are convinced there's no courtesy that is not masking some measure of blackmail or deceit."

"And what else?"

"The doltish repetition. Everyday life here is an exhausting re-run of the fable of the fox and the stork. Why doesn't the fox relent and serve the stork the cooked frog in a narrow-necked glass? Why doesn't the stork relent and serve the fox the chicken wing on a flat plate? Why doesn't the fox stroke the stork's long bill with its tail, why doesn't the stork comb the fox's fur with its bill? Why never?"

"And what else?"

"Backwoods country music that's more a caterwaul than a tune."

"Ha, ha . . ."

"I knew you'd like that one."

"And what else?"

"Conversations like this."

"Why?"

"Because this is women's talk."

"Excuse me?"

"Police interrogation."

"Unfair!"

"But true. You ask me one thing, but what you're really hoping for is something else."

"I want to know what you'd say if I said I like you."

"So soon?"

"Why not?"

"You're not very original. All women are crazy about de-miners."

"Why?"

"Because you never know whether or not they'll be coming home! Heh, heh . . ."

17.

Once when I woke at night in my Amsterdam apartment and went to the kitchen for a glass of water, I noticed a barely audible, strangely resonant and penetrating sound, much like the ping made by a crystal glass. This weird, thin ping zinged through the air and vanished, and, though it wasn't grating, it left me with a vague angst. I couldn't explain where it was from or pinpoint its cause; it dropped from somewhere like a spider spinning down its thread—and vanished. Maybe somebody somewhere in outer space had struck a tuning fork and the tone escaped and buzzed through my apartment like a crystalline fly. What starts a fissure cracking like that and when does it begin? When does the internal erosion, the crumbling, the sliding begin, when does the fall, in fact, start? Does it announce itself as a barely audible crystal ping in the silence of night, or as one of those pits that suddenly opens and yawns before us?

Rummaging through Bojan's modest collection of videocassettes, I found the old movie *Falling Down* by director Joel Schumacher. I had cut the lengths for the linen curtains I'd bought at the local shop and now I needed to hem them. I knew the job would take time, so I thought that with the movie, which I'd watched once years before, the chore of hemming would go more easily.

Bill ("D-Fens"!) Foster, a man wearing a perfectly ironed white short-sleeved short and a tie, "snaps" just as he's driving home in his car and gets stuck in traffic jammed by roadwork. It's a hot day, the air-conditioning in his car is on the fritz, a tiresome fly begins buzzing around, and the infuriated man tries to swat it out of the car. His range of vision dissolves into fragments as if following his internal downward slide. We, the onlookers, along with Foster, catch close-ups of aggressive human lips through car windows, scowling grimaces, ads with pointless messages to which we infer fateful weight, painful scenes of the socially disenfranchised (the homeless, beggars, lone demonstrators). This vortex of quick, sharp, short frames from every-day Los Angeles coincides with Foster's internal meltdown. He wants to make it to his daughter's birthday party as quickly as possible and now the roadwork is blocking his way. Incensed, he ditches his car and takes off on foot, and when asked by one of the drivers "Where do you think you're going?," he answers, simply, "Home." The whole morass of circumstances and the many people and things he meets on his way—from the out-of-order phone booth to salespeople who won't give him change for a pay phone, to a group of young gangsters out for a bruising, to dimwitted waitresses, to the owner of an army-navy surplus store—maniacal Nick the neo-Nazi—to Foster's ex-wife who, when he finally reaches her by phone, denies him access and threatens him with the police, to a police inspector who spends his last day before retirement handling his last case by obstructing Foster in his determination to go home. Foster, who doggedly defends his human dignity and minimal human rights, is finally cornered and, instead of turning himself in, settles for suicide by cop. He allows the policeman to kill him so his life insurance policy will go to his daughter. Finally a way to "go home" and give his daughter her birthday present.

It occurred to me that this film is a perfect analysis of the mechanism for how a person falls, and at the same time it's a youthful, cinematic, American twin to Krleža's novel *On the Edge of Reason*. True, Krleža's time frame may be different, as are his place, culture, and medium. The mechanics of the fall of Krleža's hero begin when, at dinner around a table where he's sitting with several other guests, he qualifies the actions of his host as "criminal, bloody, and morally diseased," which the actions truly are; the others around the table either disagree or haven't the courage to voice their agreement.

Foster is fighting almost pitifully for his fundamental freedoms: the right to speech, accountability, rationality, the freedom of choice, the right to disagree, but in the end he's beaten by the incremental chain-reaction of absurdities. It's as if the director is trying to convince us all the while that the problem lies with Foster and his frayed nerves, his failings (like losing his job), and not with what surrounds him. The surroundings behave as they always do, but instead of conforming, miming, acquiescing, evading conflict, Foster obstinately defends his right to his own opinion, to his humanity, to "normalcy." In the end, he wonders how all this could have happened, the fall, after he'd done everything he'd been told to do his whole life

The fall begins when there's no way back. (*I've passed the point of no return,* says Bill), a fall is gravity-bound, it begins when, for some reason (the trigger being, ultimately, moot), we drop out of the mainstream, step away from the crowd (that disgorges us like an irritating crumb), and venture forward as a loner. Regarding the different trajectories and velocities between us and the "rest of the world," we feel increasingly that *they* are wrong, while *they* think *we're* out of line. They see us as having broken the rules, we have no steady footing in the gravitational dynamic, we're not adapted, yet meanwhile we feel we're defending our fundamental human rights. When Nick, the crazed owner of the army-navy surplus store, tries to handcuff Foster in a violent move that threatens to escalate into sexual violence (against Foster), Foster says: "I can't." "Why?" asks Nick. "I'd fall," replies Foster calmly before he stabs Nick in self-defense.

The curtains were hemmed. I'd spent several hours stitching them by hand, but it was worth it. The whiteness of the linen gave the whole room an astonishing freshness. I've always known that well-chosen curtains do wonders on windows. And then, for some reason, I slipped the videocassette behind the other cassettes on the bottom shelf, exactly as if, by watching the movie, I was up to something I shouldn't have been doing and was covering my tracks.

Bojan noticed the curtains from the doorway as he entered the house.

"Now we know: spring has sprung," he said brightly.

He'd brought with him two pots with two little round cacti.

"Where did you get them?"

"The wife of one my colleagues sent them."

He carefully placed the pots with the cacti on the windowsill. Their spines touched.

"There," he said. "Even cacti like to cuddle, see?"

This was an odd statement. It was marked by a zest unusual for his age.

18.

"What came before . . . ?" I asked as we sat on the porch, sipping wine.

"Before what?"

"Before Kuruzovac?"

"Before Kuruzovac was . . . Kuruzovac," he said, and added, "And after Kuruzovac, Kuruzovac!"

"You don't need to talk about it if you don't want to," I said, feeling a stab of rancor, more at myself for having been caught out in my attempt to learn something that was, perhaps, none of my business.

In a generous concession, he talked. Grown-ups generally establish mutual trust by offering information about themselves: first and last name, address, married, unmarried, offspring . . . True, we were both part of the pre-internet, pre-Facebook, pre-selfie, pre-digital generation that was unaccustomed to having such things placed on display. He came half-way and swept away my uneasy feeling that I had intruded on his privacy.

He was an only child, son of a respected professor of economics, an excellent student, he graduated in record time, found a job, qualified as a judge and was confirmed, bought an apartment. In contrast to his peers he did all this without breaking a sweat. He traveled, enjoyed himself . . . And then he met her, Vesna, a doctor a few years younger, they married and had a little girl, Dora . . . The whirlwind years all swirled into a single tangled morass in 1991: the collapse of Yugoslavia, the political upheaval, the death of his mother, the new Croatia, the war, Dora's birth . . . When one spins a globe in search of the place where this all happened it's barely visible, all of Yugoslavia is no bigger than a Kuruzovac—and Croatia is a third of a Kuruzovac. Seen from that vantage point, all of our storms were teapot tempests, but proportions notwithstanding they felt like tempests to us. When he looked back at that now with the distance afforded by almost a quarter of a century (Heavens, had that much time really passed?) those were the years of the greatest risk and stress. Earlier we'd thought of our world as stable and then it began, suddenly, to crumble, an earthquake-like experience, people felt the ground shifting beneath their feet, the slideshow began and our world became intolerably transparent, we were suddenly seeing everything as if under a magnifying glass, every grimace, every facial twitch, every wrinkle, every lie flitting like a shadow across peoples' faces. This was a time when masks truly did fall away, no matter how pathetic that might sound, and naked human fear bubbled up to the surface. Encounters with human fear were something he'd gladly have avoided; this was one of the most disturbing experiences he'd had. No, he couldn't say he, himself, was afraid, he was far too shocked by the fear of the people around him to have the time for any fear himself, he could not for the life of him understand where this terror sprang from or what made people, with no visible external prompting, transform into a quaking, panting, sniveling, horrified collective. In our childhood we were nourished on fairy tales about valor, human dignity, sacrifice, the brave partisans and dastardly enemy, about honesty, sincerity, brotherhood and unity, heroism. All these tales drew on the same repertoire of morals, whether socialist or religious. And by the way, the two were not as antithetical as people liked now to think. Naked human fear was perhaps his greatest revelation, it showed us all as having a low tolerance, we're like mice that run even from a wind-up cat. And everything else was about the law of gravity. Those who joined the stampede were spared, those who flailed to keep from falling were trounced. Heroes were always trounced in the end. The mob dictated the criteria and standards, at the first available opportunity it recast its fear as courage, its transgressions as heroism, and so on . . . Vesna had healthy instincts. Her vitality quotient far outstripped his. She was on this earth to flourish and he to flounder. They were cut from different cloth. Phrases began cropping up in what she said, such as: *catch the last train out*, or *better safe than sorry*, or *when in Rome, do as the Romans*, or *money doesn't stink*, or *it's our turn now*, and he felt certain she'd taken them in some time ago at an almost visceral level, but had held off using them till now. Everything she said sounded crass and vulgar to him, though he knew the mistake was only his. She was simply destined to survive. While the whole wartime and post-war situation appalled him, she seemed, or so he thought at the time, to find it thrilling. While all "normal" people like Vesna fought to keep their heads above water, he cogitated on the vulgarity of surviving All in all, the exigencies of daily life in Croatia badly eroded their relationship. She thought he really ought to adapt, what a ninny, he should *get his shit together, get his ass in gear*; maybe they'd be better off going abroad for Dora's sake if not for his, Vesna would have no trouble adapting—everybody needs anesthesiologists, but he'd have a rockier time of it, he had to face that, it would be tough to find work in the law and he had no other talents or skills, because he *couldn't so much as change a lightbulb*. Maybe it was high time for him to *face the music, put his nose to the grindstone* and stop *asking for trouble* (*what was the point of asking for trouble?*), and besides, if he'd only open his eyes he'd see amazing opportunities all around him, things that only came up once in a million years, it was a time to be spry, no point waiting *till the fat lady sings*. Hadn't he noticed yet the people around him, his acquaintances and friends, swarming up the social ladder like *cockroaches*, so why didn't he also move up a rung or two, he should *be on his toes*! And then in a flash the pace accelerated and he could no longer slow or channel it in any way . . . He lost his job, she accused him more viciously of incompetence, inertia, inadequacy, and then there was the "incident": he had a small traffic accident when Vesna and Dora were in the car. This was the straw that broke the camel's back, or Vesna's. Dora wasn't harmed, but Vesna's collar bone was fractured, and while she was still in the hospital she demanded an expedited divorce. He sold the apartment, gave her all the proceeds from the sale, and she already had two airplane tickets to Sweden for herself and Dora where a job was waiting for her at a hospital. Since then she hadn't been in touch for . . . how long? She never looked back at the *maniac* who'd been so out of it that he'd jeopardized two lives, hers and her daughter's. Even after she left he still couldn't digest what had happened. He moved in with his father. His father asked to be placed in an old people's home, where he soon died.

It was difficult finding a job in his field; Croatia had fewer inhabitants than the city of Berlin, and word soon got around that he was not *flexible*. And he himself no longer wanted to have anything to do with the dirty dealings that were getting grimier by the day. He did not mean to suggest he was such a moral paragon, he felt *inflexibility* and *inadequacy* were his systemic errors, there was no way he could change; he was past the point of no return. True, "inadequate" people stubbornly believe they're to blame for everything. If they'd only made that extra little bit of effort, rolled up their sleeves, if they'd really applied themselves, if they'd been more flexible, if they'd done this or that, if they'd tried, truly tried, everything would have turned out differently. But everything would have been the same. And when he realized this he decided to leave Zagreb and work in de-mining. He rented out the Zagreb apartment he'd inherited from his dad. The rent he earned, though it wasn't much, he sent to Dora, to an account somewhere abroad. He was saving the apartment for her if she should come back to Zagreb one day. His friend (and my lawyer!) proposed that he stay in the village house that nobody had used for years. He squatted there with the lawyer's blessing. He needed very little. The only painful issue was Dora. He longed to see her. Sometimes she'd contact him with a brief message just to let him know she was alive. She was writing her dissertation at Goldsmiths University in London, that was the last news he'd had from her, more than a year before. He knew nothing about Vesna, just that she was prospering. People like Vesna who run on instinct are invaluable, everything pays off for them. By now he was deeply grateful to her that she'd intervened so speedily and efficiently to jettison a *life that was going nowhere fast* and save Dora. Maybe Dora would understand it all one day. In time he sorted things out in his own mind, but by then the situation was beyond repair. He knew time had left him in the dust, but, to his surprise, nothing hurt. The world was a chaotic place, we usually came to this once we'd finally exhausted all our energy persuading ourselves that we were living in the best of all worlds. And the time we lived could barely be called time, it was sticky, tasteless, insipid, amoral, a barely digestible porridge . . . There, in that sense, there wasn't much difference between him and those two Bosnians I described to him the other day. He, too, had veered off the tracks . . .

"I assume you're not going to apologize for that?"

"No. And besides, I'm not somebody people can rely on. I'm destined for the dump, not for evolution. Who knows how these global things are added and subtracted. But remember the harmless fact that millions of people the world over have stopped smoking over the last twenty years. Millions no longer inhale and exhale, and bluish clouds of cigarette smoke have ceased to be a part of our landscape. Millions have stopped using sugar and now the little sugar packets are so extraneous that they serve as mini-posters bearing the verses of forgotten poets. Millions have begun exercising, which they didn't do before, but now they do in order to keep up in the race: new technology is on the rise, life is accelerating, and there's an obsession with longevity. The first thing we should be thinking about is evolution."

"Oof, big words."

"Only now have I started to like life and what it's become. I'm doing something useful, much more useful than if I'd stayed in the judiciary. I'm learning useful things: how to garden, plant lettuce, pick mushrooms, how to make apricot jam and gooseberry preserves, how to change a light bulb . . . All in all, every day I work on my adequacy," he said with a note of irony.

"Why do I suddenly have the sense that the two of us are conversing like characters in Voltaire's *Candide*," I commented.

"Good point, the only thing left for us is to tend our garden," he answered.

We clinked our glasses to that and sipped the wine.

19.

As metaphors for lives, literary genres have been worn to tatters by overuse, but people never tire of describing human lives as *epics, dramas, tragedies, farces, thrillers, untold stories, Broadway shows,* and *heart-throb romances.* They still delight in comparing their life to a novel (*Oh, if you knew the story of my life, what a cliff-hanger!*), a play, a tale. True, we're surrounded by movie, television, and computer screens, so people live their lives by following a *scenario,* or *sit in the director's chair* of their lives. The newest selection of "life metaphors" is aligned with digital technology (*It was my avatar, not me! His life has been reduced to a tweet.*), and the digital may, one day, outstrip the literary.

The oldest "metaphors for life" are maritime, so we experience *shipwrecks,* and *perfect storms* that cast us up on *foreign shores.* People take the *rudder* and *get underway* and it's *plain sailing;* living life means steering between lust and sin, we *batten down the hatches, know the ropes,* we *hold our own* between *the Devil and the deep blue sea.* The *perfect storms* of life are retribution for our sins, *the riptides* and *choppy waters* are our life experiences, and the *beacon* on the stormy map of life symbolizes our faith in God.

It occurred to me that all these trite metaphors work as shorthand, much like today's text messages or tweets. In our *story*, Bojan's and mine, the metaphors snapped shut too quickly and easily, like handcuffs clapped onto the wrists of amateur thieves. Everything, *our story*, and I myself, was on the verge of soap opera, and even Bojan's death, no matter how real and terrible, was also on the very verge . . .

Bojan went off into the woods to the right of the road, the safe side that was not a mine suspicious area. He stepped on an anti-personnel bounding spray mine, a *Prom* that a Serbian soldier or paramilitary fighter must have put there without telling anybody. It was his little joke, his tease, a pile of shit left out by somebody's door, a Parthian shot, a real farewell gift for Auntie, bye bye, take care, no hard feelings, ta-ta and screw you, fuck all your goddamn mothers, one-two-three whoopeeeee, a little something to remember me by, ashes-ashes-we-all-fall-down, a sweet little secret to warm him, the anonymous fool, over the boring days to come, which might suddenly jolt him awake one night, leave him giggling, pleased as Punch; and who knows, maybe from the momentary surge of victory he'd pounce on the woman sleeping next to him and then fall asleep with the image of the enemy who'd be blown to bits like a clay pigeon . . . What was Bojan doing off in the woods to the right of the road? Nobody could tell me that, he probably simply went for a stroll to breathe the forest air without the constant smell of danger that permeated the area to the left side of the road.

Everything after that happened quickly, and as if in a fog. The crew published an obituary for Bojan in the papers, hoping that people he knew might see it and come forward. There were probably email addresses on his computer of the people he'd been in contact with, but they couldn't access the laptop without his password. Some of the crew made the effort, drove to Zagreb, sought the help of a computer service, but to no avail. Nobody knew Bojan's wife's surname, she might have remarried in the meanwhile or maybe was using her maiden name. Or maybe she was no longer in Sweden. Nor had he left any information about his daughter, Dora, probably because he knew nothing of her whereabouts. His crew knew he sent her money to an account abroad. The lawyer I'd called, hoping he might know something more, knew only that.

The crew had a fund to cover funeral expenses. They buried Bojan in the woods, near the place he was killed, trodding a path from the dirt road to the grave. They arranged for a permit to bury him in the woods; Bojan *would be tickled pink*, they said. We have another grave on the left side, in the work area, they said, and they took me to it to show me. They liked it that I followed them with no fear. The President of Croatia was here last year, they said, and, by God, he didn't dare . . .

The Terminator, the eldest of the de-miners, gave a thoughtful, frank, heartfelt graveside eulogy, in defiance of all expectations. The crew bought a wreath with the slightly awkward words *rest in peace your de-miners* on it, and one of them, the youngest, tossed a children's toy plastic egg into the grave. In the egg they'd put a pull ring from a hand grenade; he showed it to me before he slipped it back into the egg and tossed it in. This was his amulet, he always had it with him in the pocket of his flak jacket. "Off it goes with Bojan to help him, heaven bound, pay his tolls. Who knows, it may come in handy," he said, tipping back his chin and gazing skyward.

The crew was kind. They offered to lend a hand, on principle, they treating me like Bojan's widow. I kindly declined. They asked for my address, which I did not decline, so they could send me a photograph of the gravestone when it was made, it would be a small stone, they said, much like the one I saw on the left side, but instead of the normal rectangular shape they would order an oval stone, partly because Bojan was not religious, and party because the oval wouldn't disturb the woods, it would fit unobtrusively into the landscape. They hoped I didn't mind.

While we were talking they watched me with reserve. Although they were gracious, I knew most of them believed I'd brought Bojan bad luck.

20.

I shoved a plug-in electric burner under the old seaweed-stuffed sofa and switched it on. The dry seaweed would catch fire sooner or later, I knew, and then all the rest would go up in a blaze. I carefully shut all the windows tight. And, look, through the window facing the orchard I caught sight of an enchanting scene. There was a light breeze. Petals wafted down from the fruit trees and drifting through the air like snowflakes. The red-haired fox was bounding around the garden like a coiled spring. Breathless, I gazed out at the scene. And then, as if it had noticed me, the fox swiftly slunk through the grass into the woods.

I took the two cacti, locked the house, and tossed the key in a ditch. Off I set for Zagreb, driving along a back road, but some ten miles later I pulled over onto a side road and stopped the car by a clover field. There was no shelter nearby, but there was also nobody about. I crouched behind the car and urinated. As I straightened up I felt my knees buckle, and a sudden, overwhelming drowsiness pulled me down. Instead of lying on the car seat I stretched out in the clover field. The ground, all day in the sun, was warm.

Images from my early childhood floated to the surface of my memory: days of big plans and little wonders. Behind the modest workers housing where we lived were gardens where the residents, including my parents, had planted fruit trees and grown vegetables. As little girls we decorated our ears with cherries, sour cherries were our lipstick, and the red and pink petals were our fingernail polish. We glued the petals to our nails with our spit. We pored over the cuts we'd gotten from scraping our knees (our knees, always our knees!) as if they were magnificent craters. The little wonders—the potato beetle that laid its tiny orange eggs on the inner side of the potato plant leaf; the bluish vein gliding under the transparent skin on a child's temple; the caterpillar winding itself around a finger like a living ring; the snail leaving an opalescent trail; the heavy, fragrant peony blossom opening like a book; the golden hairs on a child's arm lit by sunlight and an ant seeking a way through the golden foliage—stirred in us a thrill that left us breathless. The world of my childhood spun from within my eyes in intoxicating, crystaline close-ups.

When I started awake from my slumber, it seemed as if a whole eternity had passed. My watch showed I'd slept barely fifteen minutes. In Kuruzovac—I now felt—I'd spent a goodly portion of my life, yet I'd been there barely three weeks. I'd spent yet another illusion, I thought, just as fast as I'd bought it.

I got up, a little groggy from the brief, deep sleep, brushed the dirt off my clothes, and plucked a clover flower that I draped over the rear-view mirror. Turning back to the car, I raised my middle finger and with it bid goodbye to *my* village. I thought back to my clueless chorus, the kids at the local café. To them, too, the finger. I closed my eyes for a moment. A magnificent sight blazed in my mind's eye. Against the lavish background of the setting sun erupted a powerful floral explosion. Millions of lilac florets, floral shrapnel, shot through the air, and the intense smell of the lilacs mingled with the smell of the conflagration. Wow, look, Auntie lit a sparkler!

I pulled out onto the main road. Beside me passed green fields dimming slowly with the day. My thoughts flew and my little niece's favorite counting song clung to me like a burr: . . . *A mousie went a-nibbling, poor little mousie, what can I do; came a cat with its kittens, ate that mouse with all its pups; came a fox with its kits, ate that cat with all its kittens; came a wolf with its whelps, ate that fox with all its kits, came a bear with its cubs, ate that wolf with all its whelps* . . . The world is a minefield and that's the only home there is. I must accustom myself to this fact, I thought, and made my way slowly to Zagreb.

PART FOUR

The Theocritus Adventure

He turned to Behemoth and said, "Come on, Behemoth, let's have the novel."

—*M. Bulgakov,* The Master and Margarita

1.

Teeth as Fine as Grains of Rice

Shocks of her hair are dyed in shades the color of honey, with one lavender streak. Using a gesture repeated oh so often she tosses her hair to the side. Always the same side. She toys with her hair the way young women do, because they love imitating each other: she scoops it up using her fingers like a hair clip at the nape of her neck and then lets it go. The gesture is coy, almost a porno tic. She's nearly forty but she looks younger. She watches me with an unabashed gaze positioned so that our eyes aim in different directions: her gaze moves from down to up. Her eyes don't yield much, she's the one controlling the field of vision, the world doesn't enter her, she enters the world.

As far as she's concerned, she knows that nothing, absolutely nothing, can be achieved without promotional strategies. She milks every option she has. She posts on Facebook, she tweets, she blogs. She figured all this out when her first book came out, which, so far, is her only book, though not for long. She gives the name of her town as "the great backward beyond." And then she adds: "That depends, of course, on which way you're facing." She laughs, flashes her teeth—fine as grains of rice. No, she says, she thinks she's no genius but she does believe she's a good writer. And besides, don't forget how writer-geniuses die in semi-anonymity. Especially "our" geniuses, who come from "our" little backwater, even the Nobel Prize doesn't help, take Ivo Andrić, she says. Who has even heard of him any more?! So I ask her why she thinks "our" geniuses merit attention, instead of, say, the geniuses of Belgium or Romania? She doesn't understand my question. And why does she, in her opinion, merit attention? Her short answer: her view of the world might be of interest to others, in her new novel, for instance, she describes her relationship and break-up with a former lover, she writes about feelings, today so few writers deal with feelings. And by the way, since she's been here she's discovered she has a body. Not only in the literary sense but literally: she sits for painters. She has so many requests, I'd be amazed! Some of them fancy themselves as painters, for others it's a pastime—painting a live model—and yet others pursue it for its therapeutic value. This is an affluent country, people can afford to amuse themselves. She spends hours on Facebook and dating sites, that's how she learns about all sorts of people, builds her characters, this all helps her in her writing. And along the way she's on the lookout for a husband. Somebody, in fact, who would help her get her papers. Her first book is rich with selfies, multimedial prose, is that the proper phrase? Her fingerprint, too, is a selfie. Everything is her fingerprint. She doesn't read as much as she used to, in fact she hardly reads at all, first of all she has no time for it, and, second, she's so bored. She's bored by the way other people see the world, she has quite enough on her hands with her own . . . view. Again she flashes her teeth, fine as rice grains. She thinks art must fight for its audience, for its readers, listeners, and viewers. Literary value is all about lobbying. Her ultimate goal is to draw the biggest number of devotees to her side. In this sense she has no morals. Anything is better than semi-anonymity. Recently she read that somewhere in America, in a hotel, they'd furnished a room as a faithful copy of Van Gogh's room, the one in Arles with the yellow wooden bed. And people are wild about spending a night there. The Dutch must be tearing out their hair because they should've been the first to come up with the idea and build a hotel near the Van Gogh museum with replicas in it of Van Gogh's rooms. How gorgeous is that, to snuggle into a famous work of art, spend the night in a "painting," and pay for it cheerfully in the morning. She'd like readers to nestle into her book the way they would into a hotel room, spend the night there, and pay in the morning. Everything matters when selling a product, and a literary work is a product. She, for example, is aware that physical appearance is a big plus. That's why she pays such close attention to her appearance. She, herself, never reads books by ugly authors. The famous artist, the queen of performance art from "our" little backwater, is absolutely right when she insists, while brushing her beautiful thick hair vehemently to the point of physical pain, that art must be beautiful . . .

I listen and meanwhile study her shapely manicured hands with their long, shiny pink nails, and try to recall how she wormed her way into my apartment where she's chatting away with me as if she's my best friend. She insinuated herself into my space like a vapor. In she oozed, odor-free, under the door. My "compatriot" asked to meet me and I felt awkward turning her away, as if I'm a socialist worker writer, some Maxim Gorky. She's never read anything of mine, I interest her only as somebody who has been successful at publishing books abroad. She doesn't say that, of course, she's polite. But she, too, would like to do the same. And she will. She waits, mouth open wide, for me to toss her a morsel, anything that might, in that sense, be of use. Her eye color is light, her eyes are glazed, nothing will stop her on her path to her goal, she's giddy with her fantasy of success, success is the drug that keeps her going. She's not pushy, she drops me a line by email from time to time, every three or four months or so, though she says she visits my building once a week, so we could be getting together for coffee weekly. She cleans the apartment for somebody she knows in my building, he pays her three times the going rate, she's very lucky, and other people also overpay her for similar jobs. This neighbor of mine is caught up in couch surfing, a collection of people trickles through his apartment and he himself is seldom home . . .

The upper part of her body is slender, she comes across as fragile, she even leans forward just a little as if about to tip over, her lower half is bulkier than her torso, as if she's put together of two separate pieces. And she draws attention to her lower half: she wears clingy leopard-skin tights and garish boots covered, on the outside, in artificial fur. Her walk is penguin-like: her torso slightly forward-thrusting as if she's about to break into a run, her lower half holding her back . . .

I listen to her and wonder where I get this feeling, justified by nothing, that I'm superior to this woman. There's no difference, in essence, between us. All of us—young and old, men and women, published and unpublished, experienced and novice, celebrated and anonymous, productive and unproductive, educated and uneducated, successful and unsuccessful, smart and stupid, fêted and unrecognized—we're all, in fact, the same. We're poised for the shot announcing the start of the race, then we each urge on our own little egg, slather it with our sperm, fertilizing ourselves. And after that we pester others to cast their eyes on the result of our perverse contrivance, our artistic offspring. And the fact that there's no difference between us, that we all have equal chances, that there are so many of us in the race, many more than there used to be, can be explained only by the absence of risk. The absence of risk makes our efforts comforting and so unimportant.

2.
Who is Doivber Levin?

Today everything is different, today everything can be fished from the blessedly de-hierarchized archive of the internet. Before, in the BG (Before Google) age, one's imagination compensated for the lack of information. Only twenty years ago the world was alluringly mysterious and vast. Today, like some divine mechanical llama, the internet spits its indifferent answers in our faces. And the answers are, in proportion to the ease with which we retrieve them, weightless, unreliable, and fluid.

Who is Doivber Levin? Doivber Levin is a writer who was, for a long time, one of the briefest of footnotes in Russian avant-garde literature. Today Doivber Levin is a somewhat longer footnote. Boris Mikhailovich Levin was born in 1904 in the small Belorus hamlet of Lyady, in the Vitebsk province. He died, some sources say, while heroically defending Leningrad in early January 1941. The date and place of his death are not reliably recorded: Russian Wikipedia, for instance, gives Levin's date of death as December 17, 1941 in the village of Pogostie. Other sources offer a date that obliges them less, saying only that Boris Mikhailovich Levin died at some point between 1941 and 1942.

In the early 1920s, Levin came to Petrograd for his studies. He enrolled in the theater department of the Institute for the History of the Arts and joined the last avant-garde literary collective, OBERIU (*Obshchestvo real'nogo iskusstva*—the Society of Real Art). Members of the art collective included Daniil Kharms, Alexander Vvedensky, Nikolai Zabolotsky, Konstantin Vaginov, Igor Bakhterev, and Doivber Levin. Levin authored several works of fiction for children and young readers, and memoirs by Levin's contemporaries—Gennady Gor and

Igor Bakhterev—tell of Doivber Levin reading fragments, at one (or more) literary soirées from his novel *The Theocritus Adventure* [*Pohozh-denie Feokrita*]. In fact, Russian Wikipedia refers to the novel as *The Origin of Theocritus* [*Proishozhdenie Feokrita*], while other sources speak of it as *The Life of Theocritus* [*Zhizn' Feokrita*].* Aside from a mention in two or three brief memoirs by his contemporaries there is no further evidence that this novel ever existed. Under the heading "orientation" (meaning Levin's literary leanings), Russian Wikipedia lists "avant-gardism." Levin added the moniker "Doivber" after discovering he had a double: there was another Boris Mikhailovich Levin.**

In the rare source (a few brief biographies), the information about each of these two writers is not always entirely separated: there are overlaps. Even the small black-and-white photographs (the only ones preserved) that appear on-line with the blurbs about Boris Mihailovich Levin and Boris Mihailovich (Doivber) Levin are sometimes jumbled. Doivber Levin was, it seems, more handsome than his double. In the cruel lottery that was spinning in those years—the revolution, the Stalinist purges, the Second World War—Doivber was granted a slightly better

---

* "In the late twenties and early thirties, Levin wrote an interesting, though unfinished novel *The Life of Theocritus*, the manuscript of which disappeared during the siege of Leningrad." (Igor Bekhterev, *Vospominania o N. Zabolotskom* [Recollections of N. Zabolotsky])

** His double, Boris Mikhailovich Levin, was born on January 5, 1899 in the town of Zagorodino in the Vitebsk province, not far from Boris Mikhailovich (Doivber) Levin's birthplace. He wrote for the satirical papers, penning witty tales of student and bureaucratic daily life. He fought in a battle between Soviet and Finnish forces near Suomussalmi. He met a heroic death on January 6, 1940, only a day after celebrating his forty-first birthday and two days before the Finnish forces vanquished the Soviets. He was buried where he fell, in Suomussalmi. Boris Mikhailovich Levin is an utterly forgotten figure in Russian literature. Under "genre" (meaning Levin's genre of choice), the Russian Wikipedia cites "melodrama."

posthumous fate than his double, thanks, ironically, to the absence, rather than the presence, of his work. This may be the very reason why Doivber Levin, and not Boris Mikhailovich Levin, is the hero of the story that follows.

3.
The Forgotten OBERIUT

Doivber Levin largely owes his posthumous life to writer and art collector Gennady Gor. In "Slow Motion," a memoir, Gor writes about the Leningrad literary and art scene in the twenties and thirties and the last Russian avant-garde group, OBERIU. In a single line of the OBERIU manifesto Levin appears as Bor. Levin: "Bor. Levin—prose writer, currently working in an experimental style." Gennady Gor recalls a literary evening at which Doivber Levin read from fragments of his work.

"OBERIU prose writer Doivber Levin [. . .] read a chapter from his novel *The Theocritus Adventure*. Levin's novel is reminiscent of a painting by Marc Chagall. In *The Theocritus Adventure*, as with Chagall, the borders are erased between what might happen and what happens only in dreams. On the ground floor of a Chagall-esque fantasy house lives an ordinary Soviet official, while on the floor above lives a mythological creature with the head of a bull. Only the ceiling separates the two epochs, modernity and antiquity, linked by the author's whimsical fancy."*

It is entirely possible that the parallel drawn between Levin's prose and Chagall's painting was inspired by the fact that Chagall and

---

* Gennady Gor, "*Zamedlenie vremeni*" ["Slow Motion"]. In: *Geometricheskii les* [*The Geometric Forest*], Leningrad, 1975.

Levin were both born in Orthodox Jewish communities in the Vitebsk province. There were Hasidic Jews living in Levin's hamlet of Lyady, and the famous Rebbe Shneur (or Schneur) Zalman hails from there. The name DovBer, which Levin chose for himself, means bear—in both Hebrew (Dov) and Yiddish (Ber). Samuil Marshak apparently nicknamed Levin "Himalayan bear." The hamlet of Lyady was eradicated; all its inhabitants were murdered in pogroms and the buildings were destroyed during the Second World War. Levin's mother tongue was Yiddish, he also knew Hebrew, and he taught himself Russian, as writer and folklorist S. Mirer, a compatriot of Levin's, penned in his memoirs. Mirer remembers Levin as a ladies' man; he recalls how the local beauty, Sonia Volkova, fell for Levin. Levin left her, dealing her, in Mirer's words, a "cruel spiritual blow." To Mirer's profound regret, the heartsick Sonia Volkova disappears without a trace after her marriage to the ambassador from Sweden.

From L. Panteleev, another compatriot of Levin's, we learn that Levin enjoyed reading Ibsen, Shakespeare, Hamsun, and Przybyszewski; that he lived on Chekhov Street in Leningrad (*He did live there yet he will no longer. Not here nor anywhere else on this earth*—L. Panteleev wrote these harsh words in his diary in 1944); he jotted down that during their last encounter, sickened with dread by the imminent world war, Levin had said: *It's over! All the lights have been snuffed out worldwide*; and that Levin had been married to a pretty Komsomol girl (*I wonder where their daughter Ira is now. How old could she be? Seven?*).

As far as OBERIU-related documents are concerned, aside from the mention in the manifesto, Doivber Levin's name comes up in a newspaper article, "A Reactionary Juggle,"* by one L. Nilvich (perhaps

---

* L. Nilvich, "Reakcionnoe zhonglerstvo" (A Reactionary Juggle), *Smena*, April 9, 1930.

the pseudonym of an informer who'd been assigned to monitor the performances put on by the "literary hooligans"). Thanks to Nilvich's article, a description of Levin's story has been preserved . . .

"Levin was the first to read. He read a story crammed with all sorts of nonsense. There was a metamorphosis of one person into two beings (one man, but two women: then one was a wife and the other a spouse), then people turned into calves, and other circus tricks." Nilvich's article also records the answer that Levin gave to a question from the audience:

"Levin said they are not understood for now, but they are the sole representatives (!) of a new art that is building its grand edifice.

"'For whom are you building it?' they asked.

"'For all of Russia,' came the typical answer."

Critic Valery Dimshits in his text *The Forgotten OBERIUT*,* written for Levin's one hundredth birthday, suggests that Doivber Levin, aside from *The Theocritus Adventure*, also authored another text, also lost, a short story entitled "Parfeny Ivanich." Dimshits does not, sadly, cite any sources that could confirm the existence of the story.

With no shortage of good will, but short on compelling arguments, Dimshits suggests that Levin's fiction for children is complex; he tries to force it into a relationship with Russian avant-garde poetics and the larger OBERIU affinity for the absurd and *zaum*. The example of *zaum* that Dimshits discerns in Levin's children's fiction is not, perhaps, entirely aligned with Khlebnikov's idea of *zaum* as the "language of the birds," the "language of the gods," and the "language of the stars" (meaning that not every instance of onomatopoeia is *zaum*), but

---

* Valery Dimshits, *"Zabytyi oberiut," Narod knigi v mire knig*, October 2004. The term OBERIUT refers to a member of the OBERIU group.

it's a laudable attempt by a critic to bring attention to this neglected writer:

"It (a rooster, op. au.) seems to have overslept and is embarrassed, so now it crows as loudly as it can muster '. . . ri-kuuuuuu!' meaning '. . . oood morning'!"

With his well-meaning yet clumsy reanimation attempt, plucking Levin from oblivion, Dimshits proposes a modernized reading of Levin's children's fiction. The main hero of Levin's novel *Shoemaker Street* is an itinerant boy, Irme the hooligan, who joins a revolutionary gang. This detail feeds the widespread (Russian?) expectation, nowadays, that revolutionaries were vagrant hooligans, which lends Levin an anticipatory halo and allows him to dovetail with today's ideological circumstances, or so, more or less, Dimshits's convoluted premise proposes.

Salamandra P. V. V.* mentions Kharms's papers, among which were preserved program notes for a group OBERIU performance in December 1928. The performance was canceled, but the program notes show that Levin was scheduled to perform "eucalic prose" (*eu*/good and *kalos*/beautiful). Another notable assertion, though in no way substantiated, is that painter Pavel Mansurov (traveling in Italy in August 1928) brought with him texts by the OBERIUTs at Kharms's urging. Among them were, supposedly, four stories by Levin.** The author of

---

* Salamandra P.V.V, "*Medved' iz Oberiu*" ["The Bear from OBERIU"]. In: *Volnie shtati Slavichi* [The Free States of Slavichi], 2013.

** These are the titles of three of Levin's stories: "A Street Beside a River" ["*Ulitsa u reki*"], "Goat" ["*Kozel*"], "Third Story" ["*Tretii rasskaz*"]. It's worth noting that G. Gor's novel, thought to be lost, was titled *Cow*. The title of Levin's lost story "Goat" ["*Kozel*"] is not far from the title of K. Vaginov's novel *The Goat Song* [*Kozlinaia pesn'*]. Such coincidences, and there are many, suggest that a

the foreword does not disclose a source to support her claim, but she does list the titles of three of the stories.

Thanks to Salamandra P. V. V.'s foreword, Levin's status has been somewhat revived. The foreword mentions, for instance, evidence— this time a little more convincing—of Levin's work on the staging of OBERIU performances.* Yet Levin remained in the background, as if merely an extra in the wings of the remarkable avant-garde experiments for which the most talented, Daniil Kharms and Alexander Vvedensky, deservedly fanned their feathers. Further, the author of the foreword attempts to term Levin's passable children's fiction a "complex formalist experiment" are a stretch at best, especially as she furnishes no arguments to support her claim. She proceeds to describe Levin's writing for young readers as "grotesquely, tightly penned prose, describing the daily life in Jewish settlements before the revolution and the civil war," saying it is prose with no "juvenile content." The true matter, she says, of Levin's children's fiction is "the gory blizzard of historical cataclysm; pernicious, absurd speech; prophetic dreams." This is far more germane to the times that gave rise to Levin's children's books than it is to the books themselves.

"*The Forgotten OBIERUT*," becomes, in Dimshits's words, "the most neglected" among the OBIERUTs, which guaranteed him, paradoxical as this may sound, a secure future within Russian literature.

---

zoological imagination was not the strong suit of the OBERIUTs, or perhaps it indicates that contemporaries are unreliable witnesses, functioning more like "broken telephone."

* During one such performance, staged by Doivber Levin, Daniil Kharms read his verses while perched on a cupboard, Alexander Vvedensky rode out onto the stage on a tricycle, Konstantin Vaginov read the verses "I am a Poet of Tragic Entertainment," while ballerina Militsa Popova performed classical ballet figures and Igor Bakhterev, after the reading was over, unexpectedly flipped over on his back.

"Manuscripts do not burn!" exclaims Woland in the novel *The Master and Margarita* by Mikhail Bulgakov.* Whether or not we choose to believe this is up to us. The only thing that cannot burn is the absence of a manuscript. And if we were to bet on eternity, perhaps it is precisely this absence of substance that would have the greater chance for victory than its presence.

4.

Foxes Prefer Deserted Places

I made the acquaintance of Mrs. Ferris at a Slavic Studies conference in Nottingham. I'd been invited to give the keynote address; I accepted. I had my reasons: first, I hadn't been in the company of Slavic scholars for some time, yet they used to be my close intellectual kin, whom I, the prodigal daughter, had deserted. Second, this was a chance to see my old friend, Asen Smirliev, who taught South Slavic: Bulgarian, Macedonian, and the literatures written in BCS (Bosnian, Croatian, and Serbian), in the Department for Russian and Slavonic Studies. He was, in fact, the one who had proposed that they invite me and pay me reasonably well. In his free time, Asen ran a tiny publishing company called "Asen" which occasionally put out a work from one of the East European literatures in English translation. The funds needed for translating the Bulgarian, Macedonian, Serbian, Montenegrin, Croatian, and Bosnian writers into English came through financial support from the ministries of culture, embassies,

---

*"Let me see it." Woland held out his hand, palm up.

"Unfortunately, I cannot do that," replied the master, "because I burned it on the stove."

"Forgive me, but I don't believe you," Woland replied, "that cannot be: manuscripts don't burn." He turned to Behemoth and said, "Come on, Behemoth, let's have the novel."

and consulates of the interested countries, as well as the occasional measly handout from English foundations.

During my lecture, my first and last name and the title of my talk were projected onto the screen behind me. Afterward several Slavic scholars clustered around me. They offered the standard compliments and mentioned the titles of my books they'd especially enjoyed. The titles were not, however, mine. The author of the titles was my, clearly more popular, colleague. I could have gracefully accepted the compliments intended for her, smiled, and let the students show off. Instead, however, I said . . .

"For God's sake, you had an entire hour to get my name right! It was there right in front of you. You could have Googled me during the talk, you all have iPhones and iPads, I assume you aren't lost in the world!" I said.

"Are you really this touchy?" sprang a young scholar of Polish immediately to their defense.

"Surprise, surprise, I am!" I snapped.

During the first day of the conference an already familiar feeling came over me that I'm no longer a player in this game; the literary-scholarly lingo is different from the parlance I knew; the way of thinking about literature has changed, the values have changed, and the interests today are altogether different. Only two panels at this three-day conference were on literary themes. All the others belonged to the broader discipline of cultural studies. The titles of the papers in the program promised they'd shed light on the culture of Russian adolescent gangs, they'd say something about film and post-Communism, post-Communism and fashion, post-Communism and pop culture, pop culture and politics, Russian celebrity culture, digital media and post-Communism, social networks and literature, social networks and democratization, the role of culture in the *branding* of young nations and nation-states. I grumbled to myself about the obvious drop in university education standards, though I was, clearly, in the wrong. Literature, whether I liked it or not, was simply no longer the focus. Even I found the panel about Russian adolescent gangs far more compelling than the papers on a publicly over-rated, effete, middle-aged post-communist writer who had created a literary universe all his own of interest to no one. So this was the bitter truth I had to make my peace with. My anger bubbled over like the head on a beer and sloshed again onto the young student of Polish who had done nothing to deserve it . . .

The brief encounter with Mrs. Ferris felt like a momentary reprieve. As soon as I gave her my first and last name, the elderly Mrs. Ferris identified me as the author of articles about Konstantin Vaginov and Leonid Dobychin. True, I'd published one of them in the Slavic journal *Russian Literature*, which had been coming out in Amsterdam for years and was regarded as the premiere place to publish Slavic-studies articles. But this was so long ago that even I could no longer remember the details. Yes, in my former life I'd been a "Slavist" but only my rare participation in gatherings such as this one brought this back to me. And, true, after a while I'd realized I lacked the motivation for a serious academic career. But I was, at least, powerfully curious at first. The times fed this, it was such a different time from our life today, the Wall was still definitively dividing Europe and this only piqued my curiosity to peer at life beyond the Wall, behind the Iron Curtain. Among other things, this was also the BG age, when my efforts, and those of others, to re-discover forgotten literary works came with a righteous thrill at rescuing texts and their authors from the jaws of Stalinist oblivion. At the time I believed there to be vortices in the history of culture. One such vortex was the Russian avant-garde. It was an explosion of new art and new thinking, but before they'd had a chance to bring it to its fullness, Stalin's iron lid clamped down on their efforts as did the Second World War, and then long years of neglect followed. Too many things happened over a short period of time: one of the greatest moments in which art flourished, yet one of the most savage scourges of artistic minds in world cultural history. Human flesh was pinioned by inconceivable hardships, right and left the reaper mowed his deadly swath.

So it transpired that my articles about Vaginov and Dobychin were among the first in the world of Russian studies to rediscover and re-evaluate these two forgotten writers of the Russian avant-garde. I knew that someone bitten by the rediscovery bug would be likely to remember such a detail.

"I, too, have always had a fondness for the avant-gardists," said Mrs. Ferris, modestly.

Irina Ferris was a memorable name especially because it sounded so much like a well-designed pseudonym. Mrs. Ferris used a cane. She spied the question in my eyes and told me how an impatient young man had knocked her down the stairs a few years before in the London Underground. He'd been rushing up, she'd been on her way down, but she'd made the mistake of using the left side instead of the right, which so infuriated the young man that he punched her and she lost her balance, fell, and fractured her hip. The operation was, apparently, mishandled. Ever since she'd been suffering from stabs of pain when she walked. She told me she was a widow; her husband, David, had also been a Slavic scholar, a linguist, but he'd died a few years before and their sons, twins, had moved to Australia where David's brother lived. She almost never saw them, especially after the bad fall. She lived in London. She'd come to the conference at Asen's urging to spice up her otherwise solitary routine. She had no right, however, to complain about anything because she'd never made much of a career for herself, she'd spent most of her life as a professor's wife, though, true, she did teach Russian language and literature now and then, but too little for her teaching to be deemed a career. She no longer had anybody left in Russia, as it was she'd only ever had her mother. She'd never known her father; he was gone before she was born, and her mother died soon after she left for England. No, she no longer had the desire, or the need for that matter, to go back "there" ever again.

There was an air of neglect about Mrs. Ferris, which clearly signaled that she no longer cared a whit about her outward appearance. She wasn't exactly untidy, but behind her trailed the subtle odor of an unaired wardrobe. When I put together her age, what student life in Moscow had been like—something I'd experienced myself, though, admittedly, only for a few months, a dozen years or so after her time there but coinciding loosely—this helped me better understand her biography, the encounter with the soft-spoken, reserved Englishman, the marriage to a foreigner that gave her "a way out." Those were days when foreigners were pursued, when young men and women, and even the middle-aged, were on the prowl, looking to trade in the non-convertible currency of their Russian life for a more convertible one. Foreigners were a sure ticket to a better life. And the foreigners often showed little or no reluctance at the prospect of leveraging their privileged status, either consciously or unconsciously, to garner profit, whether emotional, sexual, moral, or, sometimes, even financial. This was a time of lively commerce, all sorts of commodities were traded: dreams of freedom, ideas about better and worse worlds, self-confidence. Mrs. Ferris, on the other hand, was not "in pursuit." She was one of the generation of Russians for whom setting aside a month's salary to purchase a black-market copy of *The Master and Margarita* was a perfectly acceptable choice.

Mrs. Ferris and I went to a teashop not far from the conference hall for tea and English scones with raspberry jam and clotted cream. I can't say Mrs. Ferris was riveting company, but then again nothing about her had promised riveting. I recall two notable details. First, she said her two sons reminded her of camels. This curious remark, coming as it was from a parent about her own children, was most unusual. It was also a literary reference. This is how Gapa Guzhva, in a story by Isaac Babel, spoke of her daughters: they, too, looked rather a lot like camels.

Second, Mrs. Ferris mentioned living in South London; she'd moved there after her husband's death once she'd sold their home; life was less expensive there. Perhaps the neighborhood was a little less safe, but there was nothing untoward left that could happen to her.

"I'm far too old for anybody to come after me; I've lost all there is to lose," she said, perhaps a little too grimly.

She spoke of her little garden that she so enjoyed and the foxes that often dropped by . . .

"Foxes in London?" I asked.

"Oh, yes! Didn't you know?"

"I never knew foxes actually came knocking at the door . . ."

"Not in the center of town, of course . . . But in my neighborhood, yes . . ."

"And, what do you do with them?"

She didn't say . . .

"Foxes are loners. They like deserted places . . ." she added, a little absently.

Then we said our warm goodbyes. It never occurred to me or to her to exchange email addresses. I didn't even ask how this woman, who needed a cane to get about, would manage on her way back to London from Nottingham. Asen was the one who saw to that.

5.

Salieri

A young man attended an OBERIU performance at the Institute for the History of the Arts in Leningrad in 1928. Some thirty years later, this same man would be beset by flocks of Soviet and foreign Slavic scholars imploring him, in vain, to tell them, as one of the few surviving witnesses from the time of the Russian avant-garde, what really happened that evening. The man was Nikolai Ivanovich Khardzhiev. Khardzhiev graduated from the Odessa Law Faculty at the young age of twenty-two. Bios about him tell us that he is the author of the story *"Yanyichar"* [*"Janissary"*], the biography *Nedolgaia zhizn' Pavla Fedotova* [*The Brief Life of Pavel Fedotov*] about a Russian painter from the first half of the nineteenth century, and sheaves of "experimental" and humorous verses. In the late 1920s he moved from Odessa to Leningrad (later he'd live in Moscow), where—drawn by the fascinating circle of artists—he rubbed shoulders with many of this innovative crowd, including art theoreticians (formalists Yury Tynyanov, Boris Eikhenbaum, and Viktor Shklovsky), writers, and artists. His most abiding friendship was, apparently, with Aleksei Kruchenykh, a *zaumnik* and author (with V. Khlebnikov) of the libretto for the futuristic opera *Pobeda nad solntsem* [*Victory over the Sun*]. Khardzhiev also made the acquaintance of Osip Mandelstam, Anna Akhmatova, Vladimir Mayakovsky, Velimir Khlebnikov, and many others.

Nikolai Khardzhiev and Kazimir Malevich met at the OBERIU event. The encounter was a watershed moment. "It was the painters who shaped me, not the poets or the philosophers. As far as my feel for art is concerned, I owe the most to Malevich. I did socialize with Tatlin, but this I hid from Malevich. They didn't tolerate each other, so I had to hide from each of them that I spent time with the other. Fortunately, one of them lived in Moscow while the other was in

Leningrad," he said.* Khardzhiev's words exude the confidence of a person who controls and steers the game; the artists are there for him, not he for the artists. Malevich himself died seven years after they met, but Khardzhiev would stay profoundly linked to the artist, in his own way of course, until his own death.

Nikolai Khardzhiev loved fraternizing with artists—he knew how they breathed, how to get under their skin, he was always eager to lend a helping hand. At some point it struck him that an explosively talented pack of painters and writers had no one to serve as their guiding light, their archivist, their devotee, their priest, adviser, and patron, and this at a time when, as Khardzhiev put it, one could hear "the crack of splitting skulls in the air," when people were like "worms in a jar." Khardzhiev transformed his amateur love of art into a mis sion, he became an archivist, collector, guardian of Russian avant-garde art. He was cunning and sly, he knew what tone to take with weeping widows and a painter's heirs; he knew, for instance, to ask if he might make copies of certain documents and then forget to return the originals; he knew to offer to store somebody's canvasses for them and then forget to give them back.** Nadezhda Mandelstam described him as a "son of a bitch," a combination of "eunuch and marauder," a body snatcher. His appetites, power, and expertise grew, writers gave him signed copies of their books, entrusted him with editing and proofing their work, delivered manuscripts, sketches, projects, and finished canvasses to him, either for safekeeping or as gifts, grateful

---

* Irina Vrubel'-Golubkina, *Razgovory v zerkale* [*Conversations in the Mirror*].

** Nikolai Khardzhiev was different in this sense from George Costakis (or Kostaki), who was the only person on a par with Khardzhiev. Costakis, unlike Khardzhiev, actually paid for works of avant-garde artists and then he agreed to the conditions laid down by the Soviet state. In 1960, Costakis emigrated to Greece, leaving half of his collection with the Tretyakov Gallery. This concession allowed him to export the other half of his collection legally.

that somebody in those dark days was willing to take care of them. In many later newspaper articles and books, descriptions of his activities were couched in flattering terms such as *scholar, textologist, historian of new literature and art*, and *collector*.

Was Nikolai Khardzhiev the Salieri of Russian avant-garde art? According to what we're told by collector Mikhail Davidov in his book *Razgovory sa sosedom* [*Conversations with a Neighbor*], Khardzhiev "was a Mozart his whole life. Everything N. K. touched became a precious wellspring for the 'music of life.' Whether it was verse, image, word, or an ordinary, daily situation. N. K. as scholar—this was just one of his many talents. He ennobled scholarship with his resolve to be a scholar. With simple generosity he 'indebted [all of us] with his very existence.'"

The man who "ennobled" scholarship and "indebted us with his very existence" did so for nearly a century. If Salieri lived twice as long as Mozart, Khardzhiev lived almost three times as long as most of his contemporaries. He was born in 1903 in Kakhovka (Ukraine) and died in 1996 in Amsterdam. Longevity was Khardzhiev's advantage. And had he not been so long-lived, he wouldn't have had the opportunity to initiate and contribute to something (as victor or victim, or both) which many newspaper articles referred to as the "theft of the century," the "perfect crime," called by those with greater empathy "the tragedy of Nikolai Khardzhiev," and by others yet, speaking from a post-cold-war perspective, "a tragic flight to freedom."

Khardzhiev managed to amass an inestimable treasure trove of art. With the fall of the Wall, many objects were suddenly accorded value: T-shirts with Stalin's slogans and face, cheap souvenir coffee cups with Malevich designs, memoirs, documents, letters, paintings, chests, military uniforms, communist medals, Malevich paintings . . . Many collectors crossed over to became "body snatchers," there were those who hit the jackpot, others who didn't. A few of the artists, such as Daniil Kharms, were tossed up to the surface in the collective gasp of freedom—quick to become a powerful geyser—that conferred on him a cult status that reached across the borders of Russian language and literature with speed and success. Even I, visiting the newly opened and renovated Stedelijk Museum in Amsterdam to see an exhibition of Malevich's work from the Nikolai Khardzhiev collection, could not resist purchasing a souvenir at the Museum shop: an eyeglasses case with a Malevich design and a Suprematist lens cloth.

Whether Khardzhiev was a Mozart or a Salieri of Russian avant-garde art is a question of taste, but love for his contemporaries, the luminaries of the Russian avant-garde age, was certainly not his strong suit. Irina Vrubel'-Golubkina included an interview with Nikolai Khardzhiev in her book *Razgovory v Zerkale* [*Conversations in the Mirror*]. She interviewed him in early 1991 in Moscow, two years before Khardzhiev moved permanently to the Netherlands, and five years before he died.

Of his contemporary, celebrated architect and painter Vladimir Tatlin, Khardzhiev says that Tatlin had a "strange personality," that he was a "maniac," that he feared "somebody would steal his professional secrets." Khardzhiev describes Tatlin as a "wily monster," a "diabolical finagler," a man who despised Malevich with a "fierce loathing." Khardzhiev describes Aleksandr Tufanov, *zaumnik*, as an "ugly," "lame," and "hunchbacked old man," who, admittedly, was not entirely "uninteresting." His friend Nikolai Suetin, the Suprematist, was described by Khardzhiev as a "psychopath," an "unberable man with a million personal problems." Marc Chagall had a "God-help-us personality," he was "spiteful," a bad teacher who was incapable of teaching anybody anything but how to draw "flying Jews." Aleksander Rodchenko, the respected photographer, was an "amazing dreck of a man," a "ridiculous figure." Pavel Filonov was "not a painter," but a "lunatic and a mindless maniac." Even Lissitzky was "no painter." Khardzhiev socialized with Anna Akhmatova and though he referred to her as a "fine poet," her poetry was not to his liking. Osip Mandelstam was "ingenious," but not "great." Vladimir Nabokov was "overrated," and, as far as poetry was concerned, a "talentless graphomaniac." He stole the ending for his novel *Priglashenie na kazn'* [*Invitation to a Behead-ing*] from Andrei Platonov's story *"Epifanskie shlyuzy"* ["The Epifan Locks"]. As far as Andrei Platonov was concerned, Khardzhiev "can-not bear to read his prose," because of the over-abundance of "empty rhetoric" and "natural thinking," though he describes Platonov as a "decent and wise man." Nikolay Oleynikov, close to the OBERIUTs, was a poor poet, a "comedian." Alexander Vvedensky was a "card-sharp," a "gambler," who wrote shoddy children's verse for money. Evgeny Schwartz was a "fool," the "lowest of the low," in general the "Schwartzes craved possessions," they "collected porcelain" and "all manner of rubbish." This interview is rife with hints of anti-Semitism, overt misogyny, and a shocking lack of empathy toward the people Khardzhiev called his friends.

Khardzhiev was visited in 1977 by a Swedish scholar, author of a Mayakovsky biography. With Khardzhiev's blessing he took four of Malevich's paintings from Khardzhiev's collection out of the Soviet Union through a diplomatic channel. Their agreement was that the money from the sale would be waiting for Khardzhiev when he emi-grated. The Soviet authorities did not allow Khardzhiev to emigrate. Where did the four Maleviches go? The scholar sold one, suppos-edly, to the Center Pompidou in Paris, the second he donated to the Stockholm Museum of Contemporary Art, the third found its way to the Fondation Beyeler in Basel, while all trace has been lost of the fourth. Or has it? Those who work on this sort of thing will know. Mysterious are the ways that artworks travel.

A new opportunity to leave the Soviet Union arose some fifteen years later, in the form of another Slavic scholar, this time from the Netherlands. He was an expert on Velimir Khlebnikov and invited Nikolai Khardzhiev to Amsterdam. This time Khardzhiev imposed conditions: he asked for permanent residence and the possibility of exporting his entire collection. In the process, he promised that after his death he'd leave the paintings to Amsterdam museums and his rich literary archive to the Slavic Department at Amsterdam University. In September 1993, Kristina Gmurzynska, proprietor of a high-end art gallery in Cologne, Mathias Rostorfer, the director of the gallery, and the scholar all arrived in Moscow. Nikolai Khardzhiev signed a contract. The contract stipulated that Gmurzynska would take six paintings of which she'd sell two and place the other four in storage, and Khardzhiev would be given two and a half million dollars upon his arrival in Amsterdam. Khardzhiev and his wife Lidia Chaga arrived in Amsterdam in November 1993.

Three months later at Sheremetyevo, the Moscow airport, an Israeli citizen, Dmitry Jakobson, was detained and his large number of suspiciously bulky bags were inspected. In his luggage they found Velimir Khlebnikov's manuscripts, Kazimir Malevich's letters, Osip Mandelstam's and Anna Akhmatova's papers, and precious documents pertaining to Russian Futurism. Jakobson was released, the documents were confiscated. Among them was also the Galerie Gmurzynska contract. And meanwhile, as this international scandal was exploding, the remaining paintings and the archive—which Kristina Gmurzynska had already brought out—arrived in Amsterdam where they were stowed away in a safe. Khardzhiev and Chaga later claimed that many items were missing, and for this they blamed the scholar, who, they said, had access to the safe.

In the second half of 1994, a contract was signed in Amsterdam finalizing the sale of all six Malevich paintings to Galerie Gmurzyn-ska. The Khardzhievs purchased a house in Amsterdam. Having no recourse, Khardzhiev signed away to the Russian state the archive that had been confiscated at Sheremetyevo Airport. Into the lives of Khardzhiev and his wife came three "caretakers": Boris Abarov, a failed Russian actor with an Amsterdam address, his girlfriend, Bella Bekker, hired by the Khardzhiev household as a housekeeper, and Johannes Buse, who played financial adviser. In keeping with the new constellation, Khardzhiev penned a new will: now he left everything to his wife, Lidia Chaga. Soon after the will was signed, Chaga slipped on the stairs in their canal-side home, fell, and died. Now, after Khardzhiev's death, the treasure trove would go to Boris Abarov. Two days after Chaga's death, the Khardzhiev-Chaga Art Foundation was established to manage the remaining Khardzhiev collection and archive. The foundation was run by Boris Abarov and Johannes Buse.

In March 1996, Khardzhiev was visited by Vadim Kozovoi, a Russian poet living in Paris. Khardzhiev complained to Kozovoi that Abarov was essentially holding him hostage. He drew up a new will according to which he would leave everything to Kozovoi after his death, under the condition that Kozovoi move Khardzhiev to Paris. The will, however, was never certified because Abarov apparently stepped in to prevent Kozovoi, during his brief stay in Amsterdam, from having it witnessed. Kozovoi returned to Paris without finalizing the matter; Khardzhiev died in June, Boris Abarov was still the legal heir, Bella Bekker was given the house where she'd served as housekeeper,

Buse, after receiving his payout, went off to somewhere in France. Boris Abarov agreed to a payout of some ten million guilders, signed away all other pretensions to Khardzhiev's estate, and then vanished from the story. This was followed by tortuous and lengthy discussions between Dutch and Russian state negotiators about returning Khardzhiev's treasures to Russia. In 2011, the archive (or what was left of it) was returned to the Russian authorities. The valuable paintings, however, remain with the Khardzhiev-Chaga Art Foundation at its seat in Amsterdam.

This report is not complete or, I assume, fully accurate; it's merely a hasty compilation of several articles published at the height of the scandal. Much remains hidden from view. After the petty hyenas (Abarov, Bekker, and Buse) and farcical elements worthy of Mikhail Bulgakov amused the reading public for a time, the game was taken over by more serious players.

So was Nikolai Khardzhiev the Salieri of the Russian avant-garde or was he its Mozart, as an admirer claimed? The Mozart Salieri relationship is one that Russian culture has not been able to avoid. It has been raised repeatedly over the years with Pushkin's play *Mozart and Salieri*, the Rimsky Korsakov opera, Boris Pilnyak's story "A Story about How Stories Come to be Written," Vaginov's novels, Bulgakov's novel *The Master and Margarita* . . . Did Khardzhiev's long and rich biography accelerate unjustly toward its end, culminating in a brief moralistic fable? A gamblers' proverb on deadly greed? The myth of King Midas? A story of tragedy arising from the plunder of treasures (robbed = damned!)? A moralistic legend about rare diamonds that bring bad luck? A Bulgakov farce about money turning into worthless pieces of paper? To gloat over somebody's crushing defeat is in poor taste. On the other hand, not to see that Khardzhiev's story is an inseparable part of the art world (and not only the Russian art world) would be a fatal oversight.

But perhaps all is not as it seems, the secret may lie in longevity, and we barely know anything about the secret of longevity . . . "In the autumn of 1941, when the Germans were marching on Moscow, Khardzhiev and his comrade Trenin* reported to the Writers Union as volunteers. Both volunteers, in civilian garb, set out on foot for the front lines. Their city shoes soon fell to pieces, Khardzhiev ended up more or less barefoot, he caught a cold, and in a semi-conscious state he was left in a remote village far from Moscow. The entire detachment was killed, and with them, Trenin. Khardzhiev was decorated with the "For the Defense of Moscow" medal (from Russian Wikipedia).

6.
Come On, Behemoth, Let's Have the Novel!

Asen had an eye for style. The book by I. Ferris arrived in "Eastern European," retro postal packaging, wrapped in coarse, old-fashioned, brown paper, done up with string, with my address written out in a hand that pretended to a clumsy lack of familiarity with Roman-alphabet penmanship. And the book cover was retro, too, Soviet, gray, hardcover, yet nevertheless the whole effect was one of superb design. On the title page at the bottom was the name of Asen's small publishing company, *Asen*, in fine print, while across the middle of the page crawled the title: *The Magnificent Art of Translating Life into a Story and Vice Versa*. The book was not large, I don't know whether Asen had made an effort to fit everything onto the ninety-nine pages or the book simply turned out that way. I assumed numerologists assign a meaning to the number ninety-nine. An internet text I skimmed on

---

* Vladimir Trenin, literary critic and theoretician.

numerology and translated into "my" language said that ninety-nine is the number for the guardian angel, responsible, mainly, for intuition.

Leafing through the book, I noted something that surprised me: each chapter was headed with the same title, the quote from Bulgakov's *The Master and Margarita*: *Come on, Behemoth, let's have the novel!*, but printed in Russian Cyrillic. Why this quote wasn't used as the title of the entire book baffled me. I don't believe Asen would have insisted on a catchy commercial title; in his miniature publishing firm with its tiny distribution and profile, none of the books could count on enjoying big success, regardless of whether the title was *Figurae Veneris*, or *The Confessions of Stalin's Geisha*, or *The Vegetarian Bible*. I figured I. Ferris left the phrase in Russian because she felt no translation would do it justice. The peerless devil speaks, momentarily, with the voice of a plumber. And perhaps Ferris was employing *chertykhan'e* an evocation calling forth the devil. Situations in *The Master and Margarita* were rife with this trick. Perhaps she felt she needed demonic forces to spur her on with her writing. Perhaps she meant her story of the lost novel to expose the banality of Russian everyday life in the 1930s rather than something bizarre. And while the fictional Master in Bulgakov's novel burned the manuscript of his own novel about Pontius Pilate, many manuscripts were plundered by the NKVD, or, as with archives or even whole libraries, they were burned as heating fuel.

The prose of I. Ferris was not exotic, but it was also not entirely pedestrian. My first impression was that it sounded like the dispirited thesis of a librarian. The topic of the thesis was the "most neglected member of OBERIU," Doivber Levin; this hit me, briefly, as a blow to the solar plexus. I, like I. Ferris, knew a little about Levin, who had "smuggled" himself and his work into Russian literary history via his tragic fate, but voilà, she'd been the first to publish on it! My initial expectation was that this would be a modest monograph on Levin's children's fiction. His children's fiction was the only material available that one could actually work with. But his children's fiction, it turned out, was of no interest to Ferris.

Then I imagined Ferris might attempt to reconstruct the novel of Levin's mentioned by the two witnesses, Gennady Gor and Igor Bakhterev. At the outset, instead, Ferris presents her vision of the future of literature. She imagines ours as a new age in which the interest in literary reception will shift from original works to reconstruction of forgotten, burned, and lost works of world literature, a mission of literary restoration. Parallel to this process, existing canonized works will undergo a process of deconstruction, thereby resulting in a new version of *Madame Bovary, Lolita, Anna Karenina* in new multimedial forms. The literary classics will be the most quickly and efficiently transmitted to future generations as animated films, virtual reality experiences, video games . . . Ultimately, the future age will be called the age of "digital classicism" . . .

"We live in a time of the accumulation and squirreling away of rubbish," writes Ferris, "our lives are focused on the continual production of rubbish and, in parallel, we dwell on ways to handle the problems posed by rubbish. From medicine to cosmetics and so on, everything constantly reminds us that we're living in a culture centered on pollution, and, therefore, need detoxification. Our relationships with other people are *toxic*, our environment is *toxic*, the food we eat is *toxic*. *Toxic* is the key word of our times. Perhaps we need a historical time-out, production should, perhaps, be halted, we should reset, re-canonize the canonical values, hence, perhaps, we should stop having children for a while. The market persuades us of the urgency of constant production. We live in the age of the overfed, daily we serve up lotus, we've become *lotus-eaters*, and, look, we belch with satiation, why, the sound of burping is the only authentic sound we're able to make."

Ferris does not actually say as much outright, but she hints that there can be no grand works without grand risk, no literature can matter without a "sword hanging over the author's head." True, the literature of the Russian avant-garde does matter, but this is due, at least in part, says Ferris, to the authors' "dread of the sword."

"Emperor Shahryar is Scheherazade's audience, her putative executioner, her requisitioner, her misogynyst commander, her tormenter. He is not there as a literary-aesthetic mediator. He's as amoral as a child, his actions are fueled by a hunger for the story. He postpones Scheherazade's death only so he can hear the next installment of her tale. Scheherazade tells the story only because she must, in doing so delaying the moment of her own death through the art of storytelling. Over her head hangs the sword. True, Stalin was no Shahryar. Stalin was a sadist, a head-chopper, who believed himself to be God. The greatness of many of the Russian avant-garde writers is not only in their texts but in their embrace of risk, in the sword hanging over their heads, in their dread of the sword."

Ferris added numbers to her thesis, trying to prove that a great deal revolved around the number 37 at the time. Stalin destroyed the "flower of the Russian intelligentsia" in 1937. Many artists lost their lives at the age of thirty-seven: Daniil Kharms, Alexander Vvedensky, Velimir Khlebnikov, and—Doivber Levin (!). Nikolai Oleynikov, affiliated with OBERIU, died at thirty-nine, Konstantin Vaginov (true, from tuberculosis) at thirty-five, Yuri Vladimirov (also from tuberculosis) at twenty-three. Hardly any of the great figures of the Russian avant-garde made it to fifty: Isaac Babel died at forty-six, Mikhail Bulgakov at forty-nine, Osip Mandelstam at forty-seven, Boris Pilnyak at forty-five, Marina Cvetaeva killed herself at forty-nine, Sergei Yesenin at thirty, and Vladimir Mayakovsky killed himself before he reached the fatal age of thirty-seven . . . Ferris didn't venture into further explanation of the mechanisms of the Great Lottery, but she did reveal what had prompted her to write the book.

"In 1936, the right to abortion was abolished in the Soviet Union. A year later, in 1937, began the so-called Great Purge, when hundreds of thousands of people were murdered. The 'intelligentsia gene' was the first target. And then it was as if Stalin, the great engineer of human souls, knew this loss would require compensation. I was born in 1938, I was a 'child' of Stalin's decision to ban abortion. The beginning of Kharms's children's story—*I was born in the rushes. Like a mouse. My mother gave birth to me and placed me in the water*—could serve as the opening lines of my biography. All of us born between 1936 and 1955, while abortion was illegal, were born like mice. We were programmed to replenish the population vacuum, the demographic shortfall."

Ferris spends the first thirty pages of her book wandering in various directions: after her careen through literary-prophetic material, she launches into laments over contemporary culture, which she doesn't understand well; these laments are followed by autobiographical details which are, I should say, the most successful in terms of literary merit. With skill and precision, Ferris sketches the quotidian existence of Moscow student and intellectual life in the 1960s and her protracted struggle with the Soviet bureaucracy to procure for herself and her husband the papers they need to leave the country. The passages about anguished, arduous, and absurd bureaucratic everyday life are brightened by her sketches of Moscow oddballs, dreamers, liars, compromisers, informers, scoundrels, geniuses, lunatics, drunks, petty profiteers, and desperados.

Some of the finest, but also most wrenching, lines Ferris writes are dedicated to her mother. Her mother's bitterness radiates from every word, as do Ferris's youthful obstinacy and her headlong clashes with her mother; her mother's obsessive worry for her daughter and the way she is entranced by her daughter's very existence; the daughter's surges of hatred for her mother for the same reason. And between the demanding and possessive love of her mother and David's gentile reserve, Ferris chooses the reserve, leaving open the possibility that her marriage to David and departure for England are but a surreptitious avenue for escape from her mother.

Ferris speaks here and there of her present life, her life in London, the loneliness, isolation, immobility. She is a living skeleton and she knows it. All big cities like London are full of people who, like her, are half-alive. Most of them live in rundown apartments slowly succumbing to mildew, most of them do not have the financial resources to move to upscale places to die, homes for the elderly, people like this pray to God they'll sink into a blessed oblivion or simply breathe their last. The passages with the most sparkle are descriptions of a university student, a young woman to whom Ferris has offered a free room, asking in return only that the student do the shopping, which Ferris, with her limited mobility, can no longer manage. Ferris, who'd spent her whole adult life with men—her husband and two sons—describes her quiet delight in the young woman. The girl becomes the very center of her life, a substitute for the daughter Ferris never had, the grandchildren she never had, the friends who were gone. She comes to love the girl, love everything about her, love the new habit of sitting for hours in her wheelchair by the window, waiting for the young woman to come home, and, in the morning, seeing her off from the same vantage point with a long gaze still clouded by sleep. She repeats the same gaze, the same posture, with a stolid, dogged devotion. She sniffs the air when the young woman comes back, thinks up little tasks during the day to assign to her or questions she might ask just to prolong the time they spend together. The young woman is a beauty with a pale complexion, a slender face, high cheekbones, eyes that are closer than usual to the bridge of her nose, something that lends her gaze a look both alert and intent. Her movements are unusually supple and limber, she dresses in colorful clothing, unencumbered, wearing lavender socks with low-heeled green shoes, for example, and arranging her hair in wispy pigtails decorated with brightly colored clips. One time when she lies down on the sofa in the living room, she falls asleep and Ferris holds her breath, watching her: she slumbers like a child, firmly, deeply, drifting into sleep as if she were sinking into quicksand. She is soft-spoken and quiet yet deeply present. Yes, she communicates with Ferris and the space of the apartment in a way all her own. After the girl leaves the house, Ferris still feels her presence for a long time, as if she's left her shadow behind.

When I'd already given up on trying to guess where the book would go next, Ferris abruptly changes direction and begins elaborating on a wild premise . . . Since the time in which Doivber Levin lived was nightmarish and chaotic, and since there were two Levins with the same first and last name born in the same region with similar literary fates and similar dates of birth and death, and since there is no reliable information for where and when Doivber Levin was killed, and since people on all sides and in all places were dying and evading bullets by changing their identities, papers, identity cards, falsifying documents, personal histories, beliefs, faiths, and class, since all this was true, why would we not, asks Ferris, by that same logic, imagine that Doivber was not killed, but instead that he turned up elsewhere? Why, for instance, did Levin's compatriot L. Panteleev, when recalling how Levin had lived on Chekhov Street in Leningrad, write this sentence in his diary: *He did live yet no longer will he live. Not here nor anywhere else on this earth.* A person must be not only a bad writer, but a fool, writes Ferris, to claim that somebody was killed, and that therefore *no longer will he live,* and then in addition to jump up and down on the corpse, stomping on the soil with words and claiming that the corpse (Levin) will live no longer, *not here nor anywhere else on this earth.*

So what if Doivber did survive and turn up elsewhere? Just maybe, he turned *everywhere else* on earth? Daniil Kharms—the best known and most popular of the OBERIU crowd, a writer who derided many writers including himself, who ridiculed literary texts including his own and literary genres including the genre of aphorism, once wrote: *A person lives more than once. What was not finished in this life will be finished in the next.*

7.

Out of His House Went a Man

Daniil Kharms, Alexander Vvedensky, and Igor Bakhterev were arrested in 1931, having spent six months at the Leningrad investigative jail known as Shpalerka.* Kharms was given a three-year sentence (in Kursk), while Vvedensky and Bakhterev were released but banned from residing in Leningrad and Moscow and several other major cities. That same year, Yuri Vladimirov, the youngest of the OBERI-UTs, died, followed soon after by Konstantin Vaginov. Aleksandar Tufanov, a translator and a Futurist who, with Velimir Khlebnikov, had influenced members of OBERIU, was arrested that same year, 1931. During questioning by the police, he confessed that some of his *zaum* verses were, in fact, coded calls to overthrow the Soviet regime. He was sentenced to three years in prison. Igor Terentyev, a friend of OBERIU, was active in experimental theater and associated with painters Kazimir Malevich and Pavel Filonov, as well as composer Mikhail Matyushin. Terentyev was arrested that same year, 1931, and

---

* Shpalerka was on Sphalerna Street. This prison in Leningrad was as infamous as the Moscow Lubyanka.

sentenced to five years of hard labor, building the White Sea-Baltic canal. He was released early, but then arrested again in 1937 and shot at the notorious Butyrka prison in Moscow. Nikolai Oleynikov, a poet close to the OBERIU group, was arrested in 1937 and shot. Nikolai Zabolotsky was arrested in 1938 and sentenced to five years. And Vvedensky was re-arrested in 1941, after which he soon died of pleurisy. Kharms was arrested in 1941 and died in a locked-down psychiatric ward in early 1942.

Himalayan bear, Doivber Levin, sequestered himself, mouse-like, in children's literature. True, he was the quietest and least visible member of the OBERIU group, but in those days people were being put to death for lesser sins than writing "in an experimental style." Ferris was convinced that the conversation between him and his friend L. Panteleev—during which Levin uttered the fateful words: *It's over! All the lights have been snuffed out all over the world*—takes place in 1937, though L. Panteleev avers that the exchange occurred in 1939. Fears ate at Doivber Levin like pernicious bedbugs: fear of death, fear of life, fear of irrelevance, fear of fear, fear of everything . . .

For whatever reason, Ferris believes that Levin's pragmatic wife plays a crucial role in all this, a little Soviet desk-clerk armed with powerful weapons: the stamp and the seal. She obtains all the documents required for a move to Birobidzhan; this, she thinks, is the safest place in the world for Doivber. First, she knows Levin was cheating on her with a "hussy," so she feels that dispatching him to such a faraway place is fair enough as punishment; second, she is gratified at having the creative reach of Fate; third she loves her Boba, her "big bear," and she cannot tolerate the thought that any of the things happening to so many of those around him might happen to him. And, just like Fate, this little Soviet desk clerk falsifies a document, four years hence, certifying Levin's heroic death in the village of Pogostie.

Ferris's book includes a copy of the document that seems to verify Boris Mikhailovich (Doivber) Levin's death on December 17, 1941, in Pogostie, side-by-side with a copy of a document issued on December 17, 1937, permitting someone by the name of BerDov Levi to travel to the JAO, the Jewish Autonomous Oblast, the administrative seat of the future Jewish state of Birobidzhan. And a copy of his passport is included in Ferris's book as well.

These three fake documents are the only ones Ferris is able to obtain. The rest of what she writes is either truth that only she knows, or a deliberate fabrication. It is not my place to say. Ultimately, she tells us, Levin sets out for the Far East eleven years after Boris Pilnyak. And why is his departure deemed to be "after" Boris Pilnyak's? Because Levin brings Pilnyak's book *Roots of the Japanese Sun* on the trip.* Yet he isn't traveling to Japan! Ah, but he's headed eastward. And besides, his choice is not so odd if one considers just how horrified people are at the time, bracing for tragedy after tragedy, wincing at every sound. The news of each new blow travels at lightning speed. So one day before his departure, the news of Boris Pilnyak's arrest reaches even him, Doivber Levin, who matters to no one. Is it this news rather than geography that determined Levin's choice of travel reading?

"The ever-present terror on the one hand, yet the hope that life might bring rescue in the form of a merciful reversal galvanized people to the point that the lives of many actually began to resemble the very thing they'd fancied in their wildest dreams. So it was, for instance, that David Burliuk," Ferris writes, "the 'futuristic Polyphemus,' 'father of Russian Futurism,' trudged across the length of Siberia to Vladivostok, all in his secret mission to secure passage to America. With him he brought an entourage of six family members and friends. He

---

* Boris Pilnyak, *Korni iaponskogo solntsa*, 1927.

vitalized Vladivostok cultural life bringing an unheard-of intensity, turning the provincial Far-Eastern city into the world capital of Futurism. Then in the 1920s he crossed over to Japan, where he became the 'Russian father of Japanese Futurism.' During his two years in Japan, he painted some three hundred canvases, turning the Japanese into lovers of Futurist antics, and during that time he saved enough money to move with his group of six to America; they flew straight to the epicenter of art, New York City."

Doivber Levin arrives in Birobidzhan and immediately, as he knows Yiddish, is hired by the *Bilobidzhaner Stern* (an assertion which is impossible to deny, but also impossible to prove as two Levins and a Kaufman were, indeed, employed at the *Bilobidzhaner Stern* at the time), and finds work at the local Jewish theater staging performances ranging from Jewish classics to Jewish sketches adapted for the stage. Birobidzhan may be remote, but it is a lively region: after 1934 when it's proclaimed the Jewish Autonomous Oblast, and Jews, communists, and communist sympathizers begin flocking there from other parts of the Soviet Union, but also from Argentina, Poland, America, and England, seeking a place more secure and protected than what they've left behind. Some stay on but others re-trace their steps, feeling cheated. Birobidzhan is hardly the promised land; the climate is challenging, the people are hungry, and their skills—merchants, tailors, bakers, butchers, woodworkers—are not, at first, of much value. Soon begins the Second World War, and with it men are drafted into the army: many of the people of Birobidzhan die in the war.

After but a few months in Birobidzhan, where he'd make friends with Miron Belochkin, actor and poet, he sets out for Harbin in Miron's agreeable company. The two of them muddle along together for a time and then each chooses his own direction. Belochkin stays on in Harbin, seeking passage to America, while Levin goes on to

Shanghai, a free city, where no one is inspecting passports or visas. He is there, in Shanghai, in 1938, when Jews from Germany begin arriving who've been unable to secure a visa for another country. The situation changes in 1939 when Shanghai is occupied by the Japanese. Levin is moved, with thousands of other Jews who arrive in Shanghai after 1937, to a part of the city called Hongkew, a Jewish ghetto. After the defeat of the Japanese, the Jews are briefly offered hospitality in Hong Kong and from there they emigrate to South and North America, the Soviet Union, Europe, Australia. The relocation does not go smoothly or speedily. Many spend the best years of their lives waiting for their new life.

And it is right here, while Doivber Levin is waiting for his papers to move to Europe, that Ferris comes to a stop. She stops on page ninety-nine. It's unlikely that she realized the Angel No. 99 was staying her hand. Ferris leaves her hero, Doivber Levin, or BerDov Levi, or Boris Dov Kaufman, while he's housed as a refugee at the Peninsula Hotel in Hong Kong. In the hotel room, on his bedside table, lies the manuscript of an unfinished novel. The novel is titled *The Peninsula Hotel*. Even a brief glance at the first sentences shows that Levin had matured into a sophisticated writer. Ferris seems certain, for whatever reason, that life, books, and perhaps even fame still await Doivber Levin. And before she shuts the door behind her, she slips into Levin's jacket pocket a talisman for the road, the only one she can come up with: a few lines by Daniil Kharms.

> Out of the house went a man
> Out of the house he went
> With a bindle tied to a stick.
> And on a distant trek
> And on a distant trek
> Off he went on foot.

Straight along he walked and forward
Straight forward he gazed.
Not slept, nor drank,
Not drank, nor slept
Not slept, nor drank, nor ate.

Into a dark wood ventured he
In he strode one day, one dawn
From that moment
From that moment
From that moment he was gone.

If ever you should meet him
If the road should lead you on
Let us know now
Let us know now
Better now than anon.

8.

Foxes Are Loners

Asen Smirliev and I had been in touch only infrequently, but after reading the book I called him right away to thank him.

"Could you please send me Mrs. Ferris's email address? I'd like to write her. I think she'd appreciate hearing from me," I said.

"Regrettably, I cannot . . ."

"Why?"

Ira Ferris had died.

It happened not long after the conference where we'd met. She'd come to the conference to deliver her manuscript to him. He knew nothing more than what he'd heard from her twin sons, who'd come to England to see to the burial and settle her estate. Ira had been renting a room to a young woman, a student. That tragic day she saw the girl being mobbed by a throng of young neighborhood men at the front door to her house, so she'd wheeled herself hastily to the front stoop, spun her wheelchair around at an awkward angle, and plunged down the stairs.

"Heavens, what a sad story!"

"And by the way, her sons said that the girl, Dora, who'd been staying with her, was apparently from Zagreb, a student at Goldsmiths . . ."

"So is Dora still living at the apartment?" I asked, dully.

"No, the sons sold the place."

"Why is there no author bio in the book?"

"Ira preferred it that way . . ."

"And why is that?"

"I have no idea."

I could readily imagine her little row house somewhere on the outskirts of South London. I could imagine her waiting impatiently every day for the student, clutching at the young woman like a straw, fearing that if she let go she'd sink, there'd be no more reason to breathe. The girl was hounded that evening by a pack of curs by the front stoop to the house, idle young men from the neighborhood on the prowl for a thrill. When Ferris saw what was happening from her perch by the window, she hastened to the front hall in her wheelchair, and, first switching on the light, she flung open the door. The boys froze. Ferris was a terrifying, raging sight, especially when she let loose a blood-curdling shriek. She even scared herself and wondered where she'd wrenched that inhuman sound from . . . A boy from the group grabbed a tennis ball from his pocket and slammed it into her, hard. Ferris wasn't able to duck it or dodge, and, to make matters worse, in her panic she steered her wheelchair forward, tipped over, and tumbled down the stairs. The girl tore herself free, flew over to the old woman, first one neighbor came to his door, then another, then somebody called the police, the boys ran off . . .

Perhaps at the very moment of her death, Kharms's verses opened wide before Ferris's eyes: water and, on its surface, the image of the zero (Malevich's zero!), a zero that really is a circle, just as a child tosses a pebble into a puddle and the pebble makes a circle that spreads across the surface of the water, each circle giving rise to a thought, and the thought, risen from the circle, "calls forth a zero from the dark to the light."

> Yet zero is the handiwork of God;
> Zero is the kindred wheel;
> Zero is the spirit and the body;
> Boat, oar, and water . . .

Perhaps at the very moment of her death, Doivber Levin's novel finally opened its pages for Ferris. She'd been staring into it her whole life as if into a hypnotic, black blot. The novel was truly dazzling, three-dimensional, its colors more vivid than any she'd ever known. She could see the apartment building in such sharp relief, each apartment lit by a bright light, and look! the mythical creature with the head of a bull and the ordinary Soviet official were next-door neighbors after all. The tenants were shuffled like cards, they were shining onto one another, literally; the color of one left its trace like a kiss on the hues of another; in the eye of the creature with the head of a bull slept the cowering figure of the Soviet official. And the proportions were skewed; a tiny woman sat on the rim of a flowerpot on a windowsill, swinging her legs and smoking. A little, bewhiskered man slept in one of the apartments, pressed against the fat body of a cockroach twice his size . . . Ira could hear voices, they were all talking at once, intertwining as if in some divine musical composition. And then the sounds bore her aloft as if on a sudden gust of wind (like Khlebnikov's "Radio of the Future") and off she flew. The marvelous house opened like a shell and drew her in. The feeling of displacement that had dogged her for her whole life was gone. She felt relief. She was finally home.

Or maybe that's not how it happened. As I assembled the puzzle pieces and played at forensics, it occurred to me that Bulat Okudzhava's *Prayer* must have been the soundtrack of her youth. In the final reckoning, she'd had something for everybody: her husband was able, thanks to her, to enjoy the quiet and gratifying career of a diligent verb counter, counting verbs being what he most enjoyed. She loved her sons far more than they ever loved her. When she died, they sold her house and back they went to Australia with a sigh of relief. She'd looked after the girl, Dora, and, at least for a time felt close to her, the little "foreign girl," so similar to what she'd been her whole life long. She watched over the girl, prayed to the Lord of Sea-Green Eyes to give the girl wisdom and strength: let the Lord of Sea-Green Eyes dole out a little of that to everyone, yes, and let him not forget her, Ira. She granted Doivber Levin a second life, sketched his biography, whether real or fictional, and acquitted the duty she'd been carrying forward since her birth at a certain time and a certain place. And as for herself, she allowed herself an inexpensive little outing. Her adventure might be termed the poetics of absence, the poetics of the holes in Swiss cheese, the poetics of the "divine zero" . . .

9.

Sprinklers

A month or two after Ferris's book arrived at my address, I searched the internet for a review, any sign that somebody else had read it. Meanwhile, I googled Doivber Levin's name, too. I received the same results I'd come up with before, but this time I clicked on one of the websites and, reflexively, pressed print. Only the next day did I remember to go and collect the printed text from the printer. Before I tossed it into the recycling bin, I just so happened, more by chance than intent, to cast an eye over the text. It was longer than I'd expected. I checked the website on my computer monitor. Everything was as it should be: Levin was born in such and such a year, wrote such and such texts, died at such and such a time. In the printed version, however, there were other sentences interspersed. These were not like the teeth of a comb fitting snugly into the teeth of another comb: they were not interlinked. The inserted text was gibberish, noise that impeded the flow of information. For example, after the sentence *Doivber Levin enrolled at the university in Petrograd in 1922* was interposed the sentence *How remarkable that Spider-Man knew nothing of this.* And while these two could, theoretically, be linked (the second offering an amusing commentary on the first), the sentences that followed were gibberish. I tried finding some connection between the website and the gibberish, a hidden message, but to no avail, the sentences were fragments from unraveled texts, nothing was linkable to anything else. The last sentence was *Even Anastasia Stotskaya couldn't imagine such a thing.* I hoped this might be a quote from a novel or hid a riddle of some sort. I was persuaded otherwise when I ascertained that Anastasia Stotskaya was not a fictional character, but a momentarily popular Russian star.

I ran my anti-viral program, but my computer appeared to be clean. I called a few acquaintances, but none of them had ever heard of such a thing. One did suggest that what I was seeing was an earlier version that had *attached itself* to the main text: revisions are usually hidden from view on the monitor, but because of a computer error they were showing up in the print-out. "A routine glitch," said my acquaintance.

Nothing I said could convince him that these were not revisions I'd made to the text, nor that the glitch was at all "routine." It had never happened before, but I had no will to go on researching, especially because a fantastical notion had occurred to me and captured my imagination.

What if texts, imprinted on infinitesimal, transparent layers with hidden text, are overlaid one atop the other, yet we know nothing of them because they remain permanently hidden from view, and only very occasionally, as with the Doivber Levin website, do they appear to the computer user in readable form? What if there are many of these "adhered" layers, which our eye is not capable of perceiving? What if the texts are, in fact, linked to one another, but we haven't the skill we'd need to grasp their coherence? And what if we human beings are actually living, breathing texts? What if we're walking around with myriad overlays of "revisions" of ourselves about which we know nothing? What if the blurbs about other people (one, two, a thousand?) are "attached" to us, yet we are unaware of their existence? What if these texts fuse to us; what if we all, each and every one of us, has been inhabited by secret dwellers? Why did I get so *stuck* ages ago on that utterly inconsequential footnote about Doivber Levin? Why did Ferris spend all her time on Levin? Which was it? Did Ferris dream her text about Levin, or did the text about Levin dream Ferris?

Whatever the case, Ferris's fascination with Levin's biography could simply be explained by the way she perceived her own life as a footnote appended to a text rather than as a text in its own right; because of her sense of her own second-class status she wrapped herself around equally "second-class" Doivber Levin, warming it, the footnote that is, with her breath as if it were a frozen bird. Is her "restoration" of Levin's biography credible? I can't even say that. I know only that

it's plausible. It is entirely possible that things are less exalted than
we might imagine, that Doivber Levin is, indeed, Irina Ferris's real
father. Perhaps Ferris knew of her father's existence, or perhaps she
adopted Levin as a make-believe father; maybe the "pretty Komsomol
girl" who had the powerful weapon, the stamps, was, indeed, her
mother. Lest we forget, L. Panteleev, Levin's compatriot, jotted down
a few words in his diary after meeting with Doivber Levin, musing:
I wonder where his daughter Ira is now. How old could she be? Seven?

Ferris wrapped herself in her book as if it were a simple scarf she'd
knitted herself. She slipped into her book the way a mouse wiggles
into a wheel of cheese, with the intention of remaining there until its
tiny heart stops beating. Having raised Levin a "monument," she buried herself under the same tombstone. And as to the question of the
veracity of her discoveries regarding Levin's biography, this became
moot the moment Ferris moved into her own book. Though there
was nothing OBERIU-like about Ferris, her gesture was worthy of
OBERIU.*

And me, what about me? Why did this story stick so doggedly to
me? Ferris's obsession with Levin is easy enough to understand: her
native literature was Russian, her native language was Russian; and
her nightmare—in which history nibbled indifferently at human lives
like pumpkin seeds, discarding vast piles of the empty husks—was
bound to a particular moment of Russian history.

---

* Konstantin Vaginov, a member of OBERIU, master of grotesque exaggeration,
ended his little novel about the make-believe writer Svistonov:

"In the end he realized he'd been definitively shut up inside his novel.

"Wherever he went, everywhere he'd see his characters. They had other sur-
names, other bodies, other hairstyles, and they behaved differently, but he'd spot
them at once. In this way Svistonov moved entirely into his work." (Konstantin
Vaginov, *Trudy i dni Svistonova*, 1928-1929)

During the time I spent in Moscow in 1975-76, I acknowledged a key detail: I was protected from every fear not just by my youthfulness, but by an altogether fragile little item: my passport. With my Yugoslav passport I was treated like a "westerner," which meant that in Moscow, where there was nothing but shortages, I enjoyed certain advantages. So how did it happen—when there wasn't a single cloud in my sky and when, while reading *The Master and Margarita*, I sincerely believed that manuscripts don't burn—that I latched onto Doivber Levin as a trivial souvenir, a gray pebble by the roadside, a literary footnote, a few references to a non-existent novel? And then I went on cherishing him as a permanent mental possession. My empathy for Doivber Levin was not, it seems, merely empathy out of principle for a man-footnote. It turns out it was anticipation of what I was yet to experience, though I would've sworn (at the time) that such a thing could never happen to me. Only two years after the fall of the Berlin Wall my little country in the south of Europe crumbled into six even smaller countries, and our minor language split into three or four even more minor ones. And not only that, at a time when post-Communism began to flourish, "unsuitable" people disappeared, "unsuitable" articles disappeared, "unsuitable" books were taken off library shelves (including—surprise, surprise—mine!), relegated to the trash or to personal or organized bonfires; street names disappeared, monuments disappeared, governments in the itty-bitty countries in the European south were swarmed by brutal mobs who decided that all things would be tailored to their taste and their benefit. People were expelled, people were murdered, people fled in groups or singly to neighboring countries, to distant countries, families were broken up, parents found themselves in one country while their children were somewhere else. And I, too—having earlier inscribed on my inner map a random trajectory—found myself living abroad, becoming a person with two biographies, or two people with one biography, or three people with three biographies and three languages . . . All these things happened in other proportions, for other reasons, and in other ways than they did in Doivber Levin's day. From outside, it all looked as if this were happening inside a glass snow globe with the snow swirling. But, inside, instead of snow there swirled blood. When somebody picked up the globe and shook it, miniature people inside the globe conducted a miniature war, burned books as big as poppy seeds, erected miniature borders, opened their miniature camps for the ethnically unsuitable, raised fences and barbed wire, revised the school books, erased everything old and established everything new, they died in miniature, were expelled in miniature, blew up miniature homes, everything went on in miniature—and over it all flurried that soothing artificial snow. Today, a quarter of a century later, due perhaps to an optical omission, snake eggs have been breeding in the democratic incubators of the new statelets of Croatia and Serbia, in Bulgaria, Hungary, and Poland, in Russia and Romania, and also in the incubators of Greece, Italy, and Spain, Finland and Norway. Will new people hatch from these snake eggs, outfitted with masks and camouflage? Will these new people respond to the first call, or perhaps to no call at all, and begin a massacre of the refugees who are inundating Europe from all possible directions?

Whether Ira Ferris's efforts at research are credible or not matters less; what does matter is that the text remains. In Levin's case what remains is not a text, but the absence of a text, a hole, a yawn, a pale sketch that spurs the imagination. The absence of a text, of an image, of music is the flip side of the medal and the symbol of the age. The text's absence glows with a magical light, it pulses, it is every bit as authentic and alive. The story of Doivber Levin is not an OBERIU up-yours to the culture of the hierarchy of taste, to the institutions that pretend to a stable eternity. It is a metaphysical up-yours (no matter how ironic this may sound) demonstrating how the power of the imagination and creativity can outstrip the very power of words on paper. In that sense, manuscripts truly do not burn.

The first review of the book appeared in the *Nottingham Post*. I doubt it would inspire anybody to rush out and buy it, though in this day and age, with memoirs still at the top of the bestseller list—I won't swear to that. Ferris's book has a catchy title, *The Magnificent Art of Translating Life into a Story and Vice Versa,* and the author of the brief review adeptly quoted a passage that says that the real literary fun begins the moment a story slips an author's control, when it starts behaving like a rotating lawn sprinkler, firing off every which way, when grass begins to sprout not because of any moisture, but out of thirst for a near source of moisture. If the image of the rotating lawn sprinkler has stuck with me, it may stick with others, too . . .

PART
FIVE

Little Miss Footnote

Human life is but a series of footnotes to a vast obscure unfinished masterpiece.

—*Vladimir Nabokov,* Lolita

1.

Apparently only great writers (or those who will one day become great) are not afraid of banality. They strew it throughout their texts like confetti. As if they are calculating in advance that their future readers will peck at these alluring, sagacious gems (the fine paper fortune-cookie slips, future fodder for intimate diaries, yearbooks, and notebooks for pearls of wisdom) like greedy pigeons going after breadcrumbs. These gems are like the sugared fruit in a Christmas cake. Human life is but a series of footnotes—or so says Nabokov, who, after all, made his masterpiece *Pale Fire* entirely out of footnotes—we are all footnotes. Literary footnotes joust for survival like cocks trained for the fight, at one moment it all comes down to who will make whom into a footnote, who will *befootnote* whom, who will be the text and who the footnote. We are all walking texts, we stride through the world with invisible copies adhering to us, numerous revisions of ourselves, and we're ignorant of their existence, number, and content. We bear on our skin the biographies of other people about whom we know nothing. We are glued to one another like transparent layers with hidden text, we grow into one another, all of us, and each of us is being inhabited, individually, by secret dwellers, as we dwell in the homes of others.

Nabokov would seem to have been right when he said we're all pieces of a mega-text, footnotes to some vast, unfinished masterpiece.

2.

Dorothy Leuthold became an essential footnote to the history of modern literature through no effort of her own. She had no qualifications for it (Can somebody actually qualify to be a footnote? Oh, yes!), nor did she have the inclination to be anything of the kind. Leuthold is, nevertheless, a footnote appended to the great cultural text known as "Vladimir Nabokov." And while this is a cultural text that expands daily, Leuthold remains the same miserly and mysterious footnote she was at the outset, and this—in our day and age, when the number of footnotes and their size often threaten to engulf the text—is a genuine rarity.

Dorothy G. (Gretchen) Leuthold was born on April 8, 1897, in the little town of Waseca, Minnesota. Her parents, Charles and Josephine Cincthold, were of German extraction as was, indeed, half of Waseca. Apparently she never married, so why Dorothy changed her name from Cincthold to Leuthold is not clear. Her entire life is a blank except for a single detail that has propelled her from total anonymity to the literary cocktail party whose guests are condemned to revel on forever. True, at the party Leuthold would be a wallflower, a see-through figure, a person few would ever notice, the woman in the corner who'd be taken for a maidservant and prompted with a gesture to fill the glasses for the guests. Yet her name is right there on the guest list. Chance may have put Leuthold on the list, but she was no party crasher.

Dorothy Leuthold arrived in New York from Waseca in 1930. She found an apartment on Manhattan's Upper West Side and a job at one of the branches of the celebrated New York Public Library; apparently she also attended classes at Columbia University.

Andrew Field, an early biographer of Nabokov's, was one of the first to write of Dorothy Leuthold. Having arrived in the United States in 1940, Russian writer Vladimir Nabokov, an impassioned lepidopterist, planned to spend the summer of 1941 collecting butterflies with his wife Véra and son Dmitri, although to do so would be a struggle. Véra had been suffering from back pain that whole winter and they weren't sure she'd be able to undertake the trip, and besides they had no vehicle, no car of their own.

"They did go, and on their first trip across America the Nabokovs were fortunate enough to have a driver. Her name was Dorothy Leuthold, and she was the last of Nabokov's private language pupils, an unmarried American woman who had worked for years in the New York Public Library system. Nabokov had met her quite by chance, and she had expressed a desire to supplement her knowledge of Russian, which was very limited but included, for reasons Nabokov could never fathom, all the swear words, the meanings of which she evidently did not properly grasp. Then, when the Nabokovs told her that they were going to California, she offered them her car, a brand-new Pontiac that she had just bought. But neither Nabokov nor his wife had any more occasion to know how to drive a car than to understand a bank statement—both were simple enough matters abstractly, but neither had obtruded upon their lives in the course of two decades. Their friend and pupil, when she learned that, said, 'Oh, I'll drive you.' Not only did she drive them, she also planned their itinerary, which took a southerly course and included a particularly memorable stop in Arizona, for it was there, on the south rim of the Grand Canyon on a very cold day in June (they had departed on May 26), that Nabokov walked down a path into the gorge and captured a new butterfly, which he gallantly named after their chauffeur, who had made the trip just to follow her whim and improve her Russian and be kind to some newly arrived immigrants."*

Dorothy Leuthold would bring the Nabokovs to Palo Alto and then drive the car back to the East Coast. At Stanford that summer, Nabokov would offer a course on creative writing, called "The Art of Writing," as well as a course on Russian literature.

Although Dorothy Leuthold is mentioned by many authors, notably Brian Boyd, another of Nabokov's biographers, Nabokov himself, and Robert Michael Pyle in his article "Between Climb and Cloud: Nabokov among the Lepidopterists," the itinerary they followed on their trip from the East Coast to the West Coast—which Leuthold planned and pursued with a martial rigor—has stirred more interest than has the actual person of Dorothy Leuthold. The trip, which began on May 26 and lasted precisely nineteen days, was, among other things, an excellent introduction to the America of motels that Nabokov would later describe in his masterpiece, Lolita. The very names suggest the Nabokovs stayed in cheap roadside lodgings (Motor Court Lee-Mead, Cumberland Motor Court, Wonderland Motor Courts, Motor Hotel), while other names of equally cheap lodgings tend to push the reader toward the symbolism of the "memorable experience" (the hotel, for instance, where they stayed at the Grand Canyon and where Nabokov made the big "find" of his butterfly was called Bright Angel Lodge!).

3.

In her book *Véra (Mrs. Vladimir Nabokov)*, on the life of Véra Nabokov, Stacy Schiff describes the Nabokovs settling in New York, where

---

* Andrew Field, VN, *The Life and Art of Vladimir Nabokov.* New York 1986, p. 207-208.

Vladimir "began tutoring three older women studying at Columbia, with whom he was pleased. Great lovers of Russia all, they appeared to him to 'brilliantly debunk the émigré preconception of the lacquered emptiness of the American mind' . . ."*

Stacy Schiff also describes the famous episode with the butterfly, but her eyes are on Véra: "She caught some of her first American butterflies that summer, as Leuthold chauffeured the family to California, from motor court to motor court, through Tennessee, Arkansas, Texas, New Mexico, and Arizona, a trip Véra hugely enjoyed. Some of this collecting she did in a knee-length black dress with a lace collar, a garment she could hardly have purchased with this kind of expedition in mind. She looked unwell, her skin more ashen than translucent, her cheeks sunken. On a crystalline morning in early June, on the south rim of the Grand Canyon, both Nabokovs triumphed lepidopterically, each in his own way. Vladimir set off with Dorothy Leuthold down a mule trail, where after a short walk he netted two specimens of what he recognized to be an undocumented *Neonympha*. When he returned to the Pontiac, where Véra and Dmitri were attempting to warm themselves, he discovered 'that right beside the car Véra had herself caught two specimens, sluggish with the cold, with nothing but her fingers.' Nabokov named his capture after Leuthold; he commemorated his success in 'On Discovering a Butterfly,' a poem that appeared in the *New Yorker* in 1943. Véra's parallel find went undocumented. A certain competitiveness crept into their collecting, for which the passion was primarily Vladimir's. 'I've had wonderful luck. I've gotten many things he didn't get,' Véra interrupted her husband to tell his first biographer.'"**

---

* Stacy Schiff, *Véra (Mrs. Vladimir Nabokov)*, 1999, p. 110.

** *Ibid.*, p. 115.

4.

Véra decided she'd prefer waiting with Dmitri by the car instead of risking the hike down to the canyon floor with Vladimir and Dasha. Her reason was the tedious, nagging sciatica, the result of her "migrations and anxieties," as she put it.

Dorothy, too, thought it best if she didn't hike down to the canyon floor because of a foolish mistake. She'd washed her underwear the night before and left it out, before she went to bed, to dry. The garment, however, was still damp in the morning and now she had to either give up or go; anything else would require time and locating a clothing store. The day was unexpectedly brisk for June. Luckily, she'd packed long woolen stockings that reached almost up her thighs and a long, warm skirt. She donned comfortable walking shoes and a snug windbreaker . . . Without confessing, of course, to the real source of her reluctance, she urged Nabokov to go off on his own, but he answered, as expected, that there would be no giving up. She acquiesced.

The day was marvelous, the sky a brilliant blue, the air as delicious and bracing as champagne. Leuthold and Nabokov were soon flushed from the hike and Dorothy became a little giddy. "Heavens, so much oxygen!" she said. She thought of those who say that anybody who doesn't believe the world is God's handiwork should see the Grand Canyon. The ruddy cliffs lent everything a vermilion cast. Even the marvelous air that went to her head like champagne had a reddish glow.

They followed a path into the canyon. At one moment Dorothy let Nabokov walk on ahead, saying she'd catch up in a minute, and when he'd moved on she raised her skirt, crouched down, and urinated. The bite in the air chilled her thighs. So when she rose to her feet she stepped back for a moment into a little hollow and, leaning against the cliff wall, she turned to face the sun. Though the day was cold, the sun warmed her face. Slowly Dorothy lifted her skirt. The luscious sunlight bathed her crotch and she adjusted her position by tilting her hips, like a solar panel, to the source of light. She was awash in warmth and felt a powerful sensation of well-being. The icy fire licked her thighs.

Just then Nabokov appeared. Dorothy hastened to lower her skirt but he gestured for her not to, indicating she mustn't move. Dorothy dropped her eyes. On the bushy triangle between her legs there shivered a butterfly. It seemed to have become ensnared in her curls and now was fluttering its reddish wings helplessly.

Nabokov froze and stared, spellbound, at Dorothy's pubis. The black, coarse, woolen stockings pulled up almost hip-high merely accentuated the tautness and whiteness of her skin. In the middle flamed the triangle covered with silken hairs, and here, on the burning bush, fluttered a brand new species, a butterfly with its wings a warm, Renoir-like, russet hue. Nabokov had never seen the likes of it before. He knelt, holding one arm outstretched with his palm signaling to Dorothy to be still, while with the other, the one in which he held the butterfly net, he reached ruefully toward Dorothy.

And here, against the stunning backdrop of the Grand Canyon, Dorothy saw Nabokov in crisp relief. Before her knelt this comic yet tragic figure of a boy in the body of a grown man, for whom a happy alignment of the stars—literature, butterflies, and a strong woman who with her brought him both fatherhood and fame—had conferred on him the legitimacy of an adult. Dorothy spread her legs ever so slightly. The butterfly, alarmed, fluttered yet stayed in place. Nabokov blushed crimson. Holding her skirt with one hand, Dorothy moved her other down slowly toward her crotch, which flamed with an almost surreal luster, toward the triangle, worshipped by her various boyfriends; her Miron cooed to it, calling it his "little vixen" . . . Lit by the bright sunlight, the wings of the butterfly shimmered on the ginger bush like magical flames. Dorothy caught the butterfly with her free hand, slid it tamely into her fingers, lowered her cupped fist into Nabokov's net, and released it . . .

He knelt before her, bowed by humility—like a comical Gabriel kneeling before the Virgin Mary—as she dropped her babe, as light as the breath of a butterfly (an angel?), into his net. He felt himself choke with boundless gratitude, and then, for a moment, he felt as if he were, himself, the glowing orange-winged babe. He knelt before Dasha just as his ancestors, the men of his class, had knelt before their buxom housemaids with names like Dasha and Masha, expecting from them quick, earthly, backstairs delights: a breast, a squeeze, some snatch . . . And he, the boy, thanked her for his prized butterfly.

Leuthold released her skirt. It dropped with a whoosh like a theater curtain. The two of them headed back uphill toward the *Pon'ka* where they were awaited by Véra and Miten'ka. An air of triumph shone from Nabokov's tanned visage; he looked like a bronze statue in the dazzling glow of the sun. From Leuthold's face—exactly as with well-schooled spies—shone nothing at all.

5.

Mentions of Dorothy Leuthold can be found in Vladimir Nabokov's letters to Véra. In a letter to Véra on March 19, 1941:

"I have written to Miss Ward, Chekhov, Dasha, Natasha, Lisbetsha."*

Dasha (Dorothy Leuthold), Natasha (Nathalie Nabokov) and Lisbetsha (Elisabeth Thompson) were the students whom Nabokov tutored in the Russian language. Apparently they were also more than tutees: Elisabeth Thompson babysat for Dmitri and took him out for strolls in Central Park, while Nathalie was Nabokov's cousin Nicolas's ex-wife. He "appropriates," "familiarizes," adapts the "alien" environment to his own, his intimate forms of speech, the lessening of potential danger through a process of linguistic "domestication" (Why does stranger always rhyme with danger? wonders Nabokov), as a taming of the alien, foreign, strange, and unknown by collecting, amassing, naming, taxonomy, cataloguing, which also includes a kill, a pin, a dissection; these are not strategies unique to the émigré narrative. During the trip from the East Coast to the West Coast, Dorothy's Pontiac was nicknamed the *Pon'ka*—the Russian diminutive for pony—for this very reason, a pony being a horse that was already given by nature a physically diminutive form. All strategies may be benevolently interpreted as a desire to fit in, embrace a new environment with amorous pretention, seduction, but they may also be camouflaged forms of a yen for power: how do we take the alien and foreign (and, therefore, hostile) and shrink it, make it inferior to us, vulnerable to subservience. By "appropriating" their names, Nabokov was pursuing the same approach with his students that he'd pursued with the butterflies he collected: impaling them on a board with a sharp pin, spreading their wings, describing them, labeling them (with a red label!**) Dasha, Natasha, Lisbetsha . . . In science as in art,

---

* Vladimir Nabokov, *Letters to Véra* (edited and translated by Olga Voronina and Brian Boyd). New York 2015, p. 443.
** "the immortality of this red label on a little butterfly," the last line of Nabokov's poem "On Discovering a Butterfly."

one finds the same thrill and procedures for observing the world and articulating observations, a thought Nabokov shared with Stephen Jay Gould.*

In a letter to Véra, November 9, 1942:

"I am healthy, eating plenty, taking my vitamins, and read newspapers more than usual now that the news is getting rosier. St. Paul is a stupefyingly boring city, only owls at the hotel, a bar girl looks like Dasha; but my apartment is charming."**

The first sentence in Nabokov's short note sounds more like the report a son might send his mother or a concerned sister than a letter a man would send his wife: he's healthy, eating well, taking his vitamins . . . After the dismissive observation that the city where he happened to be was boring, Nabokov seems to be claiming the right to mention the girl behind the bar who looked like Dasha. Perhaps he was thinking that Dasha, being of German descent, resembled other Minnesotan women, also German. Perhaps he simply thought the barmaid was plain like Dasha. In any case he'd written something Véra would appreciate, something requiring no further explanation for the two of them.

Nabokov said, somewhere, that two people in love behave like Siamese twins: one sneezes when the other sniffs tobacco (*V ljubvy nuzhno byt' kak siamskie bliznecy, odin chihaet, kogda drugoj njuhaet tabak*), which may sound less than romantic to many a reader, indeed such a vision for a romantic relationship might even be alarming. The perfect

---

* Stephen Jay Gould, "No Science Without Fancy, No Art Without Facts: The Lepidoptery of Vladimir Nabokov." In: *I Have Landed, The End of a Beginning in Natural History*, 2011.

** Vladimir Nabokov, *Letters to Véra*, p. 482.

romantic couple is, therefore, a sort of monstrosity, and a successful romantic bond is the willing embrace of a form of invalid functionality, with one half depending on, conjoined with, subservient to the other. In this sort of symbiotic love there must be perfect coordination for the love machine to operate. Hence it is the shortest path to the functionality of domination, i.e. the muffling of the beloved. Hence Humbert Humbert wished to sedate Lolita to gain control of her, hence Nabokov pinned the butterfly to the board and spread its wings to fully savor his victory. The hunter aspires to no fame but the glory of naming, in other words, nothing short of—God's glory!

> I found it and I named it, being versed
> in taxonomic Latin; thus became
> godfather to an insect and its first
> describer—and I want no other fame.

This is how our mind works, how we all conquer and adapt the world around us, in this sense we could all wear the red label "like Dasha" . . .

In a letter to Véra on December 7, 1942:
"Saw Dasha—took her out to a restaurant—she was awfully sweet and talkative."*

He was awfully sweet and talkative. As usual, he charmed everything in reach, both the living and the non-living, including her, Dasha, the plates and silverware, the table, the tablecloth, the waitress . . . As usual he was not interested in trivialities unless they provided "nourishment." She had learned how to gauge by his facial expression the degree to which he found something "nourishing." She'd know it by the gleam in his eyes, by the flame blazing suddenly somewhere deep

---

* Vladimir Nabokov, *Letters to Véra*, p. 484.

inside his pupils, by the muscles poised, somewhere in his gullet, to launch a long, thin tongue with arrow-like speed, coil it around the prey, and snap it back into his maw. The perfect hunter, much like a Madagascar chameleon, he was equipped with a long, lithe, supple tongue that unerringly nabbed its morsel.

He didn't ask how she was doing, what was new in her life, he was not a man for "small talk," though he did inform her that Véra was not in town and then he commenced with his "magic" tricks. Yes, he had to be heard and revered, even when his audience was merely a mousy little librarian. She felt they were playing a game of his choosing in which he was teacher and she student, and he'd invented the rules as well, so every wrong answer brought with it a punishment, amicable enough, but a punishment nevertheless. And the questions, heavens, they were so childish!

How far were migrating butterflies capable of flying on their gossamer wings? What was the largest span recorded for a pair of butterfly wings? How did one distinguish male butterflies from females? Why were butterflies so splendidly beautiful? Did they know of their beauty? Did they have lungs? Do they breathe? They breathe, she declared, though she wasn't certain, but in the depths of his pupils she spotted the flame. She knew in some corner of his mind he was already toying with the Russian tongue twister . . . *Dasha dyshit, Dasha-dusha, dusha dyshit, Dasha prinimaet dush . . .*

Nabokov penned Dasha's name on the white linen napkin and by it added a small plus sign. Do butterflies have a spine? Yes, they do. Minus. How many pairs of legs do butterflies have? Four legs, two pairs. Minus. Three pairs of legs, six legs all told. Minuses . . . On the white linen napkin a childishly clumsy scrawl took shape of a butterfly sketched in pen, little numbers squiggled across the white fabric with the cocky minuses Nabokov assigned to Dasha for her wrong answers and the impish plus signs he gave her for the answers she got right. Through how many stages does a butterfly metamorphose? Two? Four. Egg, larva, pupa, and imago. Minus . . . Nabokov shook his head, feigning dismay, he sketched his butterfly and the stages of its life cycle and dealt Dasha malicious little minuses . . . Dorothy had the feeling that right there in the middle of the small restaurant, before the eyes of all the diners, she'd first roll up the white napkin and then unfurl it like a magician's silk handkerchief, though no white dove, no butterflies would flutter out from underneath, only her, Dasha's, minuses and the occasional plus . . .

On what does the butterfly feed? Not steak, I trust! Indeed! Nabokov tossed her a magnanimous plus. So on what, if not steaks, does it feed? Flowers? Minus! If there are four stages in a butterfly's life cycle, then presumably at each stage it has different nutritional requirements. It feeds on flowers, said Dasha stubbornly. A caterpillar feeds on leaves, plants, fruits. In the pupa stage it eats nothing; when the butterfly emerges from the pupa it feeds on pollen and with its proboscis it sips the nectar . . . So, a flower. What do you suppose would happen if the metamophosis proceeded the other way round, from butterfly to pupa, from caterpillar to egg, she mused aloud and then regretted her silliness . . .

I have this friend, she said suddenly, rapping her fork on the plate on which her spaghetti was cooling, as if the gesture were demanding something definitive, that she be heard. "Oh ho," said Nabokov, with a barely noticeable grimace of displeasure, not at what she'd said but at the interruption . . . Dasha dushitsa, he said. She ignored his ironic interjection. He's a good poet, she said firmly. How can you tell? She looked at him. Nabokov apologized with a rueful shrug. Can you help

him in some way? What's his name? Miron Belochkin. Where's he
from? A Russian Jew, he came here from Harbin. So was it, pray tell,
this Russian "squirrel" who taught you to swear? It was. And what
does this Belochkin from Harbin do? He's busking as a clown, on the
street. Clowning? Literally? Literally, he's also a trained actor. Should
anything occur to me, I will let you know. She knew he wouldn't. Ah,
my Dorothy, my poor, dear Dorothy . . . She recoiled. This was the
first time he'd called her Dorothy. You're alone in the world, Dasha
dushitsa. Dasha, dearest, where are your companions? My companions! The Scarecrow, the Tin Man, and the Cowardly Lion. You don't
even have a Toto! I do, too, have companions. Whatever gave you the
idea that I don't?!

The conversation shifted away from the slightly strained exercise in
pretentious banter between the two adults and abruptly assumed a
subtle tinge of bitterness, which was, obviously, Dorothy's doing. The
dinner was over. Nabokov paid the bill and they rose to their feet. Are
you not going to take the napkin with you? he asked. She looked at
him and spotted on his visage that spark of the future, the same gleam
of sure fame in his eyes she'd seen in the Grand Canyon, a gleam
like the gaze on the faces of statues, medals, coins, and even postage
stamps. Dorothy felt slightly queasy. Heavens, what a boy, he's such
a boy, she repeated to herself with a sense of despair that seemed out
of proportion to the situation, and she was impatient for the moment
when they'd leave the restaurant and part ways.

Whether she wanted to or not, Leuthold thought of Nabokov many
more times. First when she read the poem in *The New Yorker* about
the troubling dissection of the butterfly that he'd, apparently, named
after her. And her childish prattle at the restaurant over dinner on
the topic of reverse metamorphoses came back to her on April 30,
1967, two years before she died, when her birthplace, her Waseca,

was devastated by a tornado that leveled almost all the homes. Who knows, perhaps on that "Black Sunday" she, Dasha, metamorphosed into Dorothy, and proceeded back to her egg.

6.

Dorothy Leuthold died in 1969. That year, perhaps two months before her death (on July 22, 1969), Nabokov, who had been living for five years with Véra in Switzerland, wrote a short poem in Russian, which he dedicated to Véra, of course. The poem contained only two verses, and the second, inspired by Nikolai Gumilyov, reads:

> And I will die not in a summerhouse,
> From gluttony and heat,
> But with a heavenly butterfly in my net
> On the summit of some wild hill.

The poem was written in Russian and the words *obzhorstvo* (gluttony) and *zhara* (heat) deal the reader an almost physical blow with their powerful, harsh sounds. The butterfly, an angel (weightlessness, transparency, beauty, fragility, coolness, spirituality) is perhaps the most natural antithesis to *gluttony* and *heat* (the earthly, carnality, heaviness, paralysis, ugliness). The poet pictures himself at the moment of his death on the summit of a hill, far from ugly, corporal, crass humankind to which he, regrettably, belongs. He prefers a solitary fate, a death not bound by a bed, the space delimiting the fundamental human activities (to beds we are born, in them we sleep, make love, bear children, wet, bleed, die). He chooses for himself a highly aestheticized death, with an angel ticket in his pocket (a butterfly in his net!), waiting at the metaphorical airport (on the hill's summit) to soar to eternity. This chilled, aseptic image is terrifying. The lone poetic subject at the moment of his imagined death has no need of human solace, there is no place here for the warm touch of a hand from his life-long helpmate, friend, companion (or did she, in his fantasies, predecease him?). The poetic subject here is alone with his obsession, his eternal companion, the butterfly (angel). This refusal to die in a summerhouse is perhaps merely a camouflaged acquiescence, a return to two photographs (back to the egg!) taken in 1907 at Nabokov's grandfather's summerhouse in Vyra. In one, Vladimir, an appealing-looking boy with long slender legs and tender knees, in light-colored shorts and white knee socks, a white shirt, a kerchief tied round his neck, sits in an armchair with a book on his lap. In the book, spread open like a giant butterfly, one can see small images of butterflies. In another, the scenography is slightly different, his mother Elena, dressed in white, is standing next to the boy. Nabokov's grandfather deeded the boy the summerhouse after his death, but Vladimir Nabokov never saw it again. Soon he would start changing countries like "counterfeit money," "hurrying on and afraid to look back," "like a phantom dividing in two," "like a candle between mirrors sailing into the sun" (verses from the poem "Fame," 1942).

So what is left, in that image, of the two lovers, the Siamese twins, where one is sneezing while the other sniffs tobacco? The twins seem to lack gender, but if they were gendered, then, in Nabokov's vision, they'd be two little boys rather than two little girls. So what remains of the boy—with his elegant, slender head, his calm (angelic?) gaze, with his face that in the photograph looks like a water lily in bloom, with his frame as lanky as a tropical liana—what is left of him? Had Leuthold been able to read these lines, she would, we assume, have seen in the Russian word for butterfly—*babochka*—the comic sabotage of this self-flattering, melancholic (or is it merely alpinistic?) death image. But who was Leuthold to know anything about that!

7.

There are two photographs of Leuthold (they can be found in the book, *Nabokov's Butterflies*). In one, she and Nabokov are seated on a tree trunk. The first thing one notices about her is her watch, and beyond the watch, her plain summer dress draped over her generous frame. In the second photograph are the three of them—Nabokov, butterfly net in hand and summer hat on head, Leuthold wearing glasses, in that same plain dress, with a purse—she has it on her lap and holds the handle with both hands—and Véra, a slender woman in slacks wearing a fetching bandana, with sunglasses—they stand leaning on Leuthold's Pontiac. Next to the Nabokovs, Leuthold looks plain but also somewhat less real, as if she'd made every effort to adapt her demeanor to the stereotype of the obliging "old maid," the mousy librarian, who is willing to go the distance and drive a family all the way across the country, because she doesn't know how better to spend her summer vacation than be of service to a writer, a great future writer. Had it not been for the trip, she probably would have done without a vacation and spent those days where she otherwise spent her life, among books, a fat, half-blind bookworm. As it was, she earned her entry ticket to eternity, she, the *Neonympha dorothea dorothea* . . .

PART
SIX

The Fox's Widow

There was a fox's widow once
And twelve wee kits were in her brood
Into the sun her kits she led
Into the sunlight on a hill,
    Dy-lee-doe, dy-lie-lee-doe dy-lie-doe
She sat them down to pick their fleas
Picked their fleas and wept her tears
How will your mother feed you now
A wee young kit, so small and shrewd,
    Dy-lee-doe, dy-lie-lee-doe dy-lie-doe
To his mother then he said:
Oh mother dear, now don't you cry,
You'll feed us easily by and by
Into the hunter's pouch we'll go
    Dy-lee-doe, dy-lie-lee-doe dy-lie-doe
Gracing the throats of the richest folk
In the Sultan's white city of Istanbul.

              —*Bulgarian folk song*

1.

Up and down jumps the little girl in a wonderfully regular rhythm, as light as a ball as she bounces. Up and down. Up and down. Other children tire after a time, they fall, wriggle around on the trampoline, giggle, push one another, make silly faces, eye their parents who stand, the hovering supervisors, around the trampoline. My little girl seems wrapped in an invisible membrane. Her face is calm and bright. She looks not at me, but straight ahead. Her lithe little body doesn't betray the slightest effort, her muscles are relaxed, she jumps as if jumping is her natural state, she's a bouncy ball. Her straight, short hair and bangs swing up on her forehead and drop down in regular rhythm. The sunbeams play over her hair. The girl radiates light. Not far from the trampoline shines the blue sea. Other children give up, new ones climb up onto the trampoline, but my little girl doesn't stop. Up and down, up and down. With her jumping she halts time. If she were to get down from the trampoline, fall, drop to her knees, catch her breath, she'd have to be growing up. Every moment she rests she invites unknown danger. Because as long as she jumps effortlessly into the air, as long as she's absorbed in the rhythm, no danger threatens. She is safe. She's as safe as Peter Pan.

2.

After asking the flight attendant for a glass of water I swallowed another five dark-pink two-hundred-milligram tablets of Ibuprofen, though I knew my back pain wouldn't let up. I'm a veteran, I call my back pain *mine* with the knowledge that I've earned the right. I've built it into my life as if it were my closest family member, my little adoptee, I feed it with pain pills the hue of raw meat, as if it were a household pet. It's the result of my "migrations and anxieties," as Véra Nabokov said somewhere. I remembered her words, I liked them, there was a comforting ring to them even if they were not entirely accurate. I should never have gone on the trip but I did; only five days, I said to myself. Yet the particulars were troublesome. With my stubborn optimism I never expect them to be, yet they always are. So it was that as I arrived in Rome, the first stop on a five-day reading tour, Rome–Milan–Turin, my back pain began its irritating march and all because of the cheap B&B, a fourth-floor walk-up. The risers on the stairs were far too steep. True, the step itself wasn't the real cause, the spasm in my back comes on in tandem with other, less tangible signals: internal jitters that have no visible origin, uneasy qualms at a situation we find ourselves coerced into against our will, a sense of betrayal that can be sniffed in the air like rain.

I am an "economy-class" writer. Writers are either economy-class or business-class, categorized by their media exposure and what they receive for their advance. The great majority of us are economy-class, while only a negligible minority are business-class. To be honest, I'd say it seems that those whose job it is to work with us writers do everything they can to clip our wings, regardless of class. Whatever the case, I am clearly economy-class, and the economy class is a breeding ground for misanthropy. The air in economy is thick with irritation at one's fellow travelers; the symptoms—lassitude, headache, suffocation—are identical to those arising from a shortage of negative ions. For years I've not been able to comprehend why whoever sits in front of me on a plane lowers the seat, though it's perfectly obvious that when they lower the seat, the seatback will mash my knees and the coffee I'm drinking will spill all over my lap, It seldom happens that a fellow traveler in front of me mercifully forgets to lower the seat. The gadflies are fond of boasting, strutting, flapping their wings, nesting into their seat, after all they paid for it, they wedge their fellow travelers in and let everybody else know that all the others are the same worthless human beings they are. Young women who travel in economy class are fond of flicking their tresses back over the seat, whipping the person sitting behind them with their hair. And at these and other similar gestures, my sullen mood rises from my stomach to my gullet, abrading it along the way. With economy class come cheap B&Bs in which the shower or the hot-water heater doesn't work; something essential is out of order at every one. Economy class further brings with it toting my luggage on my own; paying for the cab myself. The organizers deliberately neglect to settle such matters, they're trained to squeeze every ounce out of the economy-class writer's patience like toothpaste to the very end of the tube.

I recall with a dose of implausible cheer a literary gathering in London where the organizers sought financial support from the Austrian embassy, and the embassy accommodated us (us being several participants who were coming from the former Austro-Hungarian monarchy) in the attic of their spacious building. The attic was decked out in Alpine style, its walls paneled with rustic wood planks, replete with cuckoo clocks, Alpine landscapes, and antlers. All together it came across as a sort of retro-art installation, an Alpine sabotage, the secret cell of a terrorist group for disseminating Alpine kitsch planted in the heart of elegant Belgravia . . . Okay, I admit my overactive imagination may have added the antlers, but the Embassy staff—largely

Polish, who also used the attic, smoked on the little balcony, and did everything they could to thwart our access to the bathroom and the telephone—was no embellishment. Theirs was an innocent game of torment, a bit of "teasing" that the "attic folk" had devised for us: instead of the empathy we might have met, we were put through a mild version of "cousinly" malice.

With far less cheer I recall a *writers retreat*, a one-month residency, in a Middle-European city, all under the auspices of a dubious EU cultural project. The people behind the "project" were a local figure of some sort and his female companion. Thanks to his EU connections, he started a writers' retreat in his apartment, and the rent, maintenance, and modest stipend for the visiting writer were financed by the dubious EU source. Because of the nature of his "project," the local figure arrived at the notion that he, too, could write, and in this was supported fervently by his companion, twenty years his senior, who was determined not to spend her dotage in a hole in the wall. As soon as I arrived, the local figure offered me evidence in the form of translations of his autobiographical prose into Estonian, Urdu, and Korean. He boasted that during a trip to South Korea he'd established prestigious literary connections, and after my stay the next writer would be a young South-Korean. This Dickensian couple (Wackford Squeers and wife) was running what was, in fact, a writers' orphanage, and the EU and the local authorities had given their blessings in this sluggish Middle-European town where even the town fountain sprayed in slow-motion. It wasn't as if I'd sought them out. They'd cajoled me into coming with ingratiating pleas, vaunting their "project" as a major plus both for the town and the visiting writer. I, who can never get used to the fact that culture and business have begun so handily cohabiting in a bourgeois marriage, was lured in only to flee like a bat out of hell a few days later.

The chances are slim that economy-class writers will ever cross paths with their business-class counterparts; the honoraria grow ever slimmer, the habit of failing to pay the contracted fee is fast becoming commonplace, the likelihood that the economy-class writer will throw up his hands grows more real. While an honorarium is indeed worth kicking a fuss up over, there is little point in battling over a tip. All this, of course, is well-trodden ground for the taskmasters: the publishers, those who organize the literary events, the people in charge of publicity, all those who live off literature and on literature, and all those who are cynically certain that the author's place is the lowest in the chain. And, in fact, they're right: the author's place on the food chain is indeed the lowest.

Aching bones, foul moods, gripes, backache . . . I bribe my bad back with odd tidbits, capsules of New Zealand green-lipped mussels, also called *kuku* and *kutai*, and shark's-liver oil extract. I lubricate my ossified joints because my ability to ossify in a flash has been imprinted upon my bones and my psychogram like a tattoo. I'm gradually turning to stone while I look the world in the eye and pay for my pigheadedness with larger and larger banknotes of pain. Most people look prudently away, they don't stare where they shouldn't, they don't see, they don't hear, they don't protest, they don't gripe, they keep their mouths shut, they buckle, while I'm left wrestling not only with my bad back but also with the full knowledge of the futility of all my confrontations. Never have I succeeded in budging anything, because one law alone rules this world of ours: the powerful are the sole ones in charge. Everything else is "fairy tales for little children," "claptrap," "tell me another."

True, there's also an exhilarating ingredient in the cocktail of back pain and gripes. Grumbling, grousing, moaning, whinging, groaning,

and bellyaching have a palliative effect. They act like Diazepam.
Griping brings with it a kind of mental spryness. A grumbler is so
drained after a time that he drops off to sleep in the end like a well-fed
reptile, just as I did, no longer caring a whit about the cramped seat
and thoughtless fellow travelers. And besides I was, myself, no exemplar of courtesy: I was started from my brief doze by my own snores.

3.

In the morning she gets up, enveloped in the warm fog of sleep. She's
quiet. If she's in a good mood, she waves (slender twig!), signaling
she's seen me but isn't in the mood for talk. At breakfast she always
drinks milk, only milk, though she's nearly twelve. She drinks it down
in long, powerful gulps, sometimes taking a straw and sucking it up
with strong sips. She doesn't eat, she crumbles up her bread, wads it
into balls, plays with it, chewing bores her.

She drinks her milk, she doesn't see me, as if she's still dreaming
she whispers something to herself, scribbles in the air as if writing
on an invisible computer screen. Sometimes, she, already slender,
grows wispier yet, her lavender veins show through her tender hair,
her temples go pale, her pupils darken, a gray shadow slips over her
small face and it's as if my little girl sinks. And then she pulls out of
her momentary internal slump and her energy zings.

She calls me Aunt (stern, blunt, unusual), Auntie Em (Where did
she get that from?), Super Auntie, Auntie Dearest, Aunteroo (Where
does she find them all?), or sometimes Tante (her French lessons?).
"Auntie" she saves for special intonations. She employs an endearing,
querulous tone when she'd like to tell me something but first wants
to check to see if I'm listening (Hey, Auntieee?). A scolding tone with

which she feigns reproach is used to show me she knows I'm not being serious (Auuuuntie!).

Seldom does she call me by name. We seem to use the name of a person readily only when we're not emotionally attached. I don't use her name either, I vary the substitutes, such as "pumpkin," "cupcake," "mouse" . . . Who knows, this may be a subconscious superstition at work. A name could, possibly, attract something like an evil ear. Indigenous people do not utter their spouse's given name. In indigenous communities, parents seldom praise the goodness and beauty of their children out of fear that the Evil Eye might steal a glance at their child and wreak havoc. So we use "he" and "she" and "it" for a child.

When she speaks of her grandmother (my mother), she uses words without restraint. "Grandma lives in her grave," she says. When she speaks of her mother, she's more cautious. "That's when mama was around," she'll say. Never does she say, "But that's when mama wasn't around any more." She evades facing that her mother is gone, though she likes going to the cemetery with her father, especially in May, to check and see whether the rose bush they planted by the tombstone has bloomed. And though the names of my father (with a five-pointed star above it), my mother, and her mother are carved onto the headstone, she associates the place only with her grandmother. Her grandfather she never met, he died years ago; she remembers her grandmother; she won't speak of her mother. Hence, as far as she's concerned, only her grandmother *lives* in the grave.

4.

A friend of mine once tried to explain the difference between "us" and "them," though he wasn't very clear about who the "we" and the "they" were. My friend was on his way back to Europe from a stay in the United States, and an elderly traveler sat next to him. When he asked her where she was going, she said: "To Europe. Munich . . . Isn't Munich in Europe?" And having been reassured that Munich is, indeed, in Europe she fell asleep and didn't wake until the plane landed at the Munich airport.

"See the difference? That woman wasn't sure of whether Munich was or was not in Europe, but she was one hundred percent certain she'd get there. That's why she fell asleep so cheerfully. We,"—here my friend enrolled me, without even asking, in his "club"—"we come from a different culture, we can never be sure of anything, there is nothing on which we can rely. We can't be sure that we are who we are, that tomorrow we'll be who we were today; we aren't sure of the language we speak, voilà, it turns out we're speaking three languages when we thought we were speaking only one; we can't be sure of our borders, of the regime, of our history, of our country (every so often we wake up in another country without ever having gotten out of bed!); we can't be sure whether the images playing out before our eyes are real or not. We don't trust anybody, because they're forever betraying us. Can you see what a difficult, exhausting, vast, and intransigent frustration this is? So this is why while *they* peacefully snore, *we* worry. We fret about all sorts of things! While the passenger next to me snored, I was mid-air over the ocean, rifling in my mind through all the worries of the world, all the injustices it has visited upon me, all the historical blows . . . I went back as far as my Turkish oppression. And all the while in my mind I was helping the pilot, one should never be cavalier about pilots . . . !"

My friend said all this with a healthy dose of self-irony, we chuckled, but what he said was true. This might come across as a comical exaggeration to the uninitiated ear, a breezy lie, but we knew we were victims of the truth that we trot out as a lie to give us the room to process it. Why do I think back on this episode? I notice that over the years I've come to sympathize more with my highstrung friend. I feel an instinctive bond with the "highstrung" types, the people who mutter to themselves in public, quibble loudly with invisible collocutors. The elderly traveler buffered her deep airborne sleep with ignorance of where she was headed, or simply with being at an age when people are sleeping more. I feel a bond with her, as well. Unlike my "highstrung" friend she is a healthy human being. And as far as I'm concerned, in my thoughts I, too, am helping the pilot more often these days.

Etched in my mind is a scene from a recent movie where a dead man lies on the floor in the fetal position in the half-dark of a room. By the corpse glows the little screen of his cell phone, the only living thing in the dark, a glowing heart. The dead man's hand on the floor is reaching for the device, a straw at which he's grasping, the life source. I can't say exactly why it is that this scene moves me so deeply. Even if it wasn't designed to serve as a parody, that's what it is. At night in the half-dark at my B&B, curled up in the fetal position, lit by the bluish light of my cell-phone screen, I flicked through the headlines like a madwoman . . . "Again stirs the beast"! Some thirty miles from Hekla, the stirring beast is Eyjafjallajökull, the volcano that spewed ash a few years ago over all of Europe. With the news item there was a video clip: thick smoke billows from the volcano, looking like vast mounds of sheep's wool. The clouds changed color, from sooty to dark-gray to light-gray and white. Nothing was visible but the terrifying, threatening wool. At first I thought the video had been made in black and white to satisfy a filmmaker's yen for "artistic effect." Apparently during such eruptions, where a volcano spews billows of smoke and nothing else, the surrounding area does become black and white, perhaps as it was at the moment of its origin.

Mesmerized by the scene, I played the video over and over. We live in a time of the theatricalization of everything; acting is no longer about somebody acting as somebody or something else, but about each of us being forced to act ourselves. Everything is "art"; even the photogenic volcano was acting itself to perfection. The world is inundated by "art projects," such as a heap of anonymous naked bodies in front of an artist's camera acting a heap of anonymous naked bodies, such as textile-industry workers who've been laid off acting textile-industry workers who've been laid off on a theater stage, such as executioners brandishing their swords, declaring, as they do so, why they'll be decapitating their victims . . . We are all forced to take part in "recreational, creative, therapeutic workshops," as the lingo of the modern "creative industry" would have it. Politicians act the politician, Donald Trump acts Donald Trump, Hillary Clinton acts Hillary Clinton. And refugees find themselves roped into "recreational, creative, therapeutic workshops," and there, through the ministrations of artists, they are transformed from living people into symbols and metaphors, into a "typical refugee narrative"; into *migration literature*, into *miglit*—a term that has already taken hold in the faddish slang of literary scholarship; into sculptures of human figures on which, where the head should be, there's a barbed-wire-wrapped suitcase, symbolizing, of course, unwelcoming borders. Even the cell phone is no longer a communications device, but an essential piece of refugee luggage, and sneakers are part of "migrant chic," symbolizing the migration of sixty million people according to the official count. This vast number registered briefly on the global gauge of human emotion and then at the behest of life that moves on (always at the behest of life that moves on) it faded from view. Everything is acting, the happiest moments of our lives are stage-set like performances. The births of our children are performances in which more and more guests take part; they are the favorite themes of video recordings where the baby's first whimpers are annotated with "creative" subtitles. Maybe this, too, is part of my momentary (momentary?) falling-out with my "profession." Is it that I'm not acting the role of writer well enough? Maybe I should over-play my role so the audience can play its role as it should. Why do I so doggedly insist on authenticity at a time when fakers are the only ones who are taken seriously? Am I not, after all, involved here in an "acting" task, "presenting" my new book?

Curled in the fetal position in the dark, I played the video with the raging Icelandic Eyjafjallajökull volcano as dense smoke streamed out of the crater. I played it again and again until I sank into an equally dense sleep . . .

5.

Too often I'm unable to decipher the reasons for her reactions. This is because I'm not with her all the time, and when we do get together I'm supposed to be Santa Claus, while she is the "good little girl." Never, for instance, will I be able to discover why she behaved so wildly when she and her father visited me briefly in Amsterdam. Was she nine? I took them to the Van Gogh museum, she gamboled about the museum like a restless puppy that keeps bringing a ball to its master's feet and waits for him to throw it. I couldn't grasp why she so avidly sought to draw attention to herself at the museum, as if Van Gogh were her rival. At one moment I nabbed her, steered her over to a painting, held her little head with my hands and pointed her face at the painting.

"Now, look!" I said.

In the painting was a pair of shoes, one of Van Gogh's paintings from that series. She quieted down, listened to my praise of the painting, and then I saw she'd dropped her eyes, she'd been staring down the whole time, she refused to look up. We went on to the next one and tried again. Now her father joined us, and he, too, made admiring comments, but she insisted on shutting her eyes tight. Why she so fiercely defied the ritual of a museum visit I don't know. Painting was one of her favorite activities, and "art class" her favorite subject in school.

Once my bad back kicked in so painfully that I couldn't move at all. She came solemnly to my bedside and pushed a drawing under my nose.

"What's that?" I asked.

She didn't answer, instead she asked . . .

"Are you better?"

"No."

She ran back to her room and soon returned, her drawing showing a few changes.

"How about now?"

She'd drawn a rainbow on the paper with thick layers of pastels and I finally realized what it was that I was supposed to say . . .

"Now I feel much better. Thank you, mouse."

How she'd come up with the idea that drawings have curative qualities, I don't know. There's a story by a Croatian writer about a little girl who believed that running under a rainbow would turn her into a boy, but she couldn't have heard that story yet in school, she was too young for that.

She still enjoys making pictures. Her greatest pleasure used to come from the physical, tactile side of painting. She loved big sets of wooden pencils and pastels, water colors and tempera, then the plasteline, brushes, pencil sharpeners, and erasers I brought her. Especially the erasers. Why erasers? This will remain a mystery. She complained that her erasers were always disappearing. This gave us the opportunity to devise a household sprite, the Eraser Gobbler, that snatched her erasers at night. When she was littler her favorite game was "rain."

"It's raining!" I'd shout and then we'd both reach for pencils and drum the pencil tips on the paper . . . "Rain! Rain! Rain." She loved dipping her fingers in paint and leaving fingerlines on paper or printing with stamps in different shapes that we'd carve from potatoes. Like a little enchantress who steers the winds, she was fond of flinging around the room little square drawings she called *Storm, Blizzard, Cloud Burst,* and *Chaos in the City.* Once she painted a sheet of paper in many colors and then tore it all to tiny pieces, piled the pieces in a tin box, sprinkled them with water, and shut the lid. This was her experiment, who knows how she imagined the outcome. When she was in particularly high spirits she'd draw heart after heart in electric pink colors, then cut them out and strew them along behind her, trailing little heaps of hearts in her wake.

I cheered her on, till once she told me . . .

"You like what I make only because you love me."

It was true but not entirely: I really thought her fierce little paper escapades showed an artistic gift. I have kept one, about 4" x 4" (the size she liked best), where on a cut-out sheet she arranged a somewhat smaller paper napkin with a design in such a way that she contrasted the structures of the papers and white hues. Then she sewed the two sheets of paper together, a little angled, on the diagonal, with thick black thread and big stitches.

"Kazimir Malevich couldn't have done better!" I said.

"Who's Kazimir Malevich?" she said, intrigued by the unusual first and last name. But as soon as I'd reach for a book or the internet to show her who Malevich was, she'd already lose her interest, or pretend she had.

Was she wilfully resisting growing up? After all what was so attractive in the grown-up world that she'd be so eager to hurry in that direction? Until now she could only learn that old people like her grandmother get old and die; that grown-ups like her mother can be young and still die; that grown-ups work, but they can, against their will, lose their job, as her father did; yes, all in all, the adult world is not safe, nor is it particularly fun.

I've never met a child who plays with greater zest than she. One needs a partner to play, but she wasn't choosy: the "other" could even be the battery-operated hamster she received for her birthday and with which she could play for hours without boredom. She drank in her games, they intoxicated her, she guzzled them to the last drop, to the point of physical exhaustion. Once, despite her father's explicit instructions, I let her play with other girls in the courtyard. She'd been outside for quite a while, and then there was a downpour, the voices of the children in the yard stilled, and finally there she was, drenched to the skin, shivering. She demanded an umbrella so she could go on playing under it. I refused and asked her to change her clothes. She raced for the door, I was quicker. I locked it and took the key.

She flew into a rage. Her shrieks tore at the surface of my skin, a pain, either imaginary or real, such as I'd never known before. There is only one sound that may have shocked me as deeply, the voicing of a female fox, a vixen, which I heard once on an amateur video clip. I'd be happy never to hear it again.

"I hate you! You can't keep me from playing outside! You're not my mother! My father's the only one who can make me come in . . ." she was choking with fury.

I reminded her I had let her go out despite her father's instructions to keep her in. And he'd clearly forbidden her to go out because she had homework due the next day.

She did not give up. She snatched my cell phone, threatening to call him and say I wasn't letting her go out, and then, incensed—she was stymied by not being able to figure out how to find the number—she flung the cell phone onto the floor in a rage and went on with her insufferable shrill screeching . . .

"I hate school! I won't go! I hate it! I'll never go to school again! I-i-i- haaaate iiiiit," she shrieked as she shivered.

"You'll crack the windowpanes with all this screeching! The other children will go to school and grow up. You'll have nobody left to play with," I said.

"Then I'll go to Germany and play with anybody I like!" she screamed.

I don't know where she'd picked up the notion that children in Germany can play with anybody they like.

"Kids in Germany go to school and grow up, too."

"Then I'll drink from a magic bottle and shrink down so small that I'll always be able to play with the little kids," she clutched at the comforting thought. (Aha, here we are, this she must have picked up from *Alice in Wonderland*, I thought.)

The comforting thought did give her comfort. As did the warm shower I coaxed her into, and the towel I wrapped her in, her, the angry, soaking-wet little bird against whom the laws of humankind had conspired.

6.

Publishers and other organizers of literary events are on the lookout for ways to squeeze a little money, often out of the embassies of the countries where their authors come from, and in the process they draw the author into uncomfortable situations. They scrounge as best they can to cover the costs of the translation or promotion of the book, the publishing costs or the author's honorarium. Although these are negligible sums, the embassies and the publishers have no money. Publishers explain this by saying that the books of the writers for whom they're seeking support don't sell. The embassies reply that this is not their concern, and, of course, they're right. The economy-class authors are willing victims one way or another, and they usually have no idea of the little deals struck behind their backs.

This time I happened to learn of the "deal" for the Croatian embassy in Rome to cover the expenses of my short tour through Italy. I didn't object: the ambassador was an old friend. He did his job, apparently, with competence and without patriotic delirium or the promotion of any personal business, literary, or sundry interests of his, the sort of things that usually accompany the diplomatic representatives of small, recently established statelets.

After the literary event my friend, his wife, and I spent a pleasant, warm evening filling in the gaps of some twenty years since the time when each of us had gone our separate way and the decade or so since we'd last seen each other. It was one of those "life writes novels" conversations. If our stories had been written up as a novel it would be such pulp fiction that we'd have had to pay the "pulp tax," I said. We reminisced about the Yugoslav "pulp tax," the mildest form of censorship, a tax on sleaze and sensationalism but also a helpful filter, which, in the general circulation of cultural goods, contributed somewhat to preventing the incursion of that ugly, stinking pond scum that, during the collapse of Yugoslavia, surfaced with such a vengeance. Ever since, the last twenty years or so, life has been mired in scum, in every sense of the word, sludge, slime, bilge, and murk. We've been swamped by pond scum, astonished at its tenacity. Some stopped holding their breath, meanwhile, and sank, some of us made it out onto the other shore, but most have stayed right where they were. Of these, a few have cultivated an almost inhuman capacity for survival while others have stayed on the surface by treading water quietly and unobtrusively, and a third group has come to rule the swamp, ravaging every other life form but the scum. I cannot expunge from my memory that moment when the scum surfaced, following a powerful underwater upheaval, and for a full quarter-century now I've been coming ashore and surveying the stench of the fetid swamp, exactly as if I were being paid for the job.

The Croatian consul had sent a driver (a homeland war veteran, no doubt) to meet me in Milan, the second stop on my brief Italian tour. At the bookstore where the public event was scheduled, a fellow countrywoman of mine who lived in Milan and was married to an Italian was waiting for me impatiently. I'd met her somewhere before but couldn't retrieve her name. With her was a young woman wearing a slightly pained expression, a member of the Croatian consular staff (no doubt the daughter of a homeland war veteran who'd earned her degree in Croatian Studies, funded by a scholarship for the children of homeland war veterans). The two of them perched in the front row like nuns. I now know by heart the body language and the seating strategies of my compatriots from halls at similar literary events. My countrymen generally keep their hands stuffed in their jacket pockets and seem loath to take them out, as if at any moment they might draw a gun. The Italian critic who was there to moderate the event hadn't yet opened his mouth when my countrywoman spoke up to warn me that I should know how many Croats in Italy disagreed with my thinking. I asked if we might leave the topic of differences in "thinking" for later, when the time came for questions from the audience. When the moderator asked the audience for questions, my countrywoman asked again whether I knew what Croats in Italy thought of me. She was now positioning herself as spokesperson for all the Croats in Italy, though what she was really angling for was the chance to hold forth about the little country to which the world owed such a debt of gratitude for the invention of the necktie, about Croats' feats of heroism during the homeland war, about the little, charming, exquisite, Catholic, European, patriotic land that had thrown off the fetters of totalitarianism, communism, Yugoslavism, Titoism, the Serbs, and Balkan turpitude, to return at long last to its authentic Croatian self. I asked if we might set aside questions about the Croats for the moment, as most of the people in the audience were there to discuss my book—just out in its Italian translation—rather than the Croats. I was bluffing, of course, I couldn't know what the people in the audience were there for. She quieted down, at least briefly, but as soon as I opened my mouth to respond to a question from the audience, she began chatting in stage whispers with the young staff member from the consulate.

My compatriots are often of a particular type; they trudge off to literary events of this kind, whine, gripe, froth at the mouth, but they are not capable of voicing a position of their own or defending it. They arrive, self-important, scowling, indignant, but quickly deflate and retreat, it's clear they've come wanting something, but literary events are not their ideal milieu, they're daunted by the public exposure. This is why they feel best in a pack of like-thinkers or in front of a computer screen on their Facebook page. Here they beat their chest, "share," "like," "hate," snarl, stick out their tongues, wait for their stagnant circulatory system to jolt into action, send blood to the brain, come alive, buzz, jut their proboscis, gape, bare their dog teeth . . .

This time (which I'd learn only two months hence) the internet assault was led by an Italian who professed to Croatian roots that had pushed him over the edge. He posted his "pics" on Facebook of the pages of my books (in Italian) which he'd slashed with scissors, he threatened to sue me, that I'd be banned from setting foot on Croatian soil and all its islands, that he'd skin me alive. The furious Italian, however, was charmed by Croatian women, those who use as their "Face" icon a woman's eye reflecting a Croatian flag, or something resembling it, with the national red-and-white checkerboard emblem superimposed. As a sign of support for the crazy Italian, an anonymous staff member from the Milan consulate joined in, trailing heaps of little yellow smiley faces convulsed with laughter.

All in all, I was left with no satisfaction. Had the hunt been an intelligent exchange and my hunters literature lovers there would, perhaps, have been something for me to take away from it all. They were, however, utterly ignorant. They weren't even capable of reciting a verse by one of the Croatian national bards. They were out for blood, plain and simple. And saddest of all, there was nothing free-thinking to their hunt. Only in the pack would they join in and doltishly follow the scent they knew so well . . .

"When you call people pond scum that means you're respecting them as your adversaries . . ." announced an old friend of mine from Zagreb whom I ran into while I was in Milan. We knew each other from somewhere, maybe university, I couldn't place her, and though we'd never been close, there we were, conversing about "politics." I'd grown accustomed to the way all conversations with my compatriots end up being about politics or about the visible evasion of talk about politics.

"By branding them as scum you didn't fix anything," she said, and she was right.

"You wonder how our power-mongers haven't lost steam, but it's the new, younger, stronger, and stupider ones who keep cropping up. Surely you've leafed through the Croatian schoolbooks and seen the score: Partisans out, Ustashas in. Children can no longer distinguish between Mickey Mouse and Adolf Hitler, and even if they could, their knowing would make no difference. Croats everywhere are licking church altars and practicing the knee-jerk fascist salute "Ready for the homeland" . . . And besides, neo-fascism, big deal, like so what, there's plenty to go around and extra left over for export: the Serbs, the Poles, the Hungarians, the Greeks, everybody's doing it . . . Who can fill all the holes from which the stupidity yawns?! Even if you flee one place, the stupidity will be waiting for you elsewhere, the way death lurks in the tale *When Death Came To Samarra* . . . If a person can't adapt, it's time to bite his tongue. Fascism is part of our folklore. Today it's cool to be fascist. Nobody in his right mind gets worked up about them except a handful of losers like yourself. You wield your puny paper sword and think those big strapping oafs are intimidated, guys who'd happily tattoo the checkerboard emblem on their tongue if they could! Chill, girlfriend, these things are so much shallower than you know," she said.

"Shallow?"

"Listen, when my daughter was a kid I bought her a bichon . . . Remember Fluffy, Anči?" she said to her daughter, who responded with icy silence, eyes glued to the screen of her smartphone.

"A Bichon Frise, the curly-haired Bichon, they're those adorable, little, white, playful, friendly dogs, live toys. Ours was so sweet it never even barked. The trouble began when we took it out for walks. As soon as our little Fluffy showed up on their radar, the racket would be deafening, the other dogs were poised to tear her to pieces. All the dogs behaved the same way, regardless of breed and size. We asked our vet. He told us our Fluffy was too refined and pure so the other dogs didn't think of her as one of their own; they didn't even recognize her as a dog. He advised us to roll her in dog shit. This was the only way to socialize her with her ilk. Only when they smell the shit will the dogs accept her. Pure and scentless, she was like a canine parody to them, not a dog. People are like dogs. Nobody likes being shut out. You know how good old Krleža put it . . . 'Society smells vile but it's cosy. Solitude is—empty. We know full well how things look under another's tail, but without all the sniffing there's no life' . . ." said my acquaintance, inspired suddenly by Miroslav Krleža.

Her daughter, who had perfected an uncanny ability to self-hibernate, still hadn't looked up from her smartphone.

"So did you roll her in shit?" I asked.

"Who?

"Fluffy?"

"We gave her to Grandma . . . Didn't we, Anči?" said my friend, but received no response.

My acquaintance was in Milan with her daughter visiting a graduate program at some supposedly famous design program.

"Everything today is about design . . ." I said, though what I wanted to say was, "Everybody today wants to go into design . . ." but stopped myself at the last minute, realizing this might sound a bit harsh to my acquaintance's ear. I don't know why, but while my acquaintance, her daughter, and I sat in Café Madeira, for a second I thought I'd spotted a flash, reflecting in her eye, of the red and white checkerboard emblem. I sincerely hope I was wrong. Meanwhile, I remembered where we'd met. She was a student of Indology; the study of South Asia was all the craze when I was a student and she was a friend of my boyfriend at the time who was wild about India . . .

Later I thought of her story about the bichon. I wondered how long it would take for the detail of the support provided by the Croatian embassy in Rome in promoting my tour through Italy to reach the ears of the Croatian media. Though the sum of money they provided—rubber-stamped by the municipality of Zagreb for the Rome embassy and passed on by the Rome embassy to my Italian publisher—was less than the price of the pair of shoes the previous Croatian ambassador to the United States (a poet, my colleague!) had purchased at a swanky shop on Madison Avenue in New York, a little article appeared about the subsidy in the Croatian daily press a month or two after my tour. The thrust of the article wasn't so much to raise eyebrows at the amount of support, but to let it be known that the Croatian authorities were backing my literary "internationalization." This was the ritual of the public smearing the bichon with shit. I may be flattering myself, but this might have been a signal to my old friend, the Croatian ambassador in Rome, that the time had come for him to pack his bags.

7.

I could imagine just how overjoyed she'd be when I shook a great pile of chocolates out in front of her that I'd picked up in a chocolate shop in Turin, and what fun she'd have inviting her girlfriends over for chocolate pizza, chocolate spaghetti, when she offered them a cell-phone-shaped piece of chocolate, a little chocolate purse, a chocolate key chain, a chocolate comb, toothpaste made of chocolate, chocolate lipstick . . .

"So when will you grow up?" I'd like to ask, but don't.

She looks at me, rolls her eyes, shrugs, whistles, puffs air (pooh-pooh-pooh!), giggles, scribbles words in the air, pouts, but doesn't respond. Her true answer would be: "Never!" And when I see how lively, playful, and radiant she is—my little minnow—I'm overwhelmed by the thought: What if even I don't want her to grow up!

I notice she finds it hard to give up her toys. She hasn't entirely discarded the Barbies yet, so though they aren't out on the shelves, they're still stowed away somewhere in her room. The Teletubbies, the Smurfs, Fifi, Dora, and Miffy lie hidden in real and mental boxes and are still giving signs of life. Their traces are strewn about, in the Dora shampoo bottle, on T-shirts with Miffy's face, Smurf socks . . . She's not ready to relinquish them, say her goodbyes, they're family. She still watches Tom and Jerry with the same delight. She still prefers cartoons to children's animated features. She doesn't watch movies for grown-ups, they bore her, though she is fond of the Turkish series *Suleiman the Magnificent.* By her age I'd already seen a large number of grown-up Hollywood movies, but many things were different back then. She doesn't like the feature-length, animated, 3-D hit movies; once she even burst into tears when we were at the movies, and she hasn't gone back since. With a pleasure entirely inscrutable to me, she still watches a cartoon that stars a sponge, though I could have sworn the character was a slab of Swiss cheese. "Auuuuntie, he's not cheese, he's a sponge!" she said with a reproachful tone as if the difference were vast, and then she added . . .

"And his name is Bob!"

Recently, her notebooks, drawing pads, and the walls of her room have been populated by girls; they're legion, I find it difficult to tell them apart, they all look the same, they all have big, shiny doe-eyes. All these characters come from the same "full package," including cartoons, video games, "webisodes" of a web series, books, dolls, T-shirts, souvenirs. The package is the work of a major American multinational company for producing toys (Barbie is their offspring!), which only means that millions of little girls all over the world already know who is who in this new, wide-branching family. The whole story is an indigestible eclectic salad—salted with a dash of Harry Potter—about teenage girls attending a boarding school. The school is situated in Fairy Tale World. The characters are divided into "royals," being "those who accept their fairy tale destinies," and "rebels," being "those who want to write their own." The boarding-school students are the children of famous fairy tale characters: if they break the rules and try to change their destiny, the stories they have inherited will disappear and they, too, will vanish.

Snow White's daughter attends the school, and Sleeping Beauty's daughter, the White Rabbit's daughter, the daughter of Odette (the queen of the swans in *Swan Lake*), of the Queen of Hearts (from *Alice in Wonderland*), of Beauty and the Beast, of the Cheshire Cat, Cinderella's daughter, Red Riding Hood's daughter, Alice's son (*Alice in Wonderland*), Hansel and Gretel's children, Humpty Dumpty's, Robin Hood's, and Eros's adopted daughter, who has fallen here from Olympus. The children have their parents' genes, their powers and skills, they repeat the lines of their parents, fall in love with each other, and conspire. The children are notable for their business acumen; Cinderella's daughter is already earning pocket money at the Glass Slipper Shoe Shop, Justine Dancer, daughter of Grimm's *Twelve Dancing Princesses,* plans to open a dance studio, and the daughter of a couple of unnamed narrators, herself a "narrator-in-training," also has aspirations ("Just because I'm destined to be the narrator doesn't mean I don't want to have my own story.").

The girls are represented as cloying "young ladies" and "princesses," teenage "models," "shoppers," mini-women who speak in quavering voices, just as they'll speak when they grow up, if they ever do. They are petite female clones with big heads (from a surfeit of wavy hair); they teeter along unsteadily on high high heels and "click" on their smartphones, the devices they use instead of the more traditional magic wand. The boys are no better—they all look like Justin Bieber.

As she introduced me to her new idols with delight, she breezed through the exceedingly long list of names, explaining which of these girls had mastered which skill and how I might tell them apart.

Meanwhile my head was spinning. And when I realized that each episode ends with the words "The end is just the beginning," I thought with horror that this generation of cartoon creatures will engender some future generation of cartoon creatures, and I cautiously asked my little girl whether she might be better advised to direct her attention to their "parents" and read *Alice in Wonderland* or the fairy tales by the brothers Grimm.

"You never like the things I like," she said in a sad voice.

"Not true. I like everything you like, but you'll find it easier to understand who the daughter of the Mad Hatter is if you first get to know her daddy . . ." I lied.

"But I do know who the Mad Hatter is."

"How?"

"From the cartoon."

"Okay, then, fine . . ." I said.

She heard the light, sour touch in my voice.

"So do you know my friends' names?" she asked.

"Well let's see, there's Thea . . ."

"And?"

"And the little one, and the two sisters, the ones living in the apartment above yours? Their names?"

"They live two floors above us . . ."

"Okay, a floor or two doesn't matter . . ."

"Does too!"

"Sorry, it's . . ."

"How can you not know where my best friends live?! And you don't even know their names!"

"I do, I just forgot them this minute."

"So what are their parents called?"

"I'm not going to remember what their parents are called, am I."

"Well you yourself said I should be getting to know the parents!"

"Oops, I meant the literary parents, what I meant was you should first get to know the real Alice and only then that son of hers, Elistar . . ."

"His name is Alistair."

"Okay, fine, Alistair."

"So what's my favorite cartoon?"

"I know you used to love the one about Miffy . . ."

"That one is for really little girls . . ." she said.

"Mouse, most of all I love you, and that means I love everything you love."

"Well maybe . . ." she said with a sigh. "But I don't believe you, just so you know."

I didn't answer. She was right. And why was I insisting on the literary side, when the industry of her lifetime was drawing her to the glibber, more appealing, electric variety that all her friends adored? And besides, hadn't I, some thirty years ago, at a time when I was burning with fervor, championed the literary notion of promiscuity among famous characters, so confident that I was the very first person in all the world to think up such an idea. Now my youthful concept had boomeranged back to me as infantile, a mawkish pout, a noisy mass-media spit in the face, as a farce, always as a farce.

I recalled the moment when the three of them, she, her brother, and their mother, who was convalscing just then from a grueling operation, visited me in Amsterdam. This was their first, and, in that grouping, only visit. She couldn't have been more than three. When they left, behind them yawned a physically painful void. I whimpered dog-like for her, especially for her. I'd come across the tiny toys she'd strewn about like crumbs. I picked them up, tossed them from hand to hand, warmed them with my breath, and whimpered. Some of these "crumbs" stand still today on my shelf: a rubber frog and crocodile. And a Smurf.

"Auuuuntie, you stole my Smurf . . ."

8.

I liked my Turin B&B because it was on the Via Giulia di Barolo, across from the famous "*feta di polenta*" building (the Casa Scaccabarozzi), and each time (during the two days I was there) I stepped out of my building, I'd cast a glance up at its fantastic, quirky façade, which stubbornly defied all architectural rules. A successful literary soirée was held in Turin: the audience was in fine spirits and the atmosphere was amicable. The Italian publisher had arranged for a get-together with students from one of the leading "recreational, creative, therapeutic workshops": Scuola Holden. I had heard of Scuola Holden only a few days earlier, but I did have the time to re-read Salinger's *The Catcher in the Rye*.

I arrived an hour earlier than scheduled and went looking for the administrative office, which was designed like the front desk of a hotel. At the desk I was greeted by a young staff member who seemed confused. She had no idea who I was or why I'd come, and suggested I wait for her boss, who was out at lunch. I asked if I might have a look at the curriculum for the fall semester.

"We're, you know, *green*," she said, as if surprised at my asking for such a thing, as if asking for something on "paper" at an ecologically minded school was a faux pas tantamount to requesting a cigarette lighter.

"You'll find all the information here . . ." she said brightly, and pointed to the corner where there was a table scattered with various promotional leaflets and brochures. There was also a small metal bookshelf holding several books.

The brochure, also a poster, was unusually attractive. The sketch of eight students posing as if for a school photograph, four women and four men, suggested that this was a school where there was no gender

or racial discrimination (the figure of a young woman in a sari helped
to convey this). And by the way, there was also no age discrimination
because there were courses of study offered for children and for the
over-thirty student. The main curriculum of the school was designed
for students between the ages of eighteen and thirty. The school was
international, equally accessible for anybody who could afford it, and
there were no special admissions requirements, no talent checks or
test-taking. The tuition seemed prohibitively steep. Students were
not obliged to be at lectures or seminars because communication between teacher and students could go on through virtual classrooms
and online lectures. The two-year course of study, as the brochure
promised, ended with an "Opening Doors" pitching event at which
each student had the opportunity to pitch their project and persuade
the professionals in attendance (directors, film and theater producers,
publishers, agents, and entrepreneurs) that it was worthwhile. This
was, I assumed, along the lines of the popular BBC show *Dragon's
Den*, where the beginner entrepreneur pitches his project to a group of
rich venture-capitalists, suggesting to the enchanted viewers that the
world, whether fairly or not, is split into winners and losers.

My attention was drawn to certain details on the poster. A beefy
young man with tattooed arms is holding the book *Captain Science*—a
detail implying that all varieties and genres of writing are equal, that
there is no hierarchical ordering into high and low, serious and popular literature. A second young man is perched on an old-fashioned
television set, holding a remote control. The message here, as I read
it, is that all kinds of "texts" are equal: from TV and movie screen-
plays and ideas for popular shows like *Big Brother*, to ads, cartoons,
and Facebook messages and tweets. A third young man is holding a
Penguin-editions mug emblazoned with the name Raymond Chan-
dler and his famous title *The Big Sleep*. This detail was sending the
message, I surmised, that the school had nothing against treating

literary works as souvenirs and therefore approved of all other kinds of exploitation of literary works.

The school—a latter-day corporative adaptation of the Hogwarts School of Witchcraft and Wizardry—was, according to the information provided in the brochure, organized into eight colleges. At the one called *Storytelling* the instruction was in English. And everything seemed fairy tale-like, if only my eye hadn't caught one detail: all the directors of the colleges were men, all eight, and at every single college the artistic director was also a man. The dean, however, had no artistic aspirations: he was the former coach of the Italian national volleyball team. The messages conveyed by the promotional copy—that a love for sport (speed, agility, flexibility, competitive edge, playfulness), particularly soccer, was expected of the potential students—was further reinforced by the symbolic choice of a famous sports coach as dean.

Meanwhile, the administrator who'd been on her lunch break returned. I introduced myself and she offered me a brief contract that promised a modest fee. After I signed it the administrator, glancing at her wristwatch, said I should come to her office in a half hour and she'd take me over to the hall where the meeting was scheduled with the students, and then she vanished into her office.

I leafed through brochures for a few more minutes, now already noticeably followed by the darting glances of the young staff member at the "front desk"; I felt like an intruder who'd snuck into the Pentagon without a pass. My attention was drawn to two books on the shelves, part of a series called *Rescue the Story*. The series offered a recipe for saving great literary masterpieces from oblivion (!): the works were given to the finest illustrators to illustrate and then to accomplished contemporary writers to re-tell. The credits at the end of these impressive picture books—"Special thanks to Will Shakespeare" or "Special thanks to Nick Gogol"—meant that it was only a matter of time until there'd be no credits at all. The *Rescue the Story* project did not also necessarily include a "Rescue the Author" clause.

The school is housed on the premises of a former bomb factory, with a large rectangular courtyard in the middle. That is why the promotional brochure said that the objective of the school was to "produce storytellers instead of bombs"; that the goal was "to shape a new world-wise generation of storytellers by exposing our students to a plurality of references and insights." There was also mention of "cross-fertilization," which was intended, presumably, to mean the same thing. All in all, the brochure promised that Holden was a school that "Holden Caulfield would never have been expelled from." True, the nameless author of the promotional brochure seems to have forgotten that if Holden Caulfield had never been expelled from school, there never would have been a Holden Caulfield.

The "bombastic" rhetoric of cultural management reminded me of Prof. Banerjee or Dr. Chaterjee, international clairvoyants, experts in the occult sciences, who regularly stuffed their leaflets into the mailboxes of the building where I live, promising tenants protection from spells, claiming their work to be speedy and effective, with one hundred percent satisfaction guaranteed. And these "results," they promised, would be forthcoming within two days at most.

I strolled around the courtyard and realized I'd never have guessed its initial purpose. A munitions factory? In my head rang the cheap Zen advice I'd picked up from the brochure. Holden, in the words of the unbridled brochure-writer, rose up to become "Holden Mountain," and it was expected of the students that, in the hands of the experienced "masters" (their teachers, instructors, and tutors), they'd choose their individual style and path along which they'd climb said "mountain."

I went back to the office. The administrator was waiting for me there and brought me to the hall where I was to meet the "mountaineers," who had come here to learn the mastery of writing, from the "messages on medications to the wording on a bag of potato chips." As if wishing me luck, a quote from Raymond Carver winked at me from the brochure: "That's all we have, finally, the words, and they had better be the right ones."

9.

When she was smaller she loved the use of peculiar words . . .

"For lunch we're having pitiful gnocchi and glum lettuce, just so you know . . ." I'd say.

"Why'd you say the gnocchi are pitiful?"

"Because they look pitiful. Pale. Quaking here before us on the plate."

She giggles, pleased. The "pitiful gnocchi" entrance her.

"Should we sprinkle parmesan on them?" she asks.

"Every Lady Gnoccho longs for her champion, Sir Parmesan!" I quip. "Gnoccho and Parmesan are sweethearts."

She laughs, this sort of banter tickles her.

"So why is the lettuce glum?"

"Because it's wilted, lost its verve. It's dejected, sad . . ."

"I, too, feel glum just like that," she says.

"When?"

"When we have Croatian class."

"Is it really that boring?"

"Oh, Auntie. It is sooooo boring! You, too, would wilt with me in Croatian class."

Drama queen.

"Really?"

"Auntie, you have no idea!" she sighs.

I once bought a cube that was a tool for storytelling with a symbol engraved on each face; it was called the *Rory's Story Cube*. (I have a deep-seated aversion to manufacturers who use literary tropes and figures, and I especially despise assonance!) Along the way I discovered that the toy industry offers a whole array of storytelling toys. Instead, I suggested we make our own cards from cardboard on which we'd draw the elements necessary for assembling a story: the characters, houses, towns, roads, rivers, bridges, vehicles, animals, adults, children, landscapes, witches, fairies, wizards, magic wands, and so forth. True, it took us forever to draw the cards, and the drawing amused us far more than the telling of the stories . . .

"We're not so good at spinning stories," say I.

"They turned out a teentsy bit boring . . ."

"And we spent so much time on the cards!"

"Then why did we make them?"

"So we'd have options."

"Options?"

"An option means a choice, a possibility . . . The little girl we invented . . ."

"Karamela!"

"When our Karamela decides to go on a trip she might choose to travel by: a) airplane; b) boat; c) car; d) bicycle; e) hot-air balloon . . ." I notice it's the listing of things by *a, b, c, d,* and *e* that she likes much more than the *options* themselves . . .

"Five options! And still she didn't use any . . ."

"That's because we rushed our story a little. Next time around we'll give it more time . . . But if you only knew how stories come to be written!"

"Stories come from your head. *You thinvent them up,*" she says.

My little girl fused the verbs *invent* and *think up* and coined *thinvent up*!

"We know where they come to be written, but still we don't know how . . ." I say and catch straight away that I'm betrayed by my slightly instructive tone.

And she, ever cagey, knows I'm luring her into something, though she can't tell what; she pulls quickly back, shrugs, picks up a cookie with her little fingers slender as mouse paws, holds it in both hands and nibbles, mouse-like, at it. She chews with the loudest crunch she can muster. She's acting dumb. She goofs off when she sniffs danger.

"So which fairy tales are your favorites?" I ask and can tell immediately that my question is all wrong. It smells of school . . .

"*Tom and Jerry,*" she answers, all innocence, and nibbles her cookie.

"*Tom and Jerry* is no fairy tale," say I.

"It is for me!"

"Well, my favorite part of a fairy tale are the commands!" I say slyly.

And, bingo, the cookie-crunching stops . . .

"Commands?"

"Do you know what a command is?"

"When a person says somebody has to do something . . ."

"In fairy tales there are heroes who possess powers. When they say certain words, whatever they say has to happen . . ."

"You mean like abracadabra? Words like that?"

"Right! Abracadabra is a magic word. But there are more . . ."

"Like?"

"If a hero from a fairy tale does something nice for a person or a creature, if, for instance, he saves the life of a fish, then the fish rewards him. In a Russian fairy tale, a boy named Emelya saves the life of a pike and the pike tells him it will grant his every wish. All Emelya has to do is say 'At the pike's command . . .' and then say what it is he desires."

"What's a pike?" she interrupts me.

"A kind of fish that lives in rivers."

"Hm . . ." she says.

"Or, in another fairy tale, the hero says 'Forest, bow down!' and down bows the forest so the hero can pass through without hindrance. Then he says 'Forest, arise!' and up rises the forest . . ."

"Cool," she says. By the flash in her eye I can see she likes the bit about the forest.

"Heroes in fairy tales can do all sorts of things, you know. Like slip through a keyhole . . . And watermelons speak in fairy tales!"

"So where does a watermelon speak?"

"In a Romani tale."

"The watermelon says, like, real words?"

"Not only does the watermelon say real words, but when Naza Shevkiya speaks, red carnations tumble out of her mouth!"

"Who is Naza Shevkiya?" she says, and I can already see she's relishing saying the strange name.

"She's a girl who can't be touched by evil of any kind because she's good, beautiful, and silver-tongued."

"Cool," she says. This word is currently in fashion.

"What's silver-tongued?" she asks.

"It means that when Naza speaks, her words flow out like a burbling stream . . . She doesn't hack at words like a saw . . ."

She laughs. She likes the bit about the saw.

"Do you know the Grimm fairy tale 'The Magic Table'?"

"I forget . . ."

"A boy's apprenticed to a carpenter and his master gives him an enchanted table as a gift. All the boy has to do is command it, 'Table, set thyself!' and the table is at once splendidly appointed . . ."

"What does 'splendidly appointed' mean?"

"It means that 'the table was spread in the blink of an eye with a fine damask cloth, and on it a plate, and by the plate a knife and a fork, and a serving dish filled to the brim with stewed and roasted meats, and thereupon gleamed a generous flask of ruby-red wine to touch the heart of any banqueter . . .'"

"Those words are all a little strange. Nobody talks like that."

"Well, that's exactly why they're so cool, don't you think?"

"I don't know."

"Do you remember in 'Cinderella' how she prepares for the ball? How she was able to come up with such a stunning gown?"

"Nope," she says.

"Thanks to a command. Before the ball she goes to her mother's grave, stands under a hazel tree, and commands: 'Shiver, oh tree, your slender boughs, / Down upon me cast silver and gold!'"

She likes a bit about gowns dropping from the branches, she tries to memorize the command but she's too groggy. Her eyelids droop, she struggles to keep them open.

"And those commands . . . Do they work for stories, too?" she asks.

"For stories?"

"Say I commanded, 'Story, set thyself!' Would the story . . ."

I stop her. I see she's so sleepy she can hardly say a word.

"You're tired, pumpkin, time for bed."

I help her undress, pull on her nightgown, tuck her into bed, and lie, just for a moment, next to her. Her breath is sweet, her breathing deeper and deeper.

"Auntie, we're just little blue dots in the universe," she mumbles.

"Who said that?"

"Brainy Smurf."

"Who?"

"The little one, blue, with the glasses . . ."

Her little hand nests a few more seconds in mine, and then, like a tiny mouse, it goes all soft . . .

10.

Some thirty students were sitting in the hall. I couldn't say for certain how old they were, but they looked as if they might be between the ages of eighteen and thirty. The administrator who brought me there introduced me with a few sentences she'd copied from Wikipedia. Some of them eyed me with curiosity; some, like a young man in the first row, built like a rugby player, sat with his shoulders hunched and his chin jutting, staring vacantly ahead; most of them were playing video games and glanced over in my direction from time to time. The organizers had given me nothing to go on and I started things off on an awkward note, asking them when they'd heard I'd be coming to speak. They were startled; maybe three weeks ago, they said, but they weren't sure.

"I know none of you have read my books, but did anyone at least run a search on my name?"

Silence. I assumed none of the speakers before me had been so blunt.

"How can you expect that one day somebody will show even a modicum of curiosity about you if you show no curiosity about others?"

Silence.

A man who was employed now at the school as a "cultural animator" or some such thing spoke up, and sounded as if he'd been a student of comparative literature.

"You know," he said, "the students here aren't studying just literature."

"Ah, what else then?" I asked.

"Soccer, for instance . . ."

"Soccer as a form of foot-based storytelling?"

"Yes, literally . . ."

"Ah ha! Then I trust you know all about the great writers who were soccer fans and played soccer themselves," I said.

Not a peep. Not even from the comp lit guy.

"Albert Camus, as you are all, no doubt, aware. And Vladimir Nabokov, who played soccer for a Russian émigré club in Berlin. Peter Handke, author of *The Goalie's Anxiety at the Penalty Kick*. Peter Esterhazy, a Hungarian writer whose novel *Not Art* is about his mother, a soccer enthusiast . . ."

The men in the audience snickered; the snickers were for the comp lit guy.

"Do you know who wrote the most engaging literary description of a soccer game in world literature?" After several seconds of deathly silence, I said, "Yuri Olesha, in his novel *Envy*."

"Never heard of it . . ." harumphed the comp lit guy.

"Just because you've never heard of something doesn't mean it's not so, does it?"

"If it were any good, others would know about it . . ." persisted the comp lit guy.

"And who are these 'others'?" I asked.

The conversation was not going well, so I switched gears. I began asking each in turn about his or her literary tastes. I learned that two or three of the women were studying medicine; the rugby player, the youngest, had already published a book, a historical novel about Caesar, though he was only eighteen. In the literary industry there are generously compensated literary stars writing for the lucrative Young Adults literary brand. I guessed such writers would be models for many of these students. The rugby player's model was Christopher Paolini, who, at the age of eighteen, published *Eragon*, a global bestseller. One student said his only interest was parallel worlds. When asked who her favorite writer was, one young woman gave an unconvincing, one-word answer: "Kafka!" A shrewd fellow threw me a punch when he said De Lollo was his favorite writer, figuring, quite rightly, that I'd assume he'd mispronounced Don DeLillo's name. Later I discovered that De Lollo, Lucian Lollo, was, in fact, an Argentinian soccer player. I wrote down each name the students gave me and this turned out to be useful; when I later read over the list, I saw it was far more ambitious than I'd expected. True, there wasn't a single woman among them, not even Elena Ferrante, the local superstar whose name could be heard absolutely everywhere. I struggled with the "parallel worlds," the "imaginative fiction," the unfamiliar genres and authors. Not a one of the students mentioned Salinger as a favorite writer or *The Catcher in the Rye* as a favorite book.

I was suddenly overwhelmed by a sense of the futility of my situation, which I had, indeed, brought upon myself by consenting to this brief, more random than deliberate, conversation. The artistic strutting of these affluent offspring, this school for apprentices to chic designers, which flaunted Holden Caulfield's name and upheld, in name at least, the dusty, seventy-year-old concept of "rebel without a cause," but also the notion of a new kind of writing that would interface glibly with the corporate world—none of this was my cup of tea. On the other hand, didn't the commercialization of literature begin years ago before I was paying attention? The word *industry* elbowed its way into literature and culture with the European cultural managers; with them came the vocabulary of business. So it was that the word *creative* attached itself to the word *industry*, and the literary craft began subdividing into *creative fiction, creative non-fiction, imaginative fiction, non-imaginative fiction, speculative fiction, fantasy fiction* and so forth. Digital technology spawned derivatives of the word *fiction* such as *fan-fiction, slash fiction, reality fiction,* and the word *literature* acquired its own derivatives, such as *twitterature.* The Russians coined the word *samizdat* and then it morphed, in the digital realm, into *self-publishing,* the English analog, but with an altogether different twist. Why am I so irked by the online sale of the little sado-maso trinkets mentioned in a porno novel that sold millions of copies? Why am I so appalled by the writing-tips app that an author of children's hits came up with that can be downloaded to one's smartphone? Haven't the foundations and museums of famous writers become souvenir shops for tourists? Haven't I been seeing for years how people—with far more enthusiasm than they buy books—snap up T-shirts with a famous writer's face, coffee mugs with writers' quotes, postcards, movies based on their work, audio books, toys, rag dolls with an author's face? Is there not a Freud rag doll on the shelf above my desk? And is it not right next to traditional Russian wooden dolls, *matryoshkas*, sporting the faces of Pushkin, Dostoyevsky, Gogol, Tolstoy, and Chekhov, which first appeared in Russian with Perestroika? Perhaps museum-goers will be able, soon, to enter the 3-D scene of a literary work and explore the "total" reading experience; perhaps, having ordered Hemingway's favorite *mojito*, or tea with Proust's madeleine, the visitors will be able to settle into a comfy armchair and enjoy, for instance, a visual version of Molly Bloom's monologue.

And then, as I studied the students' faces, I felt a sudden twinge of compassion for them. The names of their literary models told me nothing except that, like most people, they were susceptible to fashion, whatever was currently "cool," that they were "pumped"; that they were impressed by the fact that they were paying to study at this expensive and preeminent storytelling school, taking part in a new form of cultural power, which was being engineered by a select fraternity: a prosperous writer, a prosperous businessman, a powerful bookstore chain, and an international chain, currently chic, of restaurants and foodstores. For years now cultural power has not been stowed away in the dusty national academics and university departments where somebody was able to keep it under his thumb. I found myself wondering if the crusty old power structures were not so very attractive, why would these new-fangled ones be? What about the Scuola Holden's triumphalist slogan *Capitale Umano, Narrazione d'Impresa* (Human Capital, Corporate Identity)?

My friend Bojan, no longer among the living, said he knew time had left him in the dust, but, to his surprise, nothing hurt. I wondered whether time had left me, too, in the dust? And if it had, hadn't there been a similar social dynamic before as well, accelerated and given potency by digital technology? Because many of my literary models were no more laudatory or interesting than theirs. An early model for me (I was only ten at the time) was Minou Drouet, a little girl, a poet, who became a world-wide sensation at the age of ten. More enduring were the fame and sway of Françoise Sagan, a young rebel who published her first book at seventeen, the bestseller *Bonjour, Tristesse*, simply because it was part of the new Euro-American cultural text fabricated by the movies and books of the 1960s. This cultural text rose up from the rubble of the Second World War, the millions killed in the war, the grief, the hopelessness, the incredulity that such a thing could even happen, the clearing away of the ruins, the denial of reality, the accelerated manufacture of a future in which, of course, there would never again be war. I was born after the Second World War, the same year that Holden Caulfield spent his three December days in New York, and yet I managed to catch the rebel-without-a-cause bug and then convalesce as from the measles. In my time, "rebels without a cause" like James Dean were cool, and the division of the world into the genuine and the phony shielded my fragile self-confidence, and not just mine, from collapse. How many incongruous things were cool! I remember that I went for the rebel look Jean Seberg sported in the movie *Breathless*, though that was not why, soon after that, I wept while watching *Love Story* with Allie McGraw and Ryan O'Neal. Joyce, Proust, Bergman, Kafka,

Kurosawa, Erich Fromm, some of the values that I proudly strutted as a first-year student of comparative literature did not stop me from feeling protective about poor Allison MacKenzie in the American soap opera *Peyton Place*, just like the student who used De Lollo and DeLillo to form his ideological-aesthetic badge.

These students are showing off (so did I!) because they are insecure (I was too!). They are a generation atttending an expensive private storytelling school: the school bears Holden's name, but most of them haven't read *The Catcher in the Rye*. The fact that I, as I prepared before the trip, re-read it, doesn't give me the right to show off in front of them and pester them with questions such as: What is the name of the school from which Holden was expelled? Whose literary work does Holden refer to at the very beginning of the novel? Who is Holden's favorite writer? What are the most frequent words in Holden's vocabulary? And so forth.

To be left in the dust by time, as long as nothing hurts, is a liberating sensation. The sensation, however, is wrong, because time doesn't flow as we'd like it to, or as we imagine—in any case it doesn't age along with us. Reading *The Catcher in the Rye* again I realized that Holden Caulfield, who was seventeen in 1951 when the novel was first published, is eighty-two today. I also realized that his rebellion is actually nothing more than the puerile rant of an old codger stretching over two hundred pages. At the very beginning of the book there is a detail, where Holden says that one side of his head—the right side—is full of millions of gray hairs, which confirms symbolically that Holden is actually ageless, or that he was always in his eighties. Millions of young readers the world over took Holden Caulfield as their central focus for identification. Readers everywhere read *The Catcher in the Rye*. In Eastern Europe, for instance, it spawned "jeans prose." Other Holdens cropped up in Russia, Czechoslovakia, Poland, Yugoslavia,

East Germany; they told their stories with "lousy" vocabulary, used vernacular equivalents for Holden's "and all," experienced the world of grown-ups as "phony," acted dumb ("I'm the most terrific liar you ever saw in your life"), or only pretended to be dumb ("I'm the only dumb one in my family"). Whether he wanted it or not, Salinger also became the symbolic spokesperson for the post-war culture of "rebel without a cause." And the more these "rebels" insist that the world around them is "phony" and makes them "puke," the more efficiently the world shunts them into the mainstream. Even when I was an adolescent I found it hard to identify with Holden, perhaps because he was a boy and there wasn't a single girl in my vicinity who'd have wanted him as her boyfriend.

I started to move slowly toward the door. Nobody saw me out, not the administrator, not the comparatist. As I was leaving the school, a student, the one who'd chosen Kafka as her favorite writer, came running to the door . . .

"Sorry, I wanted to ask you . . . I don't want to be a bother, really, but . . . Can storytelling be learned? What do you think? I had the impression you're a little skeptical about the school . . . and us . . ." she said, slightly out of breath.

The girl was not, in fact, asking what she said she was asking, she was shrewdly using the same sort of mask she'd used in telling me her favorite author was Kafka. And yet her dilemmas weren't phony, she was no phony. I was the phony . . .

"Every school is good. What matters is that you're writing . . ." I said.

Why did I respond with this cheap drivel? Why didn't I show more compassion? Maybe because I had no choice. I couldn't say much about the school because I knew only what I'd gleaned from the brochures.

Even if I'd thought the school was a bad choice, it's unlikely I'd say so because she'd already invested a hefty sum in her tuition and she'd not be able to earn it back with her writing for the next ten years, unless she stumbled onto a bestseller, or unless her tuition had been paid by rich parents, which was most probably the case. I could quote her Holden: "The more expensive a school is, the more crooks it has!" but I didn't. That would have been cruel and, besides, untrue.

In his story "A Story about How Stories Come to Be Written," Boris Pilnyak says: "if the spirit of the fox enters a person, then the person's tribe is accursed. The fox is the writer's totem." How to explain to the young woman the risks of her future vocation, the profound, dangerous, and painful occupational hazards, which cannot be resolved by pain tablets the hue of raw meat. The fox in most Slavic languages, and in the large part of Slavic (as well as Chinese, Japanese, and Korean) folklore and mythological imaginary, is gendered as a female. The fox is Scheherazade. Scheherazade is a fox. Scheherazade tells about how stories come to be written. Because with each story Scheherazade is buying another day of life. Her school of creative writing lasts for one thousand and one nights, and instead of paying her tuition with cash, she pledges her head.

The fox—the totem which, according to Boris Pilnyak, is allotted to us poor writers—is cunning, a sly trickster, a deliverer of divine messages, a servant of Inari, goddess of food-production. The fox is a trafficker in dead souls; the fox is a country-fair juggler, a liar, a charlatan, a flatterer, a brownnoser, a harpy, a skinflint, a crook who risks her life for a shabby catch: a chicken's backbone, a goose leg, a nubbin of cheese dropped from another's mouth. The fox is condemned to isolation, to a life outside its kind: a brief mating period, the mothering, true, lasts a little longer, but not long enough to fill the abyss of the isolation. The fox, as a chicken thief, is the alibi and target of the more pragmatic hunters. A fox pelt is not the most highly prized, but it never goes out of style. The fox has magic powers, it can rise to the status of divine fox and be granted its nine tails, but that takes a wait of a thousand years.

My little niece and I had found our way, whether by chance or not, to the ultimate question, for which no clear answer is likely. All in all, stories will not tell themselves, just as a mirror cannot be turned into a lake, or a comb into thick grass, nor will the pike's command come true if there is no deep compulsion for it linked to serious risk. (Who knows? Maybe that's why my little girl inadvertantly murmured the wrong command, saying, *Story, set thyself!* instead of, *Story, tell thyself!*) Magic doesn't happen unless the words are uttered in vain. Hence in every story, even a fairy tale, especially a fairy tale, there must be a component of some higher "truthfulness" (and truthfulness here mustn't be confused with the truth, with cogency, with life experience, or with morals), because otherwise the story won't "work." There must be a good reason why this story, this very story, has to be told. The fox knows every trick in the book, yet still it comes up short. However, when its survival is in question (whatever that might mean)—as in the story about the poor man who steals a fox's pelt to keep it in his house as his wife—the fox drops all further negotiation and returns to its authentic self. God exists only if we believe in the phrase *do not take God's name in vain.* If we don't believe in the magic of literature, it is just a meaningless string of words.

The fox brings with it the curse of punishment; only the rare one among them is able to pass the thousand-year test and, at last, give those nine tails a swish. Still it seems that the fox cares little for a summons that could possibly come, one day, from the capricious heavens, because meanwhile it has to survive somehow: hence the rush of flattering words directed at the foolish crow up there on the branch in the hope that it just might drop that nubbin of cheese. Somebody will say, what a waste of time, wouldn't it be wiser to use one's words to glorify God, making speedier and more certain the path to redemption. Words glorifying God have no effect because God must not be corruptible, while words glorifying the conceited fool on the branch work reasonably well.

The fox's curse lies in the fact that it isn't loved. The fox neither has great strength we'd fear and submit to, nor does it have beauty to stun us and leave us breathless. How, after all, can one love a creature who shifts face and character, who's doting one moment and ready to sell us down the river the next, for whom we are not certain, what's more, whether they belong in the world of the dead or the world of the living. The fox is neither of the beasts, nor of us, people, nor is it of the gods. It is forever a stowaway, a migrant moving with ease through worlds, and when it's caught without a ticket, then it spins balls on its tail, performs its cheap tricks. The flash of admiration it receives—ah the myopic susceptibility of the fox—is its substitute for love. These are its glory days. All else is a history of fear, flight from the hunter's bullets, the constant baying of the hounds; a history of persecution, beatings, licking of wounds, humiliation, loneliness, and cheap consolation—a chicken-bone rattle.

Maybe the student with her pale complexion, her shining, wide-open eyes, the bare ghost of a smile, who is standing here before me will one day write a book, and who knows, maybe somewhere in that book she'll include a description of me. And if that happens, I would have nothing against being described as an old lady who *went out on a chilly night, prayed for the moon to give her light*, and while she slowly makes her way for many a mile, around her legs, appearing out of the dark from somewhere, twine little foxes. And look, there are more and more of them, they're skulking, forming a copper-colored royal train, until the train and the old woman are swallowed by darkness . . .

Having taken five two-hundred-milligram tablets of Ibuprofen the hue of raw meat, I decided to walk back to my B&B, although the Scuola Holden and Via Giulia di Barolo were some distance apart. My back pain let up. There was a bounce in my step, as if I'd won, as if I'd nabbed my prey (*A couple of you will grease my chin, before I leave this town-o, town-o, town-o, before I leave this town-o* . . .), though I had nothing to show for my triumph. All the more so as I suspected that the honorarium, for which I'd signed the ecologically distasteful paper contract, would never arrive . . .

August, 2016.

Dubravka Ugresic is the author of seven works of fiction, including *The Museum of Unconditional Surrender* and *Baba Yaga Laid an Egg*, along with six collections of essays, including *Thank You for Not Reading* and *Karaoke Culture*, a finalist for the National Book Critics Circle Award for Nonfiction. She has won, or been shorlisted for, more than a dozen prizes, including the NIN Award, Austrian State Prize for European Literature, Heinrich Mann Prize, *Independent* Foreign Fiction Prize, Man Booker International Prize, and the James Tiptoc Jr. Award. In 2016, she received the Neustadt International Prize for Literature (the "American Nobel") for her body of work.

Ellen Elias-Bursać has been translating fiction and nonfiction by Bosnian, Croatian, and Serbian writers since the 1980s, including novels and short stories by David Albahari, Dubravka Ugresic, Daša Drndić, and Karim Zaimović. She is co-author of a textbook for the study of Bosnian, Croatian, and Serbian with Ronelle Alexander and author of *Translating Evidence and Interpreting Testimony at a War Crimes Tribunal: Working in a Tug-of-War*, which was awarded the Mary Zirin Prize in 2015.

David Williams is the author of *Writing Postcommunism*, and translated Ugresic's *Europe in Sepia* and *Karaoke Culture*.

**OPEN
LETTER**

OPEN LETTER

WWW.OPENLETTERBOOKS.ORG